ERIN HAWKINS

UNEXPECTEDLY IN LOVE SERIES BOOK THREE

Accidentally Ours

ISBN: 978-1-7356883-9-8

Cover design by Cover Ever After covereverafter.com

Edited by Chelly Peeler inkedoutediting.com

Proofreading by Isabella Bauer

Titles by Erin Hawkins

Reluctantly Yours
Unexpectedly Mine

Best Laid Plans
Not in the Plans

CHAPTER 1

Sophie

With one last dry heave, I close the toilet lid. I swipe a finger under my eyes, the wetness there a product of my body's recent efforts, but I'm thankful the waterproof mascara I put on is doing its job. My throat burns from the mixture of coffee and stomach acid that I've just expelled. With a shaky hand, I reach out to press the flusher. I'm grateful for the plush rug under my bare knees courtesy of my brother's wife, Emma. When they first moved in together, my brother, Griffin, had been mystified by his wife's feminine decorating style, her love of soft hues and cozy textiles, since he himself had used a moving box for a nightstand for years.

On wobbly legs, I stand. In the mirror, I fix my blonde curls, then press down the length of my green shift dress and reach for my toothbrush. At least my manicure still looks good. I like to paint my nails every week and I thought the bright coral color I picked out yesterday would be the perfect color for my first week at my internship.

Who throws up on their first day of work? It's probably just nerves. Or it could have been that questionable sushi I picked up at a corner market.

The knock on the door sounds over the buzz of my electric toothbrush.

"Soph, I'm about to leave." It's Griffin. "You okay?"

It doesn't matter if I'm two or twenty-two, Griffin has always been watching over me. If he knew I'd just thrown up, he'd probably take my temperature, order me to bed and call my new boss to inform her I'm taking a sick day. That's what he would have done when we were growing up. Our mother likely working at one of the odd jobs she would only be able to hold down for a week or two at a time, or gone for a stretch of time with no phone call or note.

While my brother has been my reliable safety net for most of my life, I'm determined to change our relationship. Change the balance so I'm more like an equal, less like someone to take care of. Ultimately, I want to take the burden of my existence off his shoulders.

Step one: Kill it at my first day at my internship.

I spit and rinse, then glance at my watch. I need to leave in thirty minutes.

I open the door and give him a beaming smile as I move past him to my room across the hallway.

"A few nervous jitters. I'm sure they'll pass."

The last thing I need is for my overprotective brother to think that I can't handle this situation.

I'm chalking the stress of today up to a culmination of all the major life changes I've experienced recently. Graduating from college, moving from Las Vegas to New York City and landing a paid internship with one of the most sought-after wedding planning companies in the country.

While I made it to the city on my own, I'm currently living in Emma and Griffin's spare bedroom. As my brother pointed out shortly after I accepted my paid internship with Marion Adler Events, New York City is the most expensive place to live in the country.

Griffin leans on the doorframe while I debate the merits of

wearing heels or flats on my first day. My mind goes to the scene in *The Devil Wears Prada* when Andy shows up for her first day at *Runway* in those hideous loafers. Neither of my choices are *that* bad, and I'm interning at a wedding planning firm, not a fashion magazine, but Marion Adler is the pinnacle of wedding planners and I want to make a great first impression.

"You've got the subway directions I sent you?" Griffin asks. "And the preloaded transit card I set on the counter?"

"Yes and yes." I opt for the flats. They're stylish yet functional, and made from old water bottles, so I'm also helping the environment. I slide them on, then toss the heels into my purse. "That timed practice we did yesterday was super helpful."

"I'd think you were being sarcastic if I didn't know how much you love to be prepared."

He's right. Winging it is not my forte. I'm all about planning, knowing every detail. Knowledge is power and all that. And for me, knowledge and preparedness are key to combating the anxiety that builds in new situations.

I move around the queen-sized bed to the other side of the room where I've set up my desk that also doubles as a mirrored vanity to store jewelry and accessories.

"Headband or no headband?" I ask my reflection as I adjust the floral print knotted headband on my head.

"It's cute." Griffin offers his opinion.

I pull it from my head and set it back in the drawer.

"Yeah, that's not what I'm going for."

He lifts his hands up in surrender, the gold band on his left ring finger glints as he moves his hand.

It's still hard to believe my brother, the man who never dated or partied while he was raising me, got married in Vegas after spending one wild night with his now-wife, Emma. It's a shock to say the least.

While they had planned to annul their marriage, Emma

found out she needed him in NYC for an important interview. After spending more time together, they ended up falling in love and staying married.

None of it made sense at the time, but now it's easy to see that there was a reason they were drawn together in the first place.

"You know I'm clueless about that stuff," he says.

I shake my head, laughing. "It's a good thing your wife has impeccable taste."

"Yeah, I'm a lucky man." Griffin smiles at the mention of Emma. He's head over heels for her. He met her at his last *Rainin' Men* show in Vegas while she was there to headline a fashion show at a bridal convention, and after spending a few hours together on the Vegas strip, they got married. At the time, they were under the influence of alcohol, but as I've witnessed, the real catalyst for them ending up at the wedding chapel was their undeniable connection.

Griffin's eyes fall to the open closet door. The organized chaos that is my moving boxes.

"I can put in those shelves we talked about this weekend."

"Only if you think you'll want them for the space after I move out, otherwise I can manage."

You don't realize how much stuff you have until you try to stuff it into a New York City apartment closet.

"We'll get it set up this weekend. I've got to run." He strides over to pull me into a hug. "I'm so proud of you, Soph. Have a great first day."

"Thank you." I squeeze back, then release him.

"I'll see you after work."

"See you after," I call, watching him disappear down the hallway. A minute later, the front door clicks shut.

Once he's gone, I move to my desk and open my laptop.

I'd stayed up late last night editing my latest blog entry and I want to post it before I leave.

It's about using seed paper as a sustainable alternative for printing wedding invitations.

My blog started out as a project three years ago in a social media marketing class I took as an elective, but I enjoyed it so much that I've kept it going. Now, Sustainable Wedding Chic is for those looking for sustainable and eco-friendly practices for their wedding décor, invitations and more. The blog has grown substantially in subscribers over the years and I even have paid advertisers now. More recently, I started a YouTube channel with tutorials on DIY centerpieces and floral arrangements using upcycled glassware and vases.

My blog is a fun hobby, but working at Marion Adler Events is my dream job.

But I guess with every dream job, there is stress and anxiety, which explains my breakfast ending up in the toilet this morning. Maybe it's too perfect. Things are working out *too* well, and that's why I'm anxious. Now that I have my dream job, well, a paid internship that I plan on becoming my job once I prove to Marion that I've got what it takes to plan New York City elite's dream weddings, I'm worried it's too good to be true.

It's like when I was ten and my mom had finally quit partying and staying out all night. She'd landed a job at a retail store and we were able to make rent for the first time in years, then out of the blue Griffin came to get me out of school to tell me she had died in a car accident. She was finally becoming a better version of herself, then she was gone.

After that, Griffin and I had to figure out everything on our own, most of the adulting falling in his lap, but we both grew up quickly. While my mom's death taught me resilience, it also made me afraid to be too hopeful, too happy. And showed me how quickly something can be taken away.

I reapply my lipstick and give myself another once over

before throwing a water bottle in my purse, then lock up and head for the elevator.

Out on the street, it takes me a minute to remember which direction I need to go to catch the subway north to midtown. Begrudgingly, I pull my phone out and check the note Griffin sent to make sure I'm going the right way. Praying to the porcelain gods this morning hasn't allotted me any spare time so I can't afford to be riding the subway the wrong direction. It's only a two-block walk to the subway entrance, but New York blocks are long and I'm already feeling lightheaded when I descend the stairs. At the turnstile, I slide my transit card, then hurry to the train before its doors close.

In the subway car, I find a seat, then double check my notes again for the stop I need. While I desperately want Griffin to start treating me like an adult who can take care of herself, I realize that I might also be at fault for the imbalance in our relationship. I lean on him. A lot. I'm hoping that working and making my own money, and eventually moving out of his and Emma's apartment, will show him that I'm capable of taking care of myself. I don't want him to think that he has to take care of me. He's got Emma now, and at some point, they'll want to start a family and I don't want to be in their way. He's done so much for me, I couldn't repay him if I tried, but what I can do now is try to be less of a burden.

My phone buzzes with an incoming text from my friend, Coco.

Coco: *Thinking of you on your first day!*

Me: *Thanks. It's exciting, but I'm also really nervous.*

Coco: *I'd be stressed, too. I'm not ready for a real job and no summer break.*

Me: *Enjoy your pool days for now. Your graduate program is only a year. Next year at this time you'll be on the job hunt.*

Coco: *Ugh. Let me enjoy this.*

I smile, knowing Coco would put off adulting forever if

she could. She's been a free spirit since we met in seventh grade. We're opposites in a way, but maybe that's why our friendship works. I help her focus when she needs it, while she's always eager to remind me to let loose and have some fun.

Coco: *A few of us went out last night to Marquee. I hadn't been there since that night with you after graduation. The night you left with that hottie *wink face emoji**

I lift my eyes from the phone screen and think back to that night.

On a high after graduating at the top of my class in event planning and hospitality, and a minor in business, I was ready to let loose.

But I hadn't expected to drink that much and I hadn't expected *him*. There was something about knowing I had achieved the goals I set for myself, and that Griffin was proud of me, that I wanted one wild, reckless night, something I hadn't given myself the entire time I was in college. My entire life for that matter. It was a farewell to Las Vegas, one filled with tequila and a sexy stranger named Hunter.

Coco: *I still can't believe you told him you wanted to lick his balls.*

Feeling my cheeks heat, my eyes shift toward the woman one seat over, paranoid she can read my text exchange. She's engrossed in her romance novel and oblivious, so I turn back to my phone and type out a response.

Me: *You dared me to!*

Coco: *I didn't think you'd do it.*

I recall the warm, tingling sensation of that second tequila shot going down my throat, making me just tipsy enough to accept her dare.

She had pointed to a guy sitting on one of the VIP couches. Before I could overthink it, I walked over to him, disregarding the conversation he appeared to be in with two other men, leaned down and whispered in his ear.

I want to lick your balls.

From across the room, I had seen the way he styled his dark brown hair, a little messy, but effortlessly sexy. I had been hypnotized by his strong jaw, the dark stubble covering it and the sharpness of his nose. The way he tapped his fingers on the arm of the sofa, a slow, deliberate rhythm, made him seem content with the conversation, yet also bored. The enticing way he absently tugged on his lower lip with a single finger while his quiet attention was focused on one of the men speaking, had made me wonder how skilled those fingers might be.

But when I pulled back, I was caught off guard by the intensity in his indigo eyes. I knew he was attractive, but being that close to him, feeling the heat radiate off his skin, catching the luxurious, masculine scent of him, was a whole different experience.

His full lips twitched as he watched me retreat.

Then, I returned to the dance floor and continued dancing like I hadn't just told a stranger I wanted to put my mouth on his testicles. Coco couldn't stop laughing.

Moments later, my attention returned to him and when he raised his glass to take a drink, his eyes met mine over the rim. I've been stared at by guys plenty, but finding him watching me didn't feel creepy or unwanted. It was hot. I wanted him to see me dance. I wanted him to see me inch my already short skirt up my thighs and run my hands through my hair as I moved to the beat of the music.

It was an instant attraction that I couldn't deny. With one look from that man, my panties were soaked. I wanted him badly. And while normally I wouldn't have given in to the attraction, I would have grabbed Coco's hand and left the club, all while giggling about how funny her dare was, that night was different.

He could have been a local, or in town for business, but I didn't want to know. I wanted to have fun and not bother with names or small talk, but when his associates left and he approached me on the dance floor, Hunter, as he introduced himself, insisted we know each other's names. *So you know what name to scream when you come on my cock later,* he had whispered against my ear.

And I did scream his name. It filled his hotel room an hour later when he pinned my arms above my head and drove into me hard. The hold he had on me was borderline painful, but I liked the way it felt to be held down by him. To wrap my legs around his hips and squeeze him tighter to me. I was right about him being older. His body was toned and filled out in ways that no guy my age I'd slept with had been. His cock was long and thick, and when he buried it deep inside me, I thought it was going to split me down the middle.

My thighs squeeze together now just thinking about it.

When I woke up in his hotel room, tangled in the sheets and alone, I shouldn't have been surprised. It was what I had expected from our time together. Yet, the room was so still and empty, if the soreness between my thighs hadn't reminded me of our night together, I would have thought it didn't happen.

My phone buzzes again.

Coco: *Just wanted to remind you that you're a badass bitch and you're going to kill it today.*

Me: *Thank you!*

Coco: *Let me know how it goes. Love you! BYEEEE!*

Me: **kiss face emoji**

After I tuck my phone in my purse, my mind continues to linger on Hunter.

Sex with him was incredible.

But then again, I also don't have much to compare him to. I've only slept with two guys, so between the tequila and my lack of experience, it might not have been that great.

It was really hot, though.

Ugh, I shouldn't give this guy any more thought. Not only

because there's absolutely no point in daydreaming about a guy I will never see again, but because he turned out to be an asshole. Even though he was an older, more sophisticated, with a body chiseled to perfection by the gods kind of asshole.

It wasn't that I was expecting him to be there when I woke up. I didn't have a breakfast in bed, cuddle session, morning after scenario I wanted to fulfill. What can you really expect from a guy that you met at a club in Vegas? I wasn't picking out our kids' names or anything. It was my idea in the first place to not exchange information, so it was fine that he wasn't there.

No, everything was perfect about that night until I found the cash he left on the bedside table.

With thoughts of Hunter tucked far away, I exit the subway and walk the two blocks to Marion Adler's office. Upon exiting the elevator, the whimsical and stylishly decorated reception area greets me. Everything is white and gold, with floral arrangements adding pops of color. Large script letters, M and A, for Marion Adler, behind the reception desk are backlit with a soft pink light. A dark-haired woman in a beige dress sits at the reception desk. If I remember correctly from the new-hire packet, her name is Sabrina.

All of the interviews and orientation were done via video chat. It's odd to be walking through the doors to an office I've never been to, and now I work here.

Internally, I'm squealing.

When I approach, Sabrina holds up a finger to signal she'll be with me in a moment, but before she finishes her call, a guy appears from the side of her desk.

"You must be Sophie." While he assesses me, I observe he's fashionably dressed in gray slacks, a gray button-down vest and a white dress shirt rolled up to his elbows. His copper hair is wavy and he's got a few freckles across his cheeks. I'm tall, but he's got a good six inches on me. I mentally swat away the thought that like this guy, Hunter was tall, and I liked how he towered over me.

"That's me." I smile enthusiastically.

"I'm Johnathan, an associate wedding planner here, and your report for the summer." He extends his hand and I take it.

"Nice to meet you." I nod, recalling the orientation call where I was informed that each intern is assigned to an associate planner for the summer.

"I apologize I wasn't able to meet you at your new-hire orientation. I was on my honeymoon." He wiggles his left hand to show off a white-gold band.

"Congratulations." Suddenly I'm curious if he planned his own wedding, but before I can ask, he reads my mind.

"I don't wish wedding planning on anyone I love. And my husband is even more of a control freak than I am. We eloped."

I can't help but laugh.

"What about you?"

"Am I married? No." I shake my head.

"Don't worry. You will be. To this job." He bursts with laughter. "I'm just kidding. Kind of. No. I'm not." He catches my wide-eyed expression. "Trust me, if you made it this far, you'll be fine."

I nod and smile, hoping he's right. I wouldn't be here if I couldn't handle the job.

"All right, we've got a lot to cover this morning before the intern meeting so let's get started." He motions for me to follow him past the reception desk.

As we move down the hall, Johnathan gives an office tour, explaining how the office is set up to accommodate the two divisions at Marion Adler Events.

"On the east side, you've got the wedding planning division, and on the west, the event planning division, which covers all other events outside of weddings."

His explanation is a review of what was already covered in my online internship orientation, but it's nice to get a refresher.

As we move down the hall, he motions to the offices for the other associate wedding planners and gives me a quick rundown of their expertise and personalities.

"And this is Marietta's office." He motions to the empty office. "She hates love. I honestly don't know how she does it, but she still manages to plan some of the most idealistic, thoughtful weddings, even while detesting love as a notion."

"That's interesting."

He stops abruptly. "Before we go any further, I have to know your stance."

"My stance?" I ask.

"On love."

"Oh, pro-love. Love is great." I nod eagerly, ignoring the fact that I personally have no idea what it's like to be in love.

But, in addition to my affinity for checklists, and the creativity and patience that it takes to be a wedding planner, I love love. I want it for myself one day. One day being a good five and a half years from now, because I've got shit to do. First and foremost, take the New York City wedding planning scene by storm.

Besides, as Johnathan alluded to earlier, this internship is going to be my life for the next three months, and I need it to be the priority.

"Good. I had an intern a few years back who was a marriage cynic." He rolls his eyes. "He thought it was trendy or something. Everyone is entitled to their own opinions, but a wedding planner who doesn't believe in marriage is like a sports team manager who hopes their team loses every game.

site visits, then we've got a consultation lunch appointment at Delphino's at twelve-thirty, so you'll get to see how it all begins." He waves his hands excitedly and I can't help but share his passion.

"Get settled in, then I'll see you after the meeting with Marion."

A wave of nausea rolls over me. Ugh. I need to get this stomach thing under control.

"Sure thing."

Johnathan leaves me there at my desk, and I drop into the chair, feeling both overwhelmed and elated at the same time. I pull out my water bottle and the small framed picture of me and Griffin when we were kids, then neatly line up the notepad and gel pen set I brought.

"Are you new to the city?" I ask June.

"No, I'm from Jersey." I hear the accent the moment she says it. "What about you?"

"Las Vegas area. I lived in Henderson and went to UNLV. I moved here a few days ago."

"That's cool. Where do you live?"

"Gramercy."

Her brows lift. "How do you afford that with this internship?"

I know that Griffin and Emma's place is not the norm for a twenty-two-year-old starting out. They have two adult incomes. Emma is a designer with her bridal gown line about to launch in Bergman's department stores and Griffin is an in-house attorney for a major real estate development firm.

"I'm living with my brother and his wife right now, but I hope to move out soon. Find roommates."

"Good luck. I live in Queens with three roommates and it's still outrageous what we pay."

My phone buzzes with an incoming text.

Griffin: *Let me know you made it to work okay.*

Typical Griffin checking up on me. The devil inside me

wants to drop my phone in my purse and ignore him, but the angel knows Griffin's doing it out of love and would be truly worried if I don't respond. There have to be millions of siblings out there that wouldn't send out a search party team if their text is not answered within five minutes. Griffin is not one of them.

Me: *I'm at work now.*

Griffin: *Have a great day. I love you.*

Me: *Love you, too.*

I sigh. Why am I such a brat?

I toss my phone in my purse. I'm determined to prove that I've got everything under control, that he doesn't need to worry about me, and to start, I'm going to rock my first day at this internship.

CHAPTER 2

Sophie

After settling into my desk, I introduce myself to the other interns.

In addition to me, the rest of the wedding planning interns are Maxwell, born and raised on the Upper East Side, Jaylah from Kansas City, and Lauren from Utah. Association is how I remember lots of new people at the same time.

June and another event planning division intern, Marsala, like the wine, are having an in-depth conversation about laser hair removal. I'm trying to follow the conversation, but I'm distracted as my skin pricks with heat and a wave of nausea crashes over me. I reach for the mug of chamomile tea on my desk.

When I told June my stomach was unsettled, she showed me the tea stash in the break room. A few of the interns that were local were able to come in last Thursday to do a tour, but today is the official intern start date and meeting with Marion.

I take what I hope will be a calming sip of tea, but my stomach revolts.

I press my lips together, willing my stomach to listen to

reason and not demand that it evacuates its contents at work on my first day.

I'll feed you so much good food later, if you do this one teeny tiny thing for me.

It rejects my peace offering.

June is mid-sentence when I jump up from my desk and rush for the door. I sprint to the restroom and lock myself inside. Almost immediately, the cooler air inside the restroom pacifies my desire to rush for the toilet. I lean against the cool metal door, thankful it's a private stall where I can gather myself.

Pressing the back of my hand to my forehead to swipe at the perspiration gathered there, I take a deep, shuddering breath then release it. After a few more breaths, I push myself off the door and move toward the sink.

At the sink, I dab at my eyes and immediately regret not bringing my makeup bag to work. My mascara is holding strong, but the concealer under my eyes is nearly gone with all the wiping I've been doing.

My gaze lands on the decorative basket on the far side of the counter.

A smile tugs at my lips. Of course, the restroom of an event planning firm would be packed with all the essentials. After all, JLo's Mary Fiore in *The Wedding Planner* taught us that a wedding planner is always prepared. It's filled with anything and everything one might need. Medicine, hygiene products, hair necessities.

There's no makeup, but I do snag a travel size set of mints and down half of them. Unlike the chamomile tea, I immediately feel the refreshing peppermint calming my stomach.

I take a minute to adjust my dress and smooth my hair. I don't want to walk into the intern meeting looking disheveled.

My right hand falls to my watch, shifting it on my wrist. That's when I notice the time.

Nine-thirty-two. My eyes bulge.

Shit!

I throw open the door and rush down the hall toward the intern office. As expected, it's empty. Everyone else is at the meeting.

I want to cry. I want to run back to the restroom and throw up from the sheer panic of being late to the meeting. But instead, I race to my desk, grab my notebook and pen, then hurry out of the intern office. If I was worried about my appearance a moment ago, now I'm wishing I could get that time back. I'd rather look like a haggard mess than be late.

Right before I reach the staff lounge door, my feet slow and I take a breath. I pat my head where my hair is wild from my sprint, then enter. Ideally, I'm hoping I can sneak in and quickly take a seat, not draw attention to myself.

But...that's not what happens.

The air shifts with my arrival and everyone in the room turns their head toward me.

It's that dream where you show up at school and realize everyone is staring at you because you forgot to get dressed. I'm fully clothed, but from the wide-eyed stares, you'd think I was dressed in a full clown costume. The scary killer clown from that Stephen King book based on their horrified expressions.

With everyone's attention on me, I'm compelled to speak.

"I'm sorry I'm late," I announce.

Marion's eyes flash in my direction. Her mouth is open, telling me I've walked in mid-sentence. It's the first time I'm seeing the legendary woman in person. I'm fearful that she's going to hate me now, but I'm also internally fangirling over being in her presence. Marion is everything her weddings are known for; timeless beauty and elegance. She's in her fifties, but looks like she's a mature thirty. Wearing a lilac pantsuit with a simple Cartier necklace, her chestnut hair, cut short to accentuate her cheekbones, and her piercing gray eyes are a lot to take in.

"Please, sit down," she says curtly.

Oh, right.

My eyes dance wildly around the room looking for an open seat until they land on June motioning to a seat by her.

"I didn't know where you went," June whispers as I slip between two chairs before finally making it to the seat.

"Restroom. Thanks for the seat," I murmur back.

"Ms. Hart, is it?" Marion draws my attention again. Her brows lifted in question, her gray eyes studying me. "Not the best first impression."

With my scolding, I swear the rest of the interns straighten an inch.

I suck in a breath, my hands gripping my notebook in my lap. Should I apologize? Fall to my knees and tell her it'll never happen again? I stay silent, afraid to make my already impolite entrance worse.

A small smile forms on her lips.

"Let's see." She pulls a paper out of the stack on her lap. "Sophie Hart. *Seventeen* magazine's 2018 winner of the Perfect Prom Décor competition. Graduated from UNLV with honors in Hospitality and Event Planning. Minored in business. Worked three summers under Peyton Jacobs, head wedding coordinator at The Windsor Hotel, Las Vegas."

There's nothing more intimidating than having your boss and the woman you professionally aspire to be slowly peruse your portfolio while a room full of your peers waits silently. The only thing preventing me from hyperventilating is the fact that I was already offered the internship. I'm here, so I must belong.

"You're lucky you already made a promising first impression with your portfolio, Ms. Hart." She waves said portfolio in the air before tucking it at the bottom of the stack.

"Thank you. It won't happen again. The tardiness, I mean."

"See that it doesn't." Marion motions to Maxwell next to me.

The introductions continue, and I focus intently on everyone else's background and achievements. It's clear I'm not the only one with an impressive resumé. In fact, by the time all eight interns have introduced themselves, the self-doubt is starting to creep in. While I know I belong, it's clear so does everyone else. It's like sizing up the competition for the two-miler in track and seeing everyone has the same record time.

"As you can see, there are eight of you. Four wedding planning interns, four event planning interns. It's more than we've had before. The pool of candidates this year was outstanding, and you eight were the best of the best.

"While we were able to offer eight intern positions this summer, there are only four full-time junior associate planner positions available to stay on after September. Two in the wedding planning division and two in the event planning division. There will be a final project and presentation at the end of the summer. That, along with your job performance and professional feedback from the rest of the staff, will help in determining those who will receive a permanent job offer."

I knew the internship didn't guarantee employment after the summer, but hearing it from Marion's lips, and being face to face with all the other interns makes it more impactful. Half of the people in this room won't get a job offer at the end of the summer.

The reality sinks in, causing that queasy feeling to settle in my stomach once again.

While we're in New York City and there are likely a plethora of job opportunities in the wedding planning industry, I don't want to be anywhere else but at Marion Adler Events. Working here is my dream.

There's no other option but to land one of the junior associate wedding planner positions.

"Now, I'll go over expectations," Marion continues.

I flip open my notebook and uncap my pen. While Marion speaks, I take diligent notes and do my best to ask pertinent questions.

One that even earns me a considering look and small smile from Marion.

By the end of the meeting, I feel like I've made up for my tardiness and left a more positive impression. Marion excuses us, and we return to the intern office. At my desk, I review the rest of the day's schedule and vow to not make any more missteps today.

My feet are grateful for these recycled water bottle shoes. Johnathan and I have been walking around all morning and while my feet aren't daisy fresh, they're at least not killing me. From one meeting to the next, Upper East Side to Lower Manhattan, we've had barely enough time to catch our breath, let alone eat the apple I packed, so by the time we reach Delphino's, I'm borderline hangry. Not a great place to be when I need brain power to focus on this meeting with a potential client.

Even though the morning started off a bit shaky due to my tardiness to the meeting with Marion, our productive morning has me feeling more optimistic.

I'm grateful that I'm shadowing Johnathan. Witty and full of energy, he's a vibe. He's been talking nonstop, filling me in on office dynamics and the city's social scene. I can tell he loves his job and wants to share his knowledge with me. We're pretty much best friends now.

The waiter seats us at a window table. The early-June afternoon is warm and humid. I'm used to Las Vegas's dry heat. With all the running around today, my hair is turning into a frizzy mess. I reach in my purse to grab a ponytail holder to pull it back in what I hope is still a professional-like style of ponytail.

"Does my hair look okay?" I ask.

Johnathan turns and his eyes scan over me, taking his time to assess.

"You look gorgeous. You're giving me Keely Jones vibes but without the feathered heels."

"Thanks." I smile, knowing comparing me to a beloved Ted Lasso character is the highest compliment from Johnathan. We've only spent a few hours together, but I know he's being honest. He told a woman on the street that her tag was sticking out of her collar. I have no doubt he'd tell me if my hair didn't look good.

"Okay, a little catch up on this account. Bride is a well-known socialite and has her own jewelry line, her family is in real estate development and has money. Lots of it. Groom is a Wall Street finance guy." He pauses. "Gorgeous couple. Recently engaged and are looking to wed next summer. The budget is insane. I have so many ideas for this one." The giddiness is evident in Johnathan's voice. "This would be a huge account for me to land, so follow my lead and we'll get this one on the books."

"Of course." I take a sip of my water then smooth my hand down my ponytail. This is my favorite part. Meeting new people, listening to their vision for their event, especially weddings. They're my favorite. I'm still trying to convince Emma and Griffin to have a do-over, one that I can plan every detail of, but they're perfectly happy with their impromptu Vegas wedding.

I'm looking over the menu, hoping to decide what I want for lunch before the couple gets here, when Johnathan nudges me with his elbow.

"They're here."

I lower my menu to find the hostess leading a gorgeous, dark-haired woman with a blinding smile toward our table. Her glossy hair is past the shoulders of her cream blouse which is tucked into fitted trousers. She looks like a million bucks. Her left hand clutches the straps of her designer purse to her shoulder and it's impossible to miss the diamond that sparkles with each step she takes in her Manolo's. I'm so preoccupied by the shiny beacon that is Hannah Cartwright that it takes me a moment to turn my attention to the man following behind her.

To *him*.

Positive that I'm hallucinating, I'm forced to do a double take.

That's when it's confirmed.

The man's thick, dark hair, chiseled jaw, and full lips are all present and accounted for. And when his gaze lifts from his phone, familiar indigo eyes lock onto mine. It's the club all over again, except instead of the thrill of his eyes on me, the cold rush of horror runs through my veins as the realization hits me.

He's the groom.

I've slept with Hannah Cartwright's fiancé.

This makes my nerves this morning before work seem ridiculous. A whole four hours ago, I was blissfully unaware that I had hot, dirty sex with the groom in the first wedding I would be working on at my dream internship in New York City. *Oh God*. This can't be happening.

That feeling from this morning is back with a vengeance. The feeling like someone is wringing out my stomach like a dirty dish rag. I fight it back, praying that I can keep it together long enough to alert Johnathan to this discovery.

"Hannah." Johnathan speaks up from beside me. "It's great to finally meet you." They exchange a quick hug and air kisses. "This is Sophie, she's interning at MAE this summer and will be assisting me."

"Sophie, it's wonderful to meet you." Hannah beams. I might look like a maniacal clown, but I think I'm smiling.

"You, too," is all I can manage.

"I'm so excited to chat about my ideas. This is going to be so much fun!"

Hannah seems lovely, like a breath of fresh air, which I desperately need right now. My skin flushes like I've just finished a five-miler. Every gland in my body is sending out the alert to release the inferno of heat that is building inside me.

Poor, innocent Hannah doesn't know that it will not be wonderful to meet me when she finds out that her dirt bag of a fiancé cheated on her in Las Vegas. The dread I initially felt turns to anger just thinking about ruining this delightfully pleasant and down-to-earth woman's life.

I think I've fought back the wave of nausea, but when Hannah leans in for an air kiss, a whiff of her perfume is like a punch to the stomach.

"This is Hunter—" Hannah starts to announce, but that's when I bolt. I already know who he is and the last thing I need is to throw up all over the restaurant. All over Hannah and her expensive clothes. I refuse to do *that* on my first day.

"Excuse me." I interrupt her introduction, quickly rushing toward the restroom sign at the back of the restaurant. It feels like it takes me years to get there, but when I'm finally in the safety of a stall, I dry heave until there's nothing left. Which doesn't take long since I haven't eaten anything since the last time I threw up. Jesus. I need to get a grip and possibly a Pedialyte to rehydrate.

It's bizarre. I barely know Hunter. We spent one night together, yet somewhere in the back of my brain, the part that's attached to your gut that reads what kind of person someone is, tells me that he's not that kind of guy. It's ridiculous really. The evidence is right in front of my face. And it's not like I know him at all. We had passionate, dirty sex, not a heart to heart.

Maybe this explains his reason for leaving the cash on the nightstand. It doesn't make it right, but maybe paying for sex in some fucked up way is justified to him as less like cheating than having chemistry with someone that you meet in a club and take to your hotel room to fuck their brains out.

My perfect night in Vegas is ruined. The memories and additional fantasies I created in my head must be wiped out. I can't be thinking about what I did with another woman's fiancé. Wishing I could see him again. I have no right to those thoughts anymore. And, I have no idea how I'm going to help plan their wedding. This is a fucking nightmare.

I flush the toilet, then wash my hands. Using a paper towel, I pat the back of my neck and the edge of my hairline where my skin is clammy, then I wipe the mascara smudges out from under my eyes. I'm thankful it's a nice restaurant with paper cups and mouthwash by the sink. After I swish, I take a breath, then reach for the restroom door.

Throwing up drained me, the adrenaline from earlier is gone, but when I find Hunter waiting in the hallway, hands in his pants pockets and his 'fuck me' hair falling over his forehead, the anger rises in me again.

"Sophie, we need to talk." He pushes off the wall, one hand extended to reach for my elbow, but I shake him off and keep walking.

"Don't touch me," I bite out.

"Sophie," he calls again, hot on my heels. "Wait."

I already made my decision in the restroom. When I was staring down into the toilet bowl, the horror of what we did evidenced by the revolting stomach acid being squeezed out of me, I knew I must tell Hannah. I have to let her know what we did. What Hunter did. While it takes two to tango, I was completely unaware that he was attached and therefore will lay most of the blame at Hunter's feet.

There's an alarm bell going off in my head. It's been triggered by the girl who has just started a highly coveted internship and is wondering what admitting to this fling with Hunter could do to my career. Johnathan did say how important this account is for him and the company. But I can't stand by and plan a wedding for this cheating asshole.

"You are such an asshole," I turn to whisper-hiss at Hunter behind me.

"It was a shitty thing to do," he admits. Disappointment seizes my chest. Until this moment, I thought maybe it could be a mistake, a misunderstanding, that he didn't claim my body with his while another woman was wearing his ring. "I regret it."

Although it stings a little to have someone tell you they regret having sex with you, under these circumstances, I'm glad he's regretful.

"You think?" This guy is unbelievable. And he smells delicious, which makes me hate him even more.

After weaving through the dining room, I make it back to our table with Hunter on my heels.

"Hannah," I say breathlessly, interrupting her and Johnathan's conversation.

She smiles up at me brightly. "Yes?"

"Sophie." My attention briefly shifts to Hunter who is now beside me. I can't help it. When he says my name, it makes me weak in the knees. That's the problem. He's one of *those* guys. The kind that makes you feel like you're the only woman in the world when he looks at you. I'm sure that's how Hannah feels every day. She's too wrapped up in his charm to realize he's a lying, cheating dick. But there's nothing he can say to make me change my mind.

"Hannah, I have to tell you something," I say.

She shifts in her chair, optimistic smile still in place. Shit, this is harder than I thought it would be. She seems so happy. I don't want to ruin her day. Or her life.

"Sophie, can I—" Hunter tries to interject, but I rush my words out faster.

"I slept with Hunter." I suck in a deep breath, hoping it will give Hannah time to react and I won't have to go into all the details. I'm expecting a gaping mouth, tears, cursing, something that indicates that her world is falling apart, but there's only silence. A moment later, Hannah's eyebrows shoot to her hairline.

"I'm sorry, what?" she asks.

"We had sex," I clarify, in case she was thinking it was a platonic sleepover, a cozy movie night with matching fleece pajamas and a bowl of popcorn. "In Vegas. I used to live there and he was there, maybe for work?" I question, growing more embarrassed by the minute that my admission reveals we didn't get to know each other at all before we hooked up.

"Uh, Sophie—" Johnathan's eyes are practically bugging out of his head, but I'm not done.

"And he left five hundred dollars in cash on the nightstand. Apparently, he thought I was a prostitute, so I think even if you decide to look past the cheating, his treatment of women speaks volumes about his character." I turn to address Hunter. "Not to mention that I've lived in Las Vegas all my life and I highly doubt that was enough money for the things we did."

There. I said it all. Everything I wanted to say. The group is quiet, all eyes gravitating toward Hunter. I'm waiting for some kind of reaction, but everyone appears to be stunned into silence.

Hunter closes his eyes and pinches the bridge of his nose. I hate that now I'm thinking how perfect his nose is. How good it felt when he ran the tip of it along the column of my neck just before he sucked the tender flesh in the crook of my neck.

Jesus, Sophie. *Focus.*

Hannah looks at Hunter with amusement. Johnathan is

staring at me in disbelief. Have these people gone mad? Is this a normal occurrence that isn't cause for alarm in their impending marriage? Finally, Hunter addresses me. The look on his face is a mix of exasperation and amusement. He might be a sociopath. How unfortunate.

"The cash on the side table wasn't for you, it was for the cleaning service. The room needed..." Hunter clears his throat, "extra attention." His eyes meet my gaze and I know what he's talking about. The memories cause my whole body to flush, just like Hunter's dick when it was inside me, they're embedded so deep. I might have to undergo hypnotherapy to remove them. "I always tip the hotel cleaners with cash."

"Oh," is all I can manage. Now that he's mentioning it, that might have been why the money was in one of the hotel envelopes. Shit. I feel bad that I gave the money for the hotel staff to a woman experiencing homelessness on The Strip after keeping five dollars to buy myself a breakfast burrito from Del Taco.

Hunter's still staring at me. I try not to shrink under the weight of those pools of blue. The money is hardly the point, though. That was just a small detail.

"I think the bigger issue here is…you know…the sex." I mouth the word sex because the tables around us have started to fill up and I'm not one to create a scene. Except, I've done exactly that. I notice that a busser is discreetly listening to our conversation as he clears a nearby table, and our waitress is hovering close by, likely wondering when it's safe to take our order.

"I don't know what to say." Hannah looks to Hunter, her lips pressed together in what I can only describe as a restrained smile.

From out of nowhere, a man in a navy suit and gold flecked tie appears. He approaches Hannah from behind and upon his arrival leans in to give her a kiss on the cheek, his hands sliding over her shoulders affectionately. "Hey, babe. Sorry, I'm late." He glances around at the rest of us. "Did I miss anything?"

Hannah smiles up at the man, then introduces him. "This is James McKenzie, my fiancé."

CHAPTER 3

Hunter

"Well, that was interesting." Hannah turns to me as soon as we're in the car.

Our lunch group having just departed Delphino's, James headed back downtown and Hannah and I are sharing my car service east to my office in the Flatiron District.

"I'm not discussing it with you." I pull out my phone, hoping that working on the short drive will save me from Hannah's prying questions.

"How can you not discuss it with me? She's part of my wedding planning team. I think full disclosure is necessary."

"You're going to sign the contract?" I look up from my email.

"Of course. They were lovely. Aside from the part where Sophie accused you of cheating on me," she shivers in horror, "I think the meeting went splendid." Hannah checks her face in her compact, then drops it back into her purse. "It was quite entertaining. Although, the forty-five minutes you spent staring at her was distracting from the fact that we were there to discuss my wedding."

I rub a hand down my face because what the actual fuck just happened?

Had I been surprised to see Sophie standing there in the restaurant where I was meeting my sister's potential wedding planners? That would be an understatement. Had I been happy to see her? I'd be lying if I said no.

I had not anticipated our reunion to take place under these circumstances. Hell, I hadn't expected to see her again at all. That night, we'd only exchanged first names, no other details. Leaving my business card on the pillow before I left had been a last-minute decision.

"You like her, don't you?" I feel Hannah's gaze on the side of my face.

"What are we in, middle school?" I retort. Hannah, seven years my junior, always has a way of getting information out of me. It's a character flaw that she was gifted with at birth. She's intuitive and her meddlesomeness knows no bounds.

"I can tell. Even when she was questioning your morals, labeling you a cheater who pays women for sex, you had a look on your face."

"What look?" I know what look she's talking about. I felt it, too. But denial is best where Hannah is concerned. She's like a dog with a bone, and once she gets hold of an idea, it's hard for her to let it go.

"It's the same look you get when you close a deal. I'm not exactly sure what it is. Relief? Satisfaction? *Happiness?*"

I shake my head. "There was no look. I was surprised to see her, that's all."

"I have to admit if I woke up after a night with a guy and there was cash on the bedside table, I might have jumped to conclusions, too."

"Would you also disregard the card he left you with his phone number on it?"

"Again, in my blind rage, a note on the pillow might be overlooked. Clearly, it was in Sophie's case."

"It doesn't matter now." There's the fact that during our lunch I discovered Sophie is twenty-two. Twenty fucking two.

In Vegas, I knew she was young, but I had no idea she had recently graduated college. I just turned thirty-five. The idea of me and Sophie together is as ridiculous as Sophie thinking I was trying to pay her for sex.

She'd been right when she claimed that if I was in fact paying her for sex, I had significantly underpaid. Memories of that night with Sophie have been playing on a loop in my mind every day since.

When I fuck my hand in the shower, I think about her thighs spread wide, legs dangling over the edge of the dining table in my suite, the sweet taste of her on my tongue and my name falling from her lips when she came on my mouth. How Sophie liked it a little bit rough. My hands fisting in her hair, my teeth grazing her sensitive skin. How we covered most of the surfaces of the room, tongues licking and fingers exploring, before I pinned her to the bed and slid into her tight, wet heat. My balls ache thinking about how incredible she felt. How I kept her up most of the night, not wanting our time together to end.

It was sex between two strangers, yet it didn't feel like we were fucking for the first time. It felt honest and raw, like there was nothing holding either of us back from taking what we needed from each other. My desire to give it to her hard and fast was met with her need to take everything I could give her.

When I walked out of my hotel room hours later to catch a red-eye flight, I knew nothing about the beautiful woman with golden hair, other than her name and the scent she left on my skin, yet I hated leaving her.

"You're not going to let a little thing like false accusations stand in your way of pursuing something with Sophie, are you?" She pauses for a beat. "Oh, I guess she can't be your date for the wedding if she's working at it. Is that why you're so pissy? You're afraid you're going to get relegated to the singles table?"

"You're obnoxious." I ignore her jab.

"You love me," she says with confidence. "Thanks for coming with me, by the way. It would have been a lot more boring with Mom and Dad."

Our parents are vacationing in the south of France right now. Ever since my dad retired from Premier Real Estate Group a year ago, our mom has kept him busy traveling all over the world. Hannah thinks they're gone too much, but my mom says the only thing that will slow down her travel bug is the arrival of grandchildren. She looked pointedly at me when she said it, I don't know why. Hannah's the one who is engaged and therefore most likely to create offspring sometime within the next decade.

"I'd say it was my pleasure, but you were at the same lunch I was, and we both know it was awkward as fuck. I'll let James take it from here."

"Boring. While I love James and think he should be involved in the wedding planning process, I also think we should schedule a few more meetings with you and Sophie. The hourly rate would be worth seeing the sparks fly between you two."

"That won't be necessary. I'll manage my personal life from here."

"So, you're going to see her again?" she asks.

"Hannah, the woman did not seem pleased at all to see me."

"I think amongst the shock and horror, there was some fondness for you."

I roll my eyes. "Thanks."

"At least send her some flowers. A nice bouquet from Tiger Lily's should do the trick."

She's right. It would be a nice gesture. "I'll have Jeannie send an arrangement."

"No, you'll pick it out yourself." My sister is the queen of social etiquette. "Stefan, would you drop Hunter off at Tiger Lily's on Seventy-second?"

"Sure thing, Miss Cartwright."

"I already said I will handle it," I argue.

"Will you, though?" Hannah's lips quirk, a dubious expression on her face. "You're not exactly known for your wooing ways. Do I need to remind you how many perfectly good women have called it quits with you because you're married to your career?"

"Ironically, the same women that wanted me to buy them tits and Cartier bracelets. They can't have it both ways."

"It's not about the money and you know it." Hannah shakes her head. "Dad was a workaholic. The only reason he wasn't miserably alone was because he already had Mom before he built up the company."

"Now look at the man." I extend my phone out to show her the picture my mom just texted to us. "He's living his best life."

"Yeah, with his loving wife and soulmate." She looks at me pointedly.

My chest tightens at her reminder of my parents' perfect relationship. On one hand, it's what every child would want, to grow up witnessing the love and commitment between their parents.

On the other hand, they have set a relationship standard that feels impossible to achieve. Like attempting to climb Mt. Everest when you've only ever trained on the Adirondacks' Mount Marcy.

With the last ten years of my life being dedicated to learning the business and proving my capability to take over as CEO for Premier, I've put romantic relationships on the back burner.

I'm too focused on my career to offer anything more than a few nights a week in my bed and the occasional date to an event.

"Is this all because you're planning a wedding now? Everyone should be coupled up and in love because you are?"

"Generally, yes, but I'll also admit that I'm concerned about you."

"At least you're honest."

"You're my older brother, but I feel the need to advise you in this department. We all have gifts to offer the world. This is mine to you."

"As long as you understand your advice is unsolicited and likely not retained."

She smiles sweetly. "Even brick walls are porous."

I shake my head at her quip, eyes still on my phone as I type out a quick email response.

"Oh, here's your stop." Hannah makes a shooing motion toward the door where the car is now at the curb.

"What?" I look out the window to find the storefront of Tiger Lily's floral shop. "No, I have a meeting to get to."

"Okay, then, better make it quick." She snaps her fingers twice.

"You know this is why I refer to you as 'the accident.'"

The seven years between Hannah and myself were not planned. Hannah's conception was due to a failed vasectomy. With my dad working so much, they thought having one child was plenty, and I was resigned to the fact I would be an only child until Hannah came along.

Hannah laughs. "We've already established I'm a miracle baby."

I grumble my displeasure as I turn toward the open door Stefan is holding.

I'll pick out the flowers and sign the card, an apology for our misunderstanding, but that's where this thing with Sophie will end. We're on different paths. She's straight out of college, navigating the city and her new job. I'm thirteen years older and set in my ways.

I don't do relationships. Not because I'm heartless and unfeeling, but quite the opposite. I can't stand the look of disappointment on a woman's face when she realizes I'm not going to change. That everything I've said from the beginning is true. My career has my full attention, and my priority will never be a relationship.

Casual sex, that's what I'm interested in. It meets my needs without the messy entanglements of expectations and feelings.

My mind starts to drift back to that night with Sophie, but right now is not the time to think about how incredible it had been.

And it doesn't matter how hot the sex was. That's not the point. Sophie and I are not a match.

Hannah observes my slow exit. "You've got a meeting, right?" She waves me on.

Inside the floral shop, the saleswoman approaches me.

"Can I help you with something?" she asks.

"What kind of flowers do you get a woman when you're apologizing for making her think you were paying her for sex?"

"Excuse me?" Her eyes are wide.

"Never mind." I reach for a large arrangement of white and yellow flowers with sprigs of green. I don't know what it is about them exactly, but they remind me of Sophie. Sunshine. Sweetness. An angel with a naughty side. "I'll take these for delivery."

"Excellent choice." She hands me a small white card to fill out while she arranges them in a vase.

I uncap the pen, but hesitate over the blank card, my brain trying to come up with something to say.

It was good to see you today.

I haven't been able to stop thinking about you.

When can I see you again?

The sweet taste of your pussy is seared into my brain.

I let my brain have a moment of fantasy, thinking about what it would be like to pursue Sophie. I imagine her naked body wrapped up in my bedsheets, her satisfied smile as I crawled back up the length of her body, my lips wet with her orgasm.

I ignore it all and opt for a less personal message. I read it back. It's borderline distant, my specialty.

"I'll have these delivered today."

I sign my name, then hand her the card.

"Thank you," I say before leaving the shop to return to the car.

"It's done," I tell Hannah as we pull away from the curb. She takes it to mean the flowers are sent, but it's also me telling myself to stop thinking about Sophie. *It's done.*

My dad, Marshall Cartwright, started Premier Real Estate Group during NYC's building boom in the early 1980s. His desire to redevelop the city's abandoned buildings and warehouses shaped his plan for the company. More recently, we've expanded into new building projects which has included a winning bid for development of the second phase of The Hudson Yards Expansion, the old Long Island Railroad storage yard.

From the early years, where it was my dad and a handful others, to now, where Premier encompasses architecture and redevelopment planning, new development, and our own boutique brokerage firm.

My body is here, but my mind is somewhere between my night in Vegas with Sophie and our run-in at lunch.

"What do you think, Hunter?" Tyrell's question pulls me back to the conference room.

Thankfully, I know this project inside and out.

"If we don't concede to the neighborhood association's

demands, we would need a new site plan. That's going to set us back again and cost more money."

It's a huge project that has taken years to plan and even longer to develop. For years, it's been one step forward, two steps back. My dad intended on holding off retirement until the completion of the entire project, but after countless permit delays for the second phase, he and my mom agreed it was time to hand over the reins to me.

While I want to honor my dad's efforts by completing the project, there have been many times along the way that I've wanted to release the development, allow the headache to be taken on by someone else so I can focus on other ventures. Make my own mark on the company.

"Let's agree to the concession and move forward."

The group nods and the meeting continues. That's how the rest of my day goes. One meeting bleeds into another. By the time I make it back to my office, it's nearly six o'clock.

Jeannie, my assistant, is still working at her desk.

She looks up from her computer. "I'd ask how the Carmine meeting went, but it looks like it was a doozy." Jeannie nods in the direction of my hair. She's aware of my habit of running my hands through it when I'm intently thinking about something.

It's an old habit that started at prep school during tests and has stuck with me through the intensity of business school and now a demanding career.

My hand lifts to pat down the disheveled hair created by my restless fingers.

"Other than the fact that it probably could have been an email? Fine."

Typically, I'm calm and collected at meetings no matter how tense or tedious they are, but all afternoon, I've felt restless. I want to say it has nothing to do with seeing Sophie and everything to do with work, but I'm not convinced that is the case.

"Shouldn't you be long gone?" I motion to her desk, now lit by her lamp as most of the overhead office lights have been turned off.

With a wife and two children, I know Jeannie values her family time. I've made it clear I never expect her to stay as late as I do.

"I meant to catch you this morning, but Steph had a work emergency, so I had to take Milo to the orthodontist." She lifts a pile of mail. "We need to go over some RSVPs and your schedule."

I motion her into my office. I've got another hour of work here before I can call it a day, so I wake up my computer while she gets comfortable in my guest chair.

"I can't believe Milo is old enough for braces now. I swear he was eight yesterday."

"He's twelve now." She snorts. "And going through puberty."

"Oh, shit." I chuckle. "As a former twelve-year old boy myself, I feel the need to apologize for what is coming next. The moodiness. The odor. The dirty socks that have nothing to do with smelly feet."

She laughs. "We're already there. It's been a challenge for Steph, but I grew up with three brothers, so it's not as much of a shock to me."

Listening to Jeannie talk about her family always puts a smile on my face.

Jeannie starts through the invitations to various events and parties, using the calendar on her tablet to determine my availability.

"Everything is set for the Midtown West Towers completion celebration on Friday. Employee dinner will be at six-thirty, followed by open house and mingling at eight." She looks up from her notes. "They want a final head count by tomorrow. Are you planning on bringing a date?"

I consider the option of finding one for the occasion. Typically, I'd bring a date. A woman I'm seeing casually, but there hasn't been anyone since I hooked up with Sophie in Las Vegas.

I let that settle in for a moment. How long has it been? I glance at the calendar on my desk. Only a few weeks. *That doesn't mean anything. I've been busy.*

"No. I'll be solo on this one."

Her brows lift. "Are you sure? Natasha's still on speed dial. She asked me to call her if anything in your schedule opened."

Natasha's a nice woman, but there's nothing casual about her. She's a Park Avenue princess in her early thirties looking to settle down. I learned that on our second date and was quick to let her know that's not the direction our time together would be going.

I recall the voicemail she left me a few days ago.

"I took some time to think about what you said and I realize you're absolutely right, we should keep things casual. I'm not looking to settle down anytime soon." She paused, then laughed nervously. "I mean, what is soon anyways? Are we talking like a year, maybe two? But seriously, we shouldn't be on a timeline, right? There's no rush. I froze my eggs a few years ago so I'm not feeling pressure in any way to start a family right now. We should get to know each other, maybe take a vacation or two before we decide if we want to make a bigger commitment. I'm thinking Barbados could be fun…"

Natasha is like many of the women I've dated. They'll agree to a casual relationship thinking I'll change my mind and want more eventually. When that time doesn't come, it gets messy.

I can't pinpoint the exact reason for not wanting to settle down, to date more seriously, all I know is I have a visceral reaction to the thought of being tied to one person.

I give her a tight smile. "No, I'll go alone."

She nods and continues through the rest of her list.

My thoughts drift back to Sophie. The way her green dress set off her eyes. The look of revulsion she directed at me when she thought I'd cheated on my fiancée, then the shock when she found out my actual relation to Hannah.

I'd never been more amused and simultaneously turned on in my life.

I shouldn't be thinking about her now, but sitting across from her at lunch today makes all the memories from Vegas even more vivid.

"You've got Hannah's soft opening on Wednesday. Would you like me to send a congratulatory arrangement? Champagne?"

"Both, please."

"Got it." She makes a note, then stands. "That's all I've got for now. I'll see you in the morning."

"Okay." I nod, turning to my computer. "Have a good night."

Jeannie turns before she reaches the doorway. "Oh, and thank you for approving the extra week of vacation for me. The kids are excited to go to Disney World."

"No problem. One of the easiest decisions I've made."

She smiles. "I appreciate that you value family time even when it's not a priority for you personally."

Before I can respond, Jeannie's eyes widen.

"I didn't mean for that to sound like it's a bad thing. Everyone has different priorities, but I'm grateful that as a boss you realize that and are accommodating to those who have a life outside of work." Her palm finds the side of her head. "I didn't mean you don't have a life. Sorry, it's been a long day and I think I'm making this worse. I just wanted to say thank you."

I give her a small smile and a nod. "I understand and you're welcome."

She reaches for my office door. "Open or closed?"

Other than the cleaning staff, there's no one here but me.

"Open is fine."

A few minutes later, Jeannie's lamp clicks off and I hear her leave. The office is now quiet except for the clicking of my keyboard. I pause for a moment, leaning back in my chair to think about how I want to finalize the email I'm composing.

The time alone in my office working late usually gives me comfort.

My mind starts to wander again. I tamp down the urge to think more about Sophie, so this time, my conversation with Hannah from this afternoon in the car emerges. The comments she made about our parents having each other in the early years when our dad was establishing Premier.

My dad having a partner through it all.

That while his career took up a large part of his life, he also had my mom, and us.

Like my dad before me, I've made my career my focus. It's what I've wanted since I can remember coming to the office with him, seeing how important his job was.

I recall playing in this very office while he worked. Most of the décor and furniture have been updated, but I kept the old leather chair he had from those early days. The one I'd driven my Hot Wheels over countless times and curled up in to read Spiderman comic books.

This company was always meant to be a family business. My dad had wanted to leave a legacy for his children.

And the generations to come.

The thought has my eyes shifting to that old leather chair in the corner.

Suddenly, the silence of my office feels overwhelming. The emptiness devastating.

But I ignore the unwanted feelings and finish my email, then move to the next.

CHAPTER 4

Sophie

I close the door behind me and lean against it. The apartment is quiet. Exactly how I left it eight hours ago, before I made a fool of myself at lunch with a potential client. Scratch that, an official client. That must be the silver lining in all of this. Even after I accused her fiancé of cheating on her, and told her about the money for sex situation, Hannah, and her actual fiancé, James, did end up signing the contract with Johnathan for their wedding. I'm pretty sure that was the only reason I did not get fired today.

Johnathan was cool about the whole thing. He even gave me a 'it happens to the best of us' pep talk on our ride back to the office. It was nice of him to try to make me feel better about the situation, but the reality is, I messed up. I wanted to do the right thing and I jumped in feet first, not even bothering to collect all the facts. If I would have simply waited for Hunter to introduce himself as Hannah's brother, the whole situation could have been avoided.

It wouldn't have changed the fact that I had to sit next to him at lunch, avoiding eye contact and trying to ignore the way his mere presence had my body thrumming and my panties dampening.

I hang my bag on the hook by the door and slip off my flats. My feet are swollen and tired. I can only imagine if I would have tried to wear the heels I'd packed. If it wasn't clear before, after one workday in this city, I realize Carrie Bradshaw was one bad ass bitch walking the New York City streets in heels.

All I want to do right now is change out of my dress into comfy clothes and face plant onto my bed. I'm walking through the living room when I hear what sounds like whispers. Oh, no. The last thing I need is to walk in on Griffin and Emma having sex. That would make my day of humiliation complete.

"I'm home!" I call out, hoping that gives them enough time to pull up their pants.

"Surprise!" Emma jumps out from behind the dining room wall, followed by Griffin. Behind them I can see the dining table set, boxes of Chinese food from my favorite place (I know I've lived here for less than a week, but Emma introduced it to me, and I've declared it my favorite, no need to try out any other places).

"You guys, what is this?" I ask, pleased that the surprise is dinner on the table, not me catching them in a compromising position.

Emma pulls me into a hug. "This is your first day at your dream internship celebration dinner."

When Emma releases me, Griffin wraps his big arms around me, then whispers in my ear, "She finds any reason for a celebration. But seriously, Soph, we're so proud of you."

Tears form along my lash line and I barely manage to choke out one word. "Thanks."

Looking at the dinner spread Emma arranged, I'm immediately thankful that I didn't get fired today. That would have been a huge letdown.

"I got all of your favorites." Emma lists off the three dishes that I've tried and loved. "Now, sit down and tell us about your day."

We sit and pass the containers around the table. I'm still not quite used to seeing Griffin in his work clothes. His button-down shirt and slacks make him look like a completely different person.

"It was good," I say, scooping some rice onto my plate.

"Just good?" Emma prods.

I have to laugh. This dinner and inquisition feel like parents asking how a kid's first day of school was. While Griffin wants to put the blame on Emma for this arrangement, this has protective big brother looking for the scoop written all over it.

I humor them by telling them about Johnathan, my desk-mate, June, the excitement of running around the city for various meetings, checking out venues and meeting with vendors.

"We had lunch at Delphino's."

"I love Delphino's," Emma responds.

"Haven't heard of it," Griffin says around a mouthful of food. He's been living in the city for six weeks, so that's not a surprise.

"It was a new client meeting." I breeze over the details. You know, the fact that I threw up in the restroom, thinking I had slept with the groom, who turned out to be the bride's brother, and accused him of paying me for sex.

I also don't mention that an hour after we returned to the office, an obscenely large bouquet of flowers was delivered to me. I thought it was a mistake at first.

Johnathan had informed me this morning that many florists, caterers, and stationary businesses that want to get on the company's vendor list will send free items as a way to show off their work. He said bakeries will deliver actual wedding cakes and there is nothing more dangerous than free cake. So, when the flowers arrived at my desk, I was sure it was a florist showing off their skills that was somehow misdirected to me.

Sabrina in reception assured me the card had my name on it.

It did. Sophie was scrawled in masculine handwriting across the envelope. I don't even know what masculine handwriting is, but I knew the second I saw it who they were from.

Sophie,

I apologize for our misunderstanding in Las Vegas. Congratulations on your internship.

Wishing you well,

Hunter

I left the flowers at work. I don't need Griffin and Emma inquiring about them, and at work, everyone thought it was from friends or family congratulating me on the start of my internship. Technically, it was.

I've looked at the card five thousand, six hundred and forty-seven times. And yet, I still can't figure out what the hell *'wishing you well'* means.

It's definitely not *I want to see you again* or *I'm thinking about you.* Not that running into Hunter at the lunch meeting today was going to lead to anything. We hooked up in another city and didn't make plans to contact each other or see one another again.

"Are you not hungry?" Emma eyes my plate. The food I've piled on it hasn't been touched.

"Sorry." I wince, realizing not eating seems unappreciative of the meal. "I think I'm more tired than hungry at this point."

"No worries." She waves off my apology. "The best thing about Chinese food is how good it tastes as leftovers."

"Hey, Soph, I've got an open lunch tomorrow," Griffin addresses me. "If you're free, do you want to come by my office? We can grab sandwiches at the deli down the street."

I nod. "Yeah, that should work. I'll check with Johnathan in the morning, and let you know."

"Cool."

I watch Griffin inhale his food and try to take a few bites of my own. Emma and Griffin fall into easy conversation about their days and what they have planned for the weekend. Griffin has a work event Friday evening and he invites me to tag along with them. I know I should take advantage of a free weekend while I still have them. Part of being a wedding planner is not only planning the wedding, but being in attendance on the actual wedding day. With most couples getting married on weekends, I know I won't have much of a social life once wedding season gets underway.

Work should be my focus right now, so I push thoughts of Hunter's flowers and note away and attempt to dig into my dinner, knowing full well that while I'm telling my brain to forget about his tall, broad-shouldered frame and skilled mouth, I won't be in control of my dreams tonight.

"Good morning," I give a quick knock to Johnathan's open office door with my free hand. The other is holding Johnathan's favorite drink, an iced caramel oat milk latte, from the coffee shop on the corner and a paper bag.

When he mentioned his go-to coffee drink yesterday morning, I tucked away the information for future use. After yesterday's lunch with my false accusations and unprofessional behavior, the future is here.

Johnathan had said things were okay on the ride back to the office, but I think we were both in shock. After a restless night's sleep, I needed to make sure we're good.

I also brought him a few blueberry scones that Griffin made on Sunday. They're some of his best work.

"Come on in." He motions me toward his guest chair. "I just need a minute to finish up an email."

"Of course, take your time."

I take a seat, then glance around his office. There's a horizontal bookcase with planners and color-coded binders lined up neatly on a shelf. On top, a framed picture of him and another man. Johnathan's arms are wrapped around the other man's neck and he's giving him a kiss on the cheek. It must be his husband. They make an attractive couple. Beside the picture frame, there are multiple awards and plaques.

I lean closer to read the inscription on the rectangular shaped glass award from *Lux Magazine.*

Best Personalized Wedding Planner 2022 presented to Johnathan Murray.

A minute later, he finishes and turns his attention to me.

"Okay. What's up?"

"Best Personalized Wedding Planner by *Lux Magazine.*" I point at the award. "That's impressive."

"I pride myself on making every wedding be completely tailored to the couple. There are planners who will use ideas over and over because of trends or because it's easy to replicate an element, but I like to start with a blank slate every time."

"Speaking of blank slates." I present him with the iced latte and bag of scones. "I'm still completely mortified about yesterday."

"Is that a guilt-driven iced latte?"

I laugh. "It's an apology on a budget."

He lifts the straw to his lips and sucks.

"Divine," he says, his eyes rolling to the back of his head. "And what are these?"

"My brother's specialty. Blueberry scones."

He pulls one from the bag and takes a bite. His eyes close and a moan of satisfaction escapes his lips.

"This is the best blueberry scone I've ever had."

I smile at his delight. "I think there's an entire stick of butter in each one."

"Shh. Don't ruin it." He chews then washes it down with another sip of his drink. "I'm loving the breakfast delivery, but like I said yesterday, everyone makes mistakes."

I smile. "I appreciate your understanding and I'm grateful Hannah and James did sign the contract, but I keep thinking it could have gone differently, and I'm sorry for that. I want to assure you that I only had the best intentions and nothing like this will ever happen again."

"What won't happen again? A one-night stand or you accusing your one-night stand of cheating on his sister?" He chuckles. "If I hadn't been worried about the account, I would have been recording you, and put that shit up on YouTube. It was like watching a runaway train you knew was going to derail but there was no way of stopping it."

I wince. "Yeah, not my finest moment."

"It's all good. And not only did Hannah and James sign the contract, but Hannah sent me a note this morning." He motions to his computer. "She invited us to the soft launch of her new SoHo jewelry store tomorrow night."

"Oh, wow. That's great."

"While I wouldn't normally dictate how you spend your time outside of work hours, I think after everything yesterday, the best course of action would be for us to go."

Johnathan gives me a knowing look. I wonder if Hunter will be there. My stomach dips with nervous anticipation. Maybe it'll be a good thing to see him and clear the air. Thank him for the flowers.

And Johnathan's right. I feel so bad about yesterday, so showing up at Hannah's posh jewelry event is the least I can do to smooth things over.

He sets the drink on his desk, then studies me. "I couldn't help but notice the stunning arrangement of flowers on your desk when I walked by the intern office this morning."

"They're from Hunter."

One corner of his mouth curves up. "I had a feeling."

"It's not what you think." I rush to correct any idea he has that me and Hunter are a thing. "He sent them to apologize for the misunderstanding. That's all."

He shrugs. "If you say so, but I was there. I felt the tension crackling between you two."

I give him a tight smile.

"I know what you're talking about. It was like that in Vegas, but for the next three months, this internship is my priority."

"That's probably best." He dusts scone crumbs from his hands, his smile widening. "Okay, I've got a project for you."

My face lights. "Yeah?"

"Favors for the Delancey-Kilgore wedding."

"Oh, fun!"

He smirks. "Don't get too excited. I've given them a million options already, and they've hated everything. My notes are in their file. Put together three new ideas and have them to me by Friday."

My brain is already cranking, ready to attempt the challenge. "Okay." I nod, excitedly.

"But first, we've got to break the news to the Bradshaw-Gonzales' that the floral centerpieces they want are going to cost twice as much due to a flower shortage. I've already got back up options, but we'll need another appointment with the florist to finalize everything."

After the phone call with the Bradshaw-Gonzales,' which goes well due to Johnathan's smooth talking, I return to my desk to get started on the wedding favor project.

When I get back to the intern office, June's chair is empty. She must be out at a meeting.

My phone has several new texts from Coco, who lost her mind when I told her that I ran into Hunter yesterday. While she's certain it's kismet, I'm convinced yesterday was a stroke of bad luck.

My eyes shift to the arrangement of flowers from Hunter.

They're wildflowers. An arrangement of some of my favorites. White button chrysanthemums, snap dragons, Lily of the Incas and goldenrod. It's a coincidence, because there's no way he would know that from our one night together, but it makes me smile just the same.

Before I get distracted thinking about Hunter again, I shift my focus to my computer and get to work.

"You going to eat that?" Griffin points at my half-eaten sandwich.

"You are a bottomless pit." I offer it to him.

"I know. Problem is, I don't get as much exercise behind a desk as I used to with dancing. Hopefully Emma will still love me when I have a gut."

I have to laugh. My brother has never been out of shape a day in his life. He could eat ten sandwiches for lunch and still have a six-pack.

"You're ridiculous."

We're at a popular deli spot near Griffin's office taking our lunch break like two regular New Yorkers. My gaze snags on the line of patrons ordering sandwiches. The eclectic bunch of lunch goers that includes a twenty-something bike messenger, a mother with a toddler in a stroller, two men in business suits, and a construction worker collecting two large bags of food.

I love the buzz of the city, the constant motion and sounds. It makes me feel alive. I'm still amazed that I live here. That we live here. While I get annoyed at Griffin's protectiveness, it is comforting to be here together.

I turn my attention back to my brother who is now devouring the remains of my sandwich.

"Do you miss it?" I ask.

"Not the stage, but it's still fun to use my dance moves on Emma sometimes."

"Yeah. I don't want to know that." I scrunch my nose. "I meant Vegas."

"No. Not Vegas." He shrugs. "I miss Rita and Terrence. Chad and a few of the guys from the revue, but I'm happy here."

For the last seven years, Griffin worked as a male revue dancer at Las Vegas's premiere male revue show, *Rainin' Men*. During his time there, with the encouragement of Rita, the show's choreographer, and her husband, Terrence, a tenured law professor at UNLV, Griffin got his undergraduate degree and graduated from law school. He was positioned to take a job at Terrence's law firm when he met and married Emma.

After he realized that their marriage wasn't a mistake and they fell in love, it made sense for him to move to New York City.

I was ecstatic. A content, happy brother who gave up so much for me now living his best life while I could also pursue my dream without any guilt of leaving him behind…everything is working out perfectly.

Griffin takes another bite, while I sip on the lemon ginger iced tea that I'm finding surprisingly delicious.

"How's your second day going?" he asks.

"Good. Not as hectic as yesterday." That, and I haven't made any blunders with potential clients today so for that I'm thankful.

"I'm glad you're settling in."

"Yeah, it's good." I pause, taking another drink of my tea. "I was thinking about getting a second job."

He blinks in surprise. "Really? Why?"

"This city is expensive."

"And you're living with us to cut costs."

"It's kind of you and Emma to let me stay, but you're newlyweds and I know you need your space. I think saving up for a place of my own would be good."

"We like having you there. And it gives me peace of mind."

"Right, but when will your mind be at peace? When I'm twenty-five? Thirty? I can't live with you two forever."

Griffin is eight years older than me, but his overprotective nature and need to oversee everything in my life has become an issue between us. It was fine when I was twelve. Now that I've graduated college and landed a job, and he's in love with Emma and started down his new career path, I thought things would let up a little. That he'd realize I'm an adult, capable of using an app to navigate the subway and make my own decisions, but it feels like we're stuck in the same place we have been for years.

While I'm grateful that he and Emma are letting me live with them until I get on my feet and can manage my own apartment or find roommates, my need to break free from his watchful eyes has only increased since we moved here.

"It's not going to be forever," he argues. "It's been five days."

I can tell that Griffin doesn't like the idea of me working a second job, especially if it means I'll be moving out sooner. But my goal of moving out and becoming self-sufficient is going to require more funds. I've got waitstaff experience, so I'm hoping to find a serving job a few nights a week that could pad my savings and allow me to move out sooner.

We finish up our lunch, then start walking in the direction of Griffin's office.

"Do you have time to come up?" he asks.

I glance at my watch. "I should probably head back. I don't want to take a long lunch on my second day."

"Real quick." He motions toward the building entrance. "The view is cool."

I can't argue with Griffin's eagerness. While we're eight years apart, we're on the same timeline. Both here in a new city and starting our careers. If his excitement is anything on par with how I feel, I want to indulge his excitement to share his new office with me.

I follow him inside the building where we take the elevator up to the twenty-third floor. The office layout is similar to Marion Adler Events. Glass doors open to reception, and then long hallways on both sides house offices. The décor is more wood and metal, crisp clean lines, where Marion Adler Events office is romantic and whimsical.

Griffin introduces me to the receptionist, Rebecca, and a few other coworkers we meet along the way to his office.

In his office, he sits behind his desk and I take one of the guest chairs across from him, facing the windows. The architecture of the buildings in Midtown and the Flatiron District are some of my favorites. It's postcard-worthy and I love that this is the view he has every day.

I make a low whistling sound. "Very impressive."

"Yeah, it's pretty cool."

It's a million times better than the one I have from the interior office me and the other interns share. He looks so damn happy sitting across from me. It makes my heart swell, because he deserves this. There's nothing I can do to pay him back for the sacrifices he made to raise me, but I will be damn sure to do whatever I can to lessen the burden on him. To work hard and make him proud. To become self-reliant for once in my life.

I stand to check out the pictures lining his bookcase that he's brought in from home. There's one of him and Emma at their wedding. Emma's designer slip wedding dress, simple, yet elegant, while Griffin looks deliriously happy in his black denim and t-shirt.

I sigh, thinking about their unconventional love story. And maybe about love in general. Something I'm not familiar with. If I wasn't busting my ass getting top grades in school, I was working a part-time job. And, if a guy came anywhere near me, Griffin's big brother 'mess with my sister and I'll fuck you up' glare scared them off.

Now there is a whole city of men. I'm sure if I wasn't so focused on starting my career, it would be fun to explore the dating pool that New York City has to offer.

Hunter.

I ignore my brain's automatic reference to the gorgeous man with piercing blue eyes and a thick cock that left me deliciously sore.

There's also a picture of Griffin and me when we were kids. I must have been five or six and Griffin was a freshman in high school. Sometimes I wonder if our roles would have been reversed, if I would have had it in me to raise him. To put my needs aside and do what was best for us. The responsibility that would have required. I don't think I would have been able to do it.

A knock at Griffin's open door has both our heads swiveling toward the doorway. For the second day in a row, I do a double take.

Hunter.

At the sight of him standing there, my heart immediately stops before picking back up at a rapid-fire pace.

"Hey, Griffin," Hunter's attention is on Griffin as he waves a manila folder in the air. What the hell? I want to crawl under Griffin's desk, but my brain has short circuited and my shaky hand knocks one of the photo frames off the shelf, drawing Hunter's attention.

When Hunter's eyes land on me, there's nothing short of absolute shock in them. After all, this is the second time in two days, he's not expecting to see *me*, but he manages to recover quickly.

"I didn't realize you had company." Hunter's words are for Griffin, but his gaze never leaves me.

I could be imagining it, but Hunter's eyes narrow slightly, and his jaw tightens.

He doesn't look pleased to see me. Is he annoyed that I'm here? Does he think that I'm some obsessed woman that is trying to track him down?

I break our eye contact to pick up the fallen frame and set it back on the shelf.

"Hunter," Griffin starts, "this is my sister, Sophie."

The bulging muscle in his jaw somewhat relaxes, then Hunter confidently takes the three steps over to where I'm standing.

"Sophie, this is Hunter Cartwright. He's the CEO here at Premier Real Estate Group."

I'm too stunned to speak. In fact, I think I might squeak when Hunter's large hand wraps around mine. If my humiliation yesterday wasn't enough, looks like we're going for round two. Maybe my denial at Coco's insistence there was something cosmically at play with me and Hunter has the universe saying *hold my beer.* None of that matters right now except figuring out how to respond to this discovery. Inside my skull, my brain is playing ping pong, my thoughts bouncing all over the place.

Why is he here?

He's Griffin's boss.

Shit.

What should I say?

Should I tell Griffin that I know Hunter?

How I know Hunter?

Hell, no.

"We've met," is Hunter's response.

"Wh-what?" I stutter.

My eyes widen with panic, terrified that Hunter is about to reveal how we met.

I know Sophie. Met her at a club in Vegas where she told me she wanted to lick my balls.

Not my finest moment, but that's what tequila and pent-up sexual energy will do to you. And accepting a friend's dare.

"Yesterday. At the restaurant." Hunter's brows lift. His hand releases mine and he turns to Griffin. "Sophie is assisting with my sister's wedding planning."

"No kidding. Small world," Griffin responds before glancing between the two of us.

I do my best to quiet the sound of my heart beating inside my ears.

"It really couldn't be smaller." I laugh nervously. The fact that there are over eight million people in this city, yet my one-night stand from Vegas is my client's brother *and* my brother's boss is leaving me flustered. My anxiety is officially in the driver's seat as the word vomit falls from my mouth.

"It's like, what are the odds? Now I'll be wondering where you're going to show up next. Like, are you going to start popping out of bushes? Surprise!" I burst my hands open near my face with emphasis as a cackle escapes me. "That would be weird."

Hunter doesn't answer my delirious ramble. Instead, his lips twitch slightly before he nods.

"Nice to see you again, Sophie."

Beside me, Griffin's hand wraps over my shoulder to pull my attention to him.

"You okay?" he asks, his brows lifted.

"I'm great," I screech out before clearing my throat. "Nice to see you, Mr. Cartwright," I say, trying to deepen my voice to sound less affected, but I end up sounding like an unhinged phone sex operator.

"Call me Hunter, please."

I nod, then confirm his request. "Hunter." I mean for it to be firm and precise, but his name comes out breathier than I anticipated. And once the word leaves my mouth, there's no stopping the mind-body connection that his name on my lips triggers.

I see the moment it registers for him, too. The flare of his nostrils, the short intake of breath between his full lips.

Hunter's eyes study my face. I anticipate them dropping lower, but instead, he turns his attention to Griffin and hands him the manila folder.

"I just got back from my lunch meeting with Colson. Here are the updated contracts they've proposed." Hunter glances at his watch. "Let's circle up with Tanya at three."

"Sure thing. I'm going to walk Sophie out, then I'll take a look."

"I can walk her out," Hunter offers casually, not bothering to glance in my direction.

Griffin nods. "I'd like to get this started." He turns to me. "That okay, Soph?"

"Sure." I try to sound nonchalant, but that turkey sandwich feels like it's lodged in my throat now making my words come out low and nearly inaudible.

Griffin gives me a hug before he moves back behind his desk. "I'll see you at home."

"See you." I give him a final wave, then exit his office to follow Hunter down the hallway.

Now that I'm out of Griffin's orbit, I'm relieved. Standing in the same room with him and Hunter was something I never planned to do. And definitely didn't expect to be thrown into the situation unknowingly.

I've never had a one-night stand before, but I'm pretty sure it's not normal to have the man you slept with in Vegas end up being a new client's brother *and* your brother's boss. The statistical probability has got to be one in a gazillion bajillion. Something like that. I was never great at statistics.

For a moment, I fall into stride beside Hunter, but a group of employees walking down the hall toward us has me falling behind him in order to let them pass. We're nearly to the point where the hallway lets out to the reception area when Hunter suddenly turns around. My forward momentum sends me straight into him.

"Ow." I reach for my nose, the injured party in what felt like running into a steel door, AKA Hunter's muscular chest. Even as my nose recovers from the sharp jolt, I'm recalling the way his pecs flexed with effort when he pinned my hands above my head and thrust into me hard that night.

"Shit. I'm sorry." Hunter steadies me with his hands on my upper arms. "You okay?"

"Yeah, mostly just startled but your chest is like a steel wall. You might want to register that as a hazard."

His lips smirk at my comment, but his eyes are serious as he bends down to examine my face. His thumb brushes gently over the tip of my nose, his fingers lightly caressing my jaw.

When he doesn't find any evidence of blood or bruising, he straightens again. "Can we talk for a minute?"

I glance behind me, checking for any sign of Griffin. I'm pretty sure he would lose his shit if he knew that I had hooked up with his boss. Not that I knew Hunter was his boss when I slept with him in Vegas. But that is something Griffin should not know about.

"I've got ice packs." His lips stretch into a smile, and suddenly, nothing hurts anymore. God, I remember those lips. The warm press of them across my skin. The way they sucked and teased. Just thinking about it makes my skin tingle.

We probably should talk. Maybe share more information about ourselves, so we can better anticipate these run-ins.

"Yeah, okay." I nod.

Yesterday at the restaurant, the company around us made it impossible to talk one on one, but then he sent me the flowers and I haven't been sure what to make of them. His note was formal, if not a bit vague. Were they an apology for Vegas, a peace offering after my embarrassing declaration at lunch yesterday, or something else?

He motions toward the open door he's stopped in front of. I peer in to see a large office with panoramic views of East Manhattan. With one last glance down the hallway, I cross the threshold into his office.

If I thought Griffin's view was amazing, Hunter's is exponentially so. It's crazy how different the view is out Hunter's window just from walking down the hallway.

"How do you stand it? This view is horrible," I say with my nose practically pressed against the glass, the pain from our bump in the hallway long gone. "The Empire State Building is right there!" I point excitedly, as if I'm a five-year-old who just found their favorite princess at Disney World.

Hunter chuckles behind me. "It's nice to see it through a fresh set of eyes."

"Because you stare at it every day and think it would be such a good view if only that large building weren't in the way?" I tease.

I turn to find him watching me. He must think I'm such a tourist. I wonder when it'll start to feel like everything isn't out of a movie. That I live in this fabulous city. This is my life now.

"A set of wildly expressive green eyes."

The way he's staring at me now reminds me of how our eyes locked in the mirror when he bent me over the vanity and made me come with his cock in my pussy and his finger in my ass. How he told me to keep my eyes open so he could see how much I liked being filled with him.

He extends his hand out and I take the ice pack he hands me. The cold ice does nothing to cool the flash of heat that licks my body anytime I'm near Hunter. Clearly, the sizzle between Hunter and me in Vegas was not just due to the tequila consumed. The alcohol made me brave and carefree, but it wasn't the only reason I found myself in his bed.

I had thought I was so daring, walking up to a stranger and telling him I wanted to lick his balls. High off the thrill of being so forward, I didn't expect Hunter's response.

Is that before or after you're ass up on my bed with my cum dripping down your thighs?

Each word out of his mouth was like a stroke to my clit. That's when I realized that with Hunter, I wasn't in charge, and I didn't want to be.

There's something about his presence. A confidence that doesn't come off as arrogance. He wants what he wants and isn't afraid to say so. That's how it was the night we met in Vegas. It was easy. No games. Just open desire and uninhibited lust catapulting us into Hunter's hotel suite. Maybe that's why I let him do things that I had never done with another guy.

I pull myself out of that hotel suite and back into his office.

"You keep ice packs in your office? Are you prone to injury?"

"Bum knee. I have to ice it after I run."

I smile. I doubt he has a 'bum' anything.

"Where do you run?" I ask. The city is intimidating enough to navigate getting to work, I have yet to attempt running here on my own.

"I've got a Central Park loop I do three times a week." He rubs a hand across his jaw, still studying me. "Do you run?"

"I did in Vegas. I haven't quite gotten into a routine here yet."

"I could send you some of my routes if you'd like."

"That'd be great." I absently massage the ice pack in my hand, finally remembering I wanted to thank him for the flowers. "Thank you for the flowers. They're beautiful."

"I'm glad you liked them." Hunter lifts his gaze back to

mine. "I'm sorry about Vegas. The mix up with the cash on the nightstand...and leaving without saying goodbye."

"It's fine. I think we both know what Vegas was."

"And what was that, Sophie?" Hunter's eyes drop to my lips before returning to my eyes.

"A fun night. Blowing off steam." I smile, trying desperately to not let his closeness affect me.

"You're right. It was a fun night." The corner of his mouth pulls up in a smirk before he leans in closer to whisper, "Would you be curious to know that I've thought about that night every day since?"

The low rumble of his voice and the warmth of his breath against my ear makes my heart rate spike. When he pulls back, for a fraction of a second our lips are millimeters away and I think he's going to kiss me. His eyes drop to my mouth, and my eyes instinctively close.

"Mr. Cartwright?" A woman's voice cuts through the silence. My eyes fly open and Hunter takes a step back. There's no one there, so it must have come from the speaker on his desk phone.

Hunter walks over to his desk to press a button and speak to her. I take a large gulp of air. Air that I was deprived of being so close to him.

"The Carmine Group is here."

"Thank you, Jeannie. I'll be out in five." Hunter releases the button and glances back to me. "I've got a meeting."

I nod in understanding and start moving toward his office door.

"Sophie, wait." He studies me for a beat before continuing. "The circumstances that we find ourselves in, you planning my sister's wedding and me being your brother's boss, make it necessary for us to not see each other in that capacity again."

His lips turn down at the corners. He looks so serious, like he's delivering a eulogy. Our one-night stand is to be buried and never resurrected. While my body is mourning the loss of his wicked tongue, running my fingers through that gorgeous head of hair, and feeling him thrust inside me, I know he's right. I didn't move here to pursue a guy, I'm here for my career. *And* sleeping with Hunter now knowing he's Griffin's boss is bad news.

"You're right." I nod and adjust my purse on my shoulder.

For a quick second, his eyes narrow and I think I see his normally unshaken confidence slip, like he's confused that I'm agreeing with him.

Trust me, every cell in my body is revolting against being a mature adult about this. But that's the point. I can't think about myself here. This is Griffin's boss. The boss at Griffin's new job for his new career that he's put on hold while he raised me and put me through school. And while you could argue it shouldn't be a big deal, I worry that if Griffin found out I was involved with Hunter, it wouldn't be Griffin, the employee, that had words for Hunter, it would be big brother Griffin. The last thing I need is for Griffin to get into it with his boss over me.

He clears his throat and nods. "I am."

It's a statement, but somewhere in there, I swear I hear a question.

Hunter opens a desk drawer to pull out a card. He takes two steps to close the space between us and extends the card to me.

"My number. If you ever need anything."

"Thanks."

I reach out to take it and our fingers briefly touch. In that fleeting touch, the electrical current that passes between us is enough to light my panties on fire.

What was I saying about being an adult?

About not getting involved with this man who can turn me on with the simple caress of a digit. If this were a porno,

Hunter would swipe everything off his desk in one quick move, then lift me onto it and put his face between my thighs.

I hate that this is not a porno. It's reality. A reality where I walk out of Hunter's office and forget what it felt like for my body to be worshipped by him.

I tuck his business card in my purse and walk out of his office.

On the way back to work, I buy a giant chocolate chip cookie from a local bakery and eat every bite. It's the only guilty pleasure I'm allowing myself today.

CHAPTER 5
Hunter

I glance at my watch. I'm an hour late, but luckily the boutique is packed, so Hannah might not even notice. I lost track of time at work. The designs for Premier's up-and-coming project in Las Vegas hit my inbox right before five and I couldn't resist reviewing them.

Making my way through the crowd, I greet a few familiar faces, before I reach the bar.

"Whiskey neat, please."

"Coming right up."

The bartender pours my drink while I scan the room. The crowd is mostly women, or couples. I recognize many of Hannah's friends.

"Here's that whiskey for you."

"Thank you." I pull my wallet out and drop a tip in the jar before taking my drink.

My phone starts buzzing in my pocket. It's my mom and she's trying to FaceTime me.

I answer only because I know she'll keep calling if I don't.

"Hi, Mom."

"Hi, I'm so glad I reached you. Are you at Hannah's opening? I've been calling her, but she's not answering."

I flip the camera so she can see the crowd.

"She's a tad busy at the moment."

"Oh my goodness. What a great turnout. Oh, I wish we could have been there."

"It's the soft opening. You'll be back for the grand opening."

"I know, but we hate to miss out on things like this. We always want to be there to support."

"You're here in spirit. And via FaceTime."

"Pan me around so I can see the boutique."

"How about I walk you around so you can say hi to everyone?"

She gasps in delight. "That would be wonderful."

"I'm kidding. I'm not doing that."

"Fine, but I want a full report. And tell Hannah to call me."

"I'm sure she'll get your twenty missed calls and texts."

"I love you."

"Love you, too." I disconnect the call and pocket my phone.

Over my right shoulder, I hear my name.

"Hunter. Hey, man, I thought that was you. I didn't want to interrupt."

I turn to my right to find one of my old Princeton rowing buddies, Connor Whitlock.

"Connor, hey." I lean in and clap him on the back. "I didn't expect to see you here."

"Alice's parents are watching the kids, so we're having a date night. She wanted to stop by to see Hannah's opening, and then we're off to dinner and a show."

Alice appears at Connor's side. "Okay, I've picked out my birthday presents." She motions toward the case she was previously standing at before she glances over at me. "Hunter," her eyes light with surprise. "Oh my goodness, it's been ages." She wraps me in a hug. "I wasn't sure if you'd be here. What's new with you?"

Before I can answer, Alice continues talking.

"Oh, I saw that article last year. Your dad retired and now you're Premier's CEO. Congratulations."

"Thank you," I say, taking a drink.

"I'm sure the article declaring you to be the city's wealthiest CEO bachelor was a hit with the ladies. Anyone here with you tonight?" She scans the surrounding vicinity.

"No. Just me here supporting Hannah."

"Oh, that's nice," Alice says.

I scan the room, looking for Hannah, and that's when I see *her*.

Across the room, by one of the jewelry cases, is Sophie.

She's flanked by Johnathan and another guy. They're sipping on cocktails while they talk and peruse the jewelry.

If I thought she was off limits before, discovering Sophie is Griffin's sister should have put an end to me thinking about her, but unfortunately, that hasn't been the case. If anything, she's consumed my thoughts even more.

The group next to them shifts, blocking my view of Sophie.

"I'm going to look for Hannah. It was great to see you two."

I say my goodbyes, then make my way across the room. I should find Hannah, but my feet have me moving in Sophie's direction.

Johnathan sees me first.

"Hunter Cartwright." A huge smile takes over his face. "Nice to see you again."

"Johnathan." I nod, then shift my gaze to Sophie. "Sophie." Her name slips past my lips in a husky tone.

She's dressed in wide leg pants and a snug tank top that accentuates her full breasts and her trim waist.

"This is Marco Diaz." Johnathan introduces me to the man

next to Sophie. I've barely shook his hand when Johnathan guides him away. "And we were just going to grab another drink."

Sophie's mouth falls open, likely to protest, but Johnathan and Marco are gone before she can get a word out.

My gaze catalogs her features. The blonde curtain of silk framing her face, those responsive green eyes fixed on me. Lush pink lips wrapped around the straw of her drink.

"Hannah invited us."

One corner of my lips pulls up. "I think that's why we're all here."

"Right." She nods. "I just didn't want you to think that I'm here for any other reason."

Her tongue slides against her bottom lip and my eyes follow the movement.

"What reason would that be?" I ask.

"You know, what we discussed in your office yesterday."

I nod.

Telling her we shouldn't see each other in any capacity, particularly not repeating what we did in Vegas, was the right thing to do, but the moment the words left my mouth, I hated them.

The fact that Sophie is now there every time I turn around isn't making this easy at all.

I motion to the case nearby. The one that she had been looking at before I came over. "What do you think of the jewelry?"

"It's gorgeous. Hannah is super talented." She beams.

"Yeah, she is."

"This one is my favorite." She fingers the necklace hanging from the jewelry stand on the counter. "The delicate chain with the wildflower pendant."

"You should try it on."

Sophie shakes her head. "That's okay. It's not in my budget right now."

I ignore her refusal and reach for the necklace. Unclasping it, I lean forward to reach around her neck.

Being this close, her scent washes over me. It's light. Fig and citrus. Soft and elegant, like a new cashmere sweater.

I fasten the necklace, then gather Sophie's hair with one hand to lift it out of the loop of the chain. Gently setting down the chain on the base of her neck, I keep my hand wrapped around her hair. My fingers slide along the chain until I reach the front of the necklace. My fingertips graze the smooth skin of Sophie's chest as I position the pendant there.

Her green eyes lift to mine and I'm flooded with memories of our night together.

An image of Sophie looking up at me, her lips stretched around my cock. The memory of her velvety tongue licking the pre-cum from my tip causes my grip on her hair to tighten.

Sophie's lips part on a sharp intake of breath and I swear I can see the same memory mirrored in her heated gaze.

Sexual attraction is one thing, but my body's heightened awareness of this woman is different than anything I've ever experienced. The desire to have her again, overwhelming. With each encounter, my brain's synapses reinforce the connection to Sophie. *Mine.*

My gaze drops to those perfect pink lips. Lush and full. They're like a siren drawing me in.

Sophie's eyes close. It should be a signal of how close we are. How close our lips are.

"There you are." Hannah's voice cuts through the moment.

I blink, pulling back from Sophie. Had I forgotten we're standing in a room full of people?

I release Sophie's hair. Her hands reach up to smooth it out, her cheeks a rosy pink color now.

"Hi," Sophie says, her voice tight. "Um, Hunter was helping me try on this necklace."

"My brother is very helpful."

After giving me a knowing look, Hannah leans in to inspect the necklace I put on Sophie.

"Aw, that's one of my favorites," Hannah says.

"It's beautiful." Sophie fingers the pendant. "I love the wildflower design. How did you come up with it?"

As Hannah and Sophie discuss the necklace, I'm transfixed with Sophie. Her eyes, her smile. Her brightly-colored fingernails as she slides her fingers along the necklace chain. They're a coral color. I think back to Vegas, remembering the pretty sky-blue color they had been. How the image of her hand and those blue fingernails wrapped around my cock has been burned into my brain. The sparkly silver dress she had worn that night. The way it shimmered in the club's lights when she danced, then easily slid from her body to the floor of my suite.

Everything about her and that night is an easy recollection. It's been haunting my dreams recently.

"What do you think?" Hannah turns to me, but I've been stuck in my head and missed the entire conversation they were having.

"Huh?" I say unintelligibly.

"The necklace?"

"She's beautiful. I mean, *it's* beautiful."

At my Freudian slip, Sophie's cheeks flame and Hannah's lips twitch.

What the fuck was that?

"Thank you for having me," Sophie says, unclasping the necklace so she can place it back on the display. "Your boutique is gorgeous and I aspire to own a piece of your jewelry someday."

"That's very sweet. Thank you." Hannah gives Sophie a hug.

Sophie glances in my direction, giving me a small nod, before leaving.

"Real smooth." Hannah smirks at me. "What is going on with you?"

"Nothing." I shrug, taking a sip of my cocktail and fighting the instinct to glance in Sophie's direction. "I'm tired, that's all. It's been a busy week."

Her laugh is light and commiserating. "Isn't it always?"

She's right. This week is like no other in terms of work. The only difference being my mind's preoccupation with a certain blonde whose presence is still on my radar even when she's on the opposite side of the room.

"Okay. I've got to keep circulating." She gives me a tight squeeze. "Oh, a columnist from *The Post* is here and they want a picture of us. A *Cartwright kids, what they're doing now* type thing. Don't leave. I'll come find you in a few."

I nod, then occupy my time by making the rounds, talking with friends, and humoring Hannah's request for photos.

For the rest of the night, I make a point to steer clear of Sophie.

But it's clear, not having her again is doing something to me.

I shouldn't want Sophie, because of our age difference, because she's Griffin's sister, but with every encounter, my willpower to stay away is crumbling.

CHAPTER 6

Sophie

I've spent most of my time this week on the Delancey-Kilgore's wedding favor search. Johnathan was right. They have rejected nearly every traditional idea. We've gathered in the conference room, and after Johnathan goes over checklist items, it's my turn to present what I've come up with for favor ideas.

"Nothing." Demi Delancey does her best to lift her eyebrows, but Botox keeps them in place. *"That's* your suggestion?"

Johnathan laughs nervously. "Not *nothing*. You're giving them an unforgettable evening at the Botanic Gardens."

Johnathan's eyes flick to me, the panic evident on his face. The unspoken words there.

What are you thinking, Sophie?

"Your wedding is at the Botanic Gardens. Clearly, you enjoy nature," I say, trying to keep the confidence in my voice that I felt before Demi and Bryce started looking at me like I'd grown a horn. "What better way to commemorate your love for not only the Botanic Gardens, but our planet in general, by making a donation in every guest's name as a favor?"

"A donation?" Bryce questions.

"It'll show you care about the environment. Not only are you foregoing a traditional wedding favor that could produce waste, but also giving back to a place you enjoy spending time."

"You're saying people would throw away our favors?"

I push through. "Have you kept every wedding favor you've been given?"

Demi thinks for a moment. "You have a point."

It's a small win even if she hates my idea.

"Is it a tax write off?" Bryce asks. "The donation. Would we get the tax benefit or the person whose name the donation is in?"

"I'm not sure about the tax situation. I'm sure you could do either. Either do a large donation on behalf of your wedding guests as a whole or divide it up to each individual guest. I can check with their donations department and see what our options are."

Bryce's bottom lip juts out, his eyes narrowing as he thinks.

"It could work," he says, finally.

He turns to Demi. "What do you think?"

"It might get Maven Manchester off my back about volunteering for her Save the Barn Owl campaign. She's always giving me shade about missing it. I have nothing against the Barn Owls, I'd just rather be in the Hamptons."

"It's about balance, right?" I offer.

Demi shoots me a glance. "Good thinking." She turns to Johnathan. "I like her."

When I glance over at Johnathan, he's grinning ear to ear. "Yeah, me, too."

"I thought this was a party." I glance around at the loft space where we just arrived.

Yesterday, when I started asking in-depth questions about the real estate development firm he works for, Griffin was elated I had shown interest in his work. I felt a tad guilty knowing I was hoping to get more information about Hunter. I hoped Griffin would mention him or give me some kind of tidbit about his life. All I know is that Premier Real Estate Group buys up old commercial or residential buildings in disrepair to develop them into lofts and condos, then turns around and sells them for insane amounts of money. Like the price tag on this place. Read ten point seven million dollars.

"It's not a frat house." Griffin chuckles.

"I never went to a frat house."

"Good," he says with a satisfied nod.

"What I meant was I thought there were going to be more people." I motion to the twelve people here milling about.

When Griffin invited me to come and Emma spent two hours picking out my dress, it was under the guise that it would be a fun social event where I could meet young professionals, like myself.

The first person Griffin introduces me to is Walt, Premier's lead counsel, and his wife, Jan. Walt and Jan are in their sixties and let me know they had just returned from a Caribbean vacation, and are awaiting the arrival of their seventh grandchild any day now.

I think Griffin and Emma just felt bad leaving me home on my first Friday night in the city. Honestly, it has been an exhausting week. I wouldn't have minded curling up on the couch to watch a movie, or getting some alone time in the apartment and having a hot date with my vibrator, all before passing out in my bed by ten o'clock.

I realize how un-twenty-two-like that all sounds. I should be living it up. Trying out new restaurants and clubbing until all hours of the morning. Griffin probably wouldn't be pleased about that, but I am excited to start exploring my new city. Do all the touristy stuff that I've researched so much about.

But tonight, I'm here. Supportive sister reporting for duty.

I do a quick scan of the room, trying to appear casual, but my body is on high alert looking for Hunter.

Maybe that's why it didn't take too much twisting of my arm to come tonight. It's his company. He's got to show, right?

But this is not how I imagined it.

I'd hoped it would be a packed house situation. One where I could fade to the background, watch Hunter from afar, hidden behind throngs of people.

Hunter has been on my mind all week. It's annoying really.

Sure, there were times where I was so busy during the day, working on budget spreadsheets or setting up vendor meetings for a bride, that he wasn't at the forefront of my mind. But every night, when I climbed into my bed, I thought about him.

Thought about how he was about to kiss me at Hannah's jewelry boutique opening two nights ago. Which is crazy, because we don't want anyone to find out we hooked up in Vegas, so we shouldn't be seen kissing in public, especially after we agreed that our one-night stand would be just that.

And then there's last night, when I made myself come to the memory of him fucking me in Vegas.

Another group of people walk in.

"Oh, look, now there's twenty," I tease.

"Relax. We're here early for the dinner. More people will show up after."

Did I get the memo about dinner? My gaze drops to the hem of my dress.

The dress Emma picked out for me is insanely short. She's shorter than me, so it looks normal on her. But on me? It's barely covering my ass. Griffin scowled when he saw me in it, but Emma wrapped her arms around his waist, cuddled into his side and told him to tell me I look nice. He looked down lovingly into her eyes, then obliged. It's clear Emma is the balm to my brother's overprotective ways. I'm happy they have each other and that I now have a sweet, nurturing woman like Emma in my life.

Dinner might be a problem. The dress hits my upper thigh when I'm standing. Sitting, it will likely be above my pelvis. Oh, and the small issue that I don't have underwear on. Emma demanded I didn't wear any. It's a Balmain dress, she said, panty lines would be unforgivable. Flashing my lady parts to my brother's co-workers might be unforgivable as well.

"Griffin," a familiar male voice cuts into my thoughts and I turn to see Hunter approach us, a woman in a cream dress at his side.

When my eyes collide with Hunter's, there's a momentary look of surprise, a slight tick in his jaw, before it relaxes and he smiles.

Hunter leans in to kiss Emma on the cheek. "Good to see you, Emma."

"And you remember my sister, Sophie? You met her at the office."

"Good to see you again, Sophie." I ready myself for the feel of his lips on my cheek, the inevitable buzz that our skin-to-skin contact does to me, but he simply nods, then places his hand on the woman's lower back and gently guides her into the circle we've formed.

"This is Madeline," Hunter announces. I wait for the rest of it. Some sort of indication as to who Madeline is.

This is Madeline, my date…my girlfriend…my long-lost sister that looks nothing like Hannah and myself. I glance around. Emma and Griffin nod and smile. Apparently, no one else is dying for these details.

Everyone takes turns introducing themselves and shaking

Madeline's manicured hand. Griffin and Hunter exchange a few words about work, then Hunter excuses himself and Madeline to mingle without a glance backward. It's totally cool, I tell myself, then I beeline to the bar that's been set up in the sitting room off the foyer.

"What can I get for you?" the bartender asks.

"Tequila shots." A guy appears beside me. "Two tequila shots."

My eyebrows lift as I turn to him. "This doesn't seem like a tequila shot kind of party."

"It is when you're celebrating closing on two ten-million-dollar units." He flashes a mega-watt smile, and for the first time, I notice how handsome he is. Clean shaven, warm brown eyes, and wavy, chestnut brown hair. His nose is slightly crooked in the middle, like it's been broken before, and his grin is lopsided but charming.

"Andrew Bachman," he introduces himself with a handshake.

"Sophie Hart."

"The pleasure is all mine." His lips quirk again and I can't help but giggle. "I'm surprised we haven't met before. I'm the listing agent on the property. Do you work with Hunter?"

"No. I'm Griffin's sister." I nod toward Griffin and Emma who are across the room chatting with another couple. "I'm new to the city and he wanted me to come tonight to meet people."

Andrew's eyes light up, he points to himself. "I'm people," he says, deadpan.

I can't help but laugh. And when the bartender delivers the two tequila shots, I clink shot glasses with him and easily toss one back. The tequila makes my stomach burn. It reminds me I haven't eaten much today. Some crackers, a yogurt, half of a peanut butter and jelly sandwich and a bag of chips.

I may have graduated and started a job with an elite event

planning firm, but I still eat like a toddler. I add healthy eating to my list of adult things to do.

Suddenly, a warm flush works its way down my spine. I think it must be the tequila, but the way the heat sears into my back, it has me turning from the bar to glance around the room. A moment later, I lock eyes with Hunter. He's with a group on the other side of the room. One hand holds his cocktail glass. Long, masculine fingers gripping the edge as he holds it by his side. The other hand in his pocket, his arm occupied by Madeline's hands as she grips his forearm in a cozy, intimate gesture while she smiles and laughs with the group.

Hunter's gaze doesn't leave mine. We don't blink. It's a stare down, one that the tequila shot warming my belly has given me enough confidence to hold. I know we agreed that it was best not to explore anything with each other. I was on board with that on Tuesday. I just didn't realize I would have to subject myself to seeing Hunter with another woman. That I would want to scratch that woman's eyes out when I think about him touching her the same way he touched me.

I have the sudden urge to stick my tongue out at him. That would be super adult-like.

I need to get a grip and I need to forget about Hunter.

Beside me, Andrew is still talking.

"I'm sorry, what?" I ask, pulling my gaze away from Hunter and vowing to ignore him for the rest of the night.

"Do you want a tour of the apartment?"

"Yes. That would be great," I say, because if there's any way I'm going to ignore Hunter for the rest of the night, being in separate rooms for the majority of it will be helpful.

Andrew starts to walk me through the space, with a few other guests latching on to his tour. He provides details about the finishes but it's not a stuffy realtor tour.

From all his charming expressions and hilarious stories, I think Andrew was a stand-up comedian in a previous life.

Either that or a cartoon character. He's funny and cute, age-appropriate, and not my brother's boss. Andrew doesn't give me the electric buzz, shockwave kind of feels, but he's a guy that I think would be fun to know.

"Here's the second master." Andrew leads us in. "Floor-to-ceiling windows, travertine tile in the bath, blah blah blah." He opens a door on the wall. "*This* is really what makes this place cool."

"Andrew, there you are." The sound of Hunter's voice puts me on high alert. If only these floor-to-ceiling windows had a fire escape. "Dinner's almost ready."

"Great." Andrew claps his hands, then looks between me and Hunter. "Sophie, have you met Hunter?"

"Yes," we answer in unison.

Andrew nods, glancing between me and Hunter. "Okay. Cool. I guess we should head back to the dining room."

"I'm going to use the restroom," I announce.

"There's a powder off the hallway. I can show you." Andrew moves to put his hand on the small of my back to escort me out of the room. I watch Hunter's eyes zero in on Andrew's hand.

"Actually, Andrew," Hunter interjects. "Nessa wanted to talk with you."

"What about?" he asks.

"She wanted to follow up with the closing from yesterday. Make sure everything was good."

Andrew shrugs. "We're all good with it."

"Better double check." Hunter smiles, but it doesn't register as all that friendly. I don't know the relationship between these two, but I'd rather not get in the middle of it.

"I'll find my own way." I rush out of the room, and find the powder bath a few doors down. After doing my business, I wash my hands, but when I open the door, I find Hunter waiting in the hallway.

CHAPTER 7

Hunter

The bathroom door opens and Sophie appears. For the first time tonight, I let myself look at her. Really take her in. Our greeting earlier with Emma, Griffin and Madeline had been short, but also, I knew I couldn't let myself look at her the way I wanted to. Not with her brother standing there.

I get my fill now.

Sophie's legs stretch for miles beneath the short hem of her dress. I've thought about those legs. The smoothness of her thighs when I lifted them over my shoulders and licked her sweet pussy. How good they felt wrapped around my waist, how tight her muscles squeezed me when I drove into her hard.

My eyes move over her slender waist and up to her full, perky breasts. My hands ache to feel the weight of her breasts in my palms again, to close my mouth around a hardened peak and suck. And, fuck, I really want to come on her chest. That's not a memory from Vegas, it's a fantasy I've concocted this week while stroking myself to the thought of her. One of many I can't get out of my head.

Sophie's golden locks are styled in loose waves over her shoulders. The same way they were the night we met in

Vegas. The night I gathered them in my hand and used the leverage to angle her mouth exactly where I wanted it.

My eyes shift to that pretty mouth of hers. Right now, her full lips are parted in surprise at my presence. I remember how beautiful she looked with those lips stretched around my cock. The shape they formed when she came hard and fast, screaming my name.

The memory makes my dick swell even further, the bulge pressing uncomfortably against my zipper. Fuck. Now I'm standing here with an erection.

I rush forward toward the bathroom door.

"Hi. I guess you really need to use the bathroom," she says, bemused. She attempts to move out of my way, but I catch her elbow, pulling her back into the bathroom before I shut and lock the door behind us.

Alone in the bathroom with Sophie…it's the last place I should be, let alone at a company function, but I can't help myself. This week has been torture. Sophie is all I can think about. Knowing she's here in the city and I can't touch her is doing something to me.

"No." I lean against the door. "I don't need to use the bathroom."

"Oh." She looks around the small space before allowing her eyes to land on me. "Then what do you need?"

Her words come out breathless. I can hear the tremble of desire in them. My body was already primed from simply looking at her, hearing her voice and being this close only intensifies my craving for her. Sophie's response to me does nothing to tell me I should turn and leave. It only draws me in further.

I push off the door and take a step closer.

You. That's the answer to her question, but I don't say it aloud.

Sophie turns back to the mirror and pulls a lipstick out of her clutch. I watch her for a moment before I pull my gaze away. *What the fuck am I doing here? This is inappropriate.* My fingers thread through my hair, pulling on the styled strands until they're wild.

"I shouldn't be in here with you," I say, letting her know that I'm on edge. This is a dangerous place to be. Only feet away from her with no one else around.

"Okay." She smacks her lips together, then drops the lipstick back in her clutch. "You know where the door is."

I smirk, watching her pretend like she didn't start breathing harder the second I walked in here. It gives me some relief to know that I'm not the only one feeling this way. "That's one of the things I liked about you that night in Vegas."

"What?" she asks, her eyes trailing me in the mirror as I walk up behind her.

"Your mouth." I let myself lean into her, my front grazing her back, but I keep my hands restrained in my pockets. "I liked the sassy words that came out of it as much as I liked filling it."

When Sophie's eyes lift again, our gazes collide in the mirror.

I can see the effect my words have on her. The way her eyes dilate and her nipples harden beneath her dress. I swear I can even see the quickening pulse in her neck under the shadow of the vanity light.

"I liked how wet your thighs were from sucking my cock, how your back arched when you rode my tongue on the dining table before I bent you over the bed and fucked you hard."

I watch her swallow work itself down her slender neck, only to have the sudden urge to wrap my hand there.

The torture I've felt this week is reflected to me in the mirror. "I can't stop thinking about you, Sophie."

"And yet, you're here with another woman." She breaks our stare to tousle her hair. "That's interesting."

I've already forgotten that I brought Madeline to the party. That she asked for a ride and I obliged.

"She's a friend."

"Yes, she did look very friendly when she was hanging on your arm and rubbing her hand all over your chest."

"I know we said it would be best not to see each other—" I start, but she whips around to face me.

"Actually, *you* said that." She makes a move toward the door.

"And you agreed." I match her move. I should let her leave, end the torture that being near her causes, but I know it won't end if I walk out of this room without touching her. "Then, I see you here tonight and I can't take my eyes off you."

Behind the safety of these walls, my greedy eyes attempt to get their fill. I'm hopeful if I take in every inch of Sophie's skin, trace every curve of her body, the memories will be enough to sustain me. I already know they won't.

"I noticed," she says, her attempt at smug, but I can see the hunger I feel matched in her eyes.

I close the inches between us, pinning her against the counter, my hands gripping the edge of the cool marble.

"I've been thinking about you to the point of distraction."

"What have you been thinking?" she asks.

My forehead finds her temple. I let my lips ghost over her jaw.

"How I need to touch you. Taste you. It's driving me insane." My hands lift to her upper arms, letting my fingers lightly trail down her smooth skin. "How I'm dying to see your tight pussy stretched around my cock again."

"Hunter," she gasps.

"Fuck. Just the sound of my name on your lips, it's too much." I groan. Sophie turns her head and my lips explore that sensitive place on her neck. We should stop. But we're not even doing anything. Not really. We're standing here, both coiled tight with need. "Say it again."

I'm waiting for her to push me back and walk out the door, to remind me that touching each other again is not a good idea, but she doesn't. Her hands find my face, fingers tracing my jaw as she urges it upward until our eyes lock.

Her lips pull up at the corner. "Make me," she challenges.

My lips twitch with satisfaction.

Before we can voice what is about to happen, our desire takes over. Sophie's hands slide into my hair. A second later our lips collide on an inhale, breathing each other in. While our tongues battle, I reach for her waist and lift her onto the counter.

Now that she's seated, the hem of her dress has reached new heights. Fuck. I'm dying to touch her. My hands move along the outside of her smooth thighs, inching the hem of her dress up even farther. I need to *see* her.

Sophie seesaws back and forth on the counter to help my efforts. Finally, the dress gives way and her ass meets the countertop. Under my hungry gaze, she leans back on the counter and spreads her legs.

I take in the sight before me. The one I've been fantasizing about since Vegas. A small strip of blonde hair, and beneath that, Sophie's gloriously bare pussy.

"Sophie. Fuck. You're not wearing underwear?" My jaw tightens and my cock jolts against my zipper.

"I couldn't wear anything with this dress." She shrugs. "Emma said it would be a sin to."

I have the urge to bend Sophie over this counter and smack her ass. To punish her for making me lose my mind. Does she have any idea how hard she makes me? How much worse I will be from knowing that she walks around with no underwear on?

But I don't have time for that. I have one purpose right now. My hands connect with her inner thighs and press her open wider before I drop to my knees between them. Before either of us can come to our senses, I yank her forward and flatten my tongue against her center.

Sophie presses her lips together, but it doesn't keep her moan from escaping.

"Just like I remember, so fucking sweet," I say between licks. "You taste like sunshine and brandy and *mine*."

Sophie grinds her pelvis against my face. A rush of wetness hits my tongue. I lap up every drop.

I thrust a finger inside her, then another.

Above me, Sophie braces herself with a hand around the faucet and one on the towel hook to stay upright.

"Come all over my face, Sophie," I demand, letting my words hum against her clit. I can feel her body's response. How close she is.

I flick her clit and hook my fingers inside her.

"Oh, fuck. *Hunter*."

She clamps a hand over her mouth to muffle her cries as she comes hard. She's still pulsing around my fingers when there's a knock at the door.

CHAPTER 8

Sophie

"Sophie?" a masculine voice calls from the other side of the door.

Through the fog of my post orgasmic bliss, it takes me a moment to recognize Griffin's voice and another three breaths to feel confident enough that my voice isn't shaking to respond.

"Yes?" I finally respond, my eyes on Hunter as he stands from his position between my legs. His lips shine with my wetness and my body wars with being horrified or extremely turned on. I think I'd be turned on if Griffin wasn't right outside the door. Hunter reaches for the box of tissues on the counter, then proceeds to clean up between my legs.

"You okay?" I can hear Griffin's concern on the other side of the door.

"Yyyeah. Just finishing up. Be out in a minute."

Hunter begins working my dress back down my thighs, then helps me off the counter and we silently wash our hands. We're civilized after all, though our uncontrollable hormones would tell a different story. Even though he wiped between my legs, I can still feel how swollen my clit is, how sensitive and slick I still am from my orgasm.

As he lathers, I stare at Hunter's soapy hands, in complete shock that his fingers were inside me a moment ago. I can't believe that just happened. What the hell were we thinking?

"You go out first. I'll wait a few minutes," Hunter whispers in my ear.

I nod in confirmation, then wait for him to position himself behind the cabinet so Griffin can't see him when I open the door.

"Hey!" I greet Griffin with enthusiasm. A little too much, I think, because he gives me a strange look.

"Hi. Everything okay?" he asks.

"Yeah. I'm great. Just going pee."

"Okay." Griffin nods toward the dining room. "Dinner's being served. Emma saved you a seat."

He moves to go around me into the bathroom, and I shuffle to block him.

"What are you doing?" I ask accusingly. As if he's the one acting weird, not me.

"I need to use the bathroom." He motions to the bathroom and moves forward again.

Oh shit. He cannot go in there. While the space is beautifully decorated, it's minimalist, so unless Hunter can fold his six-foot-three body onto a floating shelf above the toilet, there's absolutely no place for him to hide. I grab the door handle and whip the door shut, nearly slamming Griffin's hand in the door jamb.

"Jesus, Soph! What are you doing?"

"I lied. It's really bad in there." I wave my hand in front of my nose to indicate an awful smell. "Something did not agree with me. I've been off dairy for a few months and let's just say that brie appetizer did not sit well." I throw my hands up dramatically to demonstrate the volcanic eruption that supposedly just took place inside this bathroom. "It went right through me."

"That's disgusting. Do you need to go home?"

"I'm fine now. A little chaffed from all that wiping."

Griffin shakes his head. "I don't need to know the details."

I'm cringing internally, and praying that Hunter is not hearing this conversation. He should be grateful I'm subjecting myself to this humiliation for the sake of trying to cover up our bathroom tryst. There's no way either of us wants to explain what we were doing in the bathroom together.

Griffin pinches the bridge of his nose. "Is there a mess?"

"No." I shake my head adamantly. "It's just the horrid smell. I sprayed some perfume and turned on the fan. It should be clear in about five to ten."

I put my arm through his and turn him away from the powder bathroom. Thankfully, he goes willingly.

"Fine. I'll use the master bath."

"Great."

I release his arm so he can continue down the hallway toward the master bedroom and ensuite bath, making sure he disappears into the room before I give the powder bath door a quick knock and whisper yell 'all clear' then make my way down the hall and out to the dining room.

The rest of the small dinner group is seated and I find my place next to Emma.

"I ordered you the chicken since I know you don't eat steak."

"Thanks." I set my clutch on the table, then slide into the high-back leather chair.

"Hey, I saw you talking to Andrew at the bar." She wiggles her eyebrows.

The side of my face warms with the weight of someone's stare. I turn to find Andrew seated at the end of the table. He smiles and gives me a small wave.

My hand lifts in acknowledgment.

"Right. He gave me a tour."

"He's very handsome and seems like a nice guy."

"Yeah." I nod, then take a sip of water.

I don't owe Andrew anything, but Emma talking about him as date potential is only making me more stressed about what Hunter and I did in the bathroom.

And everything is okay, until Hunter enters the room a few minutes later. He looks gorgeous. His hair is mussed from my hands, yet it looks intentionally styled that way. His hands are in his pockets when he moves toward his seat, giving the people at the end of the table a quick nod and casual, charming smile. That smile makes my stomach flutter and my heartbeat pound against my rib cage.

It occurs to me then that everything in the bathroom happened so fast, I never got to touch him. He'd been so intent on pleasuring me and then we were interrupted by Griffin's knock. My eyes trail Hunter as he finds his seat next to his date. That's right, I just hooked up in the bathroom with a guy who is here with another woman.

How had I completely blanked on that?

My limbs are still loose from my orgasm yet I'm watching Hunter's date lean into him, her hand on his arm, as she whispers something in his ear and all those blissful feelings drain from my body.

I'm an idiot. What the hell was I thinking? Hooking up with Hunter was a huge mistake.

If Hunter can feel me watching him, he must have stronger will power than I do to not turn and meet my gaze. Maybe it would put me more at ease if he sent me some silent message, a private look that would acknowledge what just happened between us. Andrew's over here giving me all the signals and all we've done is a tequila shot together.

"Who are you staring at?" Emma turns her attention to the end of the table where I've been tracking Madeline and Hunter's every move. "Please tell me it's not Hunter Cartwright."

"Oh, no," I say, fumbling for a response. "I like that

woman's mustard dress." I lie, then grab my fork to stab a piece of kale on my plate.

Emma turns to glance toward the woman in the mustard dress.

"It's Dior. Last season, but still might be able to get it. Do you want me to see if my assistant can locate it?"

"No." I shake my head. "It looks great on her, but it would probably wash me out. And I'm sure it's very expensive."

"Everything looks great on you." Emma nods to the dress she loaned me to wear tonight. The dress I'm going to have to dry clean after Hunter's mouth made a mess between my thighs.

"So, what's the deal with Hunter Cartwright?" I say his full name hoping the formality will keep my questioning from appearing personal. And because saying *Oh, Hunter? The guy who just had his face between my legs in the bathroom* is the last thing I can say to Emma. I love Emma, but I know she'd die if I told her something and asked her not to tell Griffin, so even though she's my only female friend in the city, I can't risk talking to her about anything that has happened with Hunter.

"He's one of the city's most eligible bachelors." Emma pauses to take a drink of her wine. She has no idea I'm on the edge of my seat. *And? And? AND? Keep talking, woman!* I want to shout.

"I know him through my cousin, Barrett. Hunter is known for serial dating and there's always a new woman on his arm."

"Oh?" I nod, trying to sound casually interested. Like she's announcing a PSA, not telling me I've just hooked up with one of New York's most eligible bachelors and he's a total player.

"He's a heartbreaker, for sure. I'd steer clear if I were you." Emma smiles. "If not for that reason, then because Griffin's head would explode if you got involved with his boss. And he's waaayyy too old for you."

"Oh, totally." I laugh and hope it sounds convincing. "He's sooo old. Like thirty, right?"

"Mid-thirties, but he doesn't look like he's settling down anytime soon."

Emma's lips twitch and she nods her head sideways in Hunter's direction where Madeline's hand is now rubbing the back of his neck, but his attention is on another woman talking to him from across the table. I'm witnessing two women vying for his attention, and yet I'm the one who hooked up with him in the bathroom and he hasn't even glanced my way. It makes me wonder if he meant what he said. Has he been thinking about me, or was he feeding me a line?

Does it even matter?

I'm not looking to land Hunter. I moved here for a career opportunity and I can't let any distractions keep me from focusing on that. I might be a lowly intern right now, but I hope to prove myself and change that. To secure one of the permanent positions at the end of the summer.

While hooking up with Hunter in the bathroom felt undeniable in the moment, I realize it was a huge mistake. Not only because of who Hunter is, but because of how it could affect my family and my goals.

And I shouldn't let my attraction to Hunter risk ruining an important evening for Griffin who has returned from the bathroom and taken his seat on the other side of Emma.

A moment later, Hunter stands to get everyone's attention and the table chatter dies down.

"Thank you all for coming tonight." For a split second, Hunter's gaze meets mine and I feel that familiar warmth rush over me. No wonder women fight for his attention, it's intoxicating. And then it's gone. "I want to thank the team that put this deal together. Walt, Rachel, Kip, and Tanya.

And Griffin, you joined us toward the end, but we're grateful for you stepping in and getting up to speed quickly."

Griffin's not one to boast or show a lot of emotion, but I can tell he's honored to be recognized by Hunter.

"Also, huge props to Andrew and Madeline for raising the bar yet again and selling this building out with another square footage increase for the neighborhood." Hunter raises his glass to toast. "Great work, team. I can't thank you all enough."

"You can thank me later." Madeline winks up at Hunter.

My mouth gapes open at her directness. I'm at the other end of the table so if I heard it, so did everyone else. Gross.

The puzzle piece clicks into place. Madeline and Hunter work together. And as he explained in the bathroom, she's a 'friend,' but she clearly wants to be more.

My stomach rolls over. Is he going to sleep with her tonight?

The thought makes my skin crawl.

I have no claim on Hunter. We sure as hell didn't make any promises to each other before his head went between my thighs. Or when we rushed up to his suite in Vegas for that matter.

But that doesn't mean I have to sit here and watch them together. Gather more mental images of what the rest of their evening will be like. I love Griffin and want to support him, but I think I'm at my limit.

"I need to go," I whisper to Emma.

"What?" Emma pulls her attention away from Hunter's end of the table. "Why?"

"I'm not feeling well. My stomach is bugging me."

She touches Griffin's arm to get his attention and informs him of the situation.

Griffin leans back in his chair to meet my gaze.

"Stomach issues." I gesture to my tummy and hope after

the little white lie I made by the bathroom earlier, he'll understand.

"You okay to get home on your own?" he asks.

I nod and grab my clutch off the table.

"Text us you made it home, okay?" Emma puts a comforting hand on my arm.

"Yeah. I will."

I don't bother to look in Hunter's direction, but I can feel his eyes on me as I move past his end of the table and quickly toward the front door.

CHAPTER 9

Hunter

The cool morning air fills my lungs, yet the high humidity has drops of sweat already gathering along my brow, clinging to my hairline, and dampening my t-shirt. It's early Saturday morning, but there are a good number of runners and walkers already hitting the paths of Central Park. I pass Bethesda Terrace and cut left to take the upper loop. My feet are on autopilot while my brain replays last night.

Seeing Sophie with her brother had been unexpected. So was the jealousy I felt when I saw her laughing and talking to Andrew. It shouldn't have bothered me. I was there with Madeline and Sophie and I had already discussed that keeping our distance under the circumstances would be best, but that didn't stop me from cornering her in the bathroom, then dropping to my knees to taste her.

And when she left? I wanted to stand up and follow her out of there. No doubt she was not pleased with the events of the evening. Why would she be? I'd given her an orgasm then returned to my seat next to Madeline, whose hands were practically groping my crotch throughout dinner. She thought I was hard because of her, having no idea I nearly came in my pants when Sophie exploded on my tongue minutes earlier.

It doesn't matter that Madeline and I aren't together. That I told Madeline that I wasn't interested, that we should keep things between us platonic, when I dropped her off at her place after the party. Even if I'm not interested in Madeline, I shouldn't be interested in Sophie.

I also shouldn't be out here running the same route that I told Sophie about when she texted me this morning. She made no mention of anything that happened last night. A simple text, *What's a good three-mile running route?*

I'd been lying in bed, debating sliding my hand in my boxer briefs to try to once again to relieve myself of the constant hard-on that is present whenever thoughts of Sophie enter my brain, which lately has been every fucking minute of every fucking day.

There is no good reason to pursue Sophie. We've already established the issues with that. And even if there was no conflict with her brother being my colleague and friend, there's the fact that she's twenty-two. I'm thirty-five. What more could we possibly have in common other than the fact that we both loved it when I slammed my cock into her tight little pussy?

So, what am I doing out here looking for her? Good question. I'm ignoring all former statements and thinking only of the latter.

The path opens and I spot a golden ponytail swaying in the distance. The woman's height, and the way she moves gracefully with each step, I immediately recognize Sophie. I pick up my stride to catch up with her, and soon, I'm a few yards away. If that ponytail wasn't already doing a good job of taunting me, finding Sophie running in tiny spandex shorts that hug her tight ass and a strappy sports bra that shows off nearly every inch of her back is enough to break my stride. I nearly trip over my own feet. I slow down and follow her for a few more strides. What the fuck am I doing? To bystanders, I probably look like a dirty pervert checking her out.

I'm about to turn around and head back the way I came when I hear her call out.

"Hunter?"

I turn to find Sophie standing there, her chest heaving, sweat glistening above her breasts. I watch, practically salivating when a drop of sweat slides from her chest down the narrow path into her cleavage.

"Hunter." Sophie snaps and I realize I'm standing here like a fool staring at her breasts, which doesn't make me a fool, because any man with eyesight would do the same, but it's rude and I can tell she's annoyed.

"Hey." I lift my gaze to her face. That doesn't help my dirty thoughts at all. Her face is glistening with sweat, her cheeks are rosy from her efforts, her green eyes alert and pink mouth wet from licking the sweat off her upper lip. "I thought that was you."

She laughs. "Then why were you turning around?"

I shrug. "I wasn't sure if you wanted company. If you were upset with me about last night."

"Upset with you? No." She shakes her head. Her ponytail sways and I can't help but imagine gripping it to angle her mouth exactly where I want it. "Maybe mad at myself."

She bites her lip and it reminds me of how she looked propped up on the bathroom counter with my face between her pretty thighs, fighting back moans of pleasure.

"I can relate." Distractedly, I drag the hem of my shirt up toward my sweaty brow and wipe. When I release my shirt, I catch Sophie's eyes quickly divert away from my stomach. Her pink cheeks darken a shade. Satisfaction fills my chest. It's good to know I'm not the only one struggling here.

"I wasn't sure which way to go now." She points ahead to where the path forks. Once you're into the heart of the park, there aren't as many signs, so it can be confusing. "Can you show me?"

"Yeah." I decide that running next to Sophie has got to be

less distracting than running behind her. And it is. Except instead of watching her toned legs stride out, or her ass bounce or ponytail sway, I get to listen to her soft breathing. Imagine it in other scenarios that involve effort.

"What do you think of the city so far?" I ask, aiming for conversation that will chase the visuals of Sophie out of my head.

"It's overwhelming and chaotic, and every subway ride makes me feel like I've conquered my worst fear, but I love it."

"Your worst fear?"

"Being enclosed in small, crowded spaces."

"Ah, so this right now," I gesture to the open space around us.

"This is my happy place." She grins.

"Good to know," I say, finally settling into stride next to her.

"It's kind of surreal that I live here now. It feels like I'm a tourist, but I haven't even had a chance to do any of the touristy stuff yet."

"What's at the top of your list?" I ask.

"Top of the Rock, the ballet, Empire State Building," she shrugs, "the usual stuff. There's so much to see and do, I don't know where to start."

"You'll get there," I say.

"I'm hoping that with my job, I'll get to see a lot of cool places."

We cut down the path to run by the Loeb Boathouse.

"Oh my God! I've seen this in so many movies!" Sophie bounces with excitement, her ponytail whipping around her head. "How cool is this?"

"Hannah and I used to come here with our parents every Sunday. We'd eat lunch, then Hannah and I would take out a rowboat."

"That's a fun tradition."

We continue running along the path. "One time, I lost the paddles in the water and my dad had to jump in to get us. He walked home dripping wet. He was not pleased."

Sophie chuckles and I love the sound, so I make it my mission to tell a story about every spot along the path.

"What about your parents? Were they upset that both you and Griffin moved to the city?"

"Our mom died in a car accident twelve years ago. And we have different dads, but neither of them were around for long."

"I'm sorry." I think about my family and how different my life would be without them. How I couldn't imagine if my parents weren't supportive or not in my life at all. If I didn't have Hannah to tease and share memories with.

"It's fine. I think moving here was the final step in moving on. We've leaned on each other for so long, we're the only family we have, that it felt necessary to move to the city together." Sophie is silent for a moment. "I guess you're partially to thank for that."

"What do you mean?" I ask.

"Emma was the main reason Griffin wanted to move here, but I know he was excited to get the job with Premier Real Estate Group. It gave him the confidence to take that step with Emma, to know he could pursue his career while staying in the city with the woman he fell in love with."

"Your brother is talented and hardworking. If he didn't end up at Premier, he would have landed somewhere else. We're lucky to have him."

We're in and out of conversation for the next mile or so. I'll point a landmark out to Sophie or she'll ask about a building or street we pass. I've never had a running partner before. It's always been easiest to go when I feel like it or can fit it into my schedule, not having to wait for someone else, but I like running with Sophie.

"Ow!" Sophie suddenly drops back, hobbling on one foot.

"You okay?" I ask, doubling back to check on her.

"It's a cramp in my calf."

She sets the foot back on the ground and starts walking gingerly.

"Shit, that hurts." She lifts it back up.

"Hold on."

I look around, then scoop her up and start walking along the path.

"Hunter, you can't carry me home."

"I'm not carrying you home. I'm going to set you down on this bench." I nod to the bench a few feet away.

"Oh."

Once I've got Sophie seated, I drop down next to her, then pull her leg into my lap. Using my thumbs to knead her tight muscles, I instruct Sophie to point and flex her foot as I work the length of her calf. Firm, yet gentle strokes.

"Wow," she sighs, "I don't know if I want to kick you or melt into a puddle."

I chuckle. "Is the pressure okay?"

"Yeah. It feels good."

I lift my eyes from Sophie's leg to find her staring at me. Focused, heated, maybe a little bit annoyed. It's the same way she looked at me last night before she left the dinner.

"I didn't sleep with Madeline last night."

Sophie moves to pull her leg away, but I use my firm grip to keep it in my lap.

"Okay." She shrugs, then looks away. "That's none of my business."

That's what she says, but I can see the way her jaw tightens and her eyes narrow.

"I've never slept with her. She's a work associate and a friend."

"Why are you telling me this?" she asks.

"Because I fucked you with my tongue last night on the

bathroom counter at my work dinner, and I meant it when I said I can't stop thinking about you."

Sophie pulls her leg back. This time I let her go. She stands up and walks toward a tree just off the path. She crosses her arms over her chest and stares at me.

"What does that even mean?" she asks.

I rise from the bench and move to where she's now leaning against the tree. I lean in close so she's the only one who will hear my words.

"Sophie, I want to press your face into a pillow and fuck you from behind, come on your tits, and leave my handprint on your ass." I clear my throat. "Among other things."

I'm not sure how she's going to react to my honesty. She might slap me, but I can't hold back from telling her what I want. I'm far past interested with Sophie. Now, I'm plain desperate to have her.

She angles her head so she can look me in the eyes. A small smile pulls at her lips.

"Hopeless romantic, huh?"

"I'm honest," I reply, pulling back so I can see all of her again. See the flush on her cheeks that is no longer from running but from hearing what I want to do to her. Maybe from thinking about what we already did in Vegas. How uninhibited we both were with each other. Strangers that had an intense connection. "That's what I liked about you in Vegas."

She laughs. "I was tipsy on tequila and thought I'd never see you again."

"Yet here we are, running into each other at every turn." I shove my hand into my hair, making my bedhead worse, I'm sure.

She bites her lip.

"Emma told me you're a player," she gives me a once over, "which is fine, I'm not looking for a boyfriend. I want to focus on my career and explore the city."

If I wasn't already turned on by the sight of Sophie, her words would do it. A sexy woman telling me she doesn't need a relationship? She's an angel sent from above.

"That's all good. I want to focus on my career and explore *you,*" I reply.

"But I'm not going to be one of many women. I didn't like that feeling last night."

"I don't have the time or energy to juggle multiple women. When I'm ready to move on, I let them know."

Sophie's brows lift. "That's simple enough."

We stand there for a moment eyeing each other.

"What's not simple is Griffin working for you and me planning your sister's wedding."

"It's our business. We'll keep it to ourselves." The words come out easy, that's how bad I want her.

"What changed? Four days ago, you were adamant we keep our distance."

She's right. But what started as a simple urge to have her again has become an insurmountable distraction. Who knows how long it will take to clear Sophie from my head. The most logical solution is to fuck her until she's out of my system.

"It was four more days of knowing that we were in the same city. Four nights of fucking my own hand and thinking about you. You can't deny there was something in Vegas." I slide my hand over her hip, my fingertips dancing along the waistband of her shorts, my thumb brushing against the smooth skin of her stomach as I pull her closer. My lips press soft kisses along her jaw. "Tell me you don't feel it."

She sighs, softening into me.

"I masturbated to the thought of you the night after Hannah's opening," she says.

Surprised, I choke on a laugh.

"Why are you laughing?" She scowls, trying to pull away.

I reach for her before she can get too far, and pin her back against the tree. "Hey, I fucking love hearing that. I didn't expect you to share that with me, that's all."

Her breath hitches when I slide my thumb underneath her waistband and my lips close around her earlobe.

"What do you think, Sophie? Do you want this?"

"I—" Sophie's hands find my chest, her fingers flexing enough to tell me she needs space. I pull back, putting distance between us and my fingers immediately yearn to touch her again.

I watch her, teeth gnawing her bottom lip, her eyes darting around, taking in the strangers passing by us. She's going to say no and I'm going to have to walk away once and for all. Fuck. Why do I hate the thought of it? Because I'd rather be fucking her than my hand. I know there are other solutions than jerking off, other women who would be happy to oblige, but that doesn't hold appeal either.

When she pushes off the tree and starts walking away, I'm ready to admit defeat.

But again, she surprises me.

She turns, her eyes finding mine. A secretive smile on her lips.

"Where do you live?"

CHAPTER 10

Sophie

"Eat this so you don't cramp up." Hunter hands me a banana, then reaches in the cabinet to grab two water glasses.

"Cute." I pull down a section of the peel while I check out his ass, already at ease with my decision to come to his condo. We're on the same page. We want to have sex but not be burdened by the time commitments of a relationship.

"That's also a good warm up for your jaw." He lifts his brows, his eyes glued to where my lips surround said banana.

I withdraw and purse my lips. "I forgot to mention, oral isn't part of the deal."

To mess with him, I suggestively wrap my tongue around the banana's end then take a huge bite. Hunter looks like he's terrified of me and I kind of like it. But then his mouth twists into a sexy smirk.

"You think I don't remember how deep you took me? How good your tongue felt on me while I fucked your sweet mouth? The way you made good on your promise to lick my balls."

I shrug, then let my eyes fall to the crotch of his running shorts. "I'm definitely not going to lick your sweaty balls."

A second later, and before I can react, Hunter rounds the

counter and throws me over his shoulder. I can't help the high-pitched squeal that comes out of my mouth. He tosses my half-eaten banana on the counter.

From my upside-down position, we pass through the living room; dark leather couches, coffee table, lamps and rug, stylish, modern, manly, yet all a blur. I don't know where he's taking me. Obviously, this is the first time I've been to his place. Is this the standard tour?

"You know this isn't punishment, right?" I grab his ass, one cheek in each hand and squeeze. Hunter's ass is round and firm. I remember the feeling of the muscles flexing under my palms while he thrust deep inside me.

"No, but this is."

In another lightning-fast move, Hunter yanks the waistband of my shorts down and smacks his palm against my bare ass.

"What the—" Before I can get the words out, or fully register the sharp sting of his hand on my skin, Hunter's thick finger presses inside my pussy and I nearly come right then. Oh my *God.* That was unexpected and so fucking hot.

Hunter stops, withdraws his hand and sets me on my feet. I'm lightheaded from being upside down and all the blood rushing from my head when he thrust his finger inside me. I miss his finger, and if I'm honest, I was hoping he was going to smack my ass again. I hadn't expected it, part of me thought he was kidding about wanting to leave an imprint on my ass, but now that I've felt that tingle of pain and how my pussy ached in response, I want him to do it again.

We're in his bathroom now. Whether it's because I had been upside down or the stimulation he'd given me made me see stars, it takes a moment for me to shake my dizziness.

His bathroom has concrete floors that look like they should be cold, but are warm under my feet, black tile shower, gray marble countertops with matte black sinks and faucets. Brass light fixtures hang above the vanity. It's masculine, yet warm.

Hunter pulls me close, his hands sliding over my backside to caress the skin he previously left hot and tingling.

"Did you like that, Sophie?" he whispers in my ear. "Did you like it when I spanked you?"

I realize if I want him to do it again, I'll have to admit that I did.

"Yes."

"Good, because I liked it a lot."

Hunter rocks his hips into me and I feel his hard length pressing into my stomach. Then, he steps back and pulls his shirt off. The way his hair sticks up haphazardly makes him look far more boyish than all the other times I've seen him with it styled.

"Your hair—" I start to giggle.

Hunter pulls off his shorts and boxer briefs, then firmly grips his erection and begins to stroke himself. I'm silenced by the fact that despite some mussed hair, there is absolutely nothing boyish about this man.

We slept together in Vegas, but dim lights and alcohol made it impossible to capture the hard edges of Hunter's body. I knew he was fit, but seeing his muscular thighs bunch to brace himself and his biceps flex while he strokes his length. Up and down. Up and down. I'm mesmerized by the action. And how rough he is with himself.

"Strip, Sophie," Hunter instructs, his dark blue eyes fixed on me, and full of heat.

Any attempt that I might have made to make undressing sexy is thwarted by the fact that everything I'm wearing is spandex and requires stretch and awkward angling of my body to escape. I half expect Hunter to be doubled over laughing by the time I finish, but he's still staring at me intently.

"Turn around and put your hands on the counter."

I do what he says, because I'm here for whatever Hunter has to offer. But then I start to think I don't exactly know what that is, everything that he's into, and I wonder if this could get kinky quick. I've only had sex with two other guys besides Hunter, so I'm up for trying new things, but I have my limits. I think. I'm sure I do. They've just never been tested.

"Wait," I turn back around, "do I need a safe word for this?"

Hunter's brows lift in surprise. "I don't think so. Do you want one?"

"I was just thinking I don't know everything you're into and I don't want to be caught off guard if it's something weird."

"Something weird?" He chuckles and I feel like an inexperienced idiot.

"Forget it." I move to turn back around, but Hunter pulls me to him. His hard body is now pressed to my soft one, or at least that's how it feels with my boobs squished into his pecs made of granite and he kisses me. Strong hands cradling my head, firm lips devouring mine. Hunter tastes me, teases me with his tongue, until I'm breathless and weak in the knees.

"There's no denying all the filthy things I've imagined doing to you. With you," he says when our lips finally part. "If I had my way, I'd pin you down and fuck you hard," his fingers slide between my thighs to rub circles against my clit. My legs shake as a result of the perfect pressure he is applying to my most sensitive place, "but we'll go slow and you can tell me what you like."

"Okay," I say, completely under the spell that Hunter's magical fingers are conjuring.

He sucks my earlobe between his lips, finally releasing it so he can whisper in my ear. "Turn around and put your hands on the counter, Sophie."

When I do that, I can see Hunter's reflection in the mirror

in front of me. A hand trails down my spine, sending a shiver through my body. And this time when Hunter's palm meets my ass, I'm prepared for the sharp sting which makes it that much more arousing. Also, seeing the desire on Hunter's face in the mirror as he watches his hand hit my ass makes my clit throb.

"Did you like that, Sophie?" Hunter soothes the sting on my skin with one hand while he uses the other to slide a single finger into me.

"Yes," I manage while my hips rock back onto his finger. The pleasure of his strokes takes away the angry heat that has started to spread on my cheek.

"I can tell." Hunter removes his finger, then uses it to spread my wetness. He circles over my clit a few times, then pulls away. "I love the way your tits bounce when I spank you. Almost as much as I like seeing how pink your ass is."

His palm comes down on the other cheek with a crack against my skin. I have to tuck my bottom lip between my teeth to stifle the moan. This time I can feel my wetness leaking out around him when he presses his finger inside.

Hunter spanks me again on both sides, each time soothing the ache with a caress of his palm and a distracting thrust of his finger inside me. I can only imagine what I look like, back arched, ass pressing back, aching for more of his touch.

He trails kisses up my spine, his hands now gliding along my sides to lift me up and set me on the counter. The cool marble feels amazing against the heat of my ass.

"That's all?" I ask, confused that he's done spanking me so soon.

"Trust me, I'd keep going if the sight of you bent over like that wasn't about to make me come."

He slides two fingers between my legs at the same time he sucks a nipple into his mouth, and I get what he means about nearly coming undone.

"I'm saving it for your throat."

"What about my tits?" I moan, rocking my hips again. So close. "I thought you wanted to come on them?"

Hunter licks across my skin to take the other nipple in his mouth. He pauses to look up with a wicked smile on his face. I grip his shoulders and curl my pelvis against his fingers.

"You didn't have plans today, did you?" he asks.

My laugh is cut short when he hooks his fingers inside me and my orgasm hits. An explosion of nerve endings radiating outward from my core to my arms and legs causing a mind-altering existence. Holy shit.

I open my eyes on a blissful sigh and find Hunter is watching me.

He grins. "I like watching you come."

I return his smile. "I like when you make me come." It feels so easy being with him like this.

The honesty. Knowing exactly what we want from each other, no complications.

Hunter scoops me up, I wrap my body around his, and he walks us into the shower. The hot water feels good on my skin which is salty from the run. For a few minutes, we lather in silence. With my back to his front, Hunter uses his fingertips to massage the shampoo into my scalp.

"You're good at this."

"Showering?" He chuckles.

"No, being sweet." I lean into him, letting my wet body slide against his, his monster erection pressed against my ass.

"Hmm, I don't think you would say that if you knew what kind of thoughts I was having about your mouth right now."

I grab the body wash off the shelf and squeeze some into my hand, then turn to start washing his chest. My hands smooth over his hard pecs, down the ripples of his abs, across his waist and along his hips where those sexy V muscles dip. If this guy ever needs a sponge bath, all the nurses would be fighting each other to do the honors.

When I finally reach my destination, his thick cock jutting

upward between us, I wrap a soapy hand around and give him a stroke. I'm nowhere near as aggressive as he was with himself, but the more I stroke, the more confident I become.

"Yes." He hisses when I rotate my thumb around his crown.

Since I want to be thorough, I use my other hand to gently massage and lather his balls. Like I said, I'm not going to be licking any sweaty balls. No, they're going to be coastal cypress and sea fennel scented according to the body wash's label. I have no idea what those are, but it smells like Hunter and I like it a lot.

When we've rinsed off, I move to lower to my knees, but Hunter catches me by the elbow.

"What—" I begin to protest.

"I'd love to see you on your knees, but not on this tile."

He walks me over to a small triangular bench in the corner.

"This will be more comfortable."

I smile up at him. "And they say chivalry is dead."

Hunter laughs before stepping in front of me to shield me from the spray. His hands gather the wet strands of my hair and move them away from my face.

"I'll enjoy thrusting my dick into your mouth more if I know you're not in pain."

His sweet gesture makes me swoon. *That's not why you're here,* I remind myself.

Hunter smiles at me while he traces his thumb across my lips.

I drop my head and lick circles around his swollen crown, immediately tasting the saltiness of pre-come on my tongue. Using my thumb, I slide the moisture around his shaft all the way to the bottom, then I trace the large vein with my tongue. Hunter's long and thick, so I wrap a hand around the base of him. I lower my mouth around his girth, circling the tip with my tongue as I work my way down his shaft.

When I can't go any farther, I pump my hand up to where my mouth ends, then with a firm hand, stroke back down to the base.

"Christ, Sophie."

One of Hunter's hands cradles my head while the other is braced against the shower wall. While I'm focused on my task of driving him wild, it's also hard not to be focused on watching him come undone. To know that I'm making his legs shake and his jaw clench as his pleasure barrels down on him. I continue my rhythm, one that Hunter has started his own chant to. *Sophie, Sophie, Sophie*. And just when I feel like I'm in my groove, I can feel his cock start to pulse.

"I'm going to come. Sophie, I've got to—" Hunter tries to pull back, but I suck him in deeper, and use a hand to hold his hip close. Too impatient to be inside me, he didn't finish in my mouth in Vegas. I want him to come in my mouth *now*. To feel the pulse of his cock as his release hits my tongue. Hunter's eyes lock with mine the moment he explodes. It's the hottest thing I've ever seen. Jaw clenched, blue eyes drowsy with pleasure as water streams down his chiseled body.

"Fuck!"

The hot liquid hits the back of my throat. Instinct has me gagging, but I manage to take a deep breath in through my nose, then swallow it all down. I had no idea that doing so would be such a turn on, but I know if I slipped my hand between my thighs, it'd be slick with arousal.

Hunter presses his thumb into my mouth, then traces my lips with the moisture. My lips are swollen from being stretched and the gentle pressure feels nice.

"Fuck, Sophie. Your mouth is so sweet."

I laugh because I think he might be teasing me about calling him sweet earlier. When I stand to do a final rinse, he captures my mouth with his and presses me to the tiled wall, his still hard cock wedged in between us.

"How are you still hard?" I gasp when the length of him rubs against my clit.

He tilts his hips, then rocks into me again, the crown of him nudging at my entrance.

"I've been dying to fuck you all week. I can't let this opportunity go to waste."

I'm aching for him, ready for him to press in farther, but he turns off the water and hands me a towel from the shelf. I've barely gotten it around my wet, shivering body when he scoops me up again and carries me to the bed.

"You know I can walk," I say, when he drops me on the pile of pillows, then climbs on top of me. He's a canopy of muscle in this soft as a cloud bed.

"I'm trying to avoid any leg cramps that might prevent me from fucking you hard."

"A true gentleman."

Hunter smiles down at me, then captures my face between his hands, kissing me until I'm breathless. "I'm happy we decided to do this."

"Me, too." I smile, because while orgasms are great, it's also nice to connect with someone that isn't obligated to hang out with me because we're related by blood or marriage, or because we work together. I don't know if saying that Hunter and I are friends is quite right, but in some way, he's the first friend in New York City that I've made on my own. Even though I happened to meet him in Vegas. Semantics, right?

He reaches for his nightstand to grab a condom. A moment later, he's positioned at my entrance. His face looks tortured as he slowly slides into me.

"Damn, Sophie. This," he slams inside, stretching me full, "is what I've been thinking about every day. Your slick, warm pussy gripping me so fucking tight."

He's right. It's so good. If I hadn't been busy with graduating, moving, and starting my new job, this probably would have been all I thought about, too.

He wedges a pillow under my ass, then lifts my knee over his shoulder, allowing himself a deeper angle. It's the perfect angle, I'm already close.

"You feel incredible. Even better than I remember."

I wrap my arms around his neck and pull him impossibly closer. I kiss along his neck and gently press my teeth into his shoulder. He licks his finger and slips it between us. I anticipate it pressing against my clit, but I should know by now that Hunter has a thing for my ass. Just the tip of his finger presses inside me, but the pressure of his cock thrusting hard is enough to send me over the edge.

"Hunter!" I scream before I can ask if his walls are well insulated.

"God, I love the feel of your pussy milking my cock. I want to feel it again."

With a growl, Hunter flips me so I'm on my hands and knees, then thrusts back into me and starts a punishing rhythm that I know will grant his wish.

I'm not sure what does it. The way he teases and pinches my nipples, his warm breath in my ear as he tells me how beautiful I look filled with his cock, or the smack of his palm against my ass, but when his finger circles my clit, I come harder than I ever have, with Hunter slamming into me one final time before he shudders his own release inside me.

"Sophie."

I'm boneless and collapse onto the bed while Hunter pulls out and takes the condom to the bathroom. A moment later, his weight dips the mattress, and he places a featherlight kiss on one butt cheek before moving to the other and doing the same. It's a stark contrast to the hard smack he delivered to the same spot minutes earlier.

"Are you alive?" Hunter chuckles near the side of my face, as he drags a hand over my back, his fingertips a soft caress.

"Barely," I mumble, my face still buried in the comforter. Too tired to move, but I know I need to get up and leave before my body permanently attaches itself to Hunter's bed. I'm searching for the energy to move my body when Hunter rolls me onto my back.

He gives a gentle press on the inside of my knee. "Open for me."

Those three words have my body on high alert because I truly don't think I can go again, but then I see the washcloth in his hand.

I spread my legs and let him clean between my thighs. The warm washcloth feels like heaven against my slick skin. And somehow the image of Hunter naked and hovering above me while he cleans me up is even hotter than when he was slick with sweat and thrusting into me a few minutes ago.

When he's done, his thumb gently brushes over the sensitive skin by my pelvic bone. "Any plans for the rest of your day?"

"Emma wanted me to go shopping with her and her friend Chloe. I'm not much of a shopper, but it should be fun. Some quality girl time." I place my hand against his chest, loving the feel of his heart beating beneath my palm. My fingers lightly trail down his chest and the smattering of dark hair there.

He grins. "That sounds like fun."

"What are you doing today?" I ask.

Hunter turns to glance at the clock. "Work."

"Oh," I say, suddenly feeling awkward. "I should go."

With a small smile, he nods. It's clear I've overstayed my welcome. It has been six minutes since my last orgasm so maybe there's only a five-minute grace period that I'm unaware of. I try not to let it bother me that he's got plans. This entire morning was unplanned, including me and Hunter deciding to start a strictly sexual relationship. That's what I should be focused on. This is sex, no cuddling or spooning.

As graceful as a baby giraffe that just learned to walk, I

slide off the side of the bed and scurry to the bathroom to pull on my sweat-damp running clothes. Hunter appears from his closet, now dressed in a pair of dark blue lounge pants. They're low slung on his hips, highlighting those V muscles that make me want to squeeze my thighs together. I make a mental note to spend more time exploring them with my tongue next time.

He's got a t-shirt in his hands. I expect him to pull it on and ruin my view, but instead he pushes it over my head.

"What's this for?" I ask, while I pop my arms through the sleeves. The gray shirt reads PRINCETON and is huge on me, the hem nearly covers my shorts. It also smells like Hunter. Delicious.

"Now I don't have to think about guys staring at you in your sports bra."

"But now it looks like I'm not wearing anything underneath." I angle my leg to the side to show the lack of shorts visible there.

Hunter frowns for a second, then gathers one corner of the shirt and knots it.

"Really?"

He shrugs. "I grew up in the nineties."

I roll my eyes. "God, you're old."

"I prefer 'experienced.'" He uses the shirt knot to pull me closer. "Same time tomorrow?"

"For running or sex?" I ask.

His other hand closes around the end of my wet ponytail, using it to guide my mouth to his. He pulls back, but then places one more kiss against my lips.

"Both."

CHAPTER 11

Sophie

"You have to get that dress," Emma exclaims when I exit the dressing room, the glass of champagne in her hand paused in front of her mouth to take me in.

"I second that," Chloe says from her place on the burgundy love seat.

We're shopping at Bergman's, an insanely expensive department store that will soon carry bridal gowns that Emma's label, Emma Belle Bridal, designed exclusively for them. I should say Emma and Chloe are shopping, while I'm wide-eyeing the prices wondering how I can justify paying that amount for one dress. Even if Emma says, and I quote, it's '*functional and fabulous.*'

"I have student loan payments cheaper than this dress," I exclaim.

Emma waves me off. "You'll get the friends and family discount."

"Bergman's has a friends and family discount?" I ask.

"Hmm?" Her brows lift.

I think by 'friends and family' she means she'll pay for it.

I look to Chloe.

She shakes her head knowingly. "More like the Emma Warner layaway plan."

Having met her only an hour ago, she's unbelievably easy to talk to and I love her quirkiness and quick wit. She's an assistant book editor at St. Clair Press and just returned from her honeymoon in Tuscany. A few weeks ago, she married Emma's cousin, Barrett St. Clair, the CEO of media titan St. Clair Media.

Emma filled me in on Chloe and Barrett's back story. How they didn't like each other, well it was mostly Chloe disliking Barrett's grumpy, workaholic persona, but during a fake dating scheme to help Barrett with a business deal, they fell in love.

"I'm not letting you buy me this dress." I march back inside the dressing room.

"You're just like your brother. So practical and conservative with money. He never lets me buy him anything." Emma pouts outside the dressing room.

I slide the side zipper down and pull the sleeves of the dress down my arms, then step out of it. Emma's right about Griffin. He's always wanted to make his own way, never wanting to take charity or help from anyone. I guess I'm the same way.

It turns out while she enjoys a few luxuries here and there, Emma doesn't care about being with someone who has money. And while she had seed money from her parents, she made her bridal gown business a success on her own.

I admire her that way, and someday would love to start my own business. Right now, I plan to soak in all the knowledge from the staff at Marion Adler Events.

I change back into my t-shirt dress, throw on my jean jacket and grab my purse.

"Thanks for humoring me," Emma says, downing her champagne before grabbing her shopping bag. "At least now I know what to get you for your birthday."

"It's in six months."

"Ooh, your half-birthday?" She smiles conspiratorially.

Chloe stands and threads her arm through mine. "You know she doesn't really need a reason, right?"

I smile watching Emma take the dress I told her not to buy me and mention something to the sales associate. Emma is the sweetest person, always wanting to do things for others. I'm grateful that Griffin found her because after all the sacrifices he's made, he deserves to have someone in his life who wants to take care of him as much as he wants to take care of her.

"Should we get lunch?" Emma asks.

Chloe's face lights. "Felice 56 is just around the corner. They have the best fettuccine Bolognese."

"Yes, please. That sounds amazing," I say. I'm glad that whatever stomach bug had plagued me this week seems to be gone and now I'm ready to eat my weight in pasta.

"How was your run this morning?" Emma asks as we exit onto Fifth Avenue. "You were gone a long time."

"Oh, yeah. I kind of got turned around and had to double back."

And detour to Hunter's apartment for sex. Oopsie.

"I'm not really a runner. I know Griffin doesn't love that you are running alone. Maybe you could join a club or something to find a partner?"

I smile at how Griffin's protectiveness of me has rubbed off on Emma. I probably shouldn't tell her that not only did I find a running partner this morning, but a fuck buddy as well. No, that probably wouldn't go over well.

"I'm no help with the running partner thing, but if you ever want to play tennis or racquetball, I'd love to take you to the club," Chloe offers.

"I've never played before, but that could be fun. I'm always up for trying new things," I tell her as we make the turn onto Fifty-Sixth Street.

"When I first started, I didn't have any skills, but I'm definitely improving. I almost beat Barrett the other day." Chloe beams, then her cheeks color and her eyes light up. "Our matches have gotten pretty intense. We always have to go straight home after if you know what I mean."

"I know what you mean and I don't really want to hear that about Barrett." Emma scrunches her nose. "He may be my cousin, but he's practically a brother to me."

I have to laugh. "So, then you'll understand my alarm when I walk in to find you and Griffin, *my* brother, fooling around on the couch."

Emma looks sheepish. "I guess that's fair."

"Here we are!" Chloe pulls open the door to the restaurant and we follow her in.

The host seats us at a four top where Emma loads the extra seat with her shopping bags. The waitress stops by to take our drink order. My head is buried in the menu, trying to decide which decadent pasta dish I want, when I hear a male voice beside our table.

"Ladies."

I drop my menu to find the guy from Hunter's dinner party last night standing at our table. He's dressed in dark jeans and a button-down shirt.

"Hi," I say, my mind blanking on his name.

Emma saves me. "Hi, Andrew. Good to see you again."

"Emma, it's my pleasure."

That's right. Andrew. He was funny and sweet and we were having a conversation about the condo he sold before I got distracted with Hunter in the bathroom.

"Chloe Anderson, well, St. Clair." Chloe waves the giant rock on her left hand, "Just haven't gotten to all the paperwork yet."

"That's right. You're Barrett St. Clair's wife. I saw your wedding announcement. Nice to meet you, Chloe."

Andrew turns his attention to me.

"Sophie, I'm sorry you had to leave early last night."

"I wasn't feeling well." I give him a small smile.

"I hope it wasn't the tequila shot."

"No, I think I was just tired with it being my first week at my new job."

"Well, you missed a fun night." Andrew pauses for a moment, eyeing Emma before returning to me. "Sophie, I was wondering if you would like to go out sometime? Grab dinner? Maybe a show?"

I can feel Emma and Chloe's eyes on me and my cheeks warm. I have no idea how to respond. Only hours ago, Hunter and I had sex, and agreed to have a no-strings-attached sexual relationship, and while we did voice that we wouldn't be sleeping with other people, we didn't address whether we could go on a date with anyone else. There's a difference, right? And if there isn't, if I'll need to choose, do I want to go out with Andrew more than I want to have sex with Hunter? Andrew's nice, but being in his presence doesn't make me deliciously horny in the best possible way. It's not like being near Hunter where every cell in my body vibrates. Hunter makes my palms sweaty and my heart race out of my chest. Not to mention the way my ovaries swoon every time his lips pull into one of those devastating smiles.

I don't want to embarrass him in front of the other ladies by saying no, but I don't know that saying yes is right either. He must pick up on my hesitation.

"Sorry to put you on the spot." Andrew reaches into his wallet and pulls out a business card. "Think about it and let me know."

"Of course," I say, taking his card and safely tucking it into my purse.

"Enjoy your lunch, ladies." He steps back from the table.

"Thank you," I say.

"Bye, Andrew." Emma gives him an enthusiastic wave before he departs.

When he's gone, Emma's brows raise as she reaches for her water glass. "That was interesting."

I shrug, trying to figure out a way to explain the situation without *explaining* the situation.

"He's handsome and seems sweet," Chloe says. "Are you not into him?"

"He's nice. I just don't know if I want to date right now. Being new to the city and my job, I think focusing on my career is probably best."

"But you could still have some fun." I swear Emma has hearts in her eyes. She thinks she's witnessing the start of a romance to be. That with her encouragement, Andrew and I could be the next great love story. "And you said you want to see the city. What could be more fun than exploring the city with a hot guy?"

She's right. I do want to explore my new city. I was already in love with New York before I moved here, and I've only been a handful of places so far. Mainly work and the subway. I know I have time to do everything, but it would be nice to have someone show me around.

"He's nice. I think we could be friends."

"*Ahh*, a friends to lovers story. Those are always the sweetest. I mean as sweet as a smutty romance novel can make them."

I laugh at Chloe's assessment. She's filled me in on her bookworm status and romance novels are her favorite.

"I'll think about it," I reply.

The waiter appears and we place our orders before he gathers the menus and retreats.

"How was work this week? I feel like I didn't get to talk to you much."

"Busy. There's so much to learn, but it's fun, you know? I

love Johnathan, the assistant planner I was assigned to. The other interns are cool, but there is a bit of tension between those of us in the same division. We know that we're competing for a limited number of job offers at the end of the summer. June is one of the event planning division interns. We share a desk area and she's nice."

"I'm glad you're settling in. I can imagine that the competition for the job offers will be stressful, but you have nothing to worry about. You're going to kill it and land one of those positions."

"Thanks. I hope so." I know it's going to take more than hope to land a job offer. It's going to be a ton of work, but I'm excited for the challenge.

"I love that we're in the same industry. It'll be fun to have someone to talk to about all the inside news. Griffin is a good listener, but he doesn't have our passion for weddings, so it's exciting we'll have each other," Emma says, then looks over at Chloe. "Sorry, Chloe."

Chloe shrugs. "I may not be in the wedding industry but I do have a say in many happily ever afters of the fictional variety."

"That's true," Emma says.

Emma's excitement is contagious. "And maybe we'll even be working with the same brides. Hannah mentioned she was going to meet with you about dress options."

"Yeah, she wants a custom dress and we've already started talking about the style. The type of fabric she wants is insanely expensive, which she can afford, but product shortages might make it difficult to get it in time. I had similar issues with getting the lace for Chloe's dress, but it worked out in the end."

Chloe sighs dreamily. "I loved my dress. Still obsessed with it. I might wear it around the house just to get more use out of it."

I laugh.

When the food comes a few minutes later, I start telling them about the true crime podcast that I just started listening to which leads to a slew of other topics including the hot pink pepper spray keychain that I accidentally drop on the floor when I reach into my purse for lip balm. The keychain was part of the collection of women's personal safety products Griffin got me for graduation.

"Is he that protective of you?" I ask Emma.

"He's definitely protective, you know, walking on the side closest to the street, and checking in if I'm later than I said I'd be, but he also knows I grew up in the city and am more familiar with my surroundings. You think a pepper spray key chain is being protective?" She motions to Chloe. "Barrett had Chloe's old apartment building re-done to make it safer."

Chloe nods. "And demanded I move into his place while it was being done."

"I think there was also a mouse involved, right?" Emma grimaces.

"Oh, yes, but that was only its first sighting. It's like Barrett's presence provoked it."

I continue to eat my pasta and listen as Emma and Chloe exchange stories about the early days with their husbands. It's especially fun to hear Emma's side of the story about her and Griffin. How he'd slept on the floor in her room because she was living with her parents but they needed to pretend their marriage was real by sleeping in the same room.

"That's why you should give Andrew a chance," Emma says. "Because you never know how something may turn out."

"That's true," Chloe agrees. "But you also have plenty of time to date, so really you should do whatever makes you happy right now."

"Hey. A moment ago, I thought you were on Team Andrew?" Emma gives Chloe an exasperated look.

Chloe shakes her head and laughs. "I'm on Team Sophie."

I point my fork at Chloe and nod my approval. "Preach."

We finish lunch, Emma gathers her bags and I lead the three of us through the door and out onto the street. I look up and down the street, trying to remember where we are. Just outside the restaurant door, while I'm debating if we need to go east or west, my gaze snags on a black SUV across the street. More importantly the man standing next to it.

Even with traffic speeding past and pedestrians passing in front of me, I can clearly see him.

It's Hunter.

And he's holding the door open for a beautiful redhead.

She's older than me, even older than Hunter. Her designer dress and bag make me feel like a twelve-year-old in my Old Navy shift dress from the clearance rack.

I watch as she laughs and places her palm on his chest, then kisses him on the cheek, before lowering into the back of the car. Sunglasses cover his eyes, but it's clear he's smiling, too.

My stomach sinks.

Work. That's what Hunter said he was doing today.

My sudden stop causes Chloe to slam into my back.

"Oh, sorry, Sophie. I didn't realize you stopped."

I pull my gaze from the car across the street and focus back on Emma and Chloe.

"Yeah, sorry. I wasn't sure which way we need to go."

"No problem. There are a bunch of clothing boutiques on Seventh Avenue. Are you up for more shopping?" Emma asks.

"Then we can get ice cream and maybe I'll convince you to give Andrew a call." Chloe winks.

I sneak a glance back across the street, but the car is gone. That's fine, I tell myself. Hunter Cartwright doesn't owe me anything, and I owe him just as much.

"What do you want to do, Sophie?" Chloe asks.

I turn back and smile. "Yeah, let's go."

~

The next morning, I find Hunter exactly where he said he would be at the exact time he said he would be. But, remembering him with the woman from the day before sends a burst of adrenaline into my blood stream. I end up running right past him without a second glance. I don't bother looking back to see if he noticed me.

It's only when I hear him calling my name that I know he's trying to catch up. I shouldn't even be annoyed with Hunter. I'm mad at myself that what is supposed to be a casual arrangement is already affecting me this way.

"Sophie!" A hand wraps around my elbow. I'd be startled if I hadn't heard Hunter calling my name the previous times, before I broke into a near sprint down the path.

"Oh, hi." I feign innocence, removing an ear bud that has absolutely nothing playing in it. I wore them so I could ignore pompous assholes who fuck women and are then seen kissing cheeks and getting into cars with other women. You know the type. Ridiculously handsome with big dicks that make you lose all your senses and agree to have a secret sexual relationship that involves universe-altering sex only to make you question everything an hour later.

"Jesus. Are you doing sprint work?" He places his hands on his knees for a moment to catch his breath.

"Just trying a new pace today." I bat my lashes. "How's your knee?"

He lifts, then moves closer and I breathe in the scent of him. Clean and manly. My body reacts immediately. It's so much easier to act indifferent when he's not right in front of me.

"I thought we were meeting at Eighty-Eighth and Central

Park?" He motions back to the block where he was waiting for me earlier.

"Oh, right. I guess I wasn't sure if you had found another running buddy since I saw you yesterday."

He narrows his eyes at me. "What are you talking about?"

"The redhead? I saw her kiss you on the cheek then you got into the car together." Hunter's expression is pure confusion, so I clarify. "I was having lunch with Emma and Chloe at Felice 56 and when we came outside, I saw you two together across the street."

Recognition lights his face and a huge smile pulls at his lips. "My Aunt Maggie?"

"Who?"

He shakes his head. "She's not technically my aunt, but Maggie's been a good friend of my mom's since I can remember. She's looking to invest in real estate so I showed her a few up-and-coming Premier projects."

"Oh."

I expect him to be annoyed that I'm accusing him of hooking up with other women, *again,* but instead he looks happy about it.

"Why are you looking at me like that?" I ask.

He leans closer, his hand wrapping around the side of my body, the spot where my skin is exposed in my sports bra and running shorts. His thumb dips under the waistband of my shorts.

"Because I'm going to enjoy fucking that thought right out of your head."

Despite my desire to appear unaffected by his words, I can't help the shiver that runs through my body. The way my pussy aches with each slow sweep of his thumb against my belly.

"I told you, I'm a one-woman guy. And right now, you're the one I want."

And there it is. The reminder that me and Hunter are temporary. Right now, I'm the one he wants. Who knows how long it will last? A few days? A week? Maybe a month. That's fine. It's what I agreed to. While I want to find love someday, I don't expect it to happen now. It's not in my five-year plan. And it wouldn't be Hunter Cartwright, a notorious bachelor thirteen years older than me, even if it was.

"Maybe I've changed my mind," I say.

"About what?" His confidence doesn't waver at my flippant attitude.

"Andrew Bachman asked me out on a date."

The muscle in his jaw tightens. "You said you weren't looking for a boyfriend."

I shrug. "He's offered to show me around the city."

Hunter lifts his gaze, staring off behind my left shoulder.

"So, let's go."

He tugs on my hand, leading me until I fall into a steady jog next to him. Now I'm confused. We run in silence, our heavy breathing muffled slightly by the sounds of the city, the birds chirping and the whooshing noise of a group of roller bladers passing by.

When we get to the south end of the park, I'm expecting that we'll keep going along the path, but Hunter motions for us to cross at the light onto Sixth Avenue. For blocks, we're dodging pedestrians and street vendors.

"Where are we going?" I ask, breathless. It's Sunday morning so not as busy as it would usually be with commuters, but it's New York. Tourists are determined to get their fill every day of the week.

Hunter finally paces back to take a left on West Fiftieth Street.

"You'll see," he says, a smile pulling at his lips.

By the time he stops in front of a building, my leg muscles are burning. It takes me a moment to notice where we are.

Top of the Rock, the engraved sign says.

"You want someone to show you the city?" he asks, clearly proud of himself for locating a tourist site I mentioned yesterday.

"Yeah, but I was hoping for a view from the top." I nod at the sign with the open hours posted on it. It's eight forty-seven. The building doesn't open until ten.

Hunter walks over to the door and taps on it with his knuckles. I want to laugh. What does he think he's going to do? Ask if they can let us up? His confidence is astounding, but if I'm being honest, it's kind of hot, too.

There's probably no one here at this hour, maybe a cleaning person and security, so I'm surprised when a woman in a dress with a nametag opens the door.

"Good morning, Mr. Cartwright." She beams at us. "We've been expecting you."

~

HUNTER

"Thanks, Sharon." I nod at her before turning to give Sophie a wink.

Her eyes narrow at the smug look on my face. I hold the door open for her to go in, then playfully swat her ass as she passes.

"Ow." She retaliates by poking me in the ribs.

"Are you sore?" I whisper in her ear as we follow Sharon to the elevator, my palm gently caressing her ass through her spandex shorts. My fingers itch to feel the flesh of her ass, but the tight-fitting shorts are a nice alternative right now.

She's killing me in this running outfit.

The moment I saw her approach, I was ready to call this outing off and drag her back to my apartment, but then she mentioned Andrew asking her out and I knew I had to bring my A game. Not that I'm competing with Bachman for Sophie's attention. I think Sophie and I both know where her interests lie. And if we weren't seeing each other secretly, Andrew would know, too.

"Yes. It's not every day that I get spanked on my bare ass," she hisses under her breath.

"Hmm, we'll need to rectify that." My lips press against the shell of her ear. I watch as my words cause goose flesh to appear on her arms.

When the elevator doors open, we enter, then Sharon waves a key card over the pad and selects the sixty-seventh floor.

"Don will take you the rest of the way," she announces.

"Thank you, Sharon." I nod.

"My pleasure, Mr. Cartwright."

The doors close on Sharon's beaming smile and I find Sophie on the opposite side of the elevator facing me. I lean against the wall, my hands lightly resting on the metal handrail behind me, while Sophie crosses her arms over her chest.

"You come here often?" she asks, trying to fight back a smile.

"Never," I deadpan. "First time."

She shakes her head and laughs.

"Just a casual Sunday morning getting a private tour at Top of the Rock?"

I shrug. "I know a few people."

She drops her arms to her sides.

"This is really nice. You didn't have to go to the trouble."

"It was easy." I made the call the moment Sophie left my apartment yesterday.

"I wish you would have told me about this." She motions to her exposed midriff and sports bra cleavage. "I would have brought a sweatshirt or something."

"Are you cold?" I ask, then close the space between us, my hands lifting to rub her upper arms in a motion that is supposed to generate heat, but sends a shudder through her instead. Her nipples pebble and strain against the fabric of her sports bra.

"That's not making it better." She laughs, moving her arms in front of her breasts.

I push her hand away and rub my thumb against the fabric of her bra, right over her tightened nipple.

"I bet my mouth would warm you right up," I say, leaning in to press my lips along Sophie's jaw. My hand moves to grip the back of her neck. Our lips connect and she softens into my touch. The elevator ride isn't long enough to do anything I want to do to her, so I settle for teasing her mouth. Kissing her breathless until I feel her pelvis seeking out mine. Cupping her ass to grind her body against me, letting her feel how ready I am for her, just to release her a moment later when the elevator rests.

The doors open and we're greeted by a man in a black security outfit.

"Mr. Cartwright. Miss?"

"Hart," Sophie fills in, her voice coming out reedy before she clears her throat.

He nods. "I'm Don. I'll be taking you up to the viewing level."

We follow Don to another elevator, filing in before he waves his key card and selects a button.

"The view is stunning today. No clouds," he comments while I slide my fingers against Sophie's palm before interlacing our fingers together. She turns to look up at me, her lips pressed together, her eyes alight with anticipation.

"That's good to hear," I reply, giving Sophie a wink.

She laughs inaudibly, then turns her attention toward Don who is deep in tour guide mode telling us about the history of the building and the architecture. I've already heard it, many times, so I opt for watching Sophie listen to him. What I see is pure joy.

When we get to the seventieth floor, Don escorts us out to the open-air deck. Still holding my hand, Sophie tugs me forward, but I indicate for her to go ahead while I hang back with Don for a minute.

CHAPTER 12

Sophie

The sun is so bright, I have to shield my eyes as I look out on New York City. The Empire State Building stands directly in front of me, but more than the iconic building, I notice the smaller ones. Apartment buildings with hundreds of windows. I'm still overwhelmed by the number of people that live here. That I'm one of them now.

The Statue of Liberty looks tiny, anchored miles away in the Hudson.

I move around to the other side, taking in the views of Central Park, where minutes ago Hunter and I were running. He finds me there.

He's got a sweatshirt and baseball hat in his hands, both adorned with Top of the Rock logos, clearly from the gift shop inside.

"For you." He holds the sweatshirt's head opening for me to push through. Once I've gotten my arms in, he lifts my ponytail to feed it through the back of the cap, then adjusts it onto my head. "Better?"

"Thank you." I smile.

"It's part of the package."

I laugh.

For a moment, my insides feel all squishy with his sweet gesture.

But then I remind myself who Hunter is. This is easy for him. It's clear from his apartment, his company, and his family, Hunter has expendable income. And connections. He could do this for any woman he was seeing. Or secretly having sex with. For all I know, he might have a standing private tour set up on Sunday mornings. The Hunter Cartwright special tour. I'm sure Don has seen a parade of women come through with Hunter.

I try not to let that thought ruin my experience. I'm the one reaping the benefit from it today and I want to enjoy it.

"Is it everything you hoped it would be?" he asks.

"It's amazing. I imagine when it's filled with people, it's a different experience. You didn't have to do this."

Hunter shrugs. "I wanted to."

"I feel bad now because I was so grumpy with you earlier and you had this planned the whole time."

"That's okay. I think we both know what that was."

I narrow my eyes at him. "What?"

"Jealousy." His voice is like gravel next to my ear. "Were you jealous, Sophie?"

I want to keep my laugh light, but it comes out flat, defensive even.

"No. I just don't want to be taken advantage of. Just because I'm younger, doesn't mean I'm naïve."

"Does it bother you that I'm older?" he asks.

"Not really. For what we're doing, it doesn't matter. Does it bother you?"

"It was a reason I told myself to stay away from you. That we're in different places in our lives. But you're right, for what we're doing, it doesn't bother me."

I nod and look back out at the view.

"The park is gorgeous. So green. I'm used to the desert, everything being beige and sandstone."

"Do you miss Vegas?" he asks.

"I miss my friends, but I knew I wanted to leave after college." My eyes fall onto a tall building in the distance. "What's that tall, skinny building blocking the view?"

Hunter chuckles. "That's one of Premier's new builds. In addition to our redevelopment projects, we're expanding into new development. It's going to be luxury condos with park views."

"Of course, it's yours." I bite back a smile. I'm starting to realize this city has the Cartwright name and influence all over it.

"There's a new technology that allows for buildings to be constructed on a smaller base—one city block for instance—yet still achieve a twenty-eight-story height." He talks about it excitedly, when he looks back at me, I can tell he's embarrassed. "You don't want to hear this, do you?"

"Yes, I do." I shake my head. "Sorry I was staring. You got excited and it was really cute."

"Cute, huh?" He slides his hand under the hem of my sweatshirt and I jump with the contact of his fingers across my bare skin. I take a breath to relax and finally, my body melts back into Hunter.

"I can't wait for autumn leaves. And snow. I've been dreaming about seeing the city decked out for the holidays. I want to see the Rockefeller tree and ice skate with hot cocoa."

"Horse and carriage ride through Central Park?" he asks.

"God, no. I feel horrible for those horses."

"No carriage rides. Noted."

I laugh. "You're taking notes? For holiday sightseeing? That's six months away." With brows arched, I turn to look at him.

"You think my sister will turn into a Bridezilla and you'll hate me by association?"

I shake my head. "She doesn't seem the type. That's why I felt awful for her when I thought you were her fiancé. I wanted her to like me and I was certain I was going to ruin her life by telling her about us."

Hunter shakes his head, a smile pulling at his lips. "She likes you. She's the one who insisted I send you flowers."

"Oh, really?" I push down the disappointment I feel knowing Hunter wouldn't have sent me flowers without Hannah's influence.

"She's far wiser than me when it comes to relationships. That's why she's the one getting married and I'm content with being secret fuck buddies. My parents have given up hope that I'll be passing on the Cartwright name. They've asked Hannah to hyphenate her and James's last name to keep the lineage."

He smiles ruefully.

"Do you want those things, Sophie? A husband? A family?"

I look back out over the city. "Someday. As we've established, I'm only twenty-two. I've got lots of goals I want to accomplish."

"Like?"

I shrug. "Being self-sufficient for starters."

"I don't know many twenty-two-year-olds who are. I wasn't at that age."

"It's in the five-year plan."

"What else is in the five-year plan?" he asks.

"Get my own apartment. Travel. Maybe start my own business."

"Wedding planning?" he asks.

"While the luxury and all out weddings of New York City's elite are fabulous, I want to offer a unique service to brides where you can share wedding supplies to cut costs. I love making sustainable centerpieces and other decorations that can be reused. And a lot of people don't know what to do with their decorations once the wedding is done, or they don't want to deal with selling them, so they trash them. My business would take the guess work out of that. And help reduce waste."

He smiles down at me. "That's clever."

Our discussion about my job serves to remind me that while this weekend has been nice, going forward, most of my weekends will be booked up.

I pull my gaze from the view and turn to Hunter.

"So, how is this going to work?" I ask.

He lowers his hands to my hips. "I thought I showed you yesterday. Multiple times."

"That's not what I mean. Should we have a schedule or something? That way we both know what to expect."

Maybe if I can put Hunter on my calendar, as an item to be checked off, a need that is fulfilled, then I can compartmentalize what we're doing.

"My weekdays are busy. I work long hours," he says.

"And I'll be working most weekends."

It was just yesterday, before we had sex, that I was firmly against a hookup with Hunter. Our schedules not aligning is the proof I need that we jumped into this without really thinking and it might not be the best idea. I should tell him it's not going to work, but the thought of him never touching me again has disappointment settling into my gut.

But that disappointment now is better than having whatever it is we're doing get in the way of my career. Or yet, finding out that I could like Hunter for more than sex. I don't even want to give headspace to that possibility.

Either way, I'm starting to wonder if I'm out of my depth with him.

Hunter is a serial dater. A master at the casual fling. I've barely dated, let alone had strictly sexual flings. I like Hunter, and I like having sex with him, but I'm not sure how to navigate this thing, this arrangement. How will I feel when he loses interest and moves on? Something he has all but assured me will happen.

I'm the shiny new toy that he was desperate to have. But the shine will wear off eventually. I refuse to rearrange my life for anyone, let alone a guy that will be moving on in a matter of weeks…months tops.

"Maybe this isn't the best idea after all," I say, pulling my hands inside the sleeves of the sweatshirt, then wrapping my arms around my middle.

Hunter pulls me against him.

"You want to see the city, and I want to see you naked. I'll have to get creative."

He doesn't realize that it's not just logistics that I'm thinking about, but I'm curious what his plan is.

"How?" I ask.

He smiles wickedly and pulls me over to the side of the viewing platform. He presses me back against the wall, his strong hands gripping my hips.

"You enjoy the view while I make you come."

"Here?!" My eyes widen with shock. "No way." I push at his chest, but he doesn't budge. "We can't."

"Don's taking an elevator ride to the lobby. I'm certain I can make you come before he gets back. In fact, I accept the challenge."

I study his handsome face. This man scheduled a private tour of Top of the Rock and now wants to give me an orgasm? What's the catch?

His thumbs are rubbing seductive circles against my hip bones, making it difficult to think of anything else. When one hand slides between my legs to cup me, I whimper. Over the fabric of my shorts, Hunter scissors a finger back and forth against my center. His nose nuzzles against the column of my neck. He's seductive and sweet in equal measure. It's absolute torture.

"I can feel how warm your pussy is beneath these tiny shorts. You're wet, aren't you, Sophie?"

With my teeth trapping my bottom lip to hold in a moan, I

give a nod for confirmation. His hand moves under the baggy sweatshirt and to the waistband of my shorts. It's a snug fit, but his hand dips inside of my shorts where he confirms what he already knew…I'm soaked.

"Damn, Sophie. So fucking wet." He runs two fingers along my seam, then slowly drags it up to my clit. His mouth trails kisses up the column of my throat and along my jaw. He captures my earlobe between his teeth, then growls. "And it's all mine."

Hunter teases me with long strokes and gentle swirls. His fingertips rimming me without ever going inside.

He flicks my clit and my hips buck forward, desperately searching for his fingers.

Just when I think I'm going to cry in frustration, Hunter thrusts two fingers inside me.

"Open your eyes, Sophie. I want you to enjoy the view when you come on my hand."

And that's exactly what I do. Seventy floors above the street, with my eyes looking out over Central Park, I come hard around Hunter's fingers.

He slowly pulls his hand out of my shorts, then sucks his index finger into his mouth.

"So fucking good."

I'm breathless and leaning against the wall.

"Open your mouth," he says.

I let my jaw drop, giving space for Hunter to slide his middle finger past my lips.

"Don't you taste sweet?" he asks, letting my lips tighten around his finger before he pulls it out.

I nod, as my own musky flavor hits my tongue.

He lowers my sweatshirt, then grabs my hand.

"We should go. I've got things to do."

"Oh, sure." I nod, then follow Hunter to the elevators where Don is waiting to escort us down to the main level. In the lobby, Sharon sees us to the door.

Out on the sidewalk, Hunter looks down at his smart watch and starts scrolling on it. I have that same feeling I did yesterday, after we had sex and I felt like I should leave his apartment.

I pull my phone out of the side pocket of my shorts and start mapping out how to get back to Griffin and Emma's apartment.

Hunter drops his arm and looks over at me. "Ready?"

"Yeah, but I think I need to go this way to get home." I motion to the right. The opposite direction that Hunter is moving toward.

He looks at me confused. "Why are you going home?"

"You said you had things to do."

"Yeah, when it comes to you, I've got a whole fucking list. Right now, it includes finishing our run, then taking you back to my place to bury myself inside you. And come on your tits. I thought we'd check that off the list today."

I let out a sharp laugh at his bluntness.

"You coming?" His brows lift suggestively as he starts backing down the sidewalk.

"I don't know. You tell me," I call back playfully.

Hunter's lips pull into a wicked smile. "Yeah, you definitely will be."

My lips twist and I shake my head at his cockiness. My body, having made the decision for me, moves to fall into step with Hunter. What is it about this man that makes it impossible for me to walk away? I giggle as he pulls me along and try to ignore the voice in the back of my mind telling me this can't last.

CHAPTER 13

Hunter

Monday morning is full of meetings. Just before noon, I make my way back to my office.

Outside my window, the sun gleams off the Empire State Building. It reminds me of how delighted Sophie was to see my view last week when I invited her into my office. How I'd been certain that she was off limits, but her mere presence in my office that day only served to entice me with a mind full of dirty thoughts about what I could do to her here. Spread her out on my desk and lick her sweet pussy. Bend her over it and spank her ass until her cheeks were pink and her arousal was dripping down her thighs. Fuck her against the window with her tits pressed against the glass. My hand over her mouth to cover up those breathy moans she makes when she's close.

So many options.

I turn away from the window and to my computer screen.

Throwing myself into work has always come easy. For me, working is breathing. Last week, I was distracted by thoughts of Sophie. Now that things with her are settled, I should be able to return my focus to work.

I'm about to do just that when Hannah calls.

"What do you need?" I ask in way of greeting.

"Hello to you, too, darling brother," she teases. "I'm simply wondering how your weekend was."

"It was fine." It was more than fine.

After our stop at Top of the Rock yesterday, Sophie and I ran a short loop around the park, then went back to my place. I could barely make it past the door, so I ate her pussy against the wall in the hallway, then fucked her on the kitchen counter. She wanted me to spank her again and damn, she gets so wet when I do. Her arousal was dripping down the inside of her thighs. I had to lay her on the bed and lick her clean again. Then I hovered over her on the bed so she could suck me, before I slammed into her tight pussy, and as I had promised, I came all over her tits.

"You there?" Hannah asks, my silence making her wonder if I've hung up.

"Yeah." I adjust myself and let the fact that I'm on the phone with my sister put a stop to the raging hard-on that threatens with the thought of Sophie.

"My weekend was lovely. I spent Saturday morning at the boutique, then James and I had a picnic in the park. Thanks for asking."

"Sorry." Guilt hits me for being short with her. "I'm glad you had a nice weekend."

"Okay. I need a favor," she says.

I groan, the guilt I felt a moment ago evaporating. "So, you do need something."

"It's a small favor."

A sharp puff of air escapes from my nostrils. "Define small."

"My friend Allison will be in town for the Two Ten gala on Friday. She needs a date."

"You told me to never date your friends."

"It's not a date-date. She just broke up with her boyfriend. She's a little down and doesn't want to be a third wheel with me and James. Unless there's someone else you plan to take?"

I can't see her face, but if eyebrows lifting had a tone, this would be it.

"No." I don't know what Sophie has planned for Friday night, but even if she is available, we wouldn't be going to the Two Ten gala together.

"Pretty please, with a bottle of Balvenie on top?"

It's my favorite scotch. But I have no trouble getting my own liquor.

"That's an insulting offer."

She grumbles. "Fine. You can have the lake house for July Fourth weekend. I know you're always complaining that James and I take over with all our couple friends, so it would be all yours this time."

Our family has a house on Lake George in the Adirondacks. It's our go-to escape from the city in the summer. Fourth of July weekend especially. If she's offering it up, she must be desperate.

Normally, that offer would pique my interest, but I don't know that I'll be headed to Lake George that weekend. If Sophie's working in the city, I might opt to stay here as well. The thought comes out of nowhere. Huh. I rub my jaw, contemplating how quickly I'm letting my need for Sophie influence my life. I never do that.

"Come on, you've got to make me a better offer than that."

Hannah sighs. "Name your price."

I take a moment to think. I could keep the lake house and not make plans with Sophie that weekend. That will help keep things in perspective. We're fucking, not a couple with date nights and holiday weekend getaways. But I could also get something to assist me in my task of showing Sophie the city.

"Actually, I'll take the Lake George house for Fourth of

July weekend and you can throw in your tickets for the ballet next week."

"You want my ballet tickets? What for?" She sounds suspicious. Again, like a dog with a bone.

"No questions necessary. Do we have a deal?"

"Yes," she quickly confirms. "Make sure you look nice; she wants to take photos and post them on social media to make her ex feel like shit."

"That'll be easy," I reply, already opening a text to Sophie to ask if she's free next Tuesday night for the ballet.

"Hunter, are you feeling okay?" Hannah asks.

"Why?" I ask, distracted as I type out the text to Sophie.

"You didn't even ask what Allison looks like."

My fingers pause over my keyboard. She's right. In this situation, if I thought there was any chance in hooking up with the woman, I would ask to see pictures. Even though Hannah doesn't want me fucking her friends, it has been known to happen on occasion. But with Sophie at the forefront of my mind, I never even considered it in this situation. I don't know if it's because my sister is calling me out on my player reputation or because I'm annoyed with myself for letting one weekend with Sophie change my habits.

"Why would that matter?" I say, the defensiveness in my voice hard to disguise. "She's your friend, and she's fresh off a breakup. I'm not going to hit on her."

"Don't get your boxers in a bunch. I'm just teasing you. You're mighty sensitive today."

"I've got a meeting. Do you need anything else?" I ask.

"That's all," she says, all cheery and satisfied. "The tickets will be under your name at the theater."

"Thanks."

We exchange goodbyes and end the call.

I stare down at my unfinished text to Sophie, second guessing sending it. I don't normally make plans with women, but that's what Sophie had wanted. Structure and planning around our busy schedules. To make it work for both of us. I want her beneath me with no complications, and she wants orgasms and to see the city. The ballet was one of the items on her growing list.

I finish texting out the details and hit send.

Sophie: *OMG!! That would be dope!*

Dope. Has that word come back into use? I decide to ignore the reminder that I became a teenager the year Sophie was born.

Hunter: *Glad you're excited. Do you have a dress to wear?*

Sophie: *I think I can get one from Emma.*

Sophie: *And thank you for giving me a heads up so I'm not in a sports bra and shorts.*

Hunter: *Please wear underwear.*

Before she responds, I type out another message.

Hunter: *Or don't.*

Sophie: *Ha! I'm not hooking up with you at the NYC ballet. It's civilized. No funny business.*

I smirk at her last text. She must not realize the lengths I'll go to fuck her. If there's any opportunity to touch Sophie, I'm going to take it.

CHAPTER 14

Sophie

The start of my second week at Marion Adler Events goes much more smoothly. My nerves and stomach are settled. And after being satiated from my weekend with Hunter, I feel ready to take on the world.

By Tuesday afternoon, I've reviewed all the files for the upcoming weddings on Johnathan's calendar. It's customary for Marion to oversee the planning while the assistant planners take on the execution of details like locking in vendors and budget management. As an intern, I'm relegated to tasks such as coffee fetching, office supply ordering, and inputting notes from client planning meetings. It's not glamorous, but from what I can tell from the other interns, Johnathan is the best at including me in all aspects of the process, even if it's not necessary. I'm grateful that he wants to show me the ropes. And that he assured me he wouldn't be telling Marion about what happened at the meeting last week.

The lunch meeting with Hannah, James, and Hunter feels like a lifetime ago. I've almost forgotten about the awkwardness of admitting I've slept with Hunter, until Johnathan informs me we've got a meeting with Hannah. The second I walk into the conference room where Marion, Hannah and Johnathan are already seated, I'm nervous Hannah might say something. While Hannah has no idea that me and Hunter have agreed to a secret fling, I'm still on edge.

"Sophie, thanks for joining us." Marion motions for me to sit beside her, across from Hannah. "Would you please take notes on our meeting?"

"Of course." I nod.

"Hi, Sophie." Hannah smiles at me. "Nice to see you again."

I try not to let my cheeks flush. Hannah doesn't know what her brother and I did this weekend, yet for some reason it feels like she can read my mind. Like every detail is written on my face. The spanking, the dirty talk, the sweaty, all-consuming sex and mind-bending orgasms her brother gave me.

I try to forget about Hunter and focus on taking detailed notes of the meeting.

As they're talking about locations for the rehearsal dinner, I get caught up in the excitement.

I gasp with the sudden idea. "You should do the dinner at Loeb Boathouse. That's where your family went for lunch every Sunday when you were growing up." The words are out of my mouth before I comprehend what I'm saying. "I, uh," I look up to find three sets of eyes on me, "I think that's what I read somewhere. You know, in my research to help better understand what you might want for your big day."

"Wow. I'm impressed with the research you've done." Hannah smiles, but I swear there's a knowing gleam in her eye. "James's parents will want to have input, but I think the Loeb Boathouse at Central Park would be perfect. It fits in well with my 'on the water' theme."

I give her an enthusiastic smile, appreciative that she doesn't ask me about the research I've done.

When the meeting concludes, Marion walks Hannah out to the reception area, while Johnathan steers me back down the hallway toward his office.

"That was impressive, but also a little stalkerish." He smirks.

"Yeah, not the best delivery."

"Do I want to know your source?" His brows lift meaningfully.

I shake my head. "If I tell you, I'll have to kill you."

Johnathan lifts his hands to his shoulders. "Then it's better if I don't know."

"Oh, before I forget, I wanted to give you this." He hands me a card. "My friend's cousin is the manager at The Penrose, a swanky cocktail lounge frequented by Wall Street types. She's looking for a waitress and you mentioned you were looking for a second job. She needs Wednesday and Thursday nights. I told her about you. It might work with your schedule?"

"Thank you. This is perfect," I say, reading the card's details before tucking it into my planner.

When I get back to my desk, I input all the notes from the meeting with Hannah into her digital file and email it to Johnathan and Marion. Then, I grab my phone and reread the texts from Hunter. I'm so excited to go to the ballet with him. I know Emma would be my best resource for a dress, but I'm wondering if she would have a million questions about where I'm going.

I'm about to put my phone away when another text from him pops up.

Hunter: *Plans this weekend?*

I type out my response.

Sophie: *I'm working a wedding on Saturday. You?*

I'm wondering if I should ask him if he wants to hang out on Friday night when his text comes through.

Hunter: *I've got an event Friday night. Dinner with Hannah and James on Sunday.*

I sigh, hating that I'm disappointed I won't see him until next Tuesday. It's the sex I'll be missing, I tell myself. It's ridiculous how horny I've been lately. But when I tried to masturbate last night, it wasn't as satisfying as usual. I wanted Hunter's fingers stroking me, his cock stretching me.

June walks in and drops into her chair. Her sigh is heavy as she shakes her mouse vigorously to wake her computer.

"How's it going over there?" I ask.

"Not great. My boyfriend was going to surprise me this weekend by flying here from Michigan."

"Why isn't that a good thing? Other than it sounds like the surprise was ruined."

"He told me his plan when I mentioned that I was working Friday night. I wasn't originally working, but I volunteered to work for Vesper because she's visiting family."

"Oh, no."

Vesper comes over from her desk.

"I'm sorry, June. I've asked Sasha and Chris, but they can't do it."

"Does it have to be an event intern? I've got no plans. I can do it."

When June's eyes connect with mine, they light up.

She clasps her hands together and holds them to her chest. "I would owe you so freaking big. Anytime you need me to fill in for you."

I'd thought about doing some sightseeing on Friday after work. There's an entire city to see, after all, but I can see the desperation in June's eyes. If I had a boyfriend visiting me from out of state, I'd want someone to help me out, too.

"What's the event?" I ask.

"A gala at Chelsea Piers. It's only a few hours, checking guests in at the front door and making sure they're set up with the donation app."

"Sure." I shrug. "That sounds easy enough."

She jumps up to hug me. "Oh my God, Sophie! Thank you! Thank you! Thank you!"

Vesper claps excitedly.

"No problem. I'm sure I'll need a day off at some point, too."

"Of course. You name it and I'll be there."

June moves back over to her desk. My phone buzzes with an unread text.

Hunter: *Looking forward to Tuesday.*

I start to text him back, but realize maybe I should play it cool and wait a few hours to respond. Then I remember that's the beauty of our arrangement. It doesn't matter if I appear eager. We both know what we want. There's no need to play games.

Sophie: *Same.*

I reply, then put my phone away and get back to work.

Friday night, I'm sitting at a table in front of the entrance to Pier 60. I have to pinch myself at how cool this job is. I'm getting paid to talk to celebrities and socialites. Checking in guests is easy and fun, and watching guests arrive and walk the red carpet is the highlight. Everyone looks stunning. Men in tuxes, women in stylish gowns looking breathtaking and dreamlike. It makes me think about what I'm going to wear to the ballet. Emma would be a great shopping resource, but now that I think about it, I realize it's best not to involve her. She'd ask too many questions. Questions I don't want to answer. While I'm waiting for the next group of guests to make their way over to the check-in table, I send June a quick text.

She replies immediately.

June: *I've got the perfect place. We'll go on lunch break Monday.*

Sophie: *Thanks!*

June: *How's the event?*

Sophie: *Fun! I love seeing all the gowns. Hope you have a great night with Allen!*

Monday doesn't give me a lot of time to find a dress, but I'm hoping June's knowledge of staying on a budget in this outrageously expensive city will come through. I tuck my phone back into my purse and look up in time to see the next group making their way over. At first, I think my brain has conjured his image. That I've projected the devilishly handsome man with his wicked smile into the sea of guests, but a double take reveals it's really him.

That tux I was excited to see Hunter in on Tuesday at the ballet? Christmas came early. Damn, he looks good. A fresh wave of lust rocks my body as I take in the perfection that is Hunter Cartwright in a tuxedo. He's devastatingly handsome with his smooth jaw, those indigo eyes and his dark hair tousled. With my eyes on Hunter, I forgot about the people standing in front of me waiting for me to check them in.

The man clears his throat.

"Sorry about that. I've got you checked in." I tap the screen on the tablet I was issued at the start of my shift, then hand the man the number I assigned him for the paddle raise.

I'm anticipating Hunter approaching my table, but then remember that he's Cartwright and would need to go to the A-L table. I don't know if I'm disappointed or relieved. I want to see him, but I don't know exactly how to act. Do I smile and wave? Act aloof, like we don't know each other? I'm debating this when he steps up to my table. With him are his sister, Hannah, her fiancé, James, and a gorgeous brunette.

"James McKenzie, party of four," James tells me, then does a double take. "Wait. Do I know you?"

Hannah turns from the brunette woman that has her arm

through Hunter's. "Sophie." She greets me with air kisses. "Good to see you."

"Sophie works at Marion Adler," Hannah reminds James and tells the brunette. "She's part of my wedding planning team."

The brunette looks me up and down. "How lovely."

I drop my gaze to the tablet screen and quickly check them in. With my index finger, I stab the box by each of their names under the reservation. James McKenzie and Hannah Cartwright. Hunter Cartwright and Allison Mulvaney.

I put on my best enthusiastic door greeter smile. "Wonderful to see you all tonight." I pull out two number paddles and hand them to James and Hunter without making eye contact.

"I'll take a separate paddle," Allison says, then leans into Hunter, "unless you're sponsoring me tonight."

Hunter gives her a tight smile, but his words are kind. "I don't mind."

Allison giggles. "What an agreeable date you are."

I don't know what I'm expecting from Hunter, but I can feel his eyes on me.

When I finally look up at him, he nods. "Sophie."

I give him a small smile. Emotions are warring in me as the group moves past my table and into the gala.

A minute later, my phone buzzes in my purse. I pull it out to find Hunter's text.

Hunter: *Allison is Hannah's friend. Hannah asked me to be her date because she recently broke up with her boyfriend. That's the only reason I'm here with her.*

I let this information sink in while I check in the next group of people. I want to say that it gives me time to calm down about the situation but it's the opposite. The fact that Hunter is offering an explanation so quickly makes my guard go up. If I hadn't been here, would he have told me? I'm feeling even more annoyed when another text from him comes in.

Hunter: *I should have mentioned it when we talked yesterday. I'm sorry I caught you off guard. I could tell you were upset.*

I take a moment for his text to settle in. He's recognizing his mistake and apologizing. That should be all the explanation I need to let this go. But what's bothering me more about the situation is my body's reaction to it. Like when I saw him across the street kissing a woman on the cheek, who I now know is his mom's friend. My stomach is uneasy and I feel out of sorts.

I want to tell him that I'm not mad. That he doesn't have that kind of effect on me, but it would all be lies. And the fact that he noticed I was annoyed? That makes me even more irritated.

More than Hunter catching me off guard by having a date tonight, I hate that I'm suddenly feeling insecure.

The few times I've been with him privately, running the trail in Central Park or behind closed doors, I'd forgotten that Hunter Cartwright is somebody in this city. When we're together, he's just an incredibly sexy man that makes me laugh and hands out orgasms like firefighters who hand out candy in a small-town parade.

Tuxedo-clad, CEO Hunter is even more droolworthy. Just seeing how gorgeous and polished he is has me questioning if our time together has merely been a fever dream that I'm going to wake up from any moment.

That man wants *me?*

My brain is struggling to compute.

The group's appearance only served to remind me that Hunter is a wealthy man that attends galas and charities, while I'm the twenty-two-year-old intern on the other side of the table greeting him.

That's the whole point, though. I'm twenty-two and starting out in my career. I need to pay my dues and learn from my mistakes. Hunter has done that already. The outcome being the impressive businessman that walked in here minutes ago. I can't compare myself to him. We're at different places in life. I don't want to fast-forward to thirty-five. I want to take my time, soak in every moment.

I push Hunter and his date out of my mind to finish my shift.

Thirty minutes later, all the guests have been checked in and my duties are done.

Andrea, the other event planning intern working the check-in table, motions me over to her table where she's starting to pack up.

"Would you take these tablets to Will inside while I clean up here? He's the guy I introduced you to earlier."

"Sure." I take her tablet and mine, then walk inside the event center to find Will. A tall guy with a bald head and dark red glasses, he's easy to spot across the room. I make my way through the space, taking in the navy carpet and neon blue lighting on the ceiling, but the best part is the twelve-foot-high doors that open up to the patio overlooking the Hudson River.

After I drop the tablets with Will, I stand and take in the view for a moment. While I'm standing there, a woman mistakes me for a waitress and hands me her empty glass. I'm in a simple black dress and heels, but compared to the other women in gowns, my outfit screams waitress, not attendee. I drop her glass off at the bar, then start to make my way toward the exit.

I'm almost outside when a strong hand grips my arm and pulls me sideways into an alcove between the event room and the exit.

My mouth is open, ready to scream, when I see that it's Hunter.

"What the hell?" My words are sharp, but being this close to him, in this small space, makes my body soften. "You don't sneak up on a woman, especially one that has been catching up on the last season of *Up and Vanished*."

"You didn't respond." He rubs his hand along his jaw, but his eyes stay locked on mine as his brow furrows. "What's *Up and Vanished*?"

I attempt to not fall under his spell by staring at his ears. Ears aren't sexy, right? Wrong. Everything about this man turns me into a puddle.

"It's a podcast about unsolved disappearances. *Women* who have disappeared."

His smile causes crinkles at the corner of his eyes. "And you're listening to that because?"

"It's interesting and it helps me unwind after a busy day."

He presses his lips together in amusement. "Yeah, it sounds relaxing."

"And it gives good tips on how to be safe and aware of your surroundings."

"That's very important. Especially in a big city."

"It never warned about hot businessmen lurking in dark alcoves."

He smirks at that. "You think I'm hot?"

I scoff. "I'm leaving now."

He takes a step back, following my move, but he's still blocking the exit. "I'm sorry. I didn't know you'd be here."

"So as long as I didn't know you and Allison would be here canoodling, everything is cool?"

He smiles. "Canoodling? You sound like my grandmother."

"Your grandmother must be in her eighties, so I don't think that's a compliment."

"My grandmother is very spirited. You two would get along great."

"Too bad I'll never meet her."

"Hmm. That is too bad." He slides a hand around my back to pull me closer.

Our bodies align and for a moment I'm completely intoxicated by Hunter. I luxuriate in the way his hard body feels pressed against mine. The way one whiff of his spicy cologne makes my panties damp. Then I push his hand away and start moving toward the alcove exit.

"I'll let you get back to your date."

CHAPTER 15

Hunter

"It's not a real date. It's a favor," I tell Sophie as I reach for her wrist to keep her in this private space with me. "Hannah asked me to come with her friend."

She turns back to look at me.

"And you agreed out of the kindness of your heart?" she asks.

"I think I'm a nice guy, but no, I got something in return."

"What?" She blinks up at me with skepticism in her eyes.

"The ballet tickets for next week. It's sold out, but Hannah has season tickets. And while I could have found resale tickets, she has a box and I thought it would be best for privacy."

Sophie's face softens. "Oh." She drops her crossed arms. "Well, that's thoughtful about the tickets, but a heads up would have been nice. I had no idea you'd be here and seeing you with another woman was even more of a surprise."

"I'm sorry. I get it. I'd feel the same way if you showed up on the arm of another guy and I didn't know the situation."

"You would?" she asks, her voice disbelieving.

"Yeah, we agreed we wouldn't be seeing anyone else while we're sleeping together."

She's quiet now, disarmed, so I lean in closer. Even under

the circumstances and the misunderstanding about my appearance with Allison, I'm happy to see her. To have this private moment together after not seeing her all week.

My hand wraps around the back of her neck. My thumb traces the smooth line of her jaw until it reaches the tip of her chin and presses underneath to tilt her gaze up to mine.

"It's good to see you." My free hand runs down the side of her body, along her ribcage, the curve of her waist.

I suck on her lip, then capture her mouth with mine. The fact that I won't see her the rest of the weekend has my body urging me closer, wanting to dive in deeper.

When Sophie wraps her arms around my neck to pull me closer, it spurs me on.

I'm desperate to feel her, and not at all gentle when I reach under her dress and slip a digit beneath the lace of her panties. She's drenched.

"So fucking wet for me. That's how I like this pussy, Sophie. Slick and swollen. Always ready for me to fuck it."

The breathy moan she makes when I sink my finger inside her is my undoing. Fuck, she feels incredible.

I growl and rock my hips into her. I'm so fucking hard now. If I don't stop touching her, I'll be walking around the rest of the night with a raging hard-on. Unless she'll let me fuck her right here. My head turns toward the alcove entrance. The main gala room is dark, and this forgotten space is even darker.

The sound of guests talking and the music playing in the background filter into our tiny space. There's no door, so we're taking a risk. While I've been known for my skills in the bedroom, I've never fucked someone at an event. Even in my twenties, I managed to make it behind a locked door. Sophie does something to me. Shuts off the rational part of my brain. I have to have her. *Now.*

"I need to be inside you," I tell her. She gasps with need, but I put my hand over her mouth to quiet her. "Shh." I kiss her jaw, her neck, trailing my tongue along the shell of her ear. "Can you be quiet, sweetheart? I can make it so good for you if you can."

Her green eyes widen and she nods urgently.

I grab the condom from my wallet, then reach for my belt. "I'm going to fuck you right here. You're going to come for me, but you're not going to make a sound."

Sophie bites her lip, and nods silently in agreement.

I roll the condom on, yank her panties aside and press the head of my cock to her entrance.

She sucks in a breath. With my eyes locked on hers, I thrust hard.

The moment she surrounds me, I'm lost to the sensation of her. Nothing feels as good as being inside Sophie.

"Hmm." Sophie's lips are pressed together to muffle her groan. I grip her ass and lift her higher on the wall, driving in deeper.

She whimpers and I give her a hard look. "Do you want everyone to hear how good I'm giving it to you? Would you like that? To let everyone here know that I'm addicted to this sweet pussy, I can't get enough of it?"

She shakes her head.

With a handful of her hair to hold her head exactly where I want it, I crush my lips to hers. And then I let go. My rhythm is punishing. I know it's rough, but I can't help it. She makes me wild. She makes me want to consume her like she's consuming me.

I pull back a moment to look at her.

My hand trails down her neck, fingers gliding over her collarbone, pushing past the neckline of her dress. I'm frustrated that I can't get to more of her skin. I squeeze her breast, tease her nipple through the thin fabric of her bra, then make my way downward.

There's not much room, but I manage to land a hard smack on the side of her ass.

Sophie stifles a moan. I can't see her skin flushing, but I can feel how much she likes it. How much wetter she gets when I spank her.

I roll my hips, grinding my pelvis into her clit. She moans, her hips bucking against me. I can feel her pussy starting to clench around my cock. She's so fucking close.

"I can feel how much your greedy pussy loves my cock. Come for me, Sophie."

And then she lets go.

"Oh...my..." I cover her mouth with mine again, swallowing the sounds of her climax.

When she constricts around me, squeezing me so fucking tight, I'm powerless to do anything but bury my head in the crook of her neck and groan out my own release.

Ecstasy rushes through my veins as I pulse deep inside Sophie's tight, wet cunt.

I want to fucking own this woman.

"Fuck." I nip at the sensitive skin where her neck and shoulder meet, trying to come down from the adrenaline rush of taking her this way. I pull back and find Sophie's eyes closed, her chest heaving, but she's not making a sound. "Are you okay?"

Her eyes open, that green gaze of hers piercing right through me. She looks shell-shocked. If we were at my place, I'd hold her, clean her up and we'd have a moment to catch our breath. But here, the sounds of the gala float back into the tiny alcove, popping our bubble of lust.

When I'm touching Sophie nothing else matters but making her feel good. While lust was driving my desire to have her, I'm seeing now that I shouldn't have done that here. I'm a guest at the gala, and Sophie is here for work. If we were to get caught, it wouldn't be me that would have consequences. And I know how important Sophie's internship is to her.

"Fuck." I press my forehead to hers. "I got carried away. I'm sorry."

She clears her throat as I pull out of her and release her to the ground.

"It's okay," she whispers.

"It's not. That was…fuck…that was," I'm searching for the right word, "intense."

"Yeah." She nods, brushing her now disheveled hair off her face.

I clean us up the best I can, using my pocket square between Sophie's legs, before wrapping it around the tied-off condom. Sophie adjusts her underwear and straightens her dress.

"Let me get you water. A cab. Something."

"Hunter," Sophie places her hand on my chest, "I'm fine."

She picks her purse up off the ground and throws it over her shoulder.

"I'm going to go."

I know she's not here for the event, and even if she was, I wouldn't be able to spend time with her. I'm here with Allison, and Sophie and I are a secret.

"Text me when you get home," I tell her.

Her brows draw down in a defiant frown.

"Please," I urge her.

She nods, then clutching her purse with both hands, leaves me standing alone in the dark alcove.

I manage to sneak out and use the restroom. Wash my hands and dispose of the condom.

When I find Hannah, James, and Allison, they're outside on the patio partaking in the gala's Vegas theme playing at one of the blackjack tables. Allison smiles up at me. I'm used to being on dates with women that I don't have a vested interest in, tonight is no exception. The only difference is there is a woman I want on my arm, and I can't have her. At least not like that.

I'm used to getting what I want. I thought that's what I was getting in this arrangement with Sophie, but watching her leave after I fucked her, now I'm not so sure.

When her text comes in thirty minutes later, I smile and tap out a response.

"What are you smiling about?" Hannah asks, eyeing me carefully.

"Nothing." I pocket the phone.

For the rest of the night, I try to not think about Sophie and focus on being a considerate date to Allison.

Later that night, I lie awake, not able to sleep.

It's after midnight, but I take a chance and reach for my phone to call Sophie.

She picks up on the third ring.

"Did I wake you?" I ask.

"Yeah." Her groggy voice is adorable. I let myself imagine her curled up in bed. The visual makes my chest ache.

"Sorry. I can let you go."

"What did you need?" she asks.

"Need?" I echo.

What did I need? To hear her voice. To know she's okay and I didn't scare her off.

"Why were you calling?" she whispers.

"I wanted to make sure you're okay."

"I'm okay, Hunter. I was being honest when I said it earlier."

"Okay." I sigh. "I couldn't sleep. I've been thinking about you."

"Sorry you can't sleep," she says, sounding more awake now. "Do you usually have trouble sleeping?"

"No. It's new. I think it's your fault. That's why I called you."

"My fault?" She laughs quietly.

"Tell me more about you."

"Because you think it'll be boring and you'll be able to fall asleep?"

"Because I like the sound of your voice. It's relaxing."

She lets out a soft hum. "What do you want to know?"

Everything.

The thought materializes out of nowhere. For a moment, I'm disoriented by it. Maybe I'm more tired than I thought. *Keep it simple.*

"When did you start running?" I ask.

"Um, in high school. I was on the cross-country team. It was part of Griffin's plan to keep me busy so I wouldn't have time for boys. My freshman year I had a huge crush on a senior guy on the team, so it wasn't successful."

"You dated the guy?"

"No. I was a nerd, always studying. And I was all awkward limbs and no boobs, not exactly a magnet for the popular guys."

"Hmm. I love your long legs. As we established tonight, it makes it easier to fuck you standing up."

"Glad you're a fan."

"I'm a fan of a lot of things. Your boobs being another."

The sound she makes is half laugh, half sigh.

"What about you? When did you start running?" she asks.

"I was a rower in prep school and college, but we ran for conditioning."

"A rower, huh? Rowing sounds like such a snobby sport. And at Princeton?" She lets out a low whistle.

I chuckle at her assessment. "I can't argue with you."

"Good thing you're so down to earth now. Living in your Upper West Side penthouse and flying on your private jet."

"It's a simple life."

She giggles, more awake now, and I love the sound. "Do you still row?"

"I get out on the water from time to time, but running is

much more accessible these days. And now that I have a running partner, it's even more enjoyable."

"We're running partners now?" she asks.

"Among other things."

Her voice goes quiet. "Thank you again for inviting me to the ballet. I'm excited."

"I'll warn you, I have a track record of not being a great date."

"I don't need you to be a great date. I'm there for the ballet, not you."

I chuckle. "Good to know."

"Were you nice to Allison tonight?" she asks.

"Nice, sure, but mostly distracted thinking about you."

She sighs. "You're not going to the Feldman-Weiser wedding tomorrow, are you?"

"No."

"Thank God." She laughs quietly. "I'll actually be able to focus on my job."

I know what she means. If she's in the vicinity, it's hard to focus on anything else. And now, even when I can't see her, I could easily talk to her until we both get no sleep tonight.

She exhales, the sound of a stifled yawn.

"You need your sleep. I'll let you go."

Another stifled yawn. "Okay."

"I'll see you on Tuesday."

"See you then," she whispers.

I hang up and toss my phone onto the charger on my nightstand. If anything, talking to Sophie has only made me more alert. More aware that I've never enjoyed a woman this much.

I flip over onto my stomach and bury my hands under my pillow. I decide not to analyze it and just enjoy it while it lasts.

CHAPTER 16

Sophie

The consignment shop June takes me to on Monday is a goldmine. The brands are designer yet the prices are reasonable. For the ballet, I find a long, flowy emerald dress that brings out the color of my eyes. I also find a fitted, red dress that I can't pass up, so I hope there is another occasion to wear it.

"Thanks again for working for me on Friday night," June says through the dressing room door.

"Of course. I was happy to do it. How was the weekend with your boyfriend?" I ask.

Her sigh carries through the door. "It was good, but Allen wants me to move to Michigan. We've been long-distance the entire two years we've dated." She pauses. "I'm not sure that's what I want. My family and life are here. And it all really depends on what happens with this internship. If I get offered a full-time position, I can't imagine turning it down."

June's mention of the full-time junior assistant positions to be decided at the end of the summer has my stomach fluttering with nerves. I haven't let myself imagine not getting offered a full-time position at Marion Adler Events. Landing one of those positions is everything I've been working for. It's the next step in my plan.

"I'm sorry." That's all I can offer. I don't have much relationship experience. Zero, in fact.

"Thanks. I'll figure it out. How was the gala? See anyone famous?"

My mind immediately draws up the memory of Hunter and our secret rendezvous at the gala. While I was technically done with work, it wasn't professional of me to have sex with him there. On the other hand, it was hands down the most erotic experience of my life.

I've been thinking about it all weekend. Even as I worked the Feldman-Weiser wedding on Saturday, I found myself distracted with thoughts of Hunter.

The fear of getting caught while we fought to keep quiet. It added another element to the already explosive sex I've experienced with him.

Hunter was afraid he was too rough with me, too demanding and harsh, but I loved the way he made me feel. Wild and free. Like I didn't have to be in control like I normally am. I don't normally allow myself to feel that way around other people, but with Hunter, when he's inside me, for some reason, I let everything go.

"It was fun. I recognized a few Bravo reality stars."

We take my dresses to the register so I can pay. I didn't share with June that I was going to the ballet, but that I want to have a few dresses in my closet in case I need to dress up for an event.

"There had to be hot guys in tuxes. That's my favorite thing about formal events."

"Yeah," I laugh. "There were plenty of men in tuxes to eyeball." My stomach dips recalling Hunter in his tuxedo.

I take the shopping bag from the associate and we exit the store.

"So, what's your status? Dating anyone?" June asks.

I hesitate, thinking about my arrangement with Hunter, and June picks up on it.

"Oh, there is someone." Her lips curve in a knowing smile.

"No," I shake my head adamantly, "I'm still trying to navigate the city and focus on work. Dating is not on my agenda right now."

"Okay, but if you ever need a wing-woman, I'm your girl."

"Thanks, I'll keep that in mind."

We get salads to go from a bistro nearby and make our way back to the office.

"How did your first wedding go?" June asks as we walk down the street.

"Honestly, it was like being on a movie set. Not that I know what that's like, but the price tag seemed in line with that of a movie budget."

"Isn't it wild the amount of money some people will spend on a one-day event? I can see a wedding getting expensive, but I'm currently working on a birthday party for a five-year-old. The budget is six months of my rent."

"Wow." I blink, thinking about the dollar amount. I've assisted a few higher-end weddings when I worked at The Windsor in Las Vegas, but it's clear that New York City is in a whole other league.

"Where was the wedding at?" June asks.

"It was at 620 Loft and Garden on Fifth Avenue overlooking St. Patrick's Cathedral."

She gasps. "I've seen that venue, it's an absolute dream."

"Yeah, it was gorgeous," I agree.

While the Feldman-Weiser wedding had all the elements of a dreamy, luxury wedding, and I enjoyed being a part of the couples' special day, I also felt overwhelmed by the over-the-top expense and most of all the waste the event had produced by the end of the night. It was a reaction I wasn't quite prepared for.

Though my part was small, I had loved the feeling of helping Demi and Bryce find an eco-friendly solution to their wedding favors. It's what I enjoy about my blog. Giving people new ideas on how to make their day special in a sustainable way. Seeing the contrast at the Feldman-Weiser wedding was eye-opening. It also inspired a new post for my blog.

June and I continue our conversation, discussing upcoming projects and our plans for the next weekend. When we get back to our desks, I use what little time is left of my lunch break to edit my latest post, then upload it. Then, I get back to work.

While I insisted that Hunter not pick me up at Griffin and Emma's in case either one of them were to see him or see me get in a car with him, he insisted that he send a car to pick me up. I've just strapped on my heels when I get the text notice that the driver has arrived, so I rush for the front door. When I see Griffin working on his laptop at the kitchen island, I try to quiet my feet, but it's impossible in heels.

"Whoa." Griffin turns around, my tiptoeing to the front door unsuccessful. "You look nice. Where are you going?"

"Out." It's a smart-ass response that I feel guilty for immediately, but I'm an adult. I've earned the right to be vague and mysterious with how I spend my time.

"With whom?" he asks. And while his tone is more curious than accusing, the fact that I'm sneaking around with Hunter only magnifies my guilt, and in turn, my annoyance. This is the issue with living with Griffin. He thinks he needs to know my every move. I know he has good intentions, like safety and all that, but sometimes a girl just needs to be wild and free. I think I've earned that.

"I'm going to the ballet with a friend. Okay. Bye!" I yank open the door and rush out before he can ask any more questions.

In the elevator, I get a text from Griffin. I brace myself for more questions, but it's not what I'm expecting.

Griffin: *Have fun. I love you.*

I sigh, a fresh wave of guilt hitting me square in the stomach. I know Griffin wants to change the dynamic of our relationship, he's been working on being less of the parent and more of the easygoing big brother, but it's been twelve years since we've been on our own, even longer since he's felt responsible for me. It's not something he can shut off overnight.

I send a quick reply.

Sophie: *Thanks! I'll be home later. Love you.*

Downstairs, I let the driver hold the door open for me so I can slide into the backseat. On the drive, I confirm my work training on Thursday with Natalie at The Penrose. After meeting with her yesterday, she offered me the waitressing job. I'm excited to start this week with the hope that I can accelerate the time frame to move out of Emma and Griffin's place.

The driver drops me off at the entrance to Lincoln Center and I check my phone again for the directions Hunter sent me. They send me down an alleyway with a dead end. I'm certain I'm going the wrong way until a door on the side of the building opens and Hunter steps out. His tux is like the one he wore on Friday night, but he's traded out a four-knot tie for a bowtie and this time when he sees me, his face lights up. Unlike Friday night where I had to act indifferent, knowing I get to talk to him and touch him tonight makes him look exponentially better.

His eyes roam over my body as I approach.

"You look beautiful," he says when I reach the top step and finally stop in front of him. His fingers curve around my hips and slide along my ass to pull me closer.

"Thank you." I reach up to playfully finger his bowtie. "You look pretty good yourself."

Hunter's hands tighten around me, lifting me, and in the next second, I'm plunged into darkness, the door he was holding open slams behind him, and I find myself pressed against a wall.

His lips drop to mine, teasing my mouth open with his tongue. It's madness for the next minute. Our mouths fused together, enjoying deep passionate kisses. By the time he pulls back, I'm panting and my clit is throbbing.

"Welcome to the New York City Ballet," he tells me while his hands roam over my hips, up my ribcage and over my breasts. The low-cut neckline means I didn't wear a bra, and when Hunter's thumbs trace over my hardened nipples, I let out a soft moan. "This is the back door where stage crew, dancers and secret fuck buddies enter."

I start to laugh, but he captures my mouth again, and the sound is lost inside him.

He releases me with a groan.

"Fuck." He grips my ass, his fingers gliding along the silky fabric of my dress. "You in this dress. You're making it very hard to not drag you out of here right now."

Hunter's ease with admitting how much I turn him on makes me brazen. My hand drops to his crotch. I palm his hard cock through the soft fabric of his pants. Feeling how thick he is makes my pussy ache with need.

"You're right. It is very hard." My fingers tease over him as I tilt my head up for another searing kiss.

For a moment, I'm lost in him. I almost forget what we're doing here. All I want to do is touch him, taste him. But Hunter pulls away.

"Okay. Let's go before we're thrown out for public indecency." He takes my hand in his, discreetly adjusts himself, then leads me toward a staircase.

I follow because I do want to see the ballet. That's the whole point of coming here tonight.

At the top of the staircase, an usher checks the tickets on Hunter's phone and hands us programs. She motions us down a hallway. Hunter takes my hand, leading me to a curtained room that once I step into, I see it's a balcony box overlooking the theater below. It has privacy curtains on the side that can be pulled so we can enjoy the performance without anyone seeing us. I know this because Hunter steps in front of me to pull them.

Then, he turns to me and places a gentle kiss against my mouth before retreating.

"Fuck. It's going to be a long two hours."

I know what he means. My body is currently pleading with my brain to ditch the performance and go back to his place, but I really want to see the ballet. So, I do my best to ignore my damp panties, choose one of the seats and start looking through the program the usher gave me.

"How many times have you been here?" I ask.

"A dozen or so, but it's been years." His arm stretches out behind my shoulders. "Why the interest in ballet? Did you dance?"

"No." I laugh. "I have zero coordination. Propelling my body forward in a straight line is the extent of my athletic abilities. That's why I run. But ballet has always been fascinating to me. The dancers are so impressive. They make it look effortless when I know it must take a ton of work. Their athleticism is awe-inspiring."

"Hannah's friend, Colette, is one of the troupe dancers," he notes as I thumb through the dancer profiles. "I'd introduce you after, but then it'd get back to Hannah, and she'd ask me a million questions."

"I get it." I tuck the program into the slot in front of me and reach for the bottle of water in the cup holder. "This is perfect. Thank you." I lean over to press a kiss to Hunter's cheek. When I start to pull back, he catches me by the back of the neck to keep me close. The possessive hold he has on my neck has me expecting a burning kiss, but his lips move lightly over mine before he retreats.

"You're welcome." His voice is full of sincerity, his fingers give my neck a light squeeze before he releases me.

The theater lights dim and a moment later, the curtain lifts.

I let myself cuddle into Hunter's shoulder as I watch the performance. Hunter points out Colette, Hannah's friend, and I find it surreal that he knows someone in one of the most prestigious ballet companies in the world. I'm in awe of the dancers; they're even more graceful than I thought they'd be. By the end of the first act, I'm nearly in tears.

When the curtain lowers, I turn to find Hunter looking at me thoughtfully.

"They're amazing. Colette is the most graceful dancer I've ever seen."

His eyes rake over me. "I'm glad you're having a good time."

"Are you having fun?" I ask.

"Staring at you in that dress?" His lips curve into a wicked grin. "Absolutely."

I let out a huff. "You're not even watching the performance?"

The corner of his mouth pulls up. It's that sweet, sexy grin of his that makes the temperature of my body ratchet up a million degrees.

"The ballet is not really my thing, but I'm happy to be here with you." His fingers wrap around my shoulder to pull me closer.

I smile at that. My belly flutters with excitement at the

thought that while he doesn't prefer to spend his evening at the ballet, Hunter still made an effort to bring me.

"What is your thing? If you weren't here tonight, where would you be?"

"Working." He shrugs. "Dinner with one of our contractors or a prospective client."

"Then what do you do for fun?" I ask.

He tilts his head down, considering my question. "Like a hobby?"

"Yeah."

"I run. You already know that. And when I have the time, I like to row on the Hudson."

"Yes, your back muscles are impressive." I recall running my hands down his bare back, feeling the ripple of muscle there while he thrusted inside me. The thought sends a shiver down my spine, and I have to refocus on our conversation. "What else?"

"Playing tennis with the guys." He thinks a moment, a cocky grin pulling at his lips. "Eating your pussy is starting to become one of my favorite past times."

"That's not a hobby." I give him a playful shove. "Seriously."

"Okay, but you're going to laugh."

My eyes light with amusement. "You think I'll laugh? Oh my God, what is it? I'm dying to know."

I'm trying to think of comical hobbies, imagining Hunter trying to balance on stilts, or his arms flailing about on a unicycle. A pair of binoculars around his neck while he bird watches in Central Park. Even those images aren't humorous. Hunter could make soap carving appear sexy.

Maybe he reads romance novels in his spare time. That's not funny, it's hot. And would explain so much about his knowledge and skills in the bedroom.

"I like having the Food Network on while I work, as background noise."

"Okay." The thought of Hunter working while shows like *Guy's Grocery Games* and *Chopped* play in the background makes me smile, but it's not the scandalous sensation he's made it sound like.

"Around the holidays a few years ago, I started watching those cookie decorating shows. Then, I wondered how hard it could be, so I got a kit from a bakery that was selling them and tried it."

"And?" My eyes are wide wondering how Hunter's cookie decorating attempt went.

"It was fucking hard." He laughs. I love watching his smile as he thinks of the memory. "The cookies looked like they'd been decorated by a four-year-old." He spreads his hands. "And I may not be giving four-year-olds enough credit. I had icing everywhere. It was embarrassing."

"That's okay. At least you tried." I pat his thigh, doing my best to ignore the way his muscles flex beneath my palm.

"Yeah, I did. And I was determined to get better. I started practicing my flooding technique, working on a steady hand to pipe details. It became a challenge. And the better I got, the more calming the art of cookie decorating became."

"Wait. So, you're good at cookie decorating now?" I ask.

He pulls out his phone and opens his photos. There he shows me some decorated sugar cookies. There's even a time lapse video for one. I know it's him. I'd recognize those hands anywhere.

"Wow." I take his phone to get a better look. "This is impressive."

He lifts a shoulder. "I like to do it when I'm stressed about work. The focus it takes helps distract me. It lets my brain shift into a different mode." He scrolls back in his photos.

Staring at Hunter, my smile is a mile wide.

"Why are you staring at me like that?" he asks.

"Because you're cute."

"Cute?" Hunter lifts his brows.

"Yeah." I lean forward and kiss him. It's a light peck on the lips. He presses forward, but I pull back. "Baking is manly. Griffin makes the best blueberry scones. They're so light in the middle and crunchy outside. Oh, and when I was growing up, he'd make happy face pancakes every Sunday."

"Happy face pancakes?" he repeats, a quizzical look on his face.

"Pancakes with a face. You know, bacon mouth, strawberry nose, and blueberry eyes. And then whipped cream hair at the top."

He smiles. "I've never heard of those."

"It was our tradition. *Is* our tradition," I correct, "but we don't make them as often now."

I sigh, thinking how busy the last few months have been for both me and Griffin.

Hunter's hand runs over my forearm, drawing my attention back to him.

"How do you spend your free time?" he asks.

"Well, as you know, I like to run and listen to true crime podcasts." He nods for me to continue. "And I collect vintage vases and jars. Items that I can upcycle for my future sustainable wedding décor business. It's challenging to find large sets, but I don't have much room to store them anyway. I have even less space now in Griffin and Emma's apartment than I did in my and Griffin's place in Henderson."

"What do you do with them? Just store them in boxes?"

"I use them for DIY tutorials on YouTube." I pull up the channel I started last year giving tips and tricks on how to make a wedding more sustainable, less wasteful, and show Hunter. "It's fun."

Hunter drops his gaze to the screen, his brows lifting in surprise.

"You've got a hundred and seven thousand subscribers?"

"Uh, yeah. And my blog, which the channel is linked to, gets around ten thousand page views a month."

"Show me." He hands back the phone and I pull up my blog, *Sustainable Wedding Chic*.

I expect him to glance at the screen, then move on, but he scrolls through the pages, then watches the videos, playing a few with the volume low.

"This is great. Why aren't you focusing on this now? If you were doing it full-time, you could have even more of an impact."

"I'm not ready for that yet. I want to gain more experience working in the industry and understanding the business."

"It looks like you already do," he says, motioning to the phone screen.

"Don't worry, I've got a plan."

He begins to hand me back the phone, not realizing it's his.

I take it anyway, navigating to his camera before holding it up for a selfie of us. Our time together is secret, but I still want to capture it. Have something to remember this moment.

"Wait." He leans back out of the frame, and my initial thought is that he doesn't want to take a photo with me, but then he pulls me into his lap. "Much better," he says, settling me between his thighs. His arms wrap around my waist and I lean back, aligning our heads. I snap a few photos of us smiling before Hunter drops his lips to my cheek.

Suddenly, the lights flicker, indicating that intermission is almost over.

I turn my attention back to the stage, however, the man next to me, tracing light, teasing circles against my back, is making it difficult to focus on the performance. I power through, though, loving the second half even more.

When the performance is over, Hunter has the car pick us up at the back entrance. In the car, Hunter's hand finds the bare skin of my leg exposed by the slit of my dress. His long fingers curve around my thigh. His fingertips brush against the sensitive skin of my inner thigh, while his thumb starts to gently caress the outside of my leg.

"What was your favorite part?" he asks.

I suppress a smile, enjoying how obvious it is that Hunter is trying to distract himself from the crackling heat between us.

"The all-male corps ballet performance was stunning," I answer, not a hint of how affected I am by him in my voice. I inch my legs apart, letting Hunter's fingers dip closer to my center. "What about you?" I ask, looking up at him innocently.

"Are you teasing me, Sophie?" His pinky brushes over the center of my panties and I bite down on my lip to suppress a moan.

"Isn't that what you're doing to me?" I lift my brows then drop my gaze again to where his hand is beneath my dress.

"No, sweetheart, I'm making sure you're ready for me." He growls. "The second we walk through the door, I'm going to fuck this hot little cunt and I need you to be ready."

My core clenches at his filthy words.

His gaze holds mine as his finger edges beneath my panties.

The moment his finger dips into my slick center, I can see the hunger take over his face. The way those indigo eyes of his darken and his already chiseled jaw tightens with restraint.

"I want these off, Sophie," he rasps, his eyes never leaving mine while he tugs against the crotch of my panties.

My gaze shifts toward the driver, then back to Hunter. A small lift of his chin gives me the courage to reach under my dress, lift my ass and yank down my underwear. Hunter leans forward to help them clear my heels, then he balls the lacy material up and puts them in his pocket.

For the rest of the ride, he plays with me. A single finger sweeping over my center, then lightly flicking my clit until

I'm practically writhing against the leather seat. My orgasm agonizingly close just for him to change his rhythm and wrench it away from me.

By the time the driver pulls over at Hunter's building, I'm so turned on, I'm afraid when I exit the car, there will be wet spot on the seat.

But I don't have time to check because Hunter is pulling me out of the car, then ushering me through the front doors of his building and into the elevator. The electricity between us is like a live wire, crackling dangerously, as we wait for the elevator to hit his floor. The tension built up in the car is almost as if we're doing this for the first time.

It feels like Vegas all over again, the strained patience I had felt radiating off him as the elevator climbed to the penthouse floor. His large hand covering mine in a sure, affirming grip.

And just like Vegas, when the elevator opens at Hunter's floor, he's quick to pull me off and rush me inside. The second the door slams behind us, we collide.

HUNTER

The moment I kick the door closed, my lips crash into Sophie's. We bump along the entryway, our kisses fevered and messy, all tongues and scraping teeth as we claw at each other's clothes.

"I'm going to fuck you so hard you're not going to be able to walk properly tomorrow," I tell her, stripping off my jacket and tossing it to the floor.

"I'd like to see you try." She looks up in challenge, her fingers busy on my shirt buttons.

Sophie knows she's asking for it. That's the point. She

wants me to be a little rough. She likes how it makes her feel uninhibited and carefree. I learned that the night of the gala.

My laugh is a rumble in my chest. I can feel my gaze darkening with every impertinent word out of her mouth.

My fingers wrap around her neck. "Now you're really going to get it, sweetheart."

"Good," she says defiantly.

She's trying to rile me up. Hell, I was already there the moment my finger slid inside her in the car.

The fingers of my other hand connect with the zipper at the back of her dress. A moment later, the material pools around her ankles and Sophie is gloriously naked except for her heels.

I take in the sight. From her long, toned legs to the sexy curve of her hips, her generously proportioned ass to her tight pink nipples just begging to be sucked. My balls ache with the perfection that is Sophie's nakedness.

Fuck. I need to *see* her.

She's working to unbutton my shirt, when I lift her up onto the entry table. Impeding her progress, she lets out a frustrated sigh. I'm right there with her. My body is racing to have her. While I finish pulling off my shirt, she reaches for my belt.

"Feet on the table, Sophie. Show me that slick cunt of yours. How badly it needs me to fuck it."

Her heels find the edge of the table and she widens her legs, letting my hungry gaze settle between them. With one hand stroking my cock, the other slides between her legs to confirm she's still ready for me.

My finger dips inside her warmth and a deep, rumbling groan of satisfaction escapes my throat. She's beyond ready.

"Damn." I groan, my fingers dragging through her center, before I lift them to my mouth to taste her.

Sophie's arousal on my tongue is like a drug. I can't get enough of it. Of her.

I reach for my wallet to grab a condom, then rip the foil packet with my teeth.

Sophie's pussy is perfection. I need to be inside her like I need air to breathe. But I also like to tease her.

I press the head of my cock against her entrance, pushing just inside.

"I love watching my cock split you open." I rock my hips, only giving her a few inches.

From the shift of her pelvis, I can tell she wants more, but I'm enjoying teasing us both.

"Hunter, please."

"You want more, sweetheart?"

I inch inside her again and she shifts her hips, trying to take more of me.

With one solid thrust, I put us out of our misery. The intrusion causes a whoosh of air to leave her lungs.

Fuck. She's so snug, my vision goes blurry for a moment.

"So fucking tight, Sophie," I growl as I fight for control.

My hand lifts to her breast, cupping her there. My fingers tease the soft flesh while my thumb works her nipple into a stiff peak.

I'm buried so deep in her, my balls smack her ass with every thrust.

"Do you know how pretty you look stretched around my cock?" I ask.

"Hunter..." Sophie moans softly.

Damn, I love the sound of my name falling from her lips. How sweet and angelic she sounds when I'm fucking her hard and dirty.

Our movements cause the lamp on the corner of the table to teeter back and forth.

"You're going to break this table." She pants. "And that lamp."

"Don't give a fuck."

I grip her ass, tilting her pelvis slightly to change the angle, then sink into her again.

The table moves rapidly in sync with my punishing rhythm. Sophie's hand reaches out toward the teetering lamp. I think she's trying to steady it, but instead, the movement knocks it from the edge. The loud crash registers, but the building would have to be on fire for me to stop.

My hand moves between us and I start rubbing perfectly pressured circles against her clit.

"Let go, Sophie. I want to feel you."

With her nails digging into my back, she comes hard, her muscles squeezing me impossibly tight.

"Ahhh." Her breathy moan echoes off the walls.

A moment later, I swell inside her, groaning my own release. We're both breathing heavily as we recover. Sophie leans back against the wall while I pull out and tie off the condom.

"I can't believe I broke your lamp," Sophie says, looking at the glass shards scattered on the hardwood floor of the entryway.

"I didn't like that lamp anyway," I assure her, tucking a strand of hair behind her ear.

"How much did it cost?" she asks.

"I have no clue. My designer picked it out."

"If you let me know, I'll pay you for it."

"I don't give a fuck about the lamp, Sophie." I lift her into my arms and start walking us down the hallway, farther into my condo.

"Shouldn't we clean it up?" she asks, clinging to my chest.

"You think I'm going to spend the precious time we have cleaning?" I chuckle. "If it will make you feel better, I can punish you for it. Will a few hard smacks on your ass make you feel better?"

Sophie's eyes light up.

"I don't know, it may take more than a few." Her lips twitch into a sexy pout. "I'm pretty upset about it."

When we reach my bedroom, I drop her onto the bed.

"All right, Sophie, flip over and give me that ass."

CHAPTER 17

Sophie

The next morning, I drop onto a barstool for breakfast only to be reminded of the tender place on my cheeks where Hunter spanked me last night. It's not sore enough to be painful while sitting, just enough of a reminder how much I like it when he leaves his handprint on my ass. Just thinking about our evening together has my panties dampening.

I'm about to let my brain replay last night with him when Emma walks into the kitchen.

"Good morning!" she says, heading straight for the coffee. "How was the ballet? Griffin said you went with a friend?"

"Um, yeah. It was great. I loved it." I take a bite of banana, deliberately pretending her second question was more of a statement.

She disappears behind the refrigerator door, a carton of creamer in her hand when she emerges.

A moment later Griffin walks in making a beeline for Emma. I watch as he greets her, one arm wrapping around her waist pulling her in close while his free hand slides to the back of her neck. What starts as a chaste kiss soon turns into a full-on make-out session against the refrigerator.

I cough loudly to let him know he's got an audience.

"Shit." He pulls back, but still holds onto Emma's waist. "Sorry, Soph. I didn't realize you were there."

"Yup, it's me. Third wheel roomie at your service." I salute.

He presses his lips together. "We're happy you're here with us."

Emma nods enthusiastically.

They're both liars, but I'm grateful for them all the same.

Emma gives Griffin a quick kiss before extracting herself to finish making her coffee.

"Yeah, well, I'm hoping it won't be for too much longer. I got a waitressing job at The Penrose. I start training tomorrow night."

"The Penrose," Emma coos. "Fancy."

"Johnathan had a connection," I say.

"Hmm." Griffin's brow furrows in concern. "Is that going to work with your internship? Because that should be your priority."

"It's still my priority."

"Eggs?" Griffin asks and I shake my head.

"Are you feeling okay?" He studies me.

"Yeah, just changing up my routine."

Emma smiles at me. "You can't be low on potassium. You've been consuming a lot of bananas."

Griffin nods, then I watch as he and Emma move around the kitchen, doing a choreographed dance of making breakfast. Griffin pulls out a pan while Emma wordlessly hands him the eggs. Emma slides a bowl over to him so he can start cracking the eggs. They're adorable. I imagine what it would be like to find a person that although you haven't known them long, you're completely in sync with.

A person that you not only can laugh with, but are so insanely attracted to that your body starts tingling anytime you're near them.

Hunter.

I had the best time with him last night. The sex was phenomenal, but so was our time at the ballet, talking and teasing each other.

"How was the ballet?" Griffin asks, whipping up the eggs.

I blink at Griffin's question, trying to clear my head.

"It was amazing. The dancers were so impressive. I mean, I can't believe the human body can do some of those moves. And we had box seats so we were overlooking the stage. It was magical. Oh, and he showed me around backstage before the show. It was really cool."

"He?" Emma snags on that tiny detail. "So, you went with a guy?"

"Um, did I say that?" I'm quickly trying to recall exactly what I said during my mindless ramble.

Emma smiles knowingly. "Was it Andrew?"

"No, just a friend," I say slowly, watching my words this time. "Not that Andrew would be more than a friend, but it wasn't a date if that's what you mean." It was a show, then sex.

"Okay. Whatever you say." She sighs, realizing I'm not going to be giving any more details.

"I'm glad you're getting out and doing things. I know you've got a whole list of things you want to do and see." He splits up the eggs among two plates, then turns to me. "Do you want to do Top of the Rock next week? I thought we could sign up for a tour."

I think about lying and going with Griffin for another tour. I loved it so much that I'd go again, but with a busy work schedule and starting my second job, and hooking up with Hunter, there aren't enough hours in the day.

"Um, actually, I've already been."

"Oh, that's cool." He sits down on the stool beside me, his piping hot eggs wafting their horrid smell in my direction.

"With the same friend?" Emma winks at me over her coffee mug.

My lips twitch at her curiosity. *I'm not giving it away that easily.*

"I've got to get going." I move to stand, careful not to wince when my tender ass cheek slides against the leather stool. "I'll see you guys later."

"See you, Soph." Griffin nods, taking a bite of his eggs.

"Have a good day!" Emma calls as I leave the kitchen area.

"You, too!" I toss out on my way toward the front door.

I can hear bits of their conversation as I slide on my shoes and reach for my purse.

Emma's laugh rings out, and Griffin's deep chuckle follows.

They're perfect together.

Watching Emma and Griffin, whose affection level is sometimes nauseating mostly because he's my brother and I don't want to see him make out with anyone, I see what it's like to be in a loving relationship. The appeal of having a person that loves you and supports you, and at the same time, wants to maul you against the refrigerator at eight o'clock in the morning because they can't help themselves.

I'm curious what that would feel like.

Not the refrigerator part, I can imagine that would be hard and cool against my back, but the rest of it.

I tamp down the thought. Relationships are work, right? They require attention and constant nurturing. The only thing I have time to nurture right now is my fledgling career.

I shut the door behind me and make my way to the elevator.

On top of my normal work hours and the weekend wedding schedule, and soon waitressing at The Penrose, I need to start thinking about my internship presentation that's due at the end of the summer. What I want to present and how I should present it.

My phone buzzes in my purse and I find a text from Hunter.

Hunter: *Good morning, beautiful. How'd you sleep?*

My stomach flutters with his sweet words. After we had sex again in his bed, I pulled my dress back on and Hunter had his driver take me home.

Sophie: *Good, but my ass is sore.*

Hunter: *I'd say I'm sorry to hear that, but the thought of your sore ass makes my balls ache. Are you wet right now?*

This man is going to ruin all my underwear.

Sophie: *When you say things like that, how can I not be?*

Hunter: *You're such a filthy girl, Sophie.*

Sophie: *Oh, next time we should have sex against the refrigerator.*

Hunter: *Is this a fantasy?*

Sophie: *Something I want to try.*

Hunter: *How domestic. Just so we're clear, I'll fuck you anywhere you want.*

Before I can second guess it, I respond.

Sophie: *Are we talking setting or body part? *peach emoji**

Hunter: *Have you done anal before?*

My throat goes dry. I guess I walked into that one.

Sophie: *No, but I'm curious.*

Hunter: *I'll take everything you want to give me, sweetheart. Your ass included.*

My cheeks warm at his last message. The idea of Hunter fucking me in the ass makes me flushed and anxious, excited, and overwhelmed.

Sophie: *We'll see.*

Hunter: **peach emoji* *eggplant emoji**

It's eight-thirty in the morning, I shouldn't be this turned on. I drop my phone in my purse and push all dirty thoughts of Hunter out of my mind.

~

Thursday night, I train at The Penrose. Not only is the extra money greatly needed, but the other workers are a lot of fun and my four-hour shift flies by. Friday morning, I'm exhausted. While most people are winding down their work week, I still have another full day tomorrow at the Rhinehart-Van Housen wedding.

After Johnathan and I return from a site check at Guastavino's, I drop into my desk chair with a thud, my barely-touched salad from a quick lunch at Bistro Vendôme next to my keyboard. I should take it to the staff lounge refrigerator, but that would take energy that I don't have.

I'm just going to close my eyes for a second. A quick power nap to get me through the rest of the afternoon.

I've just let my eyelids fall when I hear June approach.

"You look like you need this more than I do."

I open my eyes to find her setting a small coffee cup next to my salad box.

"Oh, thanks. Yeah, it's been a week."

With my hopes of a power nap dashed, I lean forward to reach for the coffee cup.

"That's right, you started at The Penrose last night. How was it?"

"For work, it's pretty fun. I like the people and taking home tips in cash is great." I open my inbox to check if Johnathan has any comments on the run sheet I sent him for tomorrow, then click into my personal email inbox. "How was your night?"

"It was good. Allen and I are trying to spice things up with phone sex. It's been a bit of a challenge, but we've progressed from awkward as fuck to somewhat enjoyable."

I'm listening to June while I click on a new message and start reading.

"Holy shit."

"I mean, it's not *that* impressive."

I leap out of my chair, adrenaline coursing through my veins. I round the desk and reach for June's hand.

"Where are we going?" she whisper-hisses as I drag her down the hallway and toward the restroom. Once inside, I slam the door and lock it behind us.

"First, I love that you and Allen had a phone sex breakthrough. That's amazing. I'm so happy for you."

"Okay." She looks around. "So why are we in the restroom?"

"I just got an email from the assistant editor at *Brides* magazine. They picked my blog as one of the eight trending wedding blogs they want to feature in their August issue."

I still can't believe it as I'm saying the words. The blog I've poured my heart and soul into is going to be recognized by a national magazine. It's part of their up-and-coming series, and I'm dying to know I made the cut.

"That's amazing, Sophie. Congratulations!" She pulls me into a hug. "I'm still not sure why we're five feet from a toilet right now."

"Oh, right. Not many people know about my blog. It's been a passion project so I haven't shared much about it and didn't want to announce it in front of everyone else."

"If it's getting recognized in *Brides,* I'd say it's legit. You're acting like it's a dirty little secret."

I shrug. "I wasn't sure it would ever amount to much. It's not a real career path, just a hobby."

"Sophie, I don't know how this all works with blogs, but I'm pretty sure this recognition is a huge deal. Even if it's a hobby."

She pulls me in for a hug. "Congratulations. This is exciting!"

Deep down, I know June is right. It's why I freaked out and rushed her to a private space to tell her. But the other reason for that is I've never let myself see my blog, *Sustainable Wedding Chic,* as anything more than a side hustle. A creative outlet to explore my passion for sustainable wedding décor and services. I've definitely never seen it as a potential career path.

It's been exciting to see the following I've built increase. To get offers from advertisers that want to partner with me. But I've always thought a nine to five (plus weekends) career was the smart track to take. It's the one Griffin has encouraged me to follow to ensure financial stability and security.

That's what I want most. To support myself and be independent.

"Let's celebrate after work," June says.

The adrenaline rush of the *Brides* feature is wearing off and I can feel the fatigue starting to creep back into my body.

"I'd love to but I'm running on fumes. Is this work schedule not exhausting to you?"

"It's a lot for sure, but I'm also not working a second job and creating content for a blog."

I sigh. "That's true." Maybe in my attempt to become self-sufficient, I've overloaded my schedule.

June reaches for the door. "One drink. We have to celebrate your accomplishment."

"Okay. One drink," I tell her as she retreats.

I should get back to work, but I take a moment to gather my thoughts.

Maybe this opportunity with *Brides* magazine is a sign that my blog could become something more. That eventually it could be a full-time business. Like I told Hunter, creating my own business is in my long-term plan, but what if I moved the timeline up? Changed my plans?

The thought is both thrilling and overwhelming.

At the mirror, I check my reflection.

I look like me, but there's something different about my eyes. There's uncertainty in them.

While I find comfort in stability, I'm discovering that there's a part of me who enjoys taking a risk.

It's the part of me that wanted to have a fun night with a sexy stranger and hooked up with Hunter in Vegas. The side of me that applied for a summer internship here in New York City when I could have easily taken a full-time position at The Windsor and stayed in Las Vegas.

I've always been so certain about what I wanted. That I was going in the right direction and if I stayed the course I'd get where I wanted to be.

But the last few weeks, I've started to feel less certain about everything.

And that risk taking side of me, that voice challenging me to deviate from the plan is getting louder. Finding out about the *Brides* feature has only given it more space to be heard.

The 'what about?' and 'could I?' thoughts I've had in the past have started to become more frequent.

But acknowledging those thoughts and desires doesn't mean I need to act on them. I can be excited that my blog is going to be included in a feature in a major magazine without derailing all my set plans.

So, I will be quietly excited about the blog feature, but stay focused on my internship. That's the plan.

With a renewed sense of determination, I fix my hair, then wash my hands and get back to work.

CHAPTER 18

Hunter

When I look up to see Sophie standing in the doorway to my office, I think it must be my tired eyes playing tricks on me. My mind conjuring up what I want to see most. She's a mirage, an oasis, in the desert of work I've been swamped with for the past week.

Even now, I'm working late. Long past the hours most of my employees keep.

"Hey," she says, moving toward me. She's in a flowy, floral skirt, it's not short or form-fitting, but the idea of being able to tease my hand underneath it puts my body on high alert.

She pulls a bag from behind her back. "I brought sustenance."

We've been texting nonstop, but between my work schedule and hers, I haven't seen her since the night of the ballet.

"Forget the food," I tell her. "Come here." I hold my hand out for her to take so I can maneuver her around my desk.

She laughs. "You don't even know what I brought."

I push my chair back, but she stops me from getting up. Setting the take-out bag and her purse on my desk, she moves between me and my computer, leaning against the edge of the desk.

"It doesn't matter. Nothing tastes better than your pussy. That's what I'm hungry for right now."

"Is everyone gone?" she asks. "Rebecca wasn't out front, so I thought the coast was clear."

"I'm the last one here." I lean forward to bury my face in her neck. "Damn. You smell good."

My hands slide up her thighs and under her skirt. I don't tease her like I normally would. It's been too long since I've had her. One week and I'm losing my fucking mind. My fingers slip beneath her panties to find her soaked.

"Fuck." I growl into her mouth, then plunge two fingers inside her. Her muscles clench around me and the sensation drives me wild. Reminds me of what I've been missing. "You're so fucking wet." I hook my fingers inside her. "I've missed feeling this slick pussy of yours." I nip at her ear. "Or should I say, *mine?*"

She moans against my ear.

"This is one of my fantasies," she tells me, her hands on my shoulders to steady her body as she lifts her hips up and down, using my fingers to pleasure herself. "I've thought about doing this in your office ever since the first day I came in here with you."

"What did you think about?" I ask, rubbing my thumb against her clit.

"You bending me over your desk."

"That can easily be arranged." I nip at the tender flesh between her collarbone and her neck. "What else?"

"Sucking your cock while you sit at your desk."

"*Mmm,* I've thought about that, too."

She pulls back, her hand exploring the growing bulge between my legs.

"You want it right now, don't you, sweetheart?"

Sophie bites her lip and nods.

I pull my hand from under her skirt and my fingers, slick with her arousal, lift to my lips, sucking off her sweetness.

Her fingers quickly unlatch my belt and pull down my zipper. It's not even a question if I'm ready for her. The moment she walked in the room, I was hard as a rock. With her hand inside my briefs, she strokes me base to tip.

She lowers down to her knees in front of me. I shift the chair back so she has enough space and won't hit her head on the desk. Like she said that first day at my condo, chivalry isn't dead.

"Fuck." I growl as her tongue swirls around my length. I watch her lashes flutter over her cheeks, her glistening lips stretching around me. She bobs down my length. Once. Twice. Then, her eyes open and lift to mine. "You look so pretty sucking my cock, Sophie."

Sophie on her knees in front of me, sucking me hard is a sight I'm entranced with, but a knock on the frame of my office door has me lifting my eyes toward the sound.

My body stiffens at the sight of Griffin. I'd thought he had already left. Hell, I thought we were completely alone in the office suite or I would never have started anything with her. I definitely wouldn't have let her drop to her knees under my desk.

"I emailed you the final contract for the Carmine Group purchase." He leans on the door, hands in his pockets. I tense for Sophie's reaction. I hope it's not to bite down on my dick. I don't look down at her, but I feel her jaw go slack around me, her tongue stops swirling.

The only way I can shield her is to push my chair closer to the desk, hoping she'll follow my lead and shimmy her body underneath.

There's a loud thump. Sophie's head hitting the top of the desk. Shit.

"You okay?" Griffin asks.

"Yeah. Just bumped my knee." I do my best to make my wince believable.

"Did you want to go over it now?" Griffin's gaze drops to his watch. "It's getting late. I told Emma that I was finishing up, but—"

He takes a step into my office and I tense. I don't know what would be worse, my stiff dick hanging out of my pants, or Sophie's mouth still around me.

"No, no. That's okay. I'll review it and we can go over it tomorrow."

"Sure." He nods. I think he's going to retreat, but he takes another step into my office. "I've been meaning to talk to you about the deadline for the Hudson Yards expansion. Do you have a minute?"

Another banging sound comes from under my desk.

Griffin's gaze falls to my desk. Then to the take-out bag and Sophie's purse. Fuck. I wonder if he'll recognize it. But lots of women have black purses. His eyes drop to the floor. I'm mentally trying to recall what my desk looks like from the front. I think there's a small gap at the bottom.

Griffin must see something because he takes a step back.

I'm a big brother. I can only imagine the horror of what it would be like to walk in on Hannah hooking up with a guy. That's something I never want to see. Even now that she's engaged to James, I don't want to be subject to their sex life.

And Griffin is my friend.

If one of my friends was hooking up with Hannah, I'd be fucking irate.

Guilt hits me hard. It's in this moment that I recall why I was going to stay away from Sophie.

Griffin clears his throat. "I can talk with you tomorrow."

I nod, grateful for his realization that now's not a good time. "Sounds good."

"Have a good night." He makes a beeline for the door, shutting it behind him.

The moment he's gone, I push my chair back and zip up my pants. I cross the room to lock the door. When I return, Sophie is crawling out from under the desk. I help her up and lift her onto my desk.

We stare at each other, both of us quiet. Until this moment, we haven't had an issue with almost getting caught.

"I shouldn't have come here. I wanted to surprise you and I completely spaced that Griffin could still be here."

I want to take it as a good sign that Sophie wanted to see me and momentarily forgot that she doesn't want her brother to know about us, but I can tell she's stressed about it now.

"Do you think he knows?" she whispers.

I shove my hands in my pockets. "That I had a woman servicing me under my desk? Yes."

"Shit." She bites her lip. "But he didn't know it was me, right?"

I shake my head. "I don't think so."

"Should I leave?" she asks.

"No. It's safer in here. You don't want to run into him in the lobby."

My hand cups her jaw and I place a gentle kiss on her lips.

My cock is still hard. I'm still dying to have her, but the mood has changed. Griffin's appearance is a reminder that we're hiding this from him, from the world, for a reason. And other than text messages, we haven't talked in a week either, so I opt to help her off the desk and open the take-out bag instead.

It's ramen from Momosan, my favorite Japanese restaurant in the city. I set the bowls of ramen at the small conference table in the corner of my office, then open the remaining box to find she ordered the sticky ribs appetizer as well.

A moan escapes my throat in anticipated pleasure of one of my favorite meals.

"I wasn't sure which ramen was your favorite, so I got two kinds. And you mentioned you like those so…" She points to the box of sticky ribs but her voice trails off, a blush working its way across her cheeks. "I hope it's okay."

I lean down to kiss her softly on the lips.

"Everything looks great. Thank you for doing this."

"Even though we almost got caught?" She smiles ruefully.

That feeling in my chest is back. The one from the ballet. It's the same tug across my sternum that I got when I watched Sophie smile in delight at the performance, but then had to deny her meeting the dancers backstage because we didn't want to be seen together.

I get that I'm older and Griffin's boss and friend. There are complications. It's only been a few weeks, but the element of secrecy in our relationship is starting to lose its appeal.

She hands me a set of chopsticks and a napkin from the bag.

"How did Griffin handle you dating growing up?" I ask, pulling my chopsticks apart.

"I didn't date much. I was always on my best behavior, wanting to be helpful, not get into trouble in school or with boys. Griffin had enough to worry about, he didn't need me to pile on with teenage girl drama."

I nod taking in a bite of noodles and pork. When I've finished chewing, I continue the conversation.

"So, how did you lose your virginity?" I ask.

She sighs. "Why are we talking about this?"

"It's conversation, Sophie."

"A guy my freshman year in college. We were dating, or I thought we were, but after, he kind of ghosted." She finally has her food arranged the way she wants and takes a bite.

"Sounds like an idiot."

She simply shrugs.

"What about you?" she asks, wiggling her brows.

"Prep school. I was sixteen."

She chews quietly, then a huge smile spreads across her

face. "So basically, you've been having sex for twenty years. Almost as long as I've been alive."

I groan. "This again? I thought you were good with the age difference."

"I am. It's just funny to think about." She laughs. "And to tease you."

"Careful." I growl, my hand finding her thigh under the table and giving it a squeeze. "My palm is feeling itchy."

"In that case, let me search up some 'you're so old' jokes." She laughs, pretending to reach for her phone, but a moment later, she returns to eating. "I'm not complaining. I get the benefit of all your practice."

I give her a cocky grin. "I'll be sure to give you multiple benefits later."

"Can't wait."

She bites her lip and her eyes light. That look has me holding on to my willpower to keep eating and not bend her over this table right now.

I look away and take another bite, then shift the conversation to something far less stimulating.

"How's work? Is Hannah driving you nuts yet?"

"Work is good. And your sister is an absolute treasure."

"How much did she pay you to say that?" I ask, grinning.

"She's a client, so she's technically paying, but even if she wasn't, I'd still think she's pretty great."

"How many weddings do you work on at once?" I reach for another sticky rib and offer it to Sophie.

"*Mmm.*" She moans around the bite.

"Good, right?"

"So good."

"It's the special sauce." I reach over and wipe the corner of Sophie's mouth where said sauce has gathered. I press my thumb against her lips and she opens her mouth, swiping the sauce off my thumb. I'm too easily distracted around her. I drop my hand and motion for her to continue. "You were saying? The number of weddings."

"Right. There are twenty weddings right now that are in some stage of planning. I've worked out a color-coded system to keep track of them based on venue."

"That's wild. What's your favorite venue so far?"

"Hmm. The Botanic Gardens were pretty, but the humid weather made it miserable. I think The Plaza Hotel is going to be idyllic. The Stephens-Lautner wedding is there this Saturday. I've only walked through it once, but it's pure magic. I can't wait to see the ballroom decorated."

I smile at her enthusiasm. "The Plaza is nice."

She smirks. "I'm sure you've stayed there a million times."

"I've been to The Palm Court for business dinners and to countless events, but never had a reason to stay."

She nods. "I guess if you've lived here all your life, it's not as fascinating."

I collect our empty bowls and the remaining trash to put them in the bag.

"Thank you again for dinner." I lean forward to capture her lips and the kiss turns hungry quickly. With the door locked and Griffin long gone, we could pick up where we left off. I could easily bend Sophie over my desk and slide between her legs, but right now, I'm in the mood to lay her out on my bed and take my time with her. I pull back and grab her purse off the table. "Come on, let's get out of here."

The pads of my fingers trace along Sophie's bare back. Every inch of her skin is silky smooth. At the base of her spine, my fingers reach the swell of her ass, gently caressing the pink flesh that my palm left in its wake. I've barely had a moment to observe how beautiful she looks, skin glistening, hair a mess from my hands before she shifts and starts moving toward the edge of the bed.

Sophie's been in my bed many times in the last few weeks, but I'm starting to hate that this is how it ends every time.

"Where are you going?" I ask, reaching my hand out to catch her wrist. She's too quick.

"Home," she says. She's completely naked as she lifts the pillows off the floor to search for her clothes that are buried beneath.

I prop myself up against the headboard to watch her. I crave Sophie's body like a starving man who can't get full. My desire for her is endless. But that's not the only thing that has me wanting to keep her here with me. There's a warmth in my chest that I get when she's nearby. I'm starting to crave that feeling, too. A hunger for more.

She doesn't see me coming when I lunge forward, grab her by the waist and pin her beneath me on the bed.

"What are you doing?" She laughs and playfully pushes at my chest. When her laughter subsides, I stare down at her intently.

"I want more."

"Oh, I'm sorry, were the two orgasms not enough for you?" She rolls her eyes and shakes her head.

"Not more orgasms. I mean, I wouldn't object to them, but that's not what I was referring to."

Her eyes drop to where I'm tracing her lips with my finger, then back up to mine.

"I don't like that you run off the second I pull out of you."

"It's not the second you pull out," she argues. "It's definitely at least three minutes post orgasm." She laughs. "Besides, I didn't think secret fuck buddies were supposed to spoon."

"The good thing about secret fuck buddies is that they can make their own rules."

"Ah, so, it's a secret fuck buddy democracy? I always thought it was more of dick-tatorship."

"Smart ass." I lower my hand to pinch her ass and she cries out, squirming to get away but unsuccessful as I hold her close.

"Are you sure you have time for cuddling?" She shifts her head toward the bedside table. "Your phone has been buzzing nonstop. It's a bit distracting."

With both hands, I reach behind me for the sheet. I pull it up and over our bodies, the air underneath causing a canopy effect. If I move to shut my phone off, she'll escape, so the goal is to drown out the buzzing she's referring to. As I pin it over our heads, Sophie's face lights up.

"My mom used to do that. I'd be lying on my bed and she would pull the sheet up and over me. It was like I was inside a balloon. I loved it. It made me feel safe."

As the air escapes, the sheet settles over us. I keep the top pinned above our heads, creating that balloon effect Sophie is talking about. I want her to feel safe here with me.

"It's my favorite memory of her. There was so much uncertainty, so many times I wasn't sure if she would even be coming home. If she was okay. If she even cared about me. So, those nights she'd tuck me in were rare moments where I felt a connection to her. I felt her love."

My palm finds her cheek, my thumb swiping at the dampness under her eye.

"I'm sorry, Sophie. No kid should feel like that."

I try to hold her gaze, but she looks away.

"Griffin had it worse. At least by the time I came along, my mom was trying to get her life together. Failing miserably, but trying. When she died, he put his life on hold to take care of me. I feel like he missed out on so much of his young adulthood. He sacrificed so much, because of me. I wish I could have done more to help."

"You were ten, Sophie."

"Yeah," she bites her lip, her fingers stalling in the hollow of my neck. "Still, I feel like I've been selfish. College without too much debt, chasing my dream to New York," her eyes lift to mine, "you."

While Sophie is thirteen years my junior, from the moment I met her, there was a confidence about her that was beyond her years. It's a maturity that she developed growing up as she did, fast by necessity. No matter how much credit she gives to Griffin, she has ultimately been the reason for her drive and success.

I wrap my arm around her waist and pull her into me, her back flush against my front.

"Ahem." She wiggles her ass against my growing erection.

"Ignore it and it will eventually go away." Just mentioning my dick has it on high alert. With Sophie's ass grinding into my crotch, it doesn't stand a chance. "Maybe. Okay, probably not. Do you want me to put on boxers?"

She yawns.

"Hmm." I nuzzle my face into Sophie's hair. It smells like her shampoo, with a faint hint of sweaty sex. Our legs tangle together. The growing appendage between my legs presses against Sophie's ass. I do my best to ignore it and soak in this moment.

It's too good. Holding her in my arms. The thought of keeping her there all night, feeling her soft body against mine, then pressing into her slick heat in the morning. We wouldn't even have to move. I could press into her from behind, my fingers teasing between her thighs while she arches her ass back into me.

I'm at peace, nearly about to doze off when she replies.

"It's fine. I can only stay for a little while anyway. I've got to work at the bar at ten."

That has my eyes popping open.

"What bar?" I ask, lifting to my elbow behind her.

"I got a second job waitressing at The Penrose."

"Why do you need a second job?" I ask.

"Because living in this city is expensive, and eventually, I want to get my own place." She laughs. "You sell condos for ten million dollars; I don't think I need to explain the astronomical cost of living here to you."

Suddenly, the peace I was feeling about holding Sophie in my arms all night evaporates.

"When did you start?" I ask.

"I went in for training last Thursday. Tonight is my first official night."

I search for the words to say I don't like this without sounding like a controlling asshole.

"But I need you here." I end up sounding like a whiny teenager instead.

"*Hmm*. I'm here, until nine-thirty."

I lift my arm to glance at my watch. It's already nine.

The temptation to offer her whatever she needs is on the tip of my tongue. The tips she'd make tonight, I could easily pull from my wallet right now. But then I remember how she thought I was paying her for sex in Las Vegas and I know it's not the right thing to do.

If she was any other woman, I'd offer her assistance to keep her here. That's what most of the women I've dated want anyways, the clout and financial benefits that come with dating a billionaire, and my dick. That's always been the most popular commodity. Come for the dick, stay for the amenities.

But Sophie isn't most women. Maybe that's why I want her to stay. Her drive and determination are qualities that attracted me to her in the first place. And I already know that she'd be highly offended, refuse my offer, then leave. She'll eventually leave tonight, but I want us to be on good terms when she does.

Secret fuck buddies, we joked a few minutes ago, but it doesn't sit well with me. Not because she's Griffin's sister and I want to be respectful. No, it's more than that. I have the urge to protect her, to take care of her. I know she doesn't want me to. Maybe that's why the thought is even more appealing.

I drop my gaze to Sophie's face. Her eyes are closed, her long lashes fanned over her cheeks. Her full, pink lips slightly parted as she breathes peacefully.

She snuggles in closer to me and sighs. "Can you set an alarm for twenty minutes?" she asks, not even opening her eyes.

"Sure," I say, then press a soft kiss to her temple.

But I don't bother to set an alarm. Instead, I spend the next twenty minutes staring at her while she rests.

At nine-thirty, I watch her get dressed and kiss her before she leaves. Then, I grab my laptop and get back into bed alone. For once, I wanted a woman to stay and she had to go.

CHAPTER 19

Sophie

Johnathan and I are on our way to The Plaza Hotel to do a site check and go over the run sheet for the wedding there on Saturday when I get a text from Hunter.

Hunter: *Want to come over after work?*

Sophie: *I'm on my period. Started this morning.*

Technically, I'm only spotting right now, but the last thing I need is to be having sex and bleed all over Hunter. The thought is mortifying.

Hunter: *Okay…*

Sophie: *So, there won't be any sex.*

I clarify in case Hunter thinks that's not an issue. For me it is. I'm all about trying new things, but period sex isn't high on the list. It's not on the list at all.

Hunter: *You should still come over.*

My to-do list is a mile long. With the *Brides* blog spotlight article coming out in August, I want to make sure I'm keeping up with new material.

Sophie: *I would, but I need to record a few videos for my vlog.*

Hunter: *Can you do that here? I'll be your cameraman. I know all the right angles. <wink emoji>*

Sophie: *Your corny jokes aren't convincing me to come over.*

I tease him, but already I'm thinking the backdrop of Hunter's apartment will be far better than my cramped room.

Hunter: *I'll order Kung Fu Kitchen.*

Sophie: *And those macarons they have?*

Hunter: *All the macarons.*

Sophie: *I'm in.*

Hunter: *See you at seven.*

Hunter greets me at the door with a steamy kiss.

"I like this," he says, sliding a finger under the thin strap of my one-piece bodysuit with shorts.

"Thanks. It's kind of a pain in the ass to pee in because I have to get completely naked, but it's so comfortable."

He chuckles. "That's exactly why I understand nothing about women's fashion trends, but as long as it makes you happy."

He shuts the door behind me and leads me into the kitchen, the dining table nearby already set with the food he ordered.

At first, being at Hunter's place without the prospect of having sex feels strange, but after we eat and I consume half the container of macarons, I realize I'm too full for sex anyways.

After dinner, I'm putting together my mobile recording setup when Hunter steps in behind me.

"So explain how this works."

"This is a camera. I know it's smaller than what your generation used. Camcorders, they were called?"

When I turn to lift my brows mockingly, I'm met with Hunter's teasing glare.

"Not the recording device." He pinches my ass playfully and I scream before dissolving into a fit of laughter. "How does your blog work? Or is it a vlog because you do videos?"

"The *Sustainable Wedding Chic* started as a blog and then I noticed I was getting more response from the few videos I was doing, like tutorials and DIY videos, so I've been working to create more content on my YouTube channel and linking it to my blog."

He nods. "That's great. How can I help?"

"It's more of a one-person operation, but you can sit and watch. Or work if you need to. I just need it to be quiet while I'm recording."

Hunter sets his phone on the counter, giving me his full attention. I glance over at his handsome face. Those captivating blue eyes and sexy grin. Maybe this wasn't such a good idea.

After a thousand and one tries because I can't talk to the camera with Hunter watching me, I finally get a good take for each video.

"That was fun. Took a bit longer than I thought it would," he says, standing to enter the living room.

I turn to glare at him. "You know it was your fault, right?"

"Me?" he asks innocently, reaching for a record from his collection and placing it on the player. A soft piano melody starts to play.

"Yes. Normally, there's no one staring intently at me from the other side of the camera."

A man starts singing, his voice deep and smokey.

"Who is this?" I ask.

"David Gray. One of my favorites."

Hunter takes my hand to pull me off the stool, then leads me into the living room. With one arm wrapped around my waist, and his other hand capturing mine, we start to sway to the music. "I liked watching you work."

Just like the night at the ballet, my chest warms at Hunter's interest in my blog. It must be why I share my news with him about the upcoming feature in *Brides.*

He pulls back to look at me. "Sophie, that's incredible."

"Yeah." I nod, smiling.

"We are talking about the bridal magazine that's on every shelf where magazines are sold, right?"

"Uh-huh."

"Am I missing something here?" he asks, looking confused.

"No, I'm ecstatic."

He studies me carefully. "Yeah, the elation is written all over your face."

"I'm trying to play it cool. It's a big deal, but also it doesn't change my plan. My blog is a hobby. It's not a secure job that I can rely on. That's what I'm working for at Marion Adler Events. So, while this is unbelievably exciting, I'm not going to let it affect my plans."

"I see." He's quiet for a moment, his arm tightening around me, before he speaks again. "Let me ask you this. If you knew you had financial security, would you feel more inclined to pursue your blog full-time? Or do you truly enjoy working at Marion Adler Events?"

"I like both. The hours of wedding planning and attending the events are intense. In Vegas, at The Windsor, it was more pre-planning for couples looking for guidance on how best to do a Vegas wedding, so I didn't spend as much of my evenings and weekends at events, and I loved advising couples on sustainable wedding practices. Not everyone is into that, and I'm respectful of each couple's choice, but ultimately, I enjoy doing both. Advising on sustainable wedding practices and helping a couple plan their big day."

"Then that's what you should work toward. You could use the upcoming feature to boost your platform and launch your own sustainable wedding planning business."

My stomach dips. I can't afford to take the risk. "You make it sound so easy."

"It won't be, but I think everything worth doing has its challenges. That's the way I feel about the new ventures I'm exploring with Premier." Hunter looks down at me, his fingers grazing my temple as he sweeps a rogue hair out of my face. "Think about it."

I nod, then turn my head to rest it against his chest. While my mind is a flurry of wavering thoughts, I let my body relax into him. I soak in his warmth, loving the feel of his strong forearm wrapped around me while my fingers tease into his hair.

"I didn't take you for a slow dancing kind of guy," I sigh.

"I'm not," he says, pulling me in closer, his words contradicting his actions as we easily sway to the music. "But I like this song and any excuse to touch you."

I'm still processing his words a moment later when he spins me out. When he pulls me back to him, I not so gracefully crash into his chest before he attempts to dip me backwards.

"What is happening right now?" I laugh, my head flung back behind me.

"We'll need to work on that one," he says, setting me upright again. His lips find my temple, pressing a light kiss there.

Feeling slightly off balance, my hands lock behind his neck to steady myself.

"Yeah," I say, still laughing at our poor execution.

But when our eyes meet a moment later, my stomach flutters at the desire I see there.

Hunter's hands leave my lower back to cup my face. I swallow the last of my laughter as his mouth descends on mine, gentle yet passionate kisses that have me going from zero to one hundred in mere seconds. My hands slip under his shirt, my fingernails lightly scratching his abs while Hunter's hands are completing a circuit over my ass and hips, up to my breasts and back down. It's different to be kissing and touching, stroking, and teasing but know it's not leading to sex.

Not breaking our kiss, Hunter lifts me into his arms. My legs easily wrap around his waist before he walks us over to the couch. He lowers me onto my back, then covers my body with his.

Even with sex off the table, I feel the urge to touch him. I slide my hand between us, to palm his erection. He lets out a low moan, rocking into my hand. But a moment later, he removes it from his crotch, pinning it above my head.

"Isn't that going to bother you?" I ask as he kisses down my neck.

"I'll take care of it later."

"Don't you want me to?" I move to sit up, but my uterus cramps, sending a sharp pain through my lower body. "Ouch." I wince, gripping my lower belly.

I drop to my back again.

"What hurts?" Hunter asks, hovering over me, his brows pinched with concern.

"My uterus." I groan. "Periods are the worst. That tampon commercial telling women to have a happy period…someone should punch their marketing team in the face."

Hunter presses his lips together to suppress a laugh. Even though my belly is cramping, I can't help but laugh, too.

When our laughter quiets, he asks, "Where does it hurt?"

I place a hand on the lower right side of my abdomen. He lowers his head and drops his lips to the spot I pointed out.

It's so sweet, now my chest aches. He should probably kiss that, too.

Hunter rotates us until we're on our sides facing each other, his fingertips tracing a path over my cheek, along my jaw and down my nose. It's relaxing and makes my eyelids flutter closed.

And that's how we spend the rest of our time together until I have to leave for my shift at The Penrose. Cuddled up on his couch, touching and kissing. Nothing has ever felt so good.

When I get home from The Penrose, it's nearly one in the morning, but Griffin is still up. It almost feels like he's waiting for me. Like a parent waiting for their child to get home for curfew.

"Hi," I say, sliding my shoes off by the door.

He sets the book he's reading down and removes his glasses.

"Hey, how was your shift?"

"Good. It was busy, which makes the time fly by." I head for the kitchen to grab a glass of water and he follows me.

"We missed you at dinner. Did you eat? I made lasagna if you want some."

"I'm okay. Thanks. I'm more tired than hungry."

"I get it. That's how most of my nights used to be."

"Why are you still up?" I ask.

"Couldn't sleep."

"I'm sorry. I don't think I'll have that problem. I'm exhausted." I start moving toward the hallway and my bedroom.

"Sophie?" he calls just before I get to my bedroom door.

I turn back. "Yeah?"

"Things are good for you here, right? You're doing well? Work and everything?"

I think about my internship at MAE, and the *Brides* feature, which I haven't shared with anyone but Hunter and June because it doesn't even feel real. I'm afraid I dreamt it up. How the clear vision of what I thought I wanted is starting to blur. And there's no way in hell I'm going to tell him about Hunter.

I press a smile to my lips. "Yeah, everything is great."

He nods. "Okay."

"Goodnight, G."

"Goodnight, Soph."

In my room, I quickly get ready for bed and pull back the covers. I know things are different between me and Griffin. I can feel it. He has Emma now, and the both of us starting our careers has completely changed our routine. My goal of becoming more independent has required me to not share everything with him like I would have before. It's a good thing, I tell myself right before I fall asleep.

CHAPTER 20

Sophie

One of the jobs of being a wedding planning assistant's intern is staying long after the wedding guests have departed to help the take down crew at the venue. I can't leave until all the vendors are packed up and gone, the final invoices have been paid, and I've collected all the items left behind by tipsy guests. With a reception ending between eleven o'clock and midnight, sometimes my job isn't done until two o'clock in the morning.

Tonight's reception location is The Plaza Hotel, so I really shouldn't complain. From the bridal rooms to the ballroom, even the bathrooms, this hotel is magical. It's been a dream of mine to visit, and while I walked through with Johnathan last week, after the Stephens-Lautner wedding today I feel like I've gotten the full tour.

Besides a vegan accidentally getting delivered a filet at dinner, and the best man having a panic attack during his speech, the wedding went seamlessly. Marion left a few hours ago, and Johnathan just did a final walkthrough, leaving me to the few remaining tasks.

After securing the couple's card box with the hotel staff to be delivered to their room tomorrow, and dropping the bride's aunt's false tooth, that she misplaced while eating dinner, at the front desk, I'm dead on my feet.

I imagine most of the wedding guests staying here are tucked into The Plaza's top-of-the-line memory foam, cloud-like mattresses, with the softest, fluffiest duvets and pillows that support your neck and head for ultimate ergonomic sleep. I'm only slightly jealous. Right now, I could sleep standing up.

I'd love to take off my heels, but I don't think that even two o'clock in the morning is an appropriate time to walk through The Plaza Hotel lobby in bare feet. There's no appropriate time for that really. I'm on my way toward the lobby entrance to wait on a ride share that is still fifteen minutes away when I spot him.

My heels skitter on the marble floor when I see Hunter leaning against one of the lobby's gold columns. He's dressed casually in jeans and a t-shirt. His hair is rumpled, like maybe he was sleeping and recently woke up.

"What are you doing here?" I ask as I approach.

"Coming to get you," he says, taking my hand.

My body sags with relief at his presence. Yes, I'm perfectly capable of getting a ride share and getting home, but I'm so tired right now, I love the thought of having someone here to help me. The fact that someone is Hunter is a bonus.

He doesn't steer us toward the exit, though. Instead, he's walking us back through the lobby, toward the elevator bank.

"I might regret saying this, but I am so tired right now, I can barely keep my eyes open. I don't know what you have planned. I'm sure it's some secret sexy rendezvous that I will be hating myself for missing out on later, but I need to go home. To bed." I yawn deeply, emphasizing my point. "To sleep."

Hunter doesn't say anything, only pulls me onto the elevator and hits a button. Inside the elevator, he tucks me into his side, supporting my exhausted body with his strong arms. He places a kiss against the top of my head.

"You heard me, right?" I yawn again. It's so intense, my eyes water.

Still holding me upright, Hunter reaches down and removes my heels, one at a time. With my heels hanging off his fingers, he scoops me up with his other arm and lifts me onto his front. I lay my head on his shoulder and cling to him with my arms around his neck. The usual feeling of being this close to him, all the tingles and zaps and electric energy that only multiple orgasms can quiet, has been muted by the comfort of his calming hold on me. My desire for him is still present, but currently sleeping under a weighted blanket of exhaustion.

I'm barefoot and my ass might be hanging out right now, but in the five minutes since I swore not to walk barefoot in The Plaza Hotel, a lot has happened. I've become exponentially more tired. And with Hunter's soothing voice and gentle kiss to my temple, it's the only permission I need to let my cares slip away.

The elevator stops and Hunter carries me off. I'm pretty much dead weight at this point. A sack of potatoes in his arms.

It's not until I hear the electronic beep and the sound of a door opening that I'm fully aware of where he's taking me. A room opens around us. A sitting area. A bar. A bed, cloud-like bedding and memory foam mattress all present.

"What…" That's all I get out.

Hunter takes me into the bathroom first. I take in the gold-plated fixtures and marble floors. They really are breathtaking. He sets me on the closed toilet lid and hands me a toothbrush. I look over to find a toiletry kit on the counter with all the products I use. Did I pack for this staycation and not remember? I can't even process what it all means. I brush, then rinse my mouth, and let Hunter lead me to the bed where he strips off my dress and bra and replaces them with one of his t-shirts. The covers are already turned down, like they've been waiting patiently for me all night. I slide in and sigh when my head hits the pillow.

Hunter joins me a moment later. The large expanse of bare skin of his torso provides warmth to the contrast of the cool sheets. It's perfect.

I feel like I should say something. *Wow, this is incredibly thoughtful. Thank you for doing this.* Anything to acknowledge how fucking awesome this moment is right now, but nothing in my body is working right now. All I can do is reach for Hunter's arm and wrap it around me tight before sleep pulls me under.

I sleep like the dead. Inelegantly, with my mouth hanging open and drool escaping out the side. At least that's how I wake up. When I remember where I am, I roll over to find an empty bed. Hunter must have decided I'm an ugly sleeper and abandoned ship. But then he walks through the door in his running clothes, sweat clinging to his forehead and glistening along the dips of his muscular arms. He yanks off his shirt, revealing his sweat-slick abs. After a night in this magical hotel bed, my libido must be fully charged because my clit starts to throb with the view of his chiseled torso.

"You went running?" Without me is implied by the hint of whininess in my tone.

He drops down onto the edge of the bed. "I couldn't wake you up. I tried, but you were sleeping hard."

I rub the sleep out of my eyes, then drop back onto the bed and stretch my arms overhead. "I feel like a new woman. Thank you for surprising me last night." My tired muscles and feet feel more rested.

He smiles. "I wanted to see you. And logistically, this made the most sense."

"Logistically, it made the most sense to book a room at The Plaza Hotel so you could pick me up from the wedding I was working last night?"

He shrugs. "Yeah."

Hunter crawls over me. "You're all sweaty." I run my palms down his abs, trying to scrunch up my nose in disgust, but I love it. It's troubling how good he smells after a workout.

His hands reach up to wrap around my wrists, keeping them pinned above my head.

"Don't worry, I'll make sure you still get your workout in today."

Hunter's nose glides along the column of my neck. The tender move is my favorite. He did it the first night we were together in Vegas, and it serves to both turn me on and make me feel safe and cared for.

"Do we have the all clear?" he asks, slipping a hand down my body to palm my ass.

"What? Oh, yes, Aunt Flo has exited the building."

My period was light and shorter than usual, but I chalked it up to stress and exhaustion.

I can already feel his erection pressing between my legs and I'm dying for it. He grinds his hips into me, giving me that delicious pressure. I'm so turned on, I could come just like this, rubbing my clit on his cock with our clothes between us. His mouth finds mine and I let him devour me, morning breath and all.

But then there's a knock on the door.

Hunter pulls back and I groan in frustration.

"That's the food," he says, rolling off me.

I really want him to stay so we can finish what we started, but the moment he mentions food, my stomach growls loudly.

His lips twitch. "Hungry?"

"Starving." I follow him off the bed and reach into the bag he packed for me to grab a sweatshirt.

He pulls his shirt back on to answer the door. A moment later, a waiter rolls in a cart and starts setting up the food at the table in the corner of the room. The fact that Hunter not only booked a room for last night to surprise me, but that he ordered room service already is going to earn him one hell of a blow job later.

When the waiter leaves, we take our seats and I lift the metal warming cover off my plate. My jaw drops at what I see there. It's a happy face pancake, complete with bacon mouth, strawberry nose, blueberry eyes and whipped cream hair. I look over at Hunter's plate. He has the same thing with the addition of a spinach and mushroom omelet.

"I know I didn't make them, but I thought it would be fun to have on a Sunday morning, like your tradition with Griffin. Did I get them right? They were a special order, so I hope they turned out okay."

Hunter surprised me with a night at The Plaza Hotel and special ordered me happy face pancakes? I stare down at the chocolate chip pancake on my plate. What is happening right now? He's quickly becoming my favorite person, that's what.

But that's not what this is, though. We agreed it would be casual. Strictly sex, with a side of Hunter showing me around the city. Other than our brief attempt at dry humping, he hasn't laid a finger on me since we walked—no, he carried me —into this room last night.

"Sophie?"

I look up to find Hunter staring at me.

"Everything okay?" he asks.

"Yeah." I nod, hoping the movement will shake loose the emotions that are clawing their way up my throat. "The pancake looks great. Thank you."

In my effort to pretend like Hunter didn't just knock the

wind out of me, I grab my fork and take a heaping bite of pancake and whipped cream.

"Is there anything you want to do today?" he asks.

"What could I possibly want to do besides imprint my body into that luxurious memory foam mattress until it's time to check out?"

Hunter chuckles and reaches out to wipe the excess whipped cream off the corner of my mouth. His touch sets off a rush of need in my body. A need to be close to him. I set my fork down and move to climb into his lap.

"Are you done eating?" His hands slide up my thighs and wrap around my hips until he's gripping my ass.

"No. I just like this seat better," I say, settling in before I turn to reach for the slice of bacon off my pancake and take a bite.

Keeping one arm around my back, Hunter reaches around me to fork another bite of his omelet. When he does it a second time, he offers it to me.

I shake my head and scrunch up my nose. "No thanks."

"You're missing out."

"Yeah, I'm okay with that."

When he laughs, the skin around his eyes crinkles and my heart stops at the sight of him.

I want to ask him what we're doing here. Is this just another stop on the Hunter Cartwright New York City sight-seeing tour?

He reaches for another bite, but I practically knock the fork out of his hand before pulling his face to mine. His hands cradle my head as our kiss turns white hot. With impatient hands, we pull at each other's clothes, and Hunter stands to carry me to the bed. A minute later, we've shed our clothes and Hunter's ripping open a condom.

I need him inside me now. I need to remind myself what we're doing here.

When he pushes inside me, I feel the tears gather at the

corner of my eyes. Not because it hurts, but because the feeling is absolutely perfect.

I close my eyes and will the liquid to evaporate. Just like I urge the knot in my chest to untangle. With every steady rock of Hunter's hips, every caress of his hand against my cheek, I feel like I'm going to break.

I press my palms to his chest. Without me saying the words, he already knows what it means. He flips us so he's now on his back, his hands gripping my hips as I straddle him. When I'm on top, I feel more in control. I can close my eyes and chase my orgasm without feeling like Hunter's closeness is about to swallow me whole. Up here I can't feel his heartbeat against my chest, and I can pretend like mine isn't setting its rhythm to his.

When my orgasm hits, I tilt my head up to the ceiling and cry out. A moment later, I can feel Hunter pulsing inside me.

I lower my gaze to find Hunter's indigo eyes staring up at me. His hand lifts to cup my cheek as his thumb traces over my lips.

"God, you're beautiful."

He says it so reverently I can feel those unshed tears pooling above my lash line again.

"Thank you." It's all I can manage as I reach for my sweatshirt. I give him a quick kiss before dismounting and rushing to the bathroom to clean up.

I pee, then wash my hands. When I glance in the mirror, I'm horrified at how disheveled I look. Messy tangled hair and chapped lips. The dark circles under my eyes don't disappear even after I've wiped my mascara off.

You're beautiful. That's what Hunter had said. He might need to get his eyes checked.

"Do you wear contacts or glasses?" I ask, exiting the bathroom after I've attempted to tame my wild hair. The rest can't be helped until I shower and I'm not in the mood for that yet. I still want to eat my pancake.

Hunter is now propped up against a pillow with his hands behind his head showing off his impressive chest and chiseled abs.

"No. I had Lasik ten years ago."

He tosses his legs over the side of the bed to pull on his briefs.

I take a big bite of pancake. It's cooler now, but still incredibly delicious.

"Hmm."

I can never tell Griffin that The Plaza Hotel's pancakes are better than the ones we make, it feels disloyal to even think it, but I'm still going to eat every bite.

Hunter walks over to the table, a robe and slippers in his hand.

I gasp at the sight of the prominent Plaza Hotel emblem embroidered on them.

"I figured you'd want the full experience."

"Yes, please!"

He holds the robe out for me and I slip my arms through the plush terry velour. He sets the slippers on the carpet so I can slide my feet inside. It's heaven.

"I'm trying to decide which is more relaxing. The orgasm you just gave me or this robe," I tease.

Hunter smirks as he pulls a matching robe on and joins me at the table.

"Is there a reason you're concerned about my vision?" he asks after swallowing a bite of his pancake.

"Oh, you said I was beautiful, then I nearly scared myself looking in the mirror, so I was concerned for you. Lasik isn't permanent, right? You might need a touch up?"

Hunter chuckles, then gazes at me tenderly. "I had my eyes checked a few months ago. I've got perfect vision."

That's the thing I'm realizing about Hunter. He's not going to justify calling me beautiful. He said it and he stands by it even when I try to shake some sense into him. It's annoying really.

Or maybe that's his way of telling me I don't need to work to impress him. This isn't that kind of relationship.

I remember friends telling me about early stages of their relationships where they'd tiptoe out of bed to brush their hair and apply lip balm before pretending to wake up looking like a perfectly angelic creature. No, I'm a groggy mess in an oversized sweatshirt and Hunter doesn't care.

So, I stuff my face with the remainder of my pancake, then eat half of Hunter's pancake. We take a shower and have sex again. This time I'm more awake and when Hunter moves me into the reverse cowgirl position so he can play with my ass I come so hard I nearly fold his dick in half.

Really, it's the perfect morning.

CHAPTER 21

Hunter

It's mid-afternoon by the time I convince Sophie to shower and get dressed. The late check-out I asked for was necessary.

"Coney Island?" she asks. "I could really go for a corndog."

She's been trying to guess where we're going since we hit the Queens Midtown Tunnel.

"Are you still hungry?" She ate nearly both of our pancakes, then a plate of fries and a chocolate milkshake before we left the hotel.

"Hey," her tone is mockingly defensive, "if we're going to be having this much sex, you have to feed me."

Her eyes go wide when she realizes her outburst in front of my driver, Stefan. All I can do is chuckle at the mortified look on her face.

"You can have anything you want," I whisper in her ear while letting my palm settle over her spandex short-clad thigh. In order to make last night a surprise, Jeannie purchased some items for Sophie. I've gotten to know her style over the last few weeks and recommended biker shorts and an oversized t-shirt with sneakers. At first, Sophie was annoyed I bought her new shoes, but when it came down to it, she was happy to not put her heels back on.

When the car pulls up in front of the shop, Sophie stares out the window, confused.

"Is this where we're going?" She turns to look at me.

I can't help the smile that pulls at my lips. Watching her reaction is like opening a gift on Christmas morning. It's my new favorite thing.

"A vintage goods shop. They're supposed to have a large selection of vases and décor items."

Stefan opens the door and I help Sophie out. The store is filled with used goods which I would normally not be a fan of, but Sophie's interest in them had me instructing Jeannie to do a search.

Inside, a woman approaches us.

"Hi there, is there anything I can help you with?" she asks.

"Hunter Cartwright," I extend my hand, "I called a few days ago. You mentioned you had a selection of vintage vases."

"That's right. I remember. Right this way."

As we follow the shop owner toward the back, Sophie threads her hands around my arm.

"You called the store?" She's practically vibrating with excitement.

"Yeah. I wanted to make sure they had what you were looking for before we drove down here."

After Jeannie gave me a list, I called six stores, and this one seemed to be the best option.

At the back of the store, there are shelves filled with vases and other vase-like glassware.

Sophie's eyes light up at the selection before us.

"This is amazing." Sophie drops my arm to move toward the shelves. "Look at this! An entire collection of Amber ridged vases."

"Those are a set?" I ask, looking at the different sizes and shapes of the vases.

"They can all go together. Like this larger one can be by itself as a centerpiece or an accent on a place card table. And these," she points to three smaller ones, "they can be a set together on a table. This color is perfect. It would look amazing with these rechargeable mini light strands I found recently."

Sophie's like a kid in a candy store, but suddenly her smile drops.

"I have nowhere to put all this stuff. My bedroom at Emma and Griffin's is overflowing already."

It suddenly occurs to me that I haven't seen Sophie's bedroom. I haven't laid eyes on any of her personal items. I don't know what her bedding looks like, or how she has her furniture arranged. While it's never been a priority in my other relationships, it feels odd to not know that about her.

"You can keep it at my place," I offer.

"Really?" Her face brightens.

"Yeah. I've got plenty of space."

"Are you sure? I don't want to be a burden."

"Hey." I pull her in close. "You're never a burden. This is fun and I want you to keep them at my place." I drop a kiss to her jaw. "It'll be a way to lure you in." I press my lips against her neck and give her a light lick. "Anytime you want to see them, you'll have to see me, too."

"Hmm. You drive a hard bargain, but I think I'll take it." She wraps her arms around my neck. "Thank you."

In the car on the way back to my place, I link my fingers through Sophie's and bring her hand to my lips. Her nails are a lavender color, but one of them is chipped.

"Before I forget." I keep her hand in mine while I reach into the bag of items Jeannie purchased for Sophie and pull out a bottle of nail polish. I place it in her hand.

Sophie looks down at the bottle.

"I figured the red would be good for next weekend."

She looks back at me, a smile pulling at the corner of her lips.

"You got me nail polish?"

"You change it every Sunday, right?" I've noticed she's had a new color on every week we've been seeing each other.

"Yeah, I do."

"Got this, too." I pull out the box.

"The Olive and June complete manicure set?" She hugs it to her chest, squeezing it lovingly before planting a kiss on my cheek. "Thank you. Or should I thank Jeannie? She's really got me dialed in. I think we would be best friends."

I chuckle at her goofy smile.

I don't bother telling her that I picked out the nail polish. That yesterday afternoon I wandered down the aisles of the Target near Times Square, which I normally avoid at all costs, and selected the polish and manicure set that I thought she'd like.

I don't need the credit; the smile on her face is enough.

"Okay…you can paint my toes." I finally give in to Sophie's persistent request to paint something on me. I'm not going to show up to work tomorrow with my fingernails painted, but toenails, I can handle.

Sophie sets the nail polish bottles on the counter, her newly painted candy apple red nails flashing as she waves her hands in their direction. "What color would you like?"

"What do you recommend?" I ask playfully.

Her lips twist to the side, thinking hard. "I think this lovely sky blue will really complement your dark toe hair."

"That's very important. I'm glad you considered that."

While Sophie was painting her nails, I opted to bring my laptop into the living room to be near her while I worked. I'm still sitting in one of my living room's overstuffed chairs when she kneels in front of me.

She smiles, shaking the bottle of polish before twisting the lid off and lifting my foot into her lap.

As she paints, I'm starting to get turned on by the visual of her kneeling in front of me.

I set my laptop on the table beside me and lean back in the chair. Her face is angled down, her nose scrunched up in concentration, her blonde ponytail draped over her shoulder.

My cock twitches.

The cool paint hits the skin around my pinky toenail and I jerk.

"Sorry, ticklish."

She moves to my other foot and with adept ease, paints those nails just as quickly.

When she sits back, I admire her work.

"Looks good."

"Now, you have to let it dry."

"So, I just sit here?"

She twists the nail polish lid on and sets the bottle on the table next to my laptop.

"It's quick dry, so you should be good to go in five minutes."

"Come here." I move to lift her into my lap, knowing five minutes will pass quickly if her lips are on mine.

She shakes her head, a mischievous smile on her face.

"Lean back," she says, pushing my legs apart so she can move between them.

I do what she says. My thighs flex as she drags her palms over them. Her red fingernails dip inside the waistband of my shorts. I aid her in their removal by lifting my hips and letting her pull them down to free my hard cock.

A moment later, I'm watching Sophie's hands, with her pretty red fingernails, stroke me.

"I like your nails, baby," I tell her. "They look so fucking good wrapped around my cock."

She smiles up at me, giving me another long stroke, her green eyes alight with desire. Her tongue flicks out to wet her lips just before she dips her head and sinks her mouth down on me.

Fuck.

I let out a groan as my hips involuntarily lift to meet her.

She swirls her tongue along my shaft, taking more of me. I love watching Sophie suck my cock, but it's starting to feel like more than a sexual act. Like she's giving me a gift. It's about vulnerability and appreciation.

My hand reaches out, teasing my fingers into her ponytail. I don't use my hold there to set the pace, I just need to be touching her somewhere. I need the connection to be more than my cock in her mouth.

The feel of her soft strands beneath my fingertips gives me a sense of calm. In contrast to the scorching heat pumping through my veins as I come down the back of Sophie's throat a minute later.

I watch as she dabs at the corner of her mouth, then presses her lips together.

"Time's up. Your nails should be dry."

This woman is ruining me.

CHAPTER 22

Sophie

An incessant buzzing sound nearby jars me awake. As I stir, I become aware of the firm warmth pressed against me. I turn so quickly, I clip Hunter in the ribs with my elbow.

"Umpff." He coughs on impact.

"Shit. I'm sorry."

"Good morning," he says, his voice adorably groggy.

My head swivels to look at the clock on the bedside table. Eight thirty. *Fuuuck.*

From behind me, Hunter wraps his arms around me, but I wrestle free.

"I'm so late!"

Adrenaline courses through my body at the sudden realization. I race to the bathroom and quickly brush my teeth, then finger-comb through my hair before pulling it back into a low ponytail.

When I rush back into the bedroom, I'm just in time to watch Hunter pull on his boxer briefs over his firm ass and impressive erection. Just the sight of him makes my body start tingling.

I'm frozen now, standing here ogling Hunter's dick when I should be rushing out the door. *What is happening to me?*

He turns to catch me staring. "I take it you're not up for a quickie?"

I glower at him. "I wasn't supposed to spend the night. This is your fault." I stab a finger in the air at him. "For being all cuddly and making me fall asleep."

"Guilty as charged." He drops his smug grin.

"Shouldn't you be at work by now?" I motion to the time while I rummage through my bag, searching for something to wear.

"I snoozed my alarm. There was no way I was getting out of that bed if you were in it."

His response is sweet, but that doesn't help the situation.

"What can I do to help you?" he calls to my retreating back.

"Build a time machine!" I yell from the bathroom where I throw on my dress from Saturday before returning to his bedroom. I don't have time to go home, so thankfully, my black dress from the wedding on Saturday is clean enough to wear.

"I'm thirty minutes late and have no clothes to wear." I look around. "My underwear. Where are my underwear?"

Hunter emerges from the closet and hands me a pair of underwear.

My brows lift. "You have women's underwear on hand?" I tease, but they're the exact brand and style that I wear, same as the ones he had packed for me at The Plaza yesterday.

He smirks. "I had Jeannie order a few extra pairs."

My heart skips a beat at his thoughtfulness. I'd kiss him if I didn't think it would derail my exit.

"Thank you." I quickly pull them on, grateful for clean underwear, then rush to grab my purse and phone.

"You should keep some things here," Hunter says from behind me.

"I'm not keeping anything here. I'm never coming back here again. It's like a black hole with no sense of time or space. I walk through the door and lose my ability to think straight."

"I think your decision-making skills here are perfect." He grins and for a moment, I'm sucked in again. Caught in the warm glow that is Hunter's gorgeous smile until my brain sends an alert.

Stop staring at him and get moving!

"Goodbye," I toss out as I exit the room, but Hunter follows.

"You'll have to come back for your vases eventually."

When my mouth drops open, his lips curve up in a sexy grin.

Gotcha.

He doesn't say it, but I know what he's thinking. He's an evil genius who knows I have a weakness for vintage glassware and his hard cock. If I thought he offered to store the vases out of the kindness of his heart, I'd be wrong. He's a fucking mastermind.

"What are you doing for the holiday weekend?" he asks, following me into the kitchen.

"Working." I grab a banana and a bottle of water on the way through.

"On July Fourth? Nobody gets married on a Monday."

"You're right, I have Monday and Tuesday off."

"Come with me to my family lake house at Lake George. It would just be the two of us."

I'm already late, but I can't seem to walk out the door. Hunter's standing there in nothing but his boxer briefs, his hands above his head holding onto the door frame, every muscle in his body defined and rippling while he watches me devour the banana.

"I'll think about it," I grumble, tossing the peel into the compost bin. Hunter got one at my suggestion. It really was a swoon-worthy moment.

"I'll have Jeannie send you a packing list."

He pulls me in for a kiss that melts my panties and my annoyance with him. It makes me want to crawl back into bed with him and forget all my responsibilities, but I can't, so I push him away and make a break for the door.

His deep chuckle is cut off by the thud of his front door closing behind me.

With some distance between me and Hunter, the panic of being late for work is setting in again. Besides my late entry to the intern meeting on the first day, I've never been late.

At the lobby, Hunter's doorwoman, Francine, waves me over.

"Mr. Cartwright called down about you needing a car service." She motions to the black car at the curb. "Stefan will take you where you need to go."

"Thank you so much."

In the car, I text Hunter.

Sophie: *Thank you for the car service.*

Hunter: *You're late because of me. And I'm trying to get back in your good graces, so you'll spend the night again.*

Sophie: *It's not your fault I overslept. I've been tired lately working two jobs, and working on my blog, and then there's all the sex we've been having...okay, maybe you are to blame.*

Hunter: *I promise to let you rest up this week...if you come to Lake George with me.*

Sophie: *If you're on your best behavior.*

Hunter: *Scout's honor.*

Me: *Were you really a Boy Scout?*

Hunter: *If I say I was, would you be more inclined to spend the holiday weekend with me?*

Sophie: *No.*

Hunter: *Let's say, I've got skills they don't give merit badges for. And I know how to light a fire...in your panties.*

I roll my eyes at Hunter's cheesy response. Stefan pulls

the car over and before I can finish my text, he's opening the door for me.

"Thank you," I tell him and step out onto the curb, clutching my purse and phone.

I'm hustling into the building when a guy on the sidewalk calls out. "Sophie!"

I turn to find one of the baristas from the coffee shop down the block that I frequent with the other interns walking toward me with two trays of coffees in his hands.

"Hey," I zone in on his nametag, "Aaron. I'm running late so—"

"I know. These are for you."

I stare at the coffees. "I didn't order anything yet."

He looks down at the receipt for the coffees, then back at me. "An order was placed under your name for delivery here."

My phone buzzes in my hand.

Hunter: *I thought coffee for the office would create a smoother landing.*

Hunter can't see me, but I'm smiling and shaking my head.

"Do you need help with these?" Aaron asks.

"No, I got it. Thank you."

I reach in my purse and grab out cash for a tip, then take the trays from him and move toward the elevator.

Twenty minutes later, I've distributed coffee to Sabrina at reception, Marietta and Johnathan, and a few of my fellow interns, who were excited for the Monday morning caffeine boost and said nothing about my late arrival. June isn't at her desk, so I leave a coffee by her computer, then I grab the last one off the tray and take a sip. Ahh. That's when I notice the message on the side of the cup.

Lake George?

Jesus, he's even recruiting the barista in his efforts.

I reach for my phone to text Hunter back.

Sophie: *Coffee was a lifesaver. THANK YOU!!!!*

Hunter: *I'm wooing you to Lake George.*

Sophie: *I'm picking up on that.*

Hunter: *Or maybe I'm just a nice guy.*

Sophie: *You? Nice? Ha! My sore ass tells a different story.*

Hunter: *You love getting spanked. It makes you so fucking wet. And since I'm such a nice guy, I always lick up the mess you make between your thighs.*

Reading Hunter's words, I nearly choke on my coffee. That conversation turned dirty real fast.

Just then, June appears at her desk.

"You okay?" she asks.

"Yup." I pat my chest. "My coffee went down the wrong pipe."

"Is this for me?" She lifts the coffee cup.

"Yes, my treat. Happy Monday!"

"Thanks. How was your weekend?"

"It was the best," I say, then realize I shouldn't be sharing anything about me and Hunter.

"You sound all dreamy and whimsical. What did you do?"

"Um," I hesitate. For the first time since I started this fling with Hunter, I wish I could talk about him to someone. To gush about the amazing Sunday we had together. Because yesterday was purely magical. I'm about to give June the details, minus who Hunter is, when my phone buzzes.

Griffin: *I'm trying to be cool here, like you asked, but I need to know that you're okay.*

My stomach falls. Shit. I forgot to respond to his text yesterday. I got busy with Hunter, then fell asleep at Hunter's.

When I asked Griffin to give me space, to treat me like a roommate and not be watching my every move, I didn't think about how it would make him feel. The amount of stress that not knowing where I am or if I'm coming home would cause him.

I quickly respond.

Sophie: *All good. At work now. Stayed with a friend last night.*

Griffin: *Okay. Can we do lunch this week? Or dinner? Just the two of us?*

Sophie: *Yes! Let's do that.*

We make plans for dinner tomorrow night, then I put my phone away.

"Sorry, my brother was texting me. I haven't been home a lot lately so he was checking in."

"Ah, so there is someone. Spill the deets."

"It's just fun, nothing serious." I try to keep my smile small, but thinking about Hunter, it spreads without my permission. "Okay, a *lot* of fun."

"What happened to the whole no dating thing?"

"We're not *dating*."

June takes a sip of her coffee.

"It's super casual. We order in dinner and hang out and have sex. Sometimes we do something touristy because I haven't done a lot. Yesterday, he took me to a vintage glassware shop and I found so many amazing pieces. I had to leave them at his place, so I won't be able to work on anything this week, but I'm super excited about them."

June lifts her brows. "That sounds like dating to me."

"There's a lot of sex, and all that other stuff," I motion with my hand, "is extra."

"Yeah, again, I think that's called *dating*."

She stands and grabs her coffee. "I've got a meeting, so we'll have to debate this later. Thanks again for the coffee."

I give her a small wave as she leaves the office, then wake up my computer. But my thoughts don't easily move on.

No, that's not what Hunter and I are doing. My schedule is even busier than it was a month ago when we made our casual arrangement. Now, I'm working at The Penrose two nights a week and am more focused on my blog and creating content.

Griffin texts me a link to a restaurant's menu.

Griffin: *Hunter recommended this for dinner tomorrow. Want to try it out?*

It's an Italian place. Hunter knows my weakness for pasta.

He knows a lot of things. Like the most sensitive places on my body, and the perfect pressure with which he should tweak my nipples. But he also knows about the *Brides* feature and my desire to start my own business. How I love a banana every morning with my coffee and my running playlists are exclusively Taylor Swift. That I don't spend much effort with my makeup, but I paint my nails religiously every week.

The other day I asked if the mole on my inner thigh looked any different to him, and he confirmed without a moment of hesitation that it looks exactly like it did the first time he went down on me.

Trust me, I'd notice, he'd said, giving me a wink. *It's my favorite one.*

My heart starts thumping against my ribcage.

It's fine. Everything is fine.

All those things don't mean we're not casual. That's bound to happen when you spend a lot of time together. And skin cancer is no joke, so I'm glad he's keeping tabs on my mole.

I type out a response to Griffin.

Sophie: *Sounds great!*

Even in my panicked, and slightly confused state, not once does it cross my mind that I should end things with Hunter. That even though my schedule has gotten busier and I have fewer hours of free time outside of work to divide among my hobbies, family, and friends, I've still managed to spend a lot of time with Hunter. If I had to prioritize my time and cut back on something, my time with him would not be the first to go. Maybe that should be the real issue.

Dinner with Griffin is more awkward than I thought it would be. The food is delicious—I'll have to thank Hunter later for giving Griffin the recommendation—and Griffin seems at ease, but every time I open my mouth to tell him how I've been spending my time, I have to filter it to not mention Hunter.

"How's work going?" I ask, searching for a safe topic.

"Work's great. We've been working on the condo deal in Las Vegas and I'll have to fly out there in a few weeks to finalize it. It's going to be strange to be back there. My life is so different now. I'm going to try to meet up with Rita and Terrence, though. Catch them for dinner or something."

"That will be fun. Give them a hug for me."

"I will." He nods, taking a bite of his chicken parmesan. "You're working this weekend, right?"

"Yeah, I've got a wedding on Saturday."

"I feel bad we'll be out of town for the holiday, but Carl and Lindsay are having a barbeque at their place. I mentioned to Carl you'd be in town and they'd love to have you join."

Exhibit A. I'm going to Lake George with Hunter on Sunday, but I *can't* tell Griffin that.

"That's okay. I've been working so much I think I'm just going to chill, maybe catch up on some shows."

"The offer stands if you change your mind."

"Thanks." I take another bite of my truffle macaroni and cheese. It's *so good.* "Is Emma excited for your weekend away?"

"Excited and constantly asking me what to pack."

Griffin is taking Emma on a surprise getaway to Bar Harbor, Maine for the holiday weekend.

I laugh. "I think she likes surprises in theory, but maybe not when it comes to her wardrobe and a limited packing list."

"You're right." He takes a sip of his water. "I think she's going to love it, though. And the place Hunter is letting us use looks phenomenal."

At the mention of Hunter, my stress ratchets up a notch.

"Oh yeah, that's great." I should steer the conversation to another topic, but curiosity gets the better of me. "How's he doing?" I ask in my most nonchalant voice before forking another large bite.

He shrugs. "Good."

It's a guy answer. Like one word can completely encapsulate all that a person is. All their thoughts and feelings. Just *good.*

"Actually, I think he's seeing someone."

I inhale sharply and a noodle lodges itself in the back of my throat causing me to choke.

Griffin springs out of his seat ready to attempt the Heimlich on me, but I lift a hand to stop him as I reach for my water and chug it to dislodge the noodle.

"I'm okay," I say, my airway clear enough to croak out the words.

I take a deep breath, willing my heart rate to calm. If Griffin knew about *me* and Hunter, he'd have more words than *I think he's seeing someone.*

"Really? Why do you think that?" I ask, careful to take a smaller bite this time.

"We were playing doubles the other day and he was smiling at his phone during a break. I wouldn't have noticed, but Barrett pointed it out and gave Hunter shit about it. Neither of us can talk because we do it with our wives, but that's what made me think it must have been a woman."

"Oh, that's interesting." Now, I'm recalling mine and Hunter's text exchanges from the week. They range from sweet and innocent to downright filthy. I'm wondering if he's got me saved in his phone as Sophie, or if he has a code name.

I make a mental note to check on that in case Griffin were to see Hunter's phone screen sometime.

"It's not a big deal. We're good enough friends that if he wanted to share something about his personal life, he would."

"Yeah, I'm sure."

I leave it at that. I don't need Griffin to have a reason to think I'm curious about Hunter's personal life. I already know I am his personal life.

With a lull in the conversation, I debate whether to tell Griffin about *Brides* magazine wanting to feature my blog. It's exciting news. I should be thrilled to share, but something has been holding me back from telling him.

I poke my fork around in my bowl. "I have some exciting news."

"Yeah?" he asks.

"My blog was selected to be featured in *Brides* magazine for an article on up-and-coming wedding planning blogs to watch."

He finishes chewing his bite of food, then reaches for his water glass.

"Wow, Soph. That's awesome. When does it come out?"

"August."

"That's so cool. Congratulations." He stands to give me a hug before we both sit back down. "Emma is going to be ecstatic. You'll have to tell her when we get home."

"Yeah. I will." I hesitate for a moment, taking a sip of water before continuing. "It's made me start thinking about adding more content and maybe redesigning the logo, you know, polishing it up before there's more traffic on the site."

"Do you have time for that? With work and everything you need to be doing for your internship?"

"I'm busy, but I'd make the time. I think the feature will give me a nice boost in visibility. I'd want to capitalize on that."

"Visibility for what?" he asks.

I shrug, trying to play it cool when my entire body is tingling with excitement just thinking about the possibilities. "I don't know. I've been thinking about ways to build a business around the blog."

"It's great that your blog is getting recognition, but it's more of a hobby, right?" Before I can answer, he continues. "I know you've got some advertisers, and that's great, but it's not a steady income. And while it sounds like this feature could be free marketing, it's not a guarantee, right?"

Griffin's words are the equivalent of a parent telling their child not to major in Art History or Latin Studies because *what are you going to do with those degrees*? The real world doesn't care about your passions, you need to pay your rent and bills.

"No, you're right." I can feel my smile dimming. "It was just a thought."

The thing is I know Griffin doesn't mean to be dismissive of my blog. He wants the best for me. He's always wanted that. But with the exposure the *Brides* feature could generate and the connections I've made so far in the industry, I'm starting to wrap my head around the idea of making this my career. A sustainable wedding planning business locally while using my blog to promote my ideas all over the world.

Maybe it's wild and impractical. I could revisit this idea in five to seven years. Make it part of the ten-year plan.

Hunter doesn't think it's unrealistic. The thought surfaces, recalling his encouraging words.

But Griffin is my brother, my support system. I value his opinion so much. And when Hunter and I aren't hooking up anymore, I doubt he'll be available for business pep talks.

Griffin asks me a few more questions about the *Brides* feature, and we order dessert which I can't stomach for some reason so we box it up to take home to Emma.

At home, I say goodnight and head to my room.

With my laptop open to my blog, I grab a notepad and

start jotting down ideas. It's after midnight before I close my computer and get into bed. I think about Griffin's concerns and Hunter's encouragement and my own desire to create something I'm passionate about until my brain is mush and eventually, I fall asleep.

CHAPTER 23

Hunter

The work week is moving at a sluggish pace. Typically, I'm engrossed in project briefings and financial meetings throughout the week so much that if I blink, it's already Friday. The fact that it's only Wednesday and there's no possibility of seeing Sophie until Sunday, I fucking hate it.

After a meeting downtown, I find myself directing Stefan toward Mercer Street and Hannah's boutique, Filigree and Facet. On my way, I stop at a coffee shop to grab Hannah's favorite iced chai latte so I don't show up empty-handed.

I've thought about getting the wildflower necklace for Sophie since the night of the soft opening, but purchasing it from Hannah will be tricky. She'll have plenty of questions about me buying jewelry for a woman, and even more inquiries if she thinks it's for Sophie. But she's my sister and I want to support her business. Not to mention, I know Sophie loves Hannah's jewelry. The wildflower necklace in particular.

When we pull up to her boutique, hanging above the white trim windows and cascading down the side of the door, there's an enormous arch of flowers in various shades of pink.

Inside, the boutique is busy with customers. I make my

way around a display table of earrings, while I overhear Hannah explaining to a customer how to layer necklaces. The conversation makes me smile. The only thing Hannah loves more than designing jewelry, is sharing her passion for accessorizing.

When I catch her eye, her brows lift in surprise. I hang back, lingering around a necklace case while she finishes her conversation. After she hands off the customer to one of her sales associates, she approaches me.

"To what do I owe this lovely surprise?" she asks.

"I was in the neighborhood," I say, handing her the chai latte.

She laughs. "That's the least believable line in the book, but thanks for the drink." She takes a sip. "What are you really doing here?"

"Can't I want to see my sister?" I motion around. "Visit her thriving business?"

"Sure, sure." She motions me into the back room, before throwing a smirk over her shoulder at me. "But on a Wednesday afternoon? Not likely."

The backroom is filled with wire shelving, boxes piled high. It's brimming full but organized. A desk and chair are tucked near the back in an alcove.

"I was downtown at a meeting and I haven't been here since the soft opening," I offer as an explanation. "How's the wedding planning going?" I ask, perusing the open binder on the desk with various styles of wedding invitations inside.

"It's going well. Do you want to know about the embossed linen texture, hand-painted wedding invitations we're looking at, or do you just want to hear about Sophie?" Her lips quirk to the side, her brows lifted in that all-knowing expression of hers.

My mouth opens to reply. When nothing comes out, she laughs.

"You're so transparent, you're practically see-through."

"I will not confirm your allegations."

"But you won't deny them either." Her smile is beaming.

I drop into the chair pushed against the wall, while Hannah takes a seat at the desk.

"Let's just say I've noticed your event attendance has reduced significantly, and when you are absolutely required to be somewhere, there's been no woman on your arm."

"And that has *what* to do with Sophie?"

She shrugs innocently. "Just an observation."

I ignore her and pretend I came all this way just to flip through this wedding invitation binder.

"You're going to the lake this weekend?" she asks.

"That's the plan."

"It should be a beautiful weekend; too bad you'll be all alone."

I keep my face neutral, giving her nothing. "I'll manage."

I lift my gaze, waiting for her to dig for more information. She stays unusually quiet.

"What are your plans for the weekend?" I ask.

"James and I are going with a few other couples to the Hamptons."

I nod. "Have you talked to Mom and Dad recently?"

"They called yesterday. Sounds like they made it back from Europe, and now, they're headed to Palm Beach." She moves to stand. "Anything else?" she prompts.

She knows I'm stalling. "Listen, I'd love to hide back here and gab with you all afternoon, but I've got a business to attend to." She's mocking me. Payback for all the times I've interrupted our conversations or rushed her off the phone for work. "So, if there's nothing else you'd like to chat about…" She motions toward the exit.

"I'd like to purchase a necklace."

"Really?" She smirks. "I didn't imagine you as a gold chain kind of guy."

I roll my eyes, already regretting this. "It's not for me."

She eyes me, her lips twitching with curiosity.

"Okay then. Let's go take a look."

I follow her out to the front. I'm aware I could have sent Jeannie or ordered it online, but I wanted to pick it out myself. Like the nail polish set. It feels more personal that way. And maybe there's a part of me that wants Hannah to know about me and Sophie. A part that wonders what it would be like if the entire world knew.

Hannah takes out a mat and places it on the glass case.

"Let's start with the basics. Design preference. Sizing. Name of and your relationship with the recipient."

I narrow my eyes at her. "Do you ask all your potential customers such intrusive questions?"

"I want to establish a mood for the type of piece. It's part of my process."

There's a silent standoff across the jewelry case, until Hannah caves.

"You could have gone somewhere else." She lifts her brows. "And avoided my questioning."

"I didn't realize that was an option. I'll be going now."

I turn to leave, but Hannah reaches for my arm.

"Okay, okay. You're right. I'd be devastated if you shopped somewhere else. I got excited, that's all."

She reaches into the case and pulls out the delicate necklace with the wildflower pendant and sets it on the mat. I didn't have to tell her that's the one I wanted. She knew.

This time when our eyes meet over the jewelry case, there's softness in her gaze, understanding. The excitement she's talking about is still there, you'd have to beat that out of her, but for the first time in our relationship, it feels like she's the older sibling. That she's the one advising, showing me a rite of passage.

I simply nod. That's *the one.*

Hannah motions to her sales associate to wrap it up.

I reach for my wallet, but Hannah waves me off.

"First one's on me. I'm sure there will be more." She gives me a secretive wink.

"Thank you."

She hands me the gift bag with the necklace inside, then throws her arms around me, squeezing tight. With a final wave, I leave her shop and head back to my office.

CHAPTER 24

Sophie

"You know this isn't a lake house, right?" I set my purse on the side table by one of the three oversized sofas flanking the stone and wood fireplace that has its own built-in firewood storage bin, and take in the view. The wall of the living room facing the lake has two large panel sliding windows that are at waist height. I know that they're sliding panels because they're pushed to one side, offering an unobstructed, panoramic view of the crystal blue waters of Lake George below. "This is a *mansion* by the water."

On the drive, Hunter informed me that while many prominent families have homes in The Hamptons, his family has been coming to Lake George since he was a toddler. Until Griffin and I started happy face pancake Sunday, I didn't have any traditions growing up. There was no consistency. It was whatever my mom could handle in the moment. Christmas with a few presents one year, not even putting up a tree the next.

Hunter comes up behind me, wrapping his arms around my waist and bending slightly so he can tuck his head next to mine.

"It's my family's lake house, but you can call it what you want."

The mention of his family has me pulling away from Hunter, and the spectacular view, to peruse the built-in bookcase nearby displaying countless photos of said family. There are a few of Hunter's and Hannah's milestones, graduations and Hannah's engagement photo, but most are candid photos taken by the lake or out on a boat.

"They're not missing it for the holiday weekend?" I ask.

"My parents are traveling. My mom has had a travel bug for a while, but even more so since my dad retired. And Hannah offered up the house's exclusivity as part of the deal we made for me attending the gala with Allison."

"You got a lot out of that arrangement. You must be a top-notch negotiator."

"You have no idea." His smile is cocky. "Now, let's see, do you want me to fuck you on the kitchen counter first or a lounger on the back porch?"

"I'm not going to defile your family's lake house."

"So, you admit it *is* a lake house."

"Oh my God." I roll my eyes. "It's going to be a long two days with your cocky ass."

Hunter tackles me playfully and drops us backwards onto one of the oversized sofas, smothering me with kisses before we're both laughing and breathless.

"Admit it, you like my cocky ass. You wanted to spend two whole days with it."

"Just to make sure we're clear, I fully expect to make it out on the boat. I'm not just going to be your sexual plaything while we're here."

"Okay, but can I be yours?" He wiggles his brows.

"*Hmm.* Only if you promise to fuck me in the ass." The moment the words are out of my mouth, I can't believe I said them. It's a reference to one of our previous text exchanges, but I didn't know until this moment that I wanted him to do it this weekend.

Hunter's eyes light up. "Seriously?"

I shrug, deciding that while there's vulnerability in admitting what I want, I also feel safe with Hunter. "We talked about it before and I'm curious."

"Do you have any idea how irresistible you are?" he asks.

"You're just excited about my ass."

He nips at my jaw. "Who wouldn't be?"

"But before there's any ass play, I need food."

"I wouldn't dream of doing anal on an empty stomach."

"You're ridiculous." I shove him playfully, finding it impossible to look away from his charismatic smile.

He lifts me up and leads me into the kitchen where he pulls out a prepared cheeseboard from the refrigerator. I'm just about to dig in when we hear a sound at the front door, and a moment later, voices are echoing off the high-vaulted entryway to where we are in the kitchen.

"The gardener did a beautiful job with the flowers out front. They're exactly what that space needed. Don't you think so, Marshall?"

"Sure, sure," a man responds as I hear luggage wheels rolling against the marble-tiled entryway.

"Fuck." Hunter groans under his breath, moving away from the cheeseboard on the counter.

"Is that—" I start.

"My parents," Hunter finishes.

My eyes widen in shock. "Are you serious? I thought they were out of town?"

"Yeah, that's what they said."

"Oh, is someone here?" the woman calls. No, not *the woman*...Hunter's mother.

A flash of panic seizes me. I look around for somewhere to hide. A closet, a cupboard. Anything will do. I could probably smoosh myself against the wall behind the drapes. I'd have to turn my feet out so they don't see them peeking out, but under the circumstances, I'm sure I could manage.

As I glance hesitantly back and forth between my options, more questions arise.

How long will I have to hide?

Will Hunter distract them so he can sneak me out the back door and take me back to the city?

I think about the four-hour drive we just made.

As long car rides go, it was a blast. It was fun to tease Hunter and make him listen to Taylor Swift as well as a few episodes of the new true crime podcast I've been into lately, but my achy muscles cry at the thought of getting back in the car right now. Not to mention, I really wanted to go out on the boat. I glance longingly at the cheeseboard. And try that smoked Gouda.

My eyes are still ping-ponging between the kitchen pantry and the dining room drapes when I realize the decision has been made for me because Hunter's mom is already in the kitchen doorway.

"Hunter, I didn't know you were here." Her eyes light at the sight of me frozen in place by the cheeseboard. "And with a guest."

Hunter embraces his mom, then releases her to move toward me.

"Mom, this is Sophie." Hunter slides one large palm around my lower back until it finds a resting place on my hip, and he pulls me close. Internally, I scowl. If Mr. Handsy over here could keep it in check, I could have said I was the cleaning lady.

"Sophie," she says, smiling, before she leans in and envelopes me in her arms. "We're huggers," she says by way of explanation. "I'm Kathryn Cartwright and it's wonderful to meet you." She squeezes my shoulders as she looks me over. "Hunter doesn't introduce us to many of his lady friends."

"Mom—" Hunter starts to interject when a man, who I'm assuming is Hunter's father, walks in.

"Ah, Hunter. We didn't expect to see you this weekend." His dad pulls him in for a hug and claps him on the back.

"I put my name in the house calendar. You know, the place we check to see if someone has reserved the lake house."

"Oh, I didn't even check it," Kathryn says, waving her hand. "We were in Palm Beach, but it was ghastly hot, so we decided to make a change of plans."

"Yeah, it would have been nice to know you were coming." Hunter's gaze locks with mine and I can see the apology there. Our private weekend is now a family reunion.

"Oh, well. The more, the merrier, right?" His mom laughs.

"And who is this?" His dad has finally caught up with the rest of the group and realized there's a new face in his lake house kitchen.

"Sophie." I extend my hand, which is shaking from the adrenaline my body primed when it was preparing to run.

His large hand envelopes mine. "Marshall Cartwright. Pleasure to meet you."

I nod and smile.

"You got a cheeseboard from Nettle Meadows?" His mom claps in delight. "That will go perfectly with the Chablis we brought."

A man brings in a handful of paper shopping bags and sets them on the counter.

"Thank you, Eugene." Kathryn starts unpacking the bags. "We should have a snack and relax on the porch. Watch the sunset." She looks up from the bags. "Unless you two had other plans?"

Hunter's eyes meet mine. My lips are pressed tightly together. I can't even let myself think about what we were planning to do before his parents showed up. Hunter's brows lift and there's a secret smile on his lips. I know he's thinking about it, too.

"That all sounds good, but I think we'll go get settled first."

~

HUNTER

"Staying in separate rooms isn't going to convince my parents that we're not together," I tell Sophie who is currently unpacking her clothes into the dresser in one of the guest rooms.

After I introduced Sophie to my parents, we brought our luggage upstairs to unpack. Sophie has now refused to sleep in the same bedroom as me. It's kind of cute that she thinks us staying in different rooms is going to stop me from sneaking in to see her.

"We aren't together. Not like that."

"You know what I mean."

A lacy thong falls from the armful of clothes Sophie is shoving into one of the drawers. I reach to pick it up. Just the sight of her underwear has my mind returning to where things were going before my parents arrived.

Sophie must pick up on my thoughts. She snatches the rogue thong from my hand and tosses it in the drawer.

"You can forget about anal. We're not even going to have missionary sex. There will be no P in the V with your parents in the house."

"I'm thirty-five years old. They don't think I'm a virgin."

"Well, I'm twenty-two and I could be one for all they know."

"Is that why you're flustered? They aren't judging you. In

fact, my mom is likely in awe of you. The first woman that I've brought to our family lake house."

"I'm not flustered," she argues, clearly full of nervous energy. "But telling me I'm the first woman you've brought here isn't helping."

I wrap my arms around her, one hand firmly against her lower back while one hand reaches up to tease my fingers into the ends of her hair.

"Okay, maybe a little. I've never done this before." Her fingers slide against the placket of my shirt, toying with a button there. "Met a guy's parents. Even though you're not like my boyfriend or anything and they probably won't even remember who I am in a few months, I have this thing where I want people to like me. I want to make a good impression. And I don't like being unprepared. Which is what is happening right now."

"Do you want to leave? I can make up an excuse about work."

My parents' arrival is not ideal, but other than the fact that Sophie is stressed about meeting them, I've warmed to the idea. My parents are cool, and the house, as Sophie mentioned earlier, is large. We'll still have time alone, and with my parents traveling now as much as they do, I'll admit, it will be nice to catch up with them.

She searches my eyes and her face softens.

"No," she shakes her head, "that's silly."

"I think we can still have fun here, but I want you to feel comfortable."

"I know. Thank you."

My effort to help put her at ease is thwarted when her eyes suddenly widen in alarm. "Are they going to tell Hannah?"

"No. I already asked them not to." I don't mention that Hannah already knows. Even without telling her outright, my necklace purchase confirmed I'm still seeing Sophie some capacity.

She pulls away and drops onto the bed.

"Ugh," she groans, "I think telling them not to tell is worse, because then they know there's a reason why we don't want people to know, and that makes it even more suspicious."

"Is that a true crime theory?" I grin.

She levels me with a glare.

"I explained that you're part of Hannah's wedding planning team and that to keep things professional, we'd like to keep our relationship quiet until after the wedding."

She shoots up off the bed.

"After the wedding? That's a year away! Surely, they don't expect us to still be together then?"

I drop to sit on the edge of the bed, my elbows resting on my knees while I look down at my hands.

"Honestly, I don't think they have any expectations for me and a woman I'm seeing. They've given up on me settling down."

I look up to find she's stopped pacing, and her face has softened. "Does that upset you?"

"It's a product of my own creation, so I can't be too upset."

Sophie steps closer, her hands find my shoulders while mine move to the backs of her thighs, loving the feel of the smooth skin under my fingertips.

"I don't think it's fair to put someone in a category and expect them to stay there. Isn't that what life is about? Growing? Changing?"

"Yeah, I agree."

"That's what I'm currently going through with Griffin. He's still in parent mode and I'm trying to live my own life."

I smile up at her. "He's a protective big brother. I don't know that you grow out of that."

"Do you still feel that way about Hannah?"

"It's different. I never had it as a full-time role like Griffin did. At this point, it's probably a reflex for him. It will take time to untrain himself."

"Have you talked to him about me?" she asks.

"Not exactly. He mentions you and loves to tell everyone at the office what you're up to. It's very informative."

"Oh, really?" Her lips quirk and brows lift.

Sophie catches me off guard, moving to straddle me. I easily fall back on the bed and bring my hands to her hips. Her cutoff jean shorts expose her long legs and I can't stop myself from running my palms up and down her thighs.

"This is one of my favorite views." My fingertips tease under the hem of her shorts, exploring the crease of her hip before moving to grip the flesh of her ass.

"Enjoy it. This is as much action as you're going to get in this bed."

"So, you'll be sneaking into my room later?" I wink at her.

She shakes her head, but when I use my grip on her hips to grind her down onto my erection, a strangled moan escapes her throat.

"Come on, Sophie. Let me feel you. I bet you're so fucking wet for me." I grind up into her, loving teasing her this way.

She leans forward, changing the angle of her center over my hard cock. I know she's enjoying the friction on her clit. Her long hair falls over her shoulders, creating a curtain around our faces. Sophie drops her lips to mine, her tongue licks into my mouth and I think I've won. Only for her to pull away a moment later.

"We're not having sex with your parents downstairs."

When she climbs off me and returns to unpacking, I groan.

I shift onto my side to prop my head in my hand and watch her. Sure, I'm disappointed. I always want her. But two days with Sophie, even without sex, still sounds pretty damn good.

CHAPTER 25

Sophie

After we unpacked, Hunter handed me a glass of wine and guided me to the screened-in back porch where there's a sitting area with oversized chairs. The cloud-like chairs with supportive cushions and matching ottomans to prop your feet on have been perfectly placed to watch the sun drop behind the endless trees surrounding the pristine lake.

As instructed, I'm trying to relax, but seeing Hunter interact with his parents is doing funny things to me.

As I watch him talking and joking with his dad while they tend to the grill, I realize it's because most of the time Hunter and I have spent together has been alone. I mean, that's the point of having a secret, strictly-sexual relationship as most of the time spent together is in bed, a random dark alcove, or private rooftop, but seeing the way he smiles and laughs with his dad is adorable. The ease of the moment feels like the most natural thing in the world. And when he turns to find me staring at him over the edge of my wine glass and winks, I feel the immediate need to get up and change my underwear.

I'm quickly regretting my no-sex rule for the weekend.

But then Hunter's mom drops down in the chair next to

mine, and I remember why I wanted to be on my best behavior. Kathryn Cartwright is a vision. I see where both Hunter and Hannah get their thick and lustrous shampoo-commercial hair. The only difference being her dark strands are elegantly highlighted with gray.

"This is perfect. Now we can have some girl time." She smiles and raises her wine glass toward mine to cheers.

I clink her glass and take a sip.

"Hunter said you're a wedding planner."

"Assistant," I correct her. "Intern, technically. But yes, I'm working at Marion Adler Events."

"And you're part of the team working on Hannah's wedding? That's how you two met?"

"Um—"

"Mom, this isn't an interrogation." Hunter's watching us across the deck, his eyes quietly checking in with me.

"I want to get to know Sophie. If she's here, she's obviously caught your attention and held it long enough to make the four-hour drive."

I think Kathryn is kidding about her son's attention span, it's a friendly jab, but it is a reminder of Hunter's history with women. She doesn't realize the unique thing about me is that unlike women of Hunter's past, I'm not trying to land him. Although we're spending a few days together over the holiday weekend, we're casual. And if they hadn't shown up, there was going to be a lot of sex. That's why Hunter invited me here, with the prospect of two uninterrupted days tangled up in the sheets.

That's not going to happen now. Not if I want to look Marshall and Kathryn in the eye tomorrow at breakfast.

"We met in Vegas, where I used to live, then reconnected when I moved to the city." I keep it vague, leaving out all the ways we reconnected: our unexpected run-in at Hannah's wedding planning lunch, and then our bathroom tryst at Premier's dinner party.

"That's nice." She adjusts her necklace while taking a sip of wine. "Is your family in Las Vegas?"

"My brother recently moved to New York City, too. It's just us. Our mom died twelve years ago in a car accident and I never met my dad."

I'm not ashamed of my circumstances. They've shaped who I am, my drive to be successful and determination to be independent. Does it suck to not have parents? Of course. But I think everything happens for a reason and the life I have now is because of everything I've gone through in my childhood.

But I also know that I confidently tell people my complete backstory because it's a defense mechanism. I use it as a shield. *Here's my damage, folks! Your move.*

My eyes are glued to Kathryn, waiting for her to react.

"I'm sorry." Her lips drop in the corners, her small smile now filled with sympathy, but among the sympathy in her blue eyes, there's understanding. "My own mother passed when I was ten. She struggled with her mental health for many years before that."

"Oh," the shock of Kathryn's own circumstances causes the single word to escape. "I'm so sorry."

"It was a long time ago, but it shaped my life as I'm sure your mother's passing has shaped yours."

I take Kathryn in with a new set of eyes. It's as if we belong to a club, not one that anyone wants admittance to, but a sisterhood of sorts nonetheless, and it drops my guard.

To hear that someone like Kathryn had a similar family situation growing up is surprising. On the outside, she looks perfect. From what I know, she and Marshall have had a successful marriage while they built a multibillion-dollar company. You'd never guess that she grew up any differently than the beautiful life she's living now.

"It's hard to grow up as a woman without a mom. My dad did an amazing job, but there've been many moments in my life where I needed a woman's advice or perspective. And whether Hannah likes it or not, I've been determined to be that person for her. The mom I didn't have."

"She's lucky to have you." I smile. "That's how I feel about my brother. He's been the best role model, but there have been things I have struggled to talk to him about. Woman things."

Kathryn's smile softens. "If you ever need anything, I'm here."

"Thank you."

It's kind of her to offer, but the second I let it sink in, I know it would be a terrible idea to get attached to Hunter's mom. To anchor myself to anyone that could so easily leave my life. *Like Hunter*.

Kathryn asks me more questions about my job and how I like living in the city compared to Las Vegas. The conversation is easy. Ten minutes in and I've forgotten how anxious I was about being here with her and Hunter's dad.

Dinner is delicious, grilled garlic shrimp with grilled veggies and a salad.

I offered many times to help, but Hunter and his dad prepared everything while his mom and I chatted on the porch with the sunset showing off in the distance.

After dinner, we all start cleaning up.

"You want to go for a walk?" Hunter asks.

"Yeah, but let's help your parents clean up first."

Marshall waves us on. "We got this. You go on."

"Thanks, Dad," Hunter says, guiding me toward the back door.

Once the sun set, it cooled off and I switched out my denim shorts for a pair of jeans.

By the back door, I pull on my sweatshirt, then follow Hunter outside and along the side of the house. With the sun gone, dusk is settling around us, making everything hazy. I expect him to head toward the asphalt driveway, but instead, he motions me toward a worn path through the trees. Inside the trees, fireflies blink around us.

"Is this a ploy to have your way with me in the woods?" I ask.

He chuckles, then loops a finger through one of the belt loops on my jeans and uses it to pull me toward him. "Do you want it to be?"

The two glasses of wine I've had is enough to let my desire for Hunter jump into the driver's seat. I wrap my arms around his neck and pull him down for a kiss. His tongue battles with mine and his hands grip my ass, pulling me closer until I can feel his erection against my stomach. I'm a moment away from asking him to fuck me against a tree when he pulls back.

"Come on, I want to show you something."

I'm about to make a joke that I've already seen his dick when he takes my hand and pulls me along the trail. I can't see where I'm going, but Hunter holds my hand tight, guiding me through the trees.

He leads me to a tree with a wooden ladder nailed into the trunk. Above us, I can see a wooden platform nestled into the branches with a hole cut out where the ladder enters it.

"Is this your treehouse?" I ask.

"A treehouse would indicate there's a roof, this is more of an open-air experience. Would you like to come up?"

"Only if I can take your mom up on her offer to look through your baby pictures," I tease.

He chuckles. "You have my full support. I was a cute baby."

"Of course, you were." I smirk, but he doesn't see it because he's already moving up the ladder.

When we reach the top of the ladder, Hunter helps me climb out onto the platform. It's everything I expect a half-finished 'tree fort' that's over twenty years old to be. Splintered wood, wobbly railings, covered in debris and bird poop. But when I turn to look out, the view—a star-filled sky reflecting off the lake—is breathtaking. We don't appear to be that high off the ground, but the location of the tree, sitting on top of an incline, gives it a height advantage over the downslope trees.

Hunter does his best to clear a spot on the platform for us to sit. He lowers himself, then pulls me down to sit between his legs. Once seated, our feet dangle over the hole for the ladder, and I lean back into Hunter to look up at the sky.

"Other than being out on the water, this is my favorite spot here," he says.

"I can see why. It's beautiful." Now that I'm used to the constant sounds of the city, I strain to hear anything but the brief, fuzzy notes of katydids. "And so quiet."

"That's why my parents wanted a house here. They wanted to give their city kids the experience of calm and space to run."

Hunter mentioning his parents reminds me of how much fun I had with them tonight.

"Your parents are great."

"Yeah, they are."

I smile because there's no 'but' following his statement. Hunter has a great relationship with his parents, and it's easy to see even after just spending a few hours with them.

"Your dad is pretty chill. For some reason, I imagined him being an uptight guy who would be grilling you about work and the company."

"A year ago, he was far more involved, but I think he's really settled into his retirement. And he trusts me."

"That's great. Your dad mentioned Premier was started as a family business. Did Hannah ever have interest in working there?"

"My dad had the vision, and together, my parents built

Premier with the idea that it would continue with Hannah and me, but Hannah wasn't interested. I think she went to business school hoping it would spark a desire to get involved, but then she ended up starting her jewelry line. That's where her passion lies."

"She's super talented."

"She is. I'm happy that she trusted her gut and is doing something she loves, but I'm also secretly hoping she and James have children that will be interested in carrying on the family business."

"Because you won't?" I ask.

"I don't know. I've never seen that for myself. I've prioritized work and never thought I could get to that place with someone."

It reminds me of our earlier conversation. Hunter thinks he's not husband material, that he's not capable of prioritizing a partner and family, but I think he's selling himself short and it's hard to hear him talk about himself that way. I can tell it's a vulnerable subject for him. A soft spot in an otherwise confident man.

"I think if a wife and family is something you want, you can have it. Don't let your past or what other people think about it affect your future, you know? You don't need anyone else's permission to change your priorities."

His arms tighten around me. "Thank you for saying that."

"Well, I mean it. I don't doubt that you would be an amazing husband and dad. You're thoughtful and sweet, caring and nurturing. Just think of the effort you've put in with me the last few weeks, and we're not even dating."

I meant to use us as an example of Hunter's ability to put time into a relationship, which he has doubted he could, but when I hear the words out loud, I realize he may think I'm reading more into the situation.

"I mean, not that this is that, that you and I are headed in that direction, but I'm sure when it happens for you, you'll know."

He lowers his lips to my ear. "And what about you?"

A shiver runs through me at the warmth of his breath against the shell of my ear.

"What do you mean?" My heart stutters, not sure where he's going with this.

"Have you thought more about running your blog full-time? Converting it into a sustainable wedding planning business like you mentioned?"

"Oh, that. I've been busy with my internship. I'm supposed to start working on my final project soon. The project along with feedback from the other planners will help Marion decide who will get permanent positions in the fall. If I want to land one, I'll need to stand out among the other interns."

"Is that what you want?" he asks.

I'm ready to give a canned response, but the way he's got his arms affectionately wrapped around me, and has shared his own vulnerability tonight, urges me to do the same.

"I don't know. I thought so, but now I'm not sure."

He's quiet and a minute passes. And just when I think he's not going to say anything, he speaks.

"You know the good news?" he asks.

"What's that?"

"You don't have to figure it all out right now."

I give a slight nod. "That's true."

"Neither of us do. We've got time."

I didn't realize the conversation was making me tense, but I notice the moment my body sags in relief at his soothing words.

We've got time.

It feels like his way of telling me he's still content with our arrangement. That while he's contemplating making a change in his personal life, it's not happening now. We can still have some fun together.

"So, what would you do up here?" I ask.

"When Hannah was little, it was my place to escape because she couldn't climb the ladder, but eventually, it became a meetup spot for the all the neighboring kids."

"Did you bring girls up here?" I ask, because teasing Hunter about his past teenage hookups is far less depressing than letting my mind wander to what his future wife might look like.

His hands move under the hem of my sweatshirt and tank top, searching until they settle on the bare skin of my stomach. His warm hand against my belly sparks a familiar ache between my legs, my full attention for his answer diminishing with the dip of his pinky finger below the waistband of my jeans.

"Only you."

He presses a kiss to my head.

Hunter has been lighthearted and easygoing, everything a casual fling should be, but I'm noticing a more serious side of him. He's still sweet and teasing one moment, rough and dirty-mouthed the next, but there's a new layer emerging. It's like a secret passageway has opened in front of me. A place he's never let anyone see. The uncharted space has me feeling both intrigued and uncertain, wondering if I enter, will I be able to find my way out? And what if I never want to?

We sit quietly for a few minutes, the darkness closing in around us before Hunter suggests we climb down. I'm halfway down the ladder when he reaches for me, strong hands on my hips steadying me until I'm safely on the ground.

Silently, he takes my hand and we keep moving on the path until we reach a clearing that leads to another house. It's as large as the Cartwrights' home, but doesn't appear to be as kept. The yard is slightly overgrown, and even in the dark, I can tell the white-paneled siding needs a fresh coat of paint.

"The Davenports' place is on the other side of ours. Colette Davenport is the dancer I mentioned at the ballet. She's good friends with Hannah."

"You all spent summers here together?" I ask.

"Yeah, all the parents were friends, playing cards and lawn games, while the kids ran around getting into trouble together."

"Who lived here?" I point to the white house.

"The Spencers. Rhys was a good friend."

"Was? What happened to him?" I ask.

"Rhys's parents died in a boating accident when he was twelve. His grandparents sent him to boarding school and we lost touch over the years. I think he's in Paris now. He's been traveling all over the world."

"That's horrible about his parents. I can relate with my mom, but it sounds like he has a nice life now. Traveling the world sounds fun."

"I don't know if he travels because it's fun or because he's restless and unhappy."

Hunter wraps his arm around my shoulders and pulls me in for a kiss.

"Should we head back?" he asks.

I nod and let him lead me toward the path.

Inside the house, we part ways at the guest bedroom door. I can tell Hunter still thinks I'm being ridiculous but I give him a quick kiss goodnight before disappearing inside to get ready for bed.

I slip between the cool sheets and settle in. Earlier, I felt tired, but now that I'm lying here, my brain is awake. After an hour of tossing and turning, I throw back the covers.

I make my way down the hall, push open Hunter's door, and tiptoe to his bed. I expected him to be asleep, but he pulls back the covers, inviting me in. I slide in next to him and against his warmth.

"We're not having sex," I remind him and myself.

"That leaves a lot of other options on the table."

Hunter shifts me beneath him, bracketing his forearms around my head.

"I've never had a girl in my bed here before."

Hunter's fingers tease the strap of my tank top off my shoulder and his lips replace it.

"Seriously?"

"You heard my mom. I've never brought a woman here. I always considered it a place for family and didn't want to bring anyone that was temporary here."

His lips ghost along my collarbone. It's featherlight, teasing. It makes me want more.

I guess you broke that rule with me.

Hunter lifts his head from my chest. Even in the darkness, I can see his sharp features, the way his eyes look at me intently. And for a moment, I'm wondering if I said the words out loud. If he somehow heard my thought or if he's having a similar one.

I'm expecting him to palm my breast, to tease my nipple between his fingers, some action that will push us toward orgasms even if we're not having sex, but instead, he lowers his lips to mine in a sweet kiss before dropping back to the mattress and pulling my back into his chest, one muscular arm wrapped around my midsection to hold me firmly to him.

"Goodnight, Sophie." His warm breath tickles the hair on my neck as his lips press against my shoulder. Internally, I consider if I should have even come to his room. We've cuddled before, but only briefly after sex. I'm not against cuddling in general, but I wonder if these tender moments with Hunter are starting to confuse what we're doing. If they're starting to confuse me.

My body easily settles in next to Hunter. Unlike my head, it's not confused. It's relaxed and never wants to leave.

I push the unwanted thought away and inhale a deep breath, letting myself relish Hunter's embrace. It's like shoveling down your favorite meal until you realize it's eventually going to be gone, so you try to savor the last few bites. I fall asleep in his arms determined not to think about the moment when feeling his strong arms around me is no longer an option.

CHAPTER 26

Hunter

I find my mom out on the screened-in porch, a mug of coffee between her hands, and a book on the table beside her. Before she assisted my dad in building the powerhouse real estate development company that is Premier Real Estate, she graduated from Columbia with an English Literature degree and dreamt of teaching high school English. Then, I came along and my parents decided together it was best for her to stay home with me. She's still an avid reader and has used her money and social standing to help with many literacy charities in New York City and beyond.

"How'd you sleep?" she asks.

"Great. You?"

"I always sleep well here. It's so peaceful." She takes a sip of her coffee, and I do the same. "How did Sophie sleep?"

"She wouldn't want me to tell you that I know the answer to that question." I can't help the smile that spreads over my face, then I add, "She's still sleeping."

Her eyes crinkle at the corners and I can tell she knows what I'm getting at.

"Happy looks good on you."

My lips twitch. "Is that your subtle way of saying you like Sophie?"

"I didn't say it was because of Sophie. That was your inference."

That's what she says, but her knowing smile gives it away.

"So, you're not going to ask me about her?"

"I don't want to jinx it."

"Jinx what?" I ask.

"Exactly."

I chuckle. "I expected you to have more to say about it."

"What more is there to say? Watching you two together is like remembering the early days with your father."

"She's younger." I throw out the bait, wondering if my mom will take it.

"I noticed, but that's not the end of the world, is it?"

Based on my history, my mom is operating under the assumption that I'd be the one with an issue around the relationship. She doesn't know that we have an agreement to keep things casual, that Sophie has her own reasons for not wanting anything serious right now.

I recall my and Sophie's conversation last night about the future. About getting married and having a family. She was encouraging that I shouldn't rule those things out, but in the same breath, it felt like she was making sure I knew it wouldn't be with her. It's hard to tell if she said that because she couldn't imagine those things with me or because she still views us as temporary. She wants those things, too, but is on a different timeline.

"I don't know," I finally answer.

She gives me a knowing smile. "Above everything else, I'm glad you've found someone you enjoy spending time with. That's important in life and I've always wanted you to see that."

I nod. "Thanks, Mom."

Leaving her to read her book, I go back inside.

After a run down to Million Dollar Beach, we take the boat to fill up with gas. When a light rain shower pushes us inside in the afternoon, I delight Sophie with the Independence Day-themed cookie decorating kit I picked up before we left the city.

Sophie teases me when her cookie looks far better than a four-year-old's on her first try, but then she's amazed by how mine turn out, pouting because she already ate hers and mine are too pretty to eat.

After dinner, we're getting ready to go out on the boat again when I pull Sophie into my lap on my bed. I hold the necklace box between us. Her eyes lift from the box to mine.

"What's this?" she asks.

"It's for you."

She reaches forward to open the box, her eyes lighting with surprise when she sees what's inside.

"Hunter," she whispers. "Oh my gosh. It's the necklace from Hannah's boutique. The one I tried on the night of her opening party." She lifts it out of the box. "It's even prettier than I remember."

I set the box aside and help her fasten it around her neck. The small pendant settles into the hollow of her neck. I lean forward, kissing her there.

"Do secret fuck buddies buy each other gifts?" she asks, toying with the pendant.

I shrug. "I was at Hannah's store and I saw it and thought of you, that's all."

She wraps her arms around my neck. "Thank you. I love it."

"You're welcome."

I stand, lifting her with me. Her legs wrap around my waist and I cup her ass. Our kiss turns heated until my dad's knock on the door lets us know it's time to head out on the boat for the fireworks and has Sophie squirming out of my arms.

We drive the boat out to the center of the lake where traditionally hundreds of boats anchor for the firework display.

Sophie's chilly in her sundress, so I wrap a blanket around her and hold her close. Her blonde hair is wavy and wild from the high humidity and letting it dry naturally, and her signature scent of citrus and spice lingers in the air.

After the show, we pull the boat back into the slip and my parents unload. I'm on the dock, holding Sophie's hand to help her off when she pulls on my hand.

"Wait," she says.

Even in the dark, I can see her eyes shimmering with lust. The way her tongue darts out to lick her bottom lip.

"We'll put the cover on," I call to my parents' retreating backs. My mom gives a half wave above her shoulder. The two glasses of wine and all the fresh air has my mom curling into my dad's side.

I hop back in the boat. After Sophie watches my parents disappear up the wooden staircase to the house, she turns to me and wraps her arms around my neck.

"I still stand by the whole not having sex with your parents in the house, but I was thinking," she lifts her eyebrows, "this isn't the house."

"No, it isn't." My lips pull into a wide smile. My dick is already doing cartwheels against my zipper.

Blanketed in the darkness of the night sky, I let my hands lift the back of her dress and find the waistband of her thong. A quick pull and the loose scrap of material is a puddle around her ankles.

I move to kiss her, but she pushes me backwards until the back of my legs hit the bench seat on the boat's side. Sophie steps out of her underwear and follows, quickly climbing over my lap. After all the touching and lingering stares from the past two days, we're like a pot that's about to boil over.

"Get your cock out, Hunter," she says between searing kisses. Her fingers pull at my hair. Fuck. I really thought I could make it the two days without fucking her, but I need her right now like I need oxygen.

The moment is a flurry of wet kisses and impatient hands as we work to free my erection. Then I'm practically growling as I search for the condom in my wallet. I've had to put a new one in multiple times since Sophie and I have been together. Our tendency for impromptu sex makes it necessary to always be prepared.

I'm going to lose my mind if I didn't replace it. But then I find it tucked beneath my driver's license and yank it out.

A moment later, Sophie lowers onto my sheathed cock. The second I'm deep inside her, it's like a sigh of relief.

She feels incredible. I immediately start wondering what it would be like to thrust into her with nothing between us. I'm already addicted to her, there's no way I'd be able to get her out of my system if I knew what that felt like. Just the thought of releasing my orgasm deep inside her, filling her up with my come threatens to end this moment quickly.

Sophie moans, slowly lifting her hips before settling back down on me. "Why did it feel like I was going to lose my mind if you didn't fuck me?"

"I feel the same." My palm finds her cheek, guiding her face back to mine. This time, our kiss is slow and searching. Now that we're fused together beneath Sophie's dress, I'm not eager to reach our release.

I let Sophie set the pace and it gives me a second to calm down.

"Hunter. *Oh, God.*"

"That's it. Ride me, sweetheart." I lift the skirt of her dress above her hips so I can see where we're joined. "I love watching my cock disappear inside you."

I can already feel her tightening around me.

Fuck. I won't be able to hold on much longer. I slip my hand between us to massage her clit. As my fingers work over her, they brush over the base of my cock. I feel where

Sophie's spread around me, where I'm splitting her open, and how wet she is.

"I need you with me, sweetheart."

"I'm so close." She moans. "Don't stop."

"I won't. Not until you come for me."

I nip her earlobe, then suck the soft flesh between my teeth.

"Let me feel you, baby."

Two more strokes and Sophie's muscles are squeezing me so fucking tight. I savor the pulsing sensation of her tight pussy around my cock before I follow, my orgasm exploding deep inside her.

When we get back to the house, Sophie doesn't bother to pretend that she's sleeping in the guest room. After changing into her pajamas and brushing her teeth, she slips under the covers and curls into my side.

"What time do we need to leave tomorrow?" she asks.

"After breakfast would be good. I've got some work to catch up on when we get back to the city."

"Okay." She adjusts her head against my chest, finding her spot. I sweep her hair behind her shoulder and let my fingers trail along her arm.

"Did you have fun this weekend?" I ask.

Sophie's legs tangle between mine. For how difficult it has been to get her to cuddle with me, I've found when she does, she's like a koala hugging a tree, wrapping herself around every part of my body.

"Yes. Did you?"

"Despite your no-sex rule, I had the best time."

Sophie laughs. "I did attack you on the boat."

"If you couldn't tell, I liked it. A lot." Gooseflesh appears beneath my fingertips as I trail my fingers up her bare arm. "And it was fun to hang out with my parents."

"Your parents are sweet."

"My mom adores you."

"Yeah?" It's a question, but Sophie smiles knowingly. "We did bond over our love of plants and true crime podcasts."

Finding out my mom is an avid true crime podcast listener as well was surprising, but I liked that she and Sophie had plenty to talk about.

In the morning, after breakfast, I load the car, then we hug my parents goodbye.

Watching my mom embrace Sophie as they discuss the care of the plant my mom has propagated for her, I know it's one of those significant life moments that will cement itself in my memories. A core memory. My brain captures the picture perfectly, etching in every detail. It's one that will be available for playback for years to come.

It's also the instant I realize that I'm not nervous that my parents will get attached to Sophie and I'll have to let them know it didn't work out between us. That my commitment to work and my inability to prioritize a relationship has gotten in the way of giving them a daughter-in-law and future grandchildren, but that Sophie could be the one to decide at any moment that we're done and I'd hate it. I'm not anywhere near done with her. This is only the beginning.

CHAPTER 27

Sophie

"I've got a whole day planned," Hunter announces from the bathroom.

My body is exhausted from work. My feet ache. My back aches. Even my boobs ache. I palm myself under the covers. They did bounce a lot last night. And Hunter did grip them hard when he was taking me from behind.

He appears with a towel wrapped around his waist. His dark hair is wet and one stray longish piece on top flops over his forehead in the most adorable curl. I don't bother to hide my stare when he drops his towel to pull on his boxer briefs and shorts. I'm checking out the way his back muscles contract with every move as he pulls on a t-shirt. I pout when the shirt hides my view, but then I'm appreciating how much I love to see his strong arms pressing against the sleeves of his shirt.

"Is it lying in bed all day?" I ask.

"No." He laughs. "It'll be more things to check off your tourist list."

"Or maybe we should stay here and I could check off some unexplored territory." I slide my hand between us to palm him through his shorts.

"Tempting, but no." He presses a kiss to my jaw, then playfully swats my ass through the covers. "Get up. We've got reservations."

"Fine." I toss the covers back, exposing my nude body.

Hunter is halfway out the bedroom door when he jerks his head back toward me. His blue eyes zero in on my breasts. When I let my knees fall open, exposing myself to him, his eyes darken and his jaw ticks. I watch as his grip on the door-frame tightens, turning his knuckles white.

"We're going," he growls, and I'm not sure if he's talking to me or himself.

"Made you look," I call, when he finally continues out the door.

I shower and get dressed. Brush my teeth and curl my hair.

When I'm ready, we leave Hunter's apartment hand in hand and walk toward Zucker's Bagels where he orders my bagel sandwich, exactly how I like it.

"What if I wanted something different today?" I ask. "Like the everything bagel with veggie cream cheese and avocado."

He smiles down at me, his warm palm rubbing slow circles against my lower back. "Did you want that instead?"

His touch is comforting. Maybe that's the problem. Our time together is getting too comfortable.

And after our weekend at Lake George, it feels like something has shifted between us.

This week, when I told June about my weekend away, we continued our 'dating' debate. She was firmly in the *'that's what dating is'* camp while I determinedly argued against it.

When I informed her our weekend together was intended to be a two-day sex marathon that got preempted by his parents showing up, she threw up her hands.

You met his parents?!

Accidentally, I'd argued.

She shook her head in disbelief, then sighed. *That is the*

furthest thing from no-strings attached I've ever heard. That's like all the strings.

After that, I didn't bother to mention the necklace he'd given me.

Now, he's being sweet and ordering my bagel just how I like it. I should swoon, but my head is a mess of confused thoughts. Not to mention, my tired, achy body just wants food while my emotions are egging on my mouth to start a fight. There's no sense to it, but I can't stop myself.

"No, but you didn't ask."

He presses a kiss to my temple. It's become a familiar gesture. His way of comforting me when I'm stressed.

Is that a thing now?

"Okay. I'll ask next time."

His response is annoying.

My brain hits the panic button. "Next time?!"

"You love Zucker's Bagels, I'm sure there will be a next time."

I don't know why, but this moment feels unsettling.

"Is this our thing now?" I huff. "Breakfast dates to Zucker's Bagels?"

Hunter's brows lift. "It's just bagels."

His reaction tells me that maybe I'm overthinking this.

I eat my bagel and immediately feel less grumpy. I must have been hangry.

"What else are we doing on this non-date?" I ask as Hunter leads me down the street. Rockefeller Center comes into view. We've already been to Top of the Rock, so I'm curious what he has planned. That's when I notice a rink below, not made of ice, but a smooth surface that people are roller skating on.

"You'll see," he says. Inside the rink entrance, Hunter retrieves a box from a worker there. "You're going to need these." He hands the box to me.

Inside the square white box, I find the prettiest pair of

lace-up roller skates in sparkly rose gold. They're the skates of my eight-year-old self's dreams. And really my twenty-two-year-old self, if we're being honest. They're perfect.

"Ahh! These are so pretty!" I gasp holding up a skate to take in all its dazzling shimmer.

Hunter smiles and presses a kiss to my lips. I'm elated to receive the skates and overwhelmed by all the planning he's done.

"Do you skate?" I ask, watching him open a second box and pull out a pair of men's black roller skates.

He shrugs. "I'm an athlete, how hard can it be?"

We move to a bench outside the rink where I pull on my new skates and tie the laces. They fit perfectly and look even better on than they did in the box. Eager to try them, I roll over to the rink's entrance, then skate out onto it. I haven't skated in a long time, but it's like riding a bike and it comes back to me quickly. I've managed to find my footing and am easily rolling around the rink backwards when Hunter moves out to join me.

He's two pushes onto the rink when he wipes out, landing hard on his ass.

"Oh, shit." Quickly, I skate over to him. "Are you okay?"

"Let's just say my ass isn't the only thing that is bruised."

I grab his hands and help pull him up.

"This is a lot harder than I thought it was going to be," he says.

"It's about balance and keeping your weight over your feet."

I watch him take smaller movements this time, all his bravado gone.

"Bend your knees, don't lock them."

He looks like Frankenstein, holding his arms straight out in front of him for balance. I press my lips together to keep from laughing. There's something about this gorgeous, and usually overly confident, man now cautiously moving around the skating rink. It's endearing to know that Hunter Cartwright, CEO, billionaire, and overall self-assured man, has a weak point.

I keep ahold of his hands and skating backwards, I lead him around. As we move, Hunter's body starts to relax.

His gaze drops to my legs. "I didn't think watching you skate would be this big of a turn on."

"Yeah?"

After a few laps around, Hunter is feeling more confident, so I drop his hands and fall into place beside him. He immediately grabs my hand.

"You're doing great," I assure him.

"I know, but I like holding your hand." He presses our palms together and a swarm of butterflies take flight in my stomach.

"This reminds me of middle school and skating around the rink with the boy I liked."

"In this case, would I be that boy?"

"No, you're his inappropriately older brother who I'm secretly crushing on."

"Scandalous." He wiggles his brows and shoots me a devilish grin. "And you're the girl I'd attempt ridiculous stunts for, trying to impress you with my athletic prowess."

Hunter drops my hand to skate ahead of me. Once he's got space, he moves one leg out to the side to spin in a circle and face me. My hands are posed for clapping at his performance, but when he pushes off to start skating again, he loses his balance and falls flat on his ass.

My breath hitches in distress before skating over to check on him.

"Are you okay?" I ask, concerned.

When he starts laughing loudly, I sigh in relief. I reach out my hand to help him up.

He takes my hand, but when I give him a pull upward, he

yanks me down to him instead. My body is now crushed against his.

"Don't be fooled, gorgeous. This is all part of the plan." He winks.

"What plan?"

"To make you fall for me."

I groan. "Oh God, if the women of New York City knew what a cheeseball you really are, they wouldn't be chasing after you."

His hand slides behind my neck, his thumb tracing my jaw.

"It's a good thing you're the only one I care about."

I want to laugh off his comment as lighthearted and just over-the-top flirtation, but when he pulls my face down for a kiss, the only thing I taste is sincerity. It makes my stomach flutter with nerves.

For a moment, I lose myself in his kiss, but then I remember where we are and pull back.

"Should we go?" I ask, trying to gain control of the situation.

"Yeah, we've got another stop."

We manage to untangle ourselves and stand up. After we take off our skates and Hunter arranges for them to be returned to his condo, I let him take my hand and lead me away from Rockefeller Center.

To make you fall for me.

I think about Hunter's words, and joking or not, he has no idea how close I am to that happening.

CHAPTER 28

Hunter

I lock the oars into place and stretch out my legs before pulling Sophie into my lap.

"I forgot how peaceful it is out here."

"It's beautiful." Sophie tilts her head up toward the sun and closes her eyes. She takes in a deep breath, then exhales, her body relaxing further into mine. "Thank you for bringing me," she whispers.

"Thank you for wearing this dress." I glide my hand up her thigh and under the hem of her dress.

"It's a skort." She flips up the skirt to reveal shorts underneath.

"Bummer," I say, pressing a kiss to her neck. "I was hoping for easy access."

"There's no way you would finger me on a rowboat in the middle of Central Park."

I smile down at her wickedly, telling her that's exactly what I would do. She just shakes her head and laughs.

"I don't think you know the power your pussy wields."

"Ah, so is this the part where you serenade me?"

"That's more a gondola in Venice thing, but I can try." I start singing a late nineties' Boys II Men ballad off key loudly.

I only get a few words out when Sophie reaches her hand up and presses it to my mouth.

"You're ruining the moment."

I lick her palm and she squeaks.

"Aren't you supposed to be the older, more mature one?" She looks at me pointedly.

"I like licking you."

"*Hmm.*" Her lips twitch, but it's impossible to miss the way her neck flushes.

She moves off my lap to take in the scenery, so I reach into the picnic basket to pull out a container of grapes.

"Are you going to feed me grapes?" she asks.

"No, I'm going to toss them at you and see if you can catch them in your mouth."

I pop one straight into the air, then lean forward to catch it in my mouth.

"All right, let me try." Her hands motion for me to toss her a grape. She leans too far forward and it bounces off her nose.

"That was a terrible toss," she pouts.

"That was a superior toss."

She rolls her eyes at me. "Try again."

This time, the grape hits her front teeth and falls into her lap.

"Come on, Sophie," I tease, "I know your oral skills are better than that."

She tosses it back at me with no intention of me trying to catch it in my mouth because it's a line drive.

"Again," she says, motioning toward me.

The look of determination on her face is adorable. I toss another one, and this time she catches it in her mouth.

"Victory!" she cheers, lifting both arms above her head before grabbing the sun hat I brought for her and placing it on her head.

Sophie laughs. Her head tilts back, one hand holds her sun

hat in place while the other presses into her chest. Being here with her, seeing her laugh and smile, it's everything.

A moment later, she's quiet, looking around the lake. "Wow. You're really bringing your A game today."

"I want to make sure I'm holding up my end of the bargain."

I say it teasingly, but the words feel hollow. That's not at all what is happening here, and I know it. It's only been a handful of weeks, but every moment we spend together only makes me eager for more time with her.

I'm used to going after what I want. In business and with women. This arrangement with Sophie was no exception. Realizing I'm falling for her has me feeling off-balance. My confidence and charm are slipping, exposing an unfamiliar sensation…vulnerability.

I turn to glance at Sophie. Her once smiling face is now gaping in horror.

"Hunter," Sophie whispers, her eyes widening at something behind me. "It's Emma. Oh my God, she's going to see you. Us. She's going to see *us*. You have to hide."

Griffin walking in while Sophie was under my desk is one thing, but being caught together on a rowboat in Central Park, I'm far less concerned. Or maybe that's what I want. To get caught. I'd be relieved. I'm tired of sneaking around. And while I'd prefer to talk to Griffin before he sees us together, I know the sooner that we address the issue, the easier it will be for me and Sophie to continue seeing each other.

I don't want to be secret fuck buddies anymore. I want her to be mine.

"Where would you like me to go?" I laugh. "We're in a boat."

"Duck. Or here. Put on my hat." She transfers her wide brim hat to my head.

"I'm not wearing your hat." I take it off and deposit it back on her head.

"Shit. There's Griffin." She folds the brim of her hat to shield her face.

If I thought she looked flustered before, now she's truly panicked.

"Let's not panic. It's going to be fine."

"What are you talking about? If they see us, it's going to be far from fine. How are we going to explain this?" She motions between us. "What are we going to say? That we're taking a break from fucking to get some fresh air?"

She stands. Her head jerks around, like she's looking for an emergency exit.

"Sophie, sit down."

Her eyes narrow at me.

"Don't use your sexy voice right now. This is serious."

She points her finger downward, but the movement causes her to wobble. Her hips shift as her legs attempt to balance in the metal boat.

When she doesn't sit, I stand up to steady her. My hand reaches out to keep her from tipping over, but instead of taking my hand or sitting down, both of Sophie's hands find my chest. I catch her glance over my shoulder at the bridge, then her eyes fall back on me.

I'm not expecting it at all. If I had I would have counter-balanced with my legs. It would have been an easy correction to make. Even though there's not much weight behind it, when Sophie's hands push into my chest, it catches me off guard. A hard shove and I'm falling sideways.

A second later, I'm surrounded by the cool water of Central Park Lake.

~

SOPHIE

I find Hunter in his bathroom. A towel wrapped around his waist, steam from the shower still lingering in the air.

"Hey." I shift on my feet in the doorway. His head is angled down. I can't see his face. Can't gauge his mood.

That's a lie. I can see the tension in his sculpted back and shoulders.

"Hey," he responds, his tone curt.

He doesn't turn around, but I shift sideways and meet his gaze in the mirror. His blue eyes are narrowed, his full lips pulled in a thin line across his face.

"I'm sorry," I say quietly.

He wipes his hands on the hand towel, then tosses it on the counter.

"You pushed me in the fucking lake, Sophie."

Everything about his body language says stay away, but I slowly move toward him anyway. I care about Hunter, and I want things between us to go back to the way they were. We forgot what we were doing. We need to put the 'secret' back in 'secret fuck buddies.' Avoid picnics in the park. Stick to dark alcoves and private rooms.

"I know. I saw Emma, and then my brother, and I panicked. I'm so sorry."

"Fuck, Sophie. This has got to stop."

My stomach nosedives at Hunter's response. He's done. With me? With us?

"We should tell Griffin about us."

If the thought of Hunter ending things wasn't distressing enough, a fresh wave of panic surges through me with the thought of telling Griffin about us. I pull back my hands, putting space between us.

"Tell him what?" I ask incredulously. Because honestly, I don't know what I would say to Griffin. "That we're sleeping together? I'm sure that's what every big brother wants to hear about his sister. That I'm fucking his boss. His *friend.*"

"I think you know it's more than that." There's a growl to Hunter's voice. I can see the frustration in his eyes, see it in the tick of his jaw.

I swallow thickly. He's right. There is more here. A lot more than I'm ready to admit.

Emotions war within me. This is exactly what I was afraid of when Hunter and I made this arrangement. Getting in too deep. Having it affect my relationship with Griffin. There's no way that Griffin finding out about me and Hunter won't change things between us. The fact that we've been sneaking around behind his back isn't going to go over well. I'm not ready for the fallout from that.

"But we decided that's all it would be, right?" There's a plea in my voice.

"Is this even about Griffin working at my company? Or is that an excuse?" He lifts his brows in question.

"We agreed, just sex. That's all I could commit to. You were happy with that. Ecstatic! Remember? Why are you trying to complicate it now?"

"You pushed me in the lake to avoid being seen with me. How is that not complicated?" His face softens. "What happens between you and me will never affect Griffin's career."

I nod, acknowledging Hunter's statement.

I know he's telling the truth. That he would keep us separate from work and Griffin, but my concerns aren't only about my brother.

Hunter is starting to overwhelm my thoughts, my dreams, my very being. I'm already teetering on the edge of something dangerous—giving him my heart.

I'm not prepared for that.

Keeping limits on our relationship was the plan. What's the point of a plan if you're going to throw it out the window and fly by the seat of your pants? It would be like disregarding the wedding day run sheet and asking the wedding guests what they'd like to do next.

Raise your hand if you'd like us to cut the cake now.

That would be complete chaos.

I'm not sure how to navigate the feelings I'm having for him, but it's impossible to walk away. I don't want to put an end to what we're doing, but I'm desperate to steer us back on course. To buy myself some time to figure out what I want.

So, I focus on the reason we started this secret relationship and let my body take over.

I press my lips against the warm skin of his back while my arms encircle his waist, and my fingers tease where his towel is fastened. "How can I make it up to you?"

He turns slowly. Beneath his towel, I can make out the impression of his thick cock. I lick my lips and lower to kneel in front of him. My hands reach up to part his towel.

Hunter reaches for my wrists.

"Sophie, stop." His words are commanding, but gentle.

"Why?" My heart drops out of my chest.

"Because you're not sucking my dick as an apology."

"What if I want to suck your dick because I like it?" I ask.

He groans and I see the thick bulge beneath his towel jerk in response. But he reaches for me instead, holding me close to him. It isn't a sexy embrace, it's gentle and soothing. Like the way he carried me to the hotel room at The Plaza Hotel a few weekends ago.

As I let his strong arms hold me close, my eyes catch on the towel bar across the room. Hunter's clothes from earlier, wet from the lake, slung over the bar to dry. Seeing his clothes dripping water into a puddle on his bathroom floor snaps something inside me.

I pushed him into the lake. What the hell is wrong with me? Now, I'm trying to suck his dick to apologize. And he's holding me tight, like he doesn't think I'm a lunatic. I squeeze my eyes shut and the tears begin to fall.

"I don't know what's wrong with me. I can't—I can't..." As the tears fall, my chest tightens, making it difficult to breathe and to speak.

"Hey, no. Baby, please don't cry." Hunter holds my head in his hands, his thumbs swipe across my cheeks as the tears attempt to cut a path down my face. Then he wraps his arms around me, holding me to his chest.

"Are y-you m-m-mad at me?" I know I sound ridiculous, but I can't help it. My emotions are all over the place. I feel like an idiot crying in front of him. He wants fun, sexy Sophie. That's what he signed up for. Not some immature crybaby who can't get ahold of herself.

He presses his lips to the top of my head, a deep sigh escaping before he answers. "No, I'm not mad."

For some reason that makes me cry harder, and now I'm a snotty, tear-streaked mess. Hunter lifts me up and carries me to his bed. He unbuttons my skort dress and helps me slip out of it, pulls back the covers and sets me underneath. He leaves, but comes back with boxer briefs on and slips under the covers with me, scooping me into his arms.

He strokes my hair and rubs comforting circles across my back.

Crying feels good, and after a few minutes, my hiccups stop and my breathing starts to even out.

Hunter grabs a tissue off the bedside table and holds it to my nose so I can blow. I can only imagine what I look like. Red, puffy, with makeup sliding down my face.

I pull back, wiping at his chest where I've left tears and mascara.

"I'm sorry. This is not how you wanted the day to end."

"Don't be sorry. Sometimes, you need to let it all out."

He places a soft kiss on my jaw. It's meant to be reassuring and sweet, but the message gets crossed in my brain and my core clenches with desire.

"What can I do to make you feel better?" Hunter asks, smoothing back my messy hair with his hand. His hand continues its way down my arm in a comforting gesture, but his thumb brushes ever so slightly against the side of my breast and it makes me gasp.

My hand slides between us to his crotch. I palm his dick, but he's not rock hard, at least not like he usually is. I can't blame him; I wouldn't be turned on by me right now either. There's a moment of panic. What if this is it? What if our fun and sexy no-strings-attached relationship is over? What if he realizes that?

Under my palm, Hunter's cock starts to grow and I breathe a sigh of relief.

"I want you," I tell him, kissing along his collarbone, up his neck. I lick along his jaw before finding his lips. "Inside me." I sigh. "Now."

"Are you sure?" His indigo eyes search mine. "I don't expect—"

"I need you. *Please*."

He nods before dropping a sweet kiss to my lips. Desperate to increase our pace, I slide my tongue past his lips, deepening our kiss.

He unhooks my bra, then we work to discard my thong and his briefs.

When Hunter's tongue circles my nipple, my back bows off the bed. My hand reaches out to stop the torture.

"Too sensitive," I tell him, pulling his face upward, toward mine.

A moment later, his fingers dive between my legs. Two thick fingers easily pressing inside me tells me how slick I am. His fingers pass through my center again, his gaze drops between my thighs where his fingers are covered in my wetness.

"Fuck, Sophie. You're soaked, sweetheart."

"I know. Hunter, now. Hurry." I pushed him in the lake now I'm demanding he fuck me. I don't even recognize myself right now.

He grabs a condom from the drawer.

Seconds later, he's sliding in slow and deep. *Thank God.* His dick is like a soothing balm to the ache between my thighs.

"Yes." I pant. I want so badly to get lost in him right now. For him to spank me, tease me, fuck me so hard I can't think anymore.

But Hunter doesn't do any of that. He rocks into me, slow and gentle. His strong arms holding me to him as he rolls his hips to find that perfect place inside me.

I want to be annoyed, but then I'm coming and it's so good, I nearly start crying again.

"*Sophie.*" He groans his release inside me.

We lie there, breathing hard even though we were barely moving. Then, Hunter pulls back, his eyes on my face. His fingers trace a line down my jaw, his thumb lightly grazing my bottom lip.

It feels different. Something is different between us. The panic I felt earlier comes rushing back.

"Sophie, I—" Hunter starts, but when his phone buzzes on the nightstand, he pauses and pulls out of me. "I'll be in Las Vegas this week."

"Oh, okay." I reach for the sheet to cover myself. I'm not usually modest around Hunter, but the shift in the mood between us has me feeling vulnerable.

"For work. Griffin and I have a meeting to go over the contract deed for Premier's new development there. He's probably mentioned it."

"Yeah. Of course." Knowing Griffin, he did tell me, but my brain hasn't been working as well lately.

Hunter walks into the bathroom to dispose of the condom,

then returns with a damp washcloth. I take a moment to capture his unabashed nakedness, the sexy way his still damp hair is mussed and hanging over his forehead.

He pulls the sheet back, his eyes roaming over my body in appreciation. A small, almost secretive smile on his lips. He dips the washcloth between my thighs and I sigh, the warm cloth and Hunter's gentle touch relaxing me. He sets the washcloth aside and pulls me into his arms.

For a moment, everything feels easy between us again. Then, Hunter speaks.

"While I'm gone this week, I think we should take a break."

My eyes fly open. *What?*

His words are shocking, considering his naked body is pressed against mine, his lips sweetly brushing over my bare shoulder.

"A break?" My brain swirls trying to understand, but I'm even more confused than I was before. My eyes widen. "Like Ross and Rachel 'on a break'?"

He shakes his head, like he knows exactly what I'm talking about.

"No, not like Ross and Rachel. Like two people who are still very much exclusive, but need to take a minute and decide what they want out of this relationship."

"Oh." It's all I can manage after the emotional roller-coaster of a day I'm having.

"You're off work next weekend, right?" he asks.

"Yeah." It's a welcome break after working every weekend for the last month and a half.

"I'll be back late Friday night. We can go for a run Saturday morning."

I give him a small smile and nod.

He's giving us a timeline. And I do love a good timeline.

"I need to get some work done before tomorrow. You want to stay? I can order in dinner."

It sounds perfect, it's what I want to do, but Hunter's right, I need time to think about what I want outside of this moment.

I shake my head. "No, that's okay. I've got some things to do, too."

I roll myself out from beneath him and pull on my clothes, then pack up the overnight bag I brought.

"Hey," he catches my wrist before I can leave. He pulls me into his bare chest. It's quickly becoming my favorite place to be. It's warm and cozy. Smells great. Makes me feel protected and safe. "Have a good week." He presses a soft kiss to my lips.

"You, too," I barely squeak out before I pull away and with the strongest smile I can muster, walk out Hunter's front door.

In the elevator, I clutch my bag to my chest. Is this how the women on *The Bachelor* feel when they pack everything up before a rose ceremony, not knowing if they'll be back again?

I push the thought away.

It's a break. With his travel for work, I wouldn't see him anyway.

When the elevator dings at the lobby, I straighten my shoulders and lift my chin before stepping off.

This week with Hunter out of town will be good, I reassure myself. A break from him will give me some time to figure out what I want. It will help me gain some perspective, because I need it, desperately.

CHAPTER 29

Hunter

In the past, I've enjoyed my visits to Las Vegas. Extravagant dinners, gambling, women. It's all at your fingertips. Being here now, I feel anxious and the only thing I like about Las Vegas is that I found Sophie here.

The Vegas Strip is like a miniature New York City in that it never sleeps. Inside the casinos, it could be five in the morning or five in the evening, there's no way to tell for sure until you step outside.

That's where I find myself, waiting for Griffin so we can go to dinner.

I pull out my phone again to check my messages. There are sixty-two there, but none are the one I want.

"Hey." Griffin appears at my side. "That was a long meeting."

His tie and suit jacket are gone now, just like mine.

"Long meeting. Long day. Long fucking week."

We walk to the curb and get in the car waiting for us there.

I push my fingers through my hair. It's only Wednesday.

"We made progress, though. That's the important thing. I'd be annoyed that we made the trip if it wasn't going well."

There's a ping sound from his phone and he smiles down at it. I'll take one guess as to why he's smiling.

His phone pings again.

"Is that Emma?" I ask.

"Yeah. She's grabbing drinks with some friends."

He shows me the photo of Emma, Chloe and another two women. My chest deflates with disappointment that Sophie isn't in the picture. That I don't get to see her. Hear any kind of update about how she's doing. Then again, it's Wednesday, so she'll be heading to work at The Penrose.

Sunday was a lot for her. The rowboat and the stress that Emma and Griffin might have seen us together. I understand that she didn't want Griffin to find out about us that way, but he needs to know about us if we're going to really do this.

That's what I want.

I think about how close I was to telling her everything. To admitting my feelings and telling her I've fallen for her.

But the sheer panic in her eyes when I stated we were more than fuck buddies held me back.

And when she cried? Fuck. My heart felt like it was being ripped out of my chest.

I didn't know what to do, so I did what she asked. Well, I made love to her, which isn't exactly what she asked since she said 'Fuck me, Hunter,' but that's all I could do. Be gentle and hold her. With her underneath me, I wanted to talk about the scary things, but she was upset and I could see the anxiety behind her expressive green eyes.

So, I didn't push. I suggested a break. And now I'm hoping that giving her some space this week will give her time to think about what she wants, and ultimately, make the decision to tell Griffin about us.

I'm so far gone for her. But there's panic, too, because I've never done this before. A relationship where I see a future.

The break seemed like a good idea at the time, but I hate

the silence. I need to see her, hear her voice, even a text. Anything that would indicate she's still in this with me.

"You okay? You seem like you're stressed. Is it the deal? From my perspective, we're solid."

"No, it's not the deal." My elbows press into my knees, and I let my head drop into my hands. "I miss…" and because I can't say Sophie, I say, "New York."

Griffin chuckles. "Not a Vegas fan? Don't worry, I won't take it personally."

"How is the city for you? And everything with Emma? You good?"

"Yeah. Everything's great." He smiles, then sighs. "Well, if I'm being honest, not everything. You know my sister, Sophie."

"Yeah," I say, trying not to show my personal interest in the subject.

"You've got a younger sister, so I thought you might be able to relate. I don't know. I guess things are just different now. And maybe I'm struggling with the fact that she doesn't need me like she used to. That I was once the parent, and now even though we're still living in the same apartment, I feel like I don't know what's going on in her life. She's career-driven, which is great, but I worry that I fucked up somehow. We're both products of the situation we were in, but I'm wondering if I should have done it differently, you know?"

"That's tough. I can't imagine being responsible for my sister when I was eighteen. Being the parent to a younger sibling. From what I know about Sophie, you did a great job."

He nods. "Yeah, she just pushes herself so hard. She got a second job, waitressing at The Penrose."

"I fucking hate that." Once the words are out, I realize I'm joining in the conversation like I know what is going on in Sophie's life, because I do. But, I shouldn't. "Place." I quickly recover. "Lots of slick Wall Street types hang out there."

"I thought Barrett mentioned you two hanging out there."

"Oh, that was before it became inundated with these twenty-something financiers who use their daddies' black AmEx."

"I didn't like it before, but geez, now you got me even more worried."

Fuck. I don't know how to backtrack, so I decide the best thing to do is ignore my slipup.

"Why'd she get another job?" I ask.

"She wants to move out, live on her own. I get it, but it still scares the shit out of me. I would have felt more comfortable with her living on her own here, but now that we're in New York, it's different."

I don't think this is an invasion of her privacy. It's two brothers talking about their sisters, right? I think about how Sophie would want me to respond to Griffin, too bad it's in direct opposition to how I feel as her man.

"Sophie seems like a strong, independent woman. If she feels like you don't think she can do something, she probably will only push harder to do it. This one time I was—" I cut myself off, remembering my place again.

"What were you going to say?" he asks.

"Just that's my experience with Hannah. Give her space, let her come to you."

That's my tactic this week, anyway. No matter how much it sucks not hearing from Sophie, not knowing how she feels. It could all blow up in my face and she could decide she would rather end things between us.

"Yeah, you're probably right." He nods. "Thanks for listening."

"Sure."

We meet up with the guys from Swinnerton, the construction company that we've slated to do the luxury condo tower project with and enjoy an extravagant five-course meal. After dinner, Jeff and Lance want to continue the evening at a club. Griffin declines so he can return to his room and call Emma. If it were up to me, I'd go back to my hotel room and stare at my phone, willing Sophie to text me back.

But this is part of the business. Before Sophie, I had no problems going out to a nightclub for a few drinks. I was open to having a good time and finding a woman to take back to my room. Hell, that's how Sophie and I met.

It's different now. I only want her. The thought of being with another woman makes my skin crawl.

Not long after we're seated at a VIP table, Jeff, the CEO of Swinnerton, invites a group of women to join us. I'm barely in the mood for work, let alone entertaining a group of women that I have no interest in.

"Should we do shots?" one of the women asks, already pouring herself a vodka drink from our bottle service.

"Shots are always a good way to start the night." Lance, Swinnerton's VP of Marketing, signals to a passing waitress to bring a round of shots.

Jeff and Lance are good guys, they're hard workers, but I also know firsthand that they like to let loose.

I pull my phone out and check my messages for the millionth. Nothing from Sophie.

"What do you do?" the blonde in the short pink dress asks.

I pocket my phone and take a sip of my Manhattan.

"I'm in real estate."

Lance laughs. "That's an understatement. Ladies, you're looking at Hunter Cartwright, the CEO of the largest real estate development firm in the country. Wealthiest one, too." He smirks. "Weren't you named sexiest bachelor in New York City or some shit?"

He's referring to the article that came out a year ago when my father retired and I became CEO.

I think Lance thinks he's helping my game, as if my obsession with my phone is a result of nervousness being around beautiful women and I need him to play wingman.

Jeff leans back on the sofa and studies me. "Wasn't it last time you were here with us that you left with a young blonde?"

I tense at Jeff's mention of Sophie. It was on a night out with them that I met her at this very club.

The blonde moves closer and places her hand on my thigh.

"So, you're into blondes?" Her lips curve into a flirtatious smile, her intentions clear.

My body bristles with her touch. I'm aware that would not have been my reaction a few months ago. But it's that awareness that has me removing her hand and giving it a gentle pat as I place it on the leather seat next to her. I can see the blush on her cheeks at the rebuff.

"I'm with someone."

"No kidding?" Lance holds his glass up toward mine. "Good for you."

When Lance and Jeff's attention turns back to the women, my body immediately relaxes.

I linger for a few more minutes to finish my drink. When I see that Lance and Jeff are settled in and have no desire to talk business any further tonight, I set my empty drink on the table and make my way out of the club.

CHAPTER 30

Sophie

I'm staring at my laptop, willing my brain to start churning out ideas for my internship project, but like any good procrastinator, instead, I click over to my blog. Reading the comment section on my latest post makes me smile.

There's a question about useful wedding party gifts and I click in the box to respond.

Emma drops down on the couch beside me. I finish typing and hit submit.

"How's it going?" she asks, folding her legs beneath her. Her petite body is swimming in one of Griffin's t-shirts and a pair of lounge shorts.

"Okay. No, that's a lie. It's terrible. I've been trying to work on my internship's final project and I'm stuck. This isn't like me. I've always thrived with projects and deadlines, but this feels different, like I can't even start." I set my laptop aside. "Do you ever feel that way? Like you can't get started on a design? Like you've got no ideas?"

Her lips press together as she considers my question.

"Not really. I'm always brimming with design ideas after I meet with a new client."

"Okay. That's not helpful at all." I laugh, but really, I want to cry.

She must hear the stress in my voice.

"But it used to happen. When I was working as a brand ambassador for a designer fashion line and I had to give presentations on brand trends and marketing strategies. I thought I was terrible at my job, but then I realized it was because I wasn't passionate about what I was doing. That's when I knew I needed to make a change. And I started designing, not just as a hobby, but as a career."

I let Emma's words sink in. Isn't she telling me what I already know? What I've felt the past few weeks? That the job I've been determined to land at Marion Adler Events isn't what I actually want.

"And that's when you started Emma Belle Bridal?" I ask.

"No, it was another year of telling myself the brand ambassador job would get better before I finally decided to start my own business. It was terrifying, but I've found, it's doing the scary things that have the most rewarding outcome. Like me and Griffin. I was so scared to tell him how I felt. To be vulnerable and risk rejection, that I almost didn't. But the risk was worth the reward." She smiles and I can tell she's thinking of Griffin. "I try to keep that in mind now when things feel scary."

I consider Emma's advice. It would be so much easier If I could nail this final project presentation and land one of the permanent positions at Marion Adler Events. But easy isn't always the right path.

"I'm still elated your blog will be featured in *Brides* and the issue hasn't even come out yet. That's so freaking cool."

"Thank you. I've been playing with the idea of using my blog to launch a sustainable wedding planning business. Maybe making it an a la carte service or be a consultant."

Her face lights. "I love that idea."

"It's just an idea. I need to be practical. You know, the whole paycheck thing is important."

"That's true. But maybe there's a way to start working toward that business while you have a steady income. You're already doing both right now."

"I know. It's a lot to think about."

"You know you can talk to me about this stuff anytime, right?"

I nod. "Yeah, thanks."

"It's been fun this week. The two of us. I think I've seen you more this week than I have since you moved in." She hesitates for a moment. "Is it because Griffin's out of town that you're around more? I don't want to get in the middle of your relationship, but I know Griffin is feeling like something is off between you two."

"It's not because of Griffin," I assure her.

It's because of Hunter and our break.

I've done everything to keep myself busy this week. To take my mind off Hunter and the fact that we are giving each other space to figure things out.

You know what I've figured out?

I miss him.

Not just the sex.

Him.

And I didn't even need the week to realize that.

Running in Central Park Tuesday morning, I passed by the bench where he massaged my calf and proposed our secret arrangement. There were people all around me, but the trail felt lonely without his sexy grin and witty commentary.

Wednesday night, I ordered in from Osteria Cotta, his favorite Italian restaurant that he introduced me to, and accidentally ordered our usual. Emma ate some, but mostly I devoured the two entrees, then crawled into bed wearing Hunter's Princeton shirt. The scent of him on the worn cotton is fading just like the printed blue letters.

Yesterday, a David Gray song was playing on the car ride to a venue tour and I started crying.

Johnathan kindly gave me his pocket square to blow my nose into.

That's yours now, honey, he'd said when I offered it back.

There's no doubt in my mind that I want to be with Hunter, but the looming conversation with Griffin still sets my stomach a flutter.

I prop my feet up on the ottoman next to Emma's and sigh. But right now, it feels good to relax.

"Do you want to eat a pound of chocolate and binge *Love is Blind*?" She shakes the open bag of Dove dark chocolates in her hand.

"Yes, please." I extend my hand in her direction, palm up.

Emma passes me a piece of chocolate. I unwrap it and pop it in my mouth. So good.

"Are you on your period, too?" she asks, unwrapping another piece of chocolate.

"Um..." I hesitate as my brain registers her question.

My period, my period...my period!

I flip through my mental calendar, struggling to recall what day of the month it is.

"I just know they can sync up when women live together. I'm on birth control, but it can happen sometimes."

"Yeah," I say slowly, still trying to evaluate the situation, "I've heard that, too."

Emma navigates the television to select the show while I pull out my phone and discreetly check my calendar.

Don't panic. Let's just take a little looksee.

I had one in May right before I moved here, and then there was the one in June. It was super light, only a bit of spotting, but I've heard stress can do that and it aligned with my cycle, so I counted it. I count the weeks.

Damn. I should have had it by now.

Oh, fuckity fuck.

My stomach drops, but my brain is still trying to rationalize.

Maybe it's a little late. Due to stress or something. I've had plenty of that lately.

But it's never been this late. I think. I've never counted the days between. It always shows up eventually. I've never had the amount of sex that I've been having with Hunter before either.

But we've always used protection. Even that night in Vegas, under the influence of alcohol, we used condoms because I remember thinking that watching Hunter roll on the condom was one of the hottest things I'd ever seen.

Let's see, I've been moody lately, and hungry and bloated. Those are all premenstrual symptoms. I discreetly Google pregnancy symptoms.

Shit. They're the same.

And there was that bout of sickness I had a month ago, when I first got to the city. I look at the list…morning sickness and nausea.

Oh, God.

I bolt up and off the couch, my night of relaxation ruined.

"Actually, I've got a thing."

"A thing?" she questions, a piece of chocolate inches from her lips.

"A friend wants to meet up."

"Oh, okay. No worries." Emma smiles. "But don't forget the dinner party tomorrow night. There's someone I want you to meet."

"Sure. Okay. Yeah," I agree without really hearing her words. My mind is not thinking straight. I know I need to get out of here. To figure out if what I think is happening is really happening. Turning back to look at Emma curled up on the couch, I have the urge to confess everything to her. To pull her into this overwhelming panicked state with me so I'm not alone, but I don't want to say anything until I know for sure.

Right now, I don't know anything, but I know I need to find out.

Johnathan opens the door and I rush past him so quickly, I don't realize I've walked into a full-blown party. There's music playing. Attractive, fashionable people with wine glasses in their hands.

"You're having a party?" I ask.

"I invited you on Monday. Isn't that why you're here?" He frowns.

His gaze drops to the CVS bag in my hand.

"Girl, I know you're twenty-two, but drug store wine is not acceptable."

"I forgot."

His brows raise. "The wine?"

"About your party." I sigh. "I've been doing that lately. Forgetting things."

Johnathan scans me from head to toe.

"You're a bit underdressed," he motions to my leggings and cropped tank, "but you're giving me blonde Kendall Jenner vibes, so I'll let it pass."

"Thanks? I guess."

"What can I get you to drink?" he asks.

"Um, just water," I say, my eyes darting around the room.

"Okay. Why are you really here?"

"Can I use your bathroom?" I ask.

He looks panicked.

"You're not going to be sick, are you?"

I shake my head. "I don't think so." It depends on what the test says.

"Down the hall."

"Thanks!" I call out as I rush in the direction he indicated.

Thankfully, no one is in the bathroom. I lock the door,

shutting out the music and the living room chatter. This isn't the ideal place to do this, but I didn't want to do it at home.

I could go to Hunter's.

He's not home from Vegas yet. And there's the nagging thought that while I've missed him all week, I have no idea how he's feeling about us. He said there was more between us on Sunday, but maybe he's changed his mind. Maybe, for him, the week was clarity that he doesn't want to deal with the emotional rollercoaster that is me trying to figure out what I want. That it would be easier to walk away.

And even if he still wants me, would he want a *baby*?

We talked about his changing thoughts on relationships and having a family, but that doesn't mean he wants that with *me*.

Enough thinking about it. I rip open the box and pull out the tests. There are two tests. One isn't enough? I need to test multiple times?

I read the instructions, uncap the test, and aim to pee on the end. I've rarely had the need to produce urine on demand. I've been drinking water lately like it's my full-time job, yet the pee barely trickles out. It's nervous. Afraid of what its presence will determine.

I cap the test, flush and wash my hands. The instructions say to wait three minutes before reading the results. That's the moment I realize, I need more time than that. The response on this stick could be life-changing. I need more than three minutes to come to terms with what it might tell me. I toss the stick in the bag and rush out the door. Just as I'm rounding the corner, Johnathan appears with a glass of water.

"Here—"

"I'm sorry, I can't stay." I give him a quick kiss on the cheek. "I'll talk to you later."

"Okay. By—" I'm out the door and jogging down the stairs. I don't know why I'm moving so quickly. Sprinting out of Johnathan's apartment like I'm carrying a lit stick of dynamite. And I know that delaying looking at the test doesn't change the results, but I need a moment to catch my breath. From the sprinting and from the thoughts that are going wild in my head.

I skitter out onto the sidewalk, then take a right to start moving toward the subway.

Everyone on the street suddenly has a baby. There's a couple walking with ice cream cones in their hands, a baby in a carrier strapped to the man's chest. A couple pushing a stroller with their leashed dog in tow. *Shouldn't these babies be in bed?* Okay, it's only eight o'clock. *When does a baby go to sleep anyway?*

That's only one of the million questions circling around in my head.

I might be pregnant. There could be a baby growing inside me. Hunter's baby.

This is so much more complicated than realizing I *missed* him this week. That I *like* him. Okay, more than like him.

This is huge. A lifetime commitment. At least eighteen years of co-parenting ahead of us.

Guilt washes over me. Everything that Griffin has done for me, everything he's wanted for me, for us—a better life, a different life than what we had growing up. I'm trying to be more independent, and now, I'm going to need even more help.

If I'm pregnant.

I scan my transit card and move toward the platform. When the train arrives, I find an empty seat near the door.

What about my job? My career aspirations? I'm trying to figure that out, and now, I might have to add the title of Mom into the mix. That throws a wrench in my five-year plan. No, not a wrench. It's more like sending the five-year plan through the paper shredder.

At Twenty-Third Street, I exit the train and climb the stairs, then I walk the three blocks to the apartment. I take the elevator up and let myself in. While I was out, Griffin arrived home and is now snuggling with Emma on the couch.

"Hey, Soph." Griffin nods.

"You're back."

"I got in an hour ago. I must have just missed you."

"How was Vegas?" I ask, my brain not even focused on his answer.

"It was good. We got a lot accomplished with the project. Hunter was pleased."

At the mention of Hunter, my attention draws back to my CVS bag and its contents.

"Emma said you were meeting up with a friend." Griffin eyes the bag.

"Yeah, Johnathan from work was having a party, so I stopped by."

"Want to join us?" Emma asks.

"No, thanks. I'm headed to bed."

"Okay, goodnight," Griffin calls as I move down the hallway toward my bedroom.

I change into my pajamas, then lock myself in the hallway bathroom, open the bag and reach for the test.

Setting it upright on the counter, I take a deep breath, then peer down at the small window.

I don't even need to pull out the instructions to determine the results. There are no lines with this one. No possible way to misinterpret what it's telling me.

Staring back at me is one word: PREGNANT.

CHAPTER 31

Hunter

"You're slow today, St. Clair."

Barrett chuckles, but the humor doesn't reach his weary eyes. "Yeah, I was up all night with Betty."

He wipes his forehead with a towel and his wedding band glints in the sun.

"So, the new puppy is keeping you up?"

Barrett and Chloe adopted Baxter, a Goldendoodle, when they first started dating, and after returning from their honeymoon in Italy, they added another Goldendoodle puppy to their family.

"Yeah, it's a good thing Betty is adorable because her need to go out at three in the morning isn't working for me." He takes a drink from his water bottle. "Betty is Chloe's response to me wanting to start trying for a baby."

"You're ready for kids?" I ask, eyebrows shooting to my hairline.

"Fuck yeah. Chloe wants to wait a few years, which I understand, she's younger and wants to focus on her career and have more time just the two of us, but I'm ready to be a dad."

"Wow. I never thought I'd hear those words come out of your mouth."

"I didn't either, but then I found Chloe, and everything changed."

I can relate. It's how I feel about Sophie.

I couldn't wait to see her this morning, but she didn't show up for our run. After several unanswered calls and texts, she finally responded.

Sophie: *Sorry, I overslept this morning. I'll call you soon.*

After a week away from her, the last thing I wanted was more space.

I've been trying to distract myself today. I attempted to work this morning, but I couldn't focus. Playing tennis with Barrett has taken up most of the afternoon.

"You want to do one more game?" I ask.

Barrett glances at his watch. "I better head out. We've got a dinner party at Emma and Griffin's tonight."

"Yeah? That's cool." I normally couldn't care less about a dinner party, but with Emma and Griffin hosting, I'm curious if Sophie will be there.

I grab my phone and text her.

Hunter: *Can you come over tonight?*

The message delivers, but nothing pops up to show me she's responding.

"What's the occasion?" I ask.

If Barrett thinks it's odd that I'm asking, he doesn't let on. I'd expect for him to give me shit, but I've noticed a change in him since he's been with Chloe. And now that they're married, he's content and far less of a grump.

Barrett shrugs. "Chloe said the dinner is a guise for Emma to set Sophie up with some guy."

My head whips in his direction.

"What guy?" My tone is far too accusatory for someone with general interest, but Barrett's too clouded by marital bliss to notice.

"Chloe just sent me this picture of Baxter and Betty." He holds his phone out so I can see the picture.

Two sandy-haired dogs curled up together in a bed.

"Cute." I acknowledge the photo before circling back to the issue at hand. "What *guy*?"

He shrugs. "Not my deal. All I have to do is remember to bring wine." He grabs his bag. "I've got to get home. I'll see you later."

"Yeah. See you." I watch him walk toward the elevator. A pang of jealousy grips my chest thinking about Sophie being set up with some guy.

Yeah, that's not happening.

With my message to Sophie still unanswered, I grab my bag and head for the showers.

I've never crashed a dinner party before. I've also never been ghosted or ignored by a woman. With a bottle of wine and flowers in my hands, I'm about to come to my senses and turn around when Emma opens the door.

"Hunter?" She looks momentarily confused, but her manners and inclusive nature take over. "Come on in."

I give her a quick kiss on the cheek, then offer her the bouquet and the bottle of wine.

"I didn't know you were—" she pauses, likely trying to recall the invite that she never made, "—able to make it."

Griffin appears with a beer bottle in his hand. If I wasn't crashing their dinner party, I might not catch the look he exchanges with Emma.

Did you invite him?

No. Did you?

I'm counting on the fact that Emma is one of the sweetest women I know and she would never turn away a guest.

"Hey, man." Griffin extends his hand. "Good to see you."

"Thanks for having me," I say.

There's an awkward beat before Emma speaks. "I'll put these in water. Hunter, what would you like to drink?"

"A beer sounds great." I nod toward the beer in Griffin's hand.

I glance around their apartment. It's a mix of soft hues and warm wood tones. There's an arrangement of framed pictures on the wall over a side table. Most are of Emma and Griffin. A few casual, a few professional ones from Chloe and Barrett's wedding. One photo is of them with Sophie in the middle wearing a cap and gown. Her college graduation, I presume.

I know I'm taking advantage of the fact that Griffin works for me. That he's not going to turn away his boss or even second guess the idea that neither him nor Emma invited me, but I need to see Sophie. And the fact that instead of us talking about the next step in our relationship, she's being set up with some guy? Not fucking happening.

Griffin hands me a beer, then motions for me to follow him through the dining room. "Everyone's out on the deck."

On our way past the table, Emma is there arranging the flowers I brought. The table is set for six.

Emma and Griffin aren't the only ones surprised to see me. As I make my way toward him, Barrett's eyes narrow in my direction.

"I didn't know you were coming," he says.

"It had slipped my mind until you mentioned it." I'm aware that I'm lying through my teeth, taking advantage of the situation, but I don't care. I need to see Sophie. When I scan the balcony and see she's not there, my chest deflates.

I'm introduced to Kevin, a guy with dark hair and dark-rimmed glasses in a polo shirt and khakis. He must be Sophie's date. When I shake his hand, I do my best not to crush it. It's not his fault he's unknowingly being set up with *my* girl.

Chloe is holding Betty, her and Barrett's Goldendoodle puppy in one arm, a wine glass in the other. I'll admit the dog is adorable. We had dogs growing up, but I've never had the inclination to get a pet in my adult life.

Would Sophie want to get a dog? The thought surfaces, but I realize before there are any pets, we need to talk.

I could stay here and make small talk until she shows up, but I'd rather find her and talk in private.

I extricate myself from the group's discussion and make my way back inside.

Emma is at the table again, this time adding another place setting.

"May I use your bathroom?" I ask.

"Second door on the left." She nods down the hallway.

I walk past the bathroom and another door that's open. A bedroom, the master. Griffin and Emma's room, I'm sure. There's a door farther down the hall on the right, but it's closed. I'm assuming it's Sophie's room. I knock quietly.

"Just a minute," Sophie calls. Her voice behind the door is all the confirmation I need to reach for the door handle.

I quickly let myself inside and close the door behind me.

For how well I've gotten to know Sophie, how much I've fallen for her, it hits me that I've never been in her space before. As I look around the room, it's exactly what I would have imagined. It's pure Sophie.

In front of me, there's a queen bed covered in a white duvet with a small yellow floral print on it. There's a bedside table with a vintage lamp and a pile of magazines. A leaning ladder bookcase with various decorative vases and an assortment of plants. The one from my mom is arranged in the middle of the shelf. Across the room is a desk with a mirror where I find Sophie.

At the sight of her, my heart beats wildly in my chest. I missed her so fucking much.

"Hunter?" Sophie startles when she sees me, dropping the necklace in her hands. "What are you doing here?"

"I wanted to talk to you," I tell her. "I *need* to talk to you."

Watching her bend down to pick up the necklace, I take her in. She's wearing a matching two-piece top and skirt, the scoop neck top fits snuggly against her chest, exposing the swells of her breasts, the skirt is fitted around her waist, then flows around her hips, in the prettiest shade of blue.

"Um, you want to talk now?" She glances past me at the closed door, likely wondering if we'll get caught in here together.

"Yes." I signal for her to turn around. She holds her hair up while I latch the necklace.

It's the delicate chain and wildflower pendant I gave her.

I'm satisfied to see it hanging there around her neck, but it also reminds me that she's getting ready to be set up with another guy.

"You've been avoiding me," I say. Our eyes meet in the mirror. In the past, I'd have avoided this conversation at all costs. Hell, I'd never even get to this point with a woman. Always keeping enough distance, making sure things didn't get messy. But that's all changed for me. I want to be messy with Sophie.

"We're on a break," she says in way of a response.

"You missed our run this morning."

She lets out an exasperated huff. "I texted you. I overslept."

"Then you didn't respond this afternoon."

"I was helping Emma get ready for tonight."

I run my hand through my hair. I feel like a lovesick teenager overanalyzing his crush's every move.

"Barrett said Emma is setting you up with a guy tonight."

Sophie's brows lift. "That's what this is about?"

I scowl thinking about the guy out on the deck. Tall,

attractive, and from what I can tell, age-appropriate. "He looks like Clark Kent."

She bites her lip, her eyes skimming the length of me until they meet mine. I can see the heat there. The way her pupils dilate. "You look like Clark Kent, minus the glasses."

Her playful response puts me somewhat at ease.

I smirk, moving closer until I can reach out and pull her to me. My frustrations from earlier immediately settled by the feel of her in my arms. My lips lower to hers, tasting her for the first time in six days. When I left the city on Monday, I had no idea I'd miss her this much. Need her this much. Or maybe I knew all along that this woman was changing everything.

"Does that make me Superman?" I ask against her ear as I rock my pelvis into hers.

She gasps before her breathy response. "You just need the red cape."

"Does that make you Lois Lane?" I move my hand beneath her skirt, letting my hand settle between her thighs, over her silk panties. I can feel the heat of her on the palm of my hand, the dampness that gathers there when I rub the heel of my hand against her. My cock throbs with the need to be inside her. I want to spread her out, kiss every inch of her body. Take my time and make love to her. I'm so fucking gone for this girl. "Or my fucking kryptonite?" I growl.

She shivers against me, but then stills my hand.

"Hunter, wait. We need to talk."

Her trembling voice registers and I extract my hand from beneath her skirt.

"I know. Sorry, I got distracted." I press my forehead against hers and breathe in her scent. "Fuck. Okay. Let's talk."

I expect her to pull away, but she flings herself at me. Her arms pull tighter around my neck, her face nuzzling against my chest as she melts into my arms. Nothing has ever felt so good.

"I missed you," she says.

She missed me.

I was wrong. Sophie's words are even better.

"I missed you, too, baby." I kiss the top of her head, holding her there.

But as I hold her, I can feel the tremble of her body against mine.

She's nervous. Unsure.

I want to make it crystal clear how I feel about her.

"I do want to end our arrangement." At my words, Sophie sucks in an audible gasp. "I don't want to keep doing what we've been doing. No more secret hookups. I want to take you out. I want you on my arm at events. I want you, Sophie. I know we agreed to keep this a secret, but I can't do that anymore. I need the whole world to know how I feel about you."

She pulls back to look up at me, her eyes filled with emotion. "How do you feel about me?" she asks.

"Sophie, I—"

Before I can confess my feelings, a loud commotion from the hallway has us pulling apart.

SOPHIE

The loud thud in the hallway pulls my attention from Hunter. From what he was about to say.

"What was that?" I ask, pulling out of his arms to move toward the door.

My heart rate was already beating erratically from Hunter's speech.

He wants us to be together.

I didn't have a chance to tell him that's what I want, too. Or tell him the news.

What if he changes his mind when he finds out I'm pregnant?

All those thoughts are swirling in my brain when I open the door to find Chloe and Emma in the hallway picking up pieces of trash littered on the floor.

"I'm so sorry, Emma," Chloe says. "Betty's been getting into everything at home. That's why we brought her, but now she's making a mess of your apartment."

"It's not a big deal," Emma responds, helping her with the pieces of shredded tissue.

Griffin appears. "What's happening?"

With everyone's attention on the clean-up from Chloe and Barrett's newest pup's trash dive, I'm hoping that no one notices that Hunter and I are coming out of my room together.

Just when I think everything is going to be okay, I see it. The pregnancy test I took last night, then buried at the bottom of the trash can. Apparently, Betty left no tissue unturned.

Before I can make a move to grab it, Chloe reaches for the stick. At first, she doesn't appear to realize what it is, but when she turns it over, her eyes widen. The result window displays the shocking news I received last night.

Chloe immediately looks to Emma, who is adding more torn up tissue to the bag that Griffin is holding. A smile a mile wide spreads on Chloe's face.

"Is this—congratulations!" Chloe bursts out, then reaches to hug Emma.

Time slows and I'm rooted in place as I watch Emma receive Chloe's embrace, then look down at the stick in her hand, her brow furrowing in confusion. Griffin leans in to look, too. I can see his brain register the word in the small window. His face lights with shock, but then he's smiling and reaching for Emma, but she shakes her head.

"That's not mine," Emma says.

"What is it?" Hunter asks from beside me, drawing everyone's attention in our direction.

Griffin's eyes find mine and I see the moment he registers whose test it must be.

I don't need to ask him his thoughts. The way his shoulders sag tells me everything I need to know. But more than Griffin's feelings about it, my gaze shifts to Hunter, wondering what his reaction will be.

Hunter's eyes drop to the stick and that tiny result window.

"Wait. Who's pregnant?" he asks, surprise evident in his voice.

This is not how I imagined this going, but nothing about this situation was planned. My heart hammers in my chest, desperately trying to keep up with my body's demand for oxygen as I take in short, choppy breaths.

"I am."

I keep my eyes on Hunter, awaiting his reaction. He looks from the test in Emma's hand to me. His eyes are wide, his mouth agape. But then he does the craziest thing. Hunter wraps his arms around me and pulls me to him. He holds me tight, then lowers his lips to mine. I let my body relax against his, releasing some of the tension my muscles have been holding since I found out last night.

It's a sweet moment. Until I hear Griffin.

"What the fuck is happening right now?" Griffin barks.

I pull back, and Hunter's hand drops possessively over my stomach. For a moment, his touch soothes the anxiety of the situation, and the fact that what I've been trying to avoid all along, Griffin finding out about us being together, is now an even messier reveal.

"Wait. Are you two..." Emma motions between Hunter and me, "...is Hunter..."

I nod slowly, this time my eyes are on Griffin to gauge his reaction. His brows draw down as he looks between me and

Hunter. The disappointment in his hazel eyes is evident. It's the exact reaction I've been trying to avoid.

"I was wondering where everyone went." My supposed date, the Clark Kent lookalike, joins us in the hallway. "Hey, Sophie, I got you a drink. White wine okay?"

Griffin's lips harden in a flat line. "Hunter, I need to see you outside."

CHAPTER 32

Hunter

Sophie's pregnant.

With *our* baby.

From the second I found out, there was no doubt in my mind that the baby is mine. *Ours.*

Holy shit.

I'm going to be a dad.

The conversation I had with Barrett this afternoon at tennis registers. I'm nowhere near ready for parenthood like he seemed to be. I never even considered it an option. There's never been a woman I'd imagined settling down with, let alone having a family. Until Sophie.

I'm still trying to process the news, my brain full of thoughts, but the way Griffin is glowering at me from the other side of the balcony, I decide to put those on pause to focus on him.

Because he's furious. That's what I've concluded from his pacing.

I don't want to be here right now, I want to be with Sophie, but I know that if there's any hope in salvaging our friendship and him accepting me and Sophie together, I need to talk to Griffin. Clear the air.

"You've been sleeping with my sister and you got her pregnant? She's twenty-fucking-two. What the fuck is wrong with you, Hunter?"

I followed him out onto the deck, leaving everyone else inside. I'm wondering if this was a good idea. I'm also wondering if Griffin might try to throw me off the balcony.

"I—" I start to answer but he cuts me off.

"How long has this been going on?" he growls.

"We met in Vegas. At a club. Before she moved here."

Griffin's eyes narrow. Even without the details, it's clear what must have happened between Sophie and me in Vegas.

"When I found out she was your sister, we said we weren't going to see each other again, but then—"

"Emma has filled me in on your reputation. You've told me yourself that you don't do relationships. So, what was your plan with Sophie? Was she just another woman you were going to discard when you got bored?"

"There was no plan," I answer honestly.

He laughs sardonically. "I get it. You were just taking it one screw at a time."

I thought being honest and talking it out would bring Griffin's anger to a simmer, but with each passing moment, I can see his body tighten, his jaw clench tighter with rage. While I'm focused on his face, his right hook sneaks up on me.

The pain radiates through my jaw and I stumble backwards.

"Fuck." I push him back. "That's not what I meant."

I think about what I'd do if a guy was fucking around with Hannah and got her pregnant. How I'd think the guy was a creep if he was thirteen years older than her.

And I know Griffin is protective of Sophie. Hadn't I expected this?

Now that it's clear Griffin wants to pummel me, I decide

the best course of action is to defend myself without engaging him.

I look around the deck. All the furniture is placed on the periphery, there's nothing between us. While we're both athletes, and I've got a few inches on him, Griffin's five years younger, and a good fifteen pounds heavier. Not to mention the adrenaline that must be coursing through his veins looking at the guy who snuck around behind his back and got his little sister pregnant. I'm well aware my company position means nothing right now.

"She's twenty-two! You never should have touched her!"

He lunges at me, but I dodge him, then grab a pillow from the couch and throw it at him. He catches the pillow and tosses it aside.

This is ridiculous. I don't want to fight him, but I will defend myself.

"It was never like that. I'm aware of our age difference, but she's a consenting adult."

He comes at me again. I dodge his tackle, but my shoe gets tangled up in the deck rug and I trip. It's an easy way for him to gain an advantage and he does. Rolling on top of me, he swings his arm back for another punch. My palm flattens against his fist, stopping it from connecting with my nose.

At this point, it feels like pounding me into dust would be Griffin's preferable course of action.

I scramble from beneath him, but he swings an arm out, hitting my shin and knocking me back down. My body weight is caught by my bad knee and I hiss in pain. *Fuck.*

With my knee throbbing now, I desperately want to retaliate, but I swallow my anger.

"Can you calm down and we'll talk like adults?" I ask.

That doesn't go over well. Griffin lands a punch at my side and I wheeze, trying to take in air, but his punch counteracts my efforts to breathe.

"And I talked to you about her in Vegas. You knew why Sophie was always busy. She was sneaking around with you!"

"We were waiting to find the right time to tell you."

Even with his anger, I see his brain working. His eyes narrow with the moment of realization.

"Was she the woman under your desk? The one I walked in on you with?"

I can't lie. That would only make things worse. But admitting Sophie was on her knees at our office sucking my dick with him only feet away is going to do nothing to assuage Griffin's anger.

"Yes," I admit, my body primed for his reaction.

He shakes his head. "I thought we were friends." Beneath the anger, I can see the disappointment, the hurt.

"We are friends," I assure him.

"No, a friend wouldn't go after my little sister." His jaw is still tight. He lunges again.

"I love her." I barely get the words out before Griffin's fist meets my stomach. "Fuck." I gasp for air, trying to recover from his punch.

The balcony door slides open and I hear Sophie calling from a distance. "Griffin! Stop!"

"What did you say?" He ignores Sophie's pleas, his focus solely on me.

My insides are burning, but I manage to get the words out. "I'm in love with her."

Griffin staggers back, my words seeming to temporarily extinguish the fury in him. "You mean that?"

I'm aware of Sophie's proximity. That this isn't the scenario in which I want to reveal my feelings for her.

My words are quiet as I look Griffin in the eyes. "I haven't told her yet, but yeah, I do."

He moves closer again, but this time, his hands are by his sides.

"I don't care that you're my boss. If you hurt her, the company's going to need a new CEO."

I nod. "Yeah, I'd expect that."

Griffin gives me one last hard look before he walks past Sophie and back into the apartment.

Sophie hands me an ice pack for my lip.

"Griffin shouldn't have done that," she says, dropping down beside me on her bed. Her thumb gently grazes the skin under my lower lip as she examines the cut there.

"I would have done the same thing for Hannah. He's protective of you, like a good big brother would be."

"But still, no one should have gotten hurt over this." She inhales deeply. "I'm sorry."

"There's no reason for you to be sorry."

"Were you at the same dinner party I was? What a mess."

She lies back on her bed, her cropped shirt lifting to expose a section of skin above her skirt. Even with my busted lip, I can't help but lower down and place a gentle kiss against her belly. I hear her breath hitch with my featherlight touch.

"This is so unexpected. We were supposed to be having fun and now I'm having a baby."

I move up to see her face. The tears rimming her eyes make my chest squeeze.

"*We're* having a baby," I correct her. "Did you miss what I said earlier? I want you for more than sex. Before I knew about the baby, I wanted us to be together."

"And now?" she asks.

"I still want you. And the baby."

She lets out a momentary sigh of relief.

"The baby doesn't change anything," I assure her.

"The baby changes everything!" she wails. "Last night, I

researched pregnancy. My body is going to change completely."

I drop my gaze to her body and place my hand against her bare stomach. I can see her now, belly swollen with our baby. I don't think the visual should be making me hard, but it is.

"You say your body is going to change like it's a bad thing."

"What are you saying? That my body could use improvements?" Sophie snaps. "Pregnancy will do it some good? Widen my narrow hips? Make my mediocre boobs bigger?"

"That's not—" I start.

I think I've stepped on a landmine. I want to exit this part of the conversation, but I realize any way I do it, shit is going to blow up.

"How am I going to do this?" Sophie curls into me, apparently no longer annoyed, but sad.

With my thumb, I brush a rogue tear from her cheek.

"*We* are going to start with a doctor's appointment, then go from there."

She nods and offers me a small smile. "Okay."

I should tell her how I feel. What I told Griffin. What I planned to say this morning when she didn't show for our run, but the timing is off. I don't want her to think that I'm saying 'I love you' because she's pregnant. Like it's the 1950s and I'm trying to do the honorable thing. I would gladly drop to one knee right now if I thought she'd say yes. But she's not there yet. And we have time.

"I'm still so confused about how it happened." She bites her lip. "We used condoms every time."

She's right. Though the urge to have her bare was always in the back of my mind, we did use protection.

"These things happen." I stroke her hair. "How have you been feeling?"

"A little nausea, but I think I had more of that weeks ago.

Now, my boobs are tender. I'm tired. And it's like a faucet down there."

"What do you need?" I ask, kissing her temple. "A foot rub? A nap?"

Sophie looks up at me, her lower lip between her teeth. Her hand covers mine and pushes it down below her skirt.

"I want you to touch me."

"Yeah?" I ask, already growing hard at the thought. She doesn't have to ask me twice.

If this is a favor to anyone, it's me. And I'm happy to fulfill her request.

I slide my hand up her thigh and pull on the waistband of her underwear. She shimmies side to side to aid me in pulling them down.

"What do you need, Sophie?" I kiss the corner of her mouth gently, as I slide a finger down her wet center. "You want my mouth? My fingers? My cock deep inside you?"

"I want everything."

"Then that's exactly what you'll get."

She moans when I slip two fingers inside her. She's so fucking wet. I can't wait to lick her up. My thumb finds her swollen clit and starts moving in circles.

"Ahh. It's sensitive."

"Can you keep quiet?" I press a gentle kiss to her lips, knowing full well that the rest of the group is out in the living room. That I don't need her brother to hear her moaning when her orgasm hits.

"Isn't that what your other hand is for?" She smirks at me.

I pull a pillow from the head of her bed and hand it to her. "You'll need this." Then I drop to my knees between her thighs and lift her legs over my shoulders. Sophie is sweeter than she's ever been, which I didn't think was possible. I flatten my tongue against her lips and lick up her center. Above me, she's crushed the pillow over her face. A tragedy because I love seeing her face when she comes, but if all her writhing and grinding her pelvis against my face tells me anything, it's that she's moments away from screaming. And the pillow is necessary.

I hook my fingers inside her and feel the familiar clench of her muscles before a muffled moan erupts from beneath the pillow. Sophie comes hard. All over my face. The wetness from her orgasm leaking out of her. I can't resist a final swipe of my tongue to taste her again.

She knees me in the jaw. A knee-jerk reaction if there ever was one.

"Ow."

"Sorry!" She props herself up on her elbows to look down at me. "I'm sensitive."

"I got that," I chuckle, rubbing my jaw, which was already sore from Griffin's punch.

I climb back over her and she reaches for my belt.

"I missed you this week. Did I mention that?" I ask.

After a miserable week away, being here with her now feels incredible. And, knowing our baby is growing inside her, tethering us together, gives me a sense of calm.

"Yes. I missed you, too." She pushes my pants and briefs down my hips. My hard cock springs free, and Sophie's hand strokes me as she impatiently guides me to her entrance.

With one push, I'm inside. Sophie's slick pussy envelopes me. Bare. Nothing between us. It's official. She's ruined me for any other woman. It doesn't matter. There's only her.

"Fuu—" I begin to groan when Sophie's hand shoots up to cover my mouth.

"Shh," she whispers. "It's awkward enough that my brother knows we've had sex. I don't want him to hear it."

I flex my hips until I'm fully seated. I hold myself still inside her and think about how fucking good it feels to be this close to her. Then, I lower my mouth for a slow, exploratory kiss. When I pull back, Sophie opens her eyes. Those expressive green eyes have my heart in a chokehold.

Underneath me, Sophie digs her heels into the bed, pressing up into me, trying to create friction. I know she wants me to move.

I want that, too, but I choose that moment to let my thoughts fall out of my mouth.

"Move in with me," I say, finally starting to move inside her.

"What? Oh, God." She digs her heels into the mattress and arches her back, meeting my thrusts. "*Mmm.* Yes."

I kiss her neck.

"That's a yes?"

"No, I can't move in with you."

"Why not?" I roll my hips, giving her the perfect amount of pressure in the sensitive spot I know she needs.

"Because..." Sophie grinds up into me. I pull down her shirt along with the cup of her bra, exposing her breast. Carefully, I wrap my mouth around her hardened peak and suck. Testing that sensitivity she was talking about.

"Ahh." Her fingers push through my hair and grip the ends tightly.

It hurts so good.

"Give me a good reason."

"We've only been together a month. And we weren't officially together."

"But we are now," I argue.

"What?" She pants.

"Officially together."

"Can we talk about this another time? I just...oh...right there. YE—"

I clamp my hand down over Sophie's mouth. Her eyes momentarily open to give me a grateful look.

A second later, she's pulsing around me. The rhythm of her muscles milking my cock pulls me over the edge. I groan into the crook of her neck before emptying deep inside her. Fuck. It takes a full minute for my breathing to even out and for me to pull my face away from the smooth skin of Sophie's neck.

I push myself up to look down at her. I want to make sure we're on the same page.

"Sophie Renee Hart, will you officially be my girlfriend?"

She laughs at the formality. But with my questioning look, she nods. "Yes."

One down, one to go.

"What will it take for you to say yes to moving in? Unlimited orgasms? Foot rubs? Name it and it's yours."

Her hand finds my cheek. When her thumb lightly grazes my bottom lip, I kiss it.

"Let me think about it."

I hate her answer, but I respect it.

I pull out of her, then reach for the tissues on her nightstand to clean us up.

I can't wait to get her back to my place where she can make all the noise she wants, even if it's not permanent yet.

As I lie back on Sophie's bed with her cuddled up in my arms, I realize I didn't ask the most important question.

"I know it's a surprise and a lot to process. The baby, I mean. But do you want to keep it? Or are you thinking…"

My words trail off because it's hard to get them out. I respect Sophie and her right to choose. For us to talk about all the options there are. But I can't deny that the moment I found out the baby was ours, I was happy. I'm also thirty-five and in love with her. What if this isn't what Sophie wants? If she's not ready, I wouldn't blame her. She's younger and has a whole life to live that may not include a baby right now.

Her fingertips trail over my bare chest. "Honestly? I was terrified when I found out. But your reaction," she tilts her head up at me, "was comforting. My mom was a young mother with Griffin. I couldn't imagine being a mom at twenty on my own."

"You'll never be on your own," I say reassuringly.

But then she starts to cry.

"You're right. I'm never going to have my own apartment. I'll never live alone." She shakily sucks in air through her tears.

"*Shh*. Hey. We'll figure it out," I say soothingly. "I'll take the baby to the lake house for a weekend and you can pretend you live in the condo by yourself. Maybe not right away, but at some point."

"You'd do that?" she whispers through her tears.

I'd do just about anything to make her happy. To show her how much she means to me. How much I want us to be a family.

"Sophie, I want to make you happy. I want you to feel supported. If me time is what you need, then that's what you'll get."

"I just didn't expect this. The baby. You. None of it was in the five-year plan."

"I know." I rub her back. It wasn't in my five-year plan either. Hell, I don't have a five-year plan. Besides work to anchor me, I'd been floating through life. Now that I have Sophie, and the prospect of being a dad, I can see the years laid out before me.

Our wedding, family vacations. I can even imagine walking our child into their first day of kindergarten. One tiny hand in mine, the other one in Sophie's. At that point, there might be another baby, maybe two. I know I'm getting ahead of myself, but what once was impossible to imagine, now I can't stop coloring in the details of the life that I want with Sophie.

CHAPTER 33

Sophie

I roll over in bed, pulling the covers up under my chin. My body is sluggish and my head hurts. The moment my eyes open, I remember.

I'm pregnant.

I close my eyes again. It still doesn't feel real.

"Good morning." I follow the sound of Hunter's voice to the doorway.

My stomach flutters at the sight of him walking toward me. How gorgeous he is with his thick, dark hair, stunning indigo eyes, and hypnotizing smile. Seeing him has me wondering what our baby is going to look like. What characteristics he or she will have of mine, and which ones they'll get from their dad.

His reaction to the news yesterday was everything. Finding out I was pregnant was shocking, but knowing that Hunter was supportive and even excited gave me a sense of calm. It allowed the sliver of excitement I was feeling to expand, right before Griffin's response to the news crushed it.

Hunter is dressed in running shorts and a t-shirt. I'm not even annoyed he went running without me. There's no way I would have gotten out of this bed earlier. He's got a plastic bag in one hand and glass of water in the other.

He sets the bag and water on the nightstand, then sits down on the edge of the bed, his palm starting to rub soothing circles on my back.

"Hi." I give him a small smile, trying to blink the sleep out of my eyes.

"How'd you sleep?" he asks.

"Okay. It took me a while to fall asleep. Lots going on in my brain." I sigh and rub my temples. "And now I have a headache."

He offers me the glass of water. "You probably need to drink more water. Your body is increasing its blood supply and water is important."

"How do you know that?" I ask, sitting up so I can drink.

"I ran out and got some books."

"And you already read them?"

"I'm a quick study." He winks and I can't help but melt a little.

"I also got these." He pulls a bottle from the bag.

Prenatal vitamins.

He opens the bottle and hands me two capsules. I swallow them down, then drain the rest of the water.

It's such a small thing, but the fact that he's already jumping in to figure out what I need eases the tension in my shoulders.

"Emma and Chloe are here."

My eyes widen. "Really? This early?"

He chuckles. "It's ten o'clock."

"Oh, gosh, I didn't realize I'd slept so late." I reach for my phone. He's right, it's just after ten. So much for a productive Sunday. I had wanted to work on my internship project this weekend, but since finding out I'm pregnant Friday night, I haven't had a moment or the brain power to focus on it.

"It's okay. You clearly needed the sleep. Do you want to see them? Or should I tell them you're resting?"

I bite my lip, still thinking about yesterday. The chaos of everyone finding out the way they did, Griffin and Hunter's fight, then me and Hunter leaving before dinner.

Even though I told Hunter I wasn't ready to move in, I did pack some things to stay at his place. I know I need to talk to Griffin at some point, but right now, I'm just trying to figure everything out with me and Hunter and the pregnancy.

"No, I want to see them."

I pull on some lounge pants and a sweatshirt.

"I'm going to take a shower, then you want to grab brunch?"

"Sure." I nod, moving toward the door.

"Hey," he pulls me back to him, his arms encircling my waist. "I'm happy you're here. And in case there was any question in your mind when you woke up this morning, I want this with you."

He drops a sweet kiss to my lips, then before he releases me, he gives my ass a playful swat.

I find Emma and Chloe in the living room. At first, I'm not sure what to expect, but the moment Emma sees me, she stands to envelope me in a hug.

"We didn't get a chance to talk much yesterday with everything that was happening, but we wanted to come by and offer you whatever support you need."

Chloe steps forward next, giving me a gentle squeeze. "I'm so sorry that your pregnancy was revealed that way. I feel horrible that Betty's trash digging made an already delicate situation more stressful for you."

"You don't have to apologize," I say. "Obviously, it wasn't intentional."

"I know, but I still feel bad."

"We brought you some essentials." Emma motions to the basket on the table.

It's filled with books and snacks, there's a silk robe and cozy slipper set, flowers and what looks like a gift card to a spa.

"We didn't know what your plans are and we didn't want to assume..." Emma's words trail off.

"I'm keeping the baby."

Emma smiles and nods. "I think that's wonderful."

"So exciting." Chloe beams.

I can't stop myself from asking. "And what does Griffin think?"

Emma sighs. "I don't even think he knows. It was a shock. Your pregnancy, but also that you and Hunter were seeing each other behind his back. He was blindsided and needs some time to process."

"Yeah, I get it. That's not how I wanted him to find out. And obviously, the baby wasn't planned, but I needed him, you know?" Saying the words out loud, voicing how I hoped things had gone when Griffin found out, causes all the emotion I've been feeling to bubble up to the surface, and the tears start to flow.

Emma moves to sit beside me, wrapping her arms around me.

"I'm sorry, Sophie. I know Griffin loves you so much and wants the best for you."

"We all want that." Chloe moves to my other side, wrapping her arms around both of us, a difficult feat for her petite size.

"Thank you." I sniffle.

Emma hands me a tissue and I wipe at the tears streaming down my face. It feels amazing to have these two women rallying around me, but I can't help but wonder if in my desire to prove my independence, I ended up pushing Griffin too far away.

~

Monday morning, I go straight to Johnathan's office.

"Hey."

"Good morning. How was your weekend?" he asks.

"Um, it was eventful."

"Yeah? Your drive-by of my party on Friday was interesting." He eyes me with suspicion. "Want to tell me what was going on?"

"I feel bad. It slipped my mind and then I was in a weird headspace when I was there."

"No kidding. I wanted to introduce you to Beau, but you were in and out quicker than a man with no foreplay skills."

I smile at Johnathan's comparison, but I feel bad that I didn't get the chance to meet his husband.

"I'm sorry," I hand him the pastry bag I'm holding. "I didn't have time to grab you a coffee, but I can go make you one in the break room."

"You're forgiven." He waves me off. "No coffee necessary as long as this is a chocolate croissant."

I smile when he opens the bag and his face lights up.

He pulls the flaky pastry from the bag and takes a bite, the chocolate filling oozing out.

Damn, I should have gotten one for myself.

"I need your advice."

"Is this a bribe?" He chews a bite. "Because I can't give any help on your internship project, if that's what you're looking for. I'm supposed to be unbiased and subjective."

"I'm pregnant." The words tumble past my lips.

He's midbite when his eyes go wide and he makes a choking sound.

"Oh, no. Are you okay?" I stand to help, but he motions me to sit.

After a coughing fit, he reaches for his water bottle. A minute later, he gives a final cough before he speaks.

"Honey, don't deliver shocking news while someone's eating a flaky pastry. The tiny flakes of buttery crust went down the wrong pipe." He takes another drink of water and clears his throat before eyeing me. "That's exciting?"

It's a question because I'm not exactly radiating enthusiasm.

"It's a surprise, that's for sure."

"And the father?"

All I have to do is nod because Johnathan knows about Hunter. Or at least he has suspected since the flowers.

His jaw drops. "You're having Hunter Cartwright's baby?!"

I glance toward his door. "*Shh.*"

"And you need advice from me?" His smile is nervous. "I don't know exactly what I can contribute to this particular subject, other than offering my services as a fabulous Guncle." His jaw drops. "Wait. I did see the cutest Barefoot Dreams onesie set at Neiman's the other day. It had a Peter Pan collar and the little ruffle socks were adorable." He closes his eyes, like the mere memory is blissful.

I smile at Johnathan's excitement over baby clothes. He's like Emma and loves any reason to shop.

"It's not about the baby. At least, not directly. But I wanted you to know that's why I've been a bit scattered lately. That's why I showed up out of the blue Friday night, then left just as quickly. I'm pregnant and hormonal and generally a bit of a mess right now." I sigh. "I was feeling unsure before I found out I was pregnant, but knowing there's a baby on the way has made me realize I need to figure out my career path. I didn't want to tell you this because you're honestly my favorite thing about working here, but I don't know if I want to pursue a permanent position here."

I fill him in about my blog and the forthcoming *Brides* feature. My ideas for continuing the blog and using it to start my own sustainable wedding planning business.

"I was so excited to get the opportunity to intern at Marion Adler Events," I motion with my hands wide to describe the magnitude of it, "It's what I thought I wanted for so long, that I didn't realize this job wouldn't be a good fit for me."

"Oh, I already knew that."

I stare at him, stunned. "What? Why didn't you say something?"

"Because I've found that people do better when they come to a realization like this on their own." He tucks the rest of the croissant away in its wrapper. "And selfishly, I love having you here, so I was in a little bit in mourning over your unhappiness, but if I know you as well as I think I do, you're not going to quit. You'll finish the internship and the presentation and give it everything you have."

"You're right. I'm not quitting. I'll finish the internship, but I'm stumped on what to present. The presentation is in hopes of landing a permanent position, and if that's not what I want, then I don't know how to use it to my advantage."

"Don't you, though?" He smirks.

"While I feel like this whole wise, yet cryptic mentor vibe suits you, it's very frustrating when I just need you to say what you mean."

"Present on what you're passionate about."

"I'm passionate about starting my own business for sustainable wedding planning. I doubt Marion wants to hear about that."

"Are you sure about that?"

He lifts his brows, encouraging me to think about it.

I let my mind wrap around what he's saying.

Johnathan's right. If I'm not angling for a permanent position but want to get my business idea out there, using my internship presentation would be the perfect opportunity to get honest, critical feedback.

Johnathan stands and envelopes me in a hug. "You got this."

"Thank you," I tell him.

"Of course. And congratulations. On the baby."

"Thank you. It's wild to think that Hunter and I wanted a casual fling, and now we're doing the least casual thing two people can, have a baby together."

"I'm jealous of that baby. They'll get to call Hunter Cartwright 'Daddy.'"

I roll my eyes. "That's what you would be thinking about now."

"Trust me, I won't be the only one."

"Oh," I stop at the doorway, "I'll look forward to reviewing your Guncle application."

"Puh-lease, I'm a shoo-in." His smirk makes me laugh.

With an idea forming in my head, I make my way to the intern office and get to work.

CHAPTER 34

Sophie

Being pregnant at this stage is weird. I'm not showing, and besides some moodiness and a few cravings, nothing feels different, yet *everything* has changed.

Tuesday night, Hunter and I make our first public appearance as a couple at a charity function Hannah's boutique, Filigree & Facet, is sponsoring. Hunter had offered to take me shopping or have Hannah's stylist pick out something for me, but I don't want to trouble anyone, so I planned to wear the red dress that I previously picked up at the consignment shop with June.

An hour ago, I realized that with pregnancy, how a dress fits in the morning is very different than how it fits in the evening. A lot can happen in twelve hours. Hell, I felt that way *before* I was pregnant.

So, after a minor breakdown upon which Hunter offered to close Bergman's so I could shop for a dress, I opted to rewear the green, less fitted dress from the ballet.

"You look gorgeous," Hunter whispers in my ear as we pose on the red carpet outside the venue, his hands possessively pulling me close to him.

"Hunter, who is the lucky lady?"

"My girlfriend, Sophie Hart," he responds proudly.

Hunter's announcement starts another flurry of camera flashes, followed by a slew of questions.

"How long have you been together?"

"Hunter, is she the one?"

"Miss Hart, who are you wearing?"

My mouth gapes open unintelligibly. I'm certain I look like a wooden doll, all stiff limbs and a vacant expression. Hunter doesn't respond to the rest of their questions, but ushers me along with a hand on my lower back.

"You okay?" he asks once we're inside.

"Yeah, it's just odd that anyone cares about me."

"I care, that makes everyone else curious."

Inside, we meet up with Hannah and James. Upon our approach, Hannah's lips are pressed together, her eyes wide, but friendly. She looks like she's about to burst at the seams.

"I'm so happy to see you two together," she says, pulling me into an embrace. "You make a stunning couple."

"Thank you."

"And nothing is more satisfying than seeing my brother obsessing over a woman," Hannah teases.

"Are you ready to pull back the curtain and find out how obnoxious the elegant Hannah Cartwright can be?" Hunter ribs her back.

"Oh, I think I'm going to enjoy being around you two," I say.

I laugh at their teasing; it reminds me of my relationship with Griffin. Just the thought of him has the unease of the rift between us settling back in my stomach.

I haven't spoken to him since I left the apartment on Saturday night.

Hannah laughs, then her attention shifts and she motions with her hand above her shoulder. "Sophie, I want you to meet my friend Colette Davenport."

A woman emerges from behind Hunter. With dark hair

and crystal blue eyes with such fair skin, she looks like a porcelain doll. Her frame is petite, yet defined by lithe muscle.

Hunter leans in. "She's the dancer I wanted to introduce you to at the NYC ballet."

My eyes light. "Yes, I remember. Oh my gosh, it was such a stunning performance."

Hannah's lips quirk and she elbows Hunter in the ribs. "Now I know why you wanted my tickets."

"Colette, this is my girlfriend, Sophie Hart." It's the second time tonight he's introduced me that way, but I think it will take a million times more to feel real. That our once secret relationship is now out in the open.

I shake Colette's hand. "You're an amazing dancer. So graceful. I loved every minute of the performance."

"Thank you," she says, an angelic smile on her face.

"Do you have the night off?" I ask.

"We had our final performance for the season a few weeks ago."

"Oh, I didn't realize," I say. "I guess everyone needs time off. I'm sure it's a lot of strain on your body."

"We take a break every summer after the spring session ends to prep for the fall season."

"Lettie is trying out for a lead role in the fall session," Hannah offers.

"Lettie?" I question.

"That's my nickname," she responds.

"Oh, that's lovely. And exciting about the lead role. I'm sure you'll get it."

Colette's smile tightens slightly. "We'll see."

A waiter approaches with a tray of champagne flutes filled with bubbly.

"For you, Miss." He hands me a flute from the tray.

"Um," I stutter. Other than diverting June from a happy hour earlier this week, this is the first time I'm in public and having to deal with the fact that I can't drink alcohol. Like this entire pregnancy thing, I didn't prepare for this moment.

Hunter leans in, brushing my hair off my shoulder. "That one is just for you," he whispers discreetly before pressing a kiss to my jaw.

I nod to the waiter and accept the drink. Upon tasting, it's obvious that it's sparkling grape juice.

Thank you, I mouth to Hunter, knowing he must have arranged the drink switch ahead of time. He's the most thoughtful, dirty-talking, ass-spanking man there is. My chest tightens and my pussy clenches. My body equally swooning and lusting after this man. I fight the urge to leap into his arms and maul him; instead, I focus on the conversation around me.

"We spent summers together at Lake George," Hannah offers. "Our families have neighboring houses there."

"That's right. Hunter mentioned that."

Hannah beams, glancing between Hunter and me.

"Summers at Lake George are some of my fondest childhood memories," Colette says with a whimsical look on her face.

"Oh my God, do you remember when you were begging your parents for a cat and Rhys gave you one, only come to find out he stole it from the elderly couple a few houses down?" Hannah shakes her head, laughing.

"My first pet cat." Colette turns to me. "Only lasted for six hours before the owners knocked on our door and took her away."

"How heartbreaking, but Rhys probably shouldn't have taken someone else's cat," I say.

"No, he shouldn't have, but Rhys was always compelled to do whatever it took to make Colette happy." Hannah's lips twitch, recalling the memory.

"We were good friends," Colette counters. "He was like a brother to me. Same as Hunter."

"Sure, sure." Hannah doesn't sound convinced.

"Doesn't matter now. He's not the guy he used to be."

After a thoughtful pause, the conversation moves on.

Later, we peruse the auction items, then make our way to the bar. I thank the bartender for my soda water with lime while Hunter accepts his scotch on the rocks.

God, he looks incredible in a suit. The way his fingers grip his glass. His hair is styled in that perfectly disheveled way that looks like I could run my hands through it while he sucks on my clit and no one would even know. I didn't know I could be even more attracted to him than I already was.

These pregnancy hormones are something. It's like they're in the driver's seat and I'm just along for the ride.

Hunter gets his drink and I immediately grab his hand, pulling him out into the mezzanine as I desperately search for an empty room, a closet, anywhere I can maul this man.

"Are you feeling okay?" he asks, concern filling his voice. "The restrooms are down the other hallway," he says, still allowing me to drag him in the opposite direction.

I fling open a door and *bingo*! It's a small supply closet. I'm so relieved, I nearly trip over a broom.

"Easy, sweetheart." Hunter grips my waist to keep me on my feet.

I press the light switch, then pull the door closed behind us.

"What are we doing here?"

"I need you to touch me. Please."

I'm already gathering the skirt of my dress into my hands.

"Here?" he asks, setting his glass on the shelf next to the bulk paper towels.

"Yes, here. It's an emergency."

Hunter chuckles. "An orgasm emergency?"

"Yes! Exactly." I'm glad he's understanding my plight.

He gets right to work, hooking his fingers into the waistband of my underwear and taking them with him as he lowers to his knees.

I grab a set of disposable dust rags from the shelf and drop them to the ground.

"For your knee," I tell him. He's been icing his bad knee since he tripped and fell on it during the fight with Griffin on Saturday.

He grins up at me, likely remembering that first day in his shower when he didn't want me kneeling on the hard tile to give him a blow job.

"You're so good to me." He winks and if I wasn't already pregnant, that would do it.

A moment later, he lifts my leg over his shoulder and flattens his tongue against me and I already know this is going to be a record for fastest orgasm.

"Fuck, baby, you're so wet." He swirls his tongue over my clit, and my hands push through his hair.

"I can't help it," I groan.

"I love it. I'm going to enjoy licking up every last drop."

And he does.

A minute later, I shatter on his skilled tongue.

He stands, replacing the dust towels back on the shelf. Then, he starts to guide my underwear back over my heels.

"I can't put those back on. They're too wet."

Without question, he tucks my panties into his pocket, then uses some of the paper towels bundled on the shelf to clean me up.

"Better?" he asks, placing a kiss against my jaw.

"The orgasm was top notch, but I think the situation between my thighs is actually worse now." I pout.

"I'm sorry. We can say goodbye to Hannah and James, then leave if you want."

"Okay."

He kisses me thoroughly before taking my hand and leading me out the door. At least I'm feeling more relaxed now, that is, until we walk back into the ballroom and right into Emma and Griffin.

Emma's face lights with surprise, but she recovers quickly and pulls me into a hug.

"Hi! You look gorgeous," she says. "I love that dress."

"Thank you. You look stunning." I lean into her warm embrace.

I knew there was a chance they would be here. They're in the same social circle, and Emma is designing Hannah's wedding gown, but I wasn't prepared for this moment. Seeing them out socially when things are strained between me and Griffin.

While Emma pulls Hunter in for a hug, I glance at Griffin. He's studying something over my shoulder, not meeting my eyes.

Hunter releases Emma, then wraps his arm around my waist to pull me in close to his side. I'd normally love the feeling of his hands on me, but under Griffin's unhappy gaze, I feel deflated.

"Griffin, good to see you, man." Hunter sticks out his hand for a shake, but Griffin doesn't move his hands from his pockets.

Instead, he gives Hunter a terse nod, then grunts. I've never seen him do that in my life.

It's giving fuck-off Roy Kent vibes. Johnathan would be thoroughly impressed.

Hunter retracts his hand slowly, and the awkwardness hanging between our foursome ratchets up to a ten.

"Well, it's so good to see both of you. I think we're going to go browse the auction items." It's impossible to miss the terse look she aims at Griffin before she gives me a sympathetic smile and they turn to leave.

The whole encounter is an out of body experience. As I watch them walk away, my heart sinks.

Part of me thought we'd see each other and everything would be fine. I've never fought with Griffin.

But maybe that's the problem, growing up we were always on our best behavior, trying to make the others' life easier in the situation we were in. And everything is changing now.

"Does he hate me now?" I ask.

"Hey," Hunter catches my chin with his finger. "He could never hate you. Give him some time. It's only been a couple of days."

"Hello?" I point to my belly. "I'm still processing over here and it's happening to me."

"I know," he kisses me gently. "Do you want to go process at home in bed?"

"Yes." I nod, excited to take off this dress and stretch out on Hunter's king-size bed.

On the way home, Emma texts me.

Emma: *I'm sorry that was awkward. Griffin isn't handling this well.*

Sophie: *Yeah, I know he and I need to talk but tonight was not the time.*

Emma: *How are you feeling? I didn't want to ask at the event.*

Sophie: *Okay. Bloated and tired. I'm going to the doctor on Friday.*

Emma: *I hope you can get some rest. And that everything goes well at the doctor. Will you let me know how it goes?*

Sophie: *Of course.*

Emma: *Sweet dreams!*

Sophie: *Have a good night.*

When I finally climb into bed, my body is exhausted, but my brain is swirling with thoughts. Griffin, my pregnancy and upcoming doctor's appointment, my internship and future career. Not to mention all the logistics and financial burdens of having a baby.

A to-do list that isn't easily checked off. The worst kind.

Hunter turns the lamp off and pulls me close.

"I can hear you thinking," he says.

"I'm overwhelmed. Between my internship and thinking about starting my own business, and the pregnancy, and Griffin not speaking to me. There's a lot going on."

"I know. The last few days have been tough. Tomorrow, we'll make a plan. I know how much you love checklists."

"I do, especially if they're color coded."

He chuckles. "Then that's what we'll do."

In Hunter's arms, I do my best to push all my worries aside and get some much-needed sleep.

CHAPTER 35

Hunter

Sophie: *I'm so horny. Come home and fuck me please.*

I stare at her text. I should be focused on the *horny* and *fuck me* parts of it. That's a no-brainer. But, *come home* stands out. *Home.*

Hunter: *On my way.*

I type out my response, then grab my suit jacket on the way out of my office.

When Jeannie sees me exit, she looks up from her computer.

"Have a good night," I tell her as I pass her desk.

"Oh," she startles, checking her watch, then appears confused with the time it offers her, "um, goodnight."

When I get home, she's already there, lying on the bed with her legs spread wide. Her eyes are closed, her finger circling over her clit as her breasts lift and fall with each deep breath.

Not breaking stride on my way to her, I toss my suit jacket on the chair then yank at my tie to loosen it. My already hard cock twitches eagerly against my zipper.

My eyes drop between her legs. At the wetness dripping along her seam.

"Christ, Sophie."

Her eyes fly open. "I started without you."

"I can see that."

My fingers start working the buttons of my shirt while I stand there taking her in. Appreciating how beautiful she looks with her hair spread over the pillow. She's still tan from our weekend at the lake. Her skin kissed with a bronze glow in places that her swimsuit doesn't cover.

My gaze drags over her body.

Her full breasts and tight pink nipples.

The indent of her waist and curve of her hips.

Her belly where I've started to notice the slightest bump developing.

Those who don't know she's pregnant wouldn't be able to tell, but I know Sophie's body so well, I can see the change happening. The swell of her stomach is a reminder that just like our baby developing inside her, my feelings for Sophie have grown.

I toss my shirt aside, then drop my pants and step out of my boxer briefs.

I give myself a stroke, then crawl over until I'm hovering above her.

"Did you make yourself come?" I ask, joining her hand between her thighs to tease her.

She shakes her head. "I want you inside me."

I move to lower myself between her legs, but Sophie quickly lifts and flips over to her hands and knees.

"I want you to fuck me from behind."

I'm happy to oblige. My fingers slide over her pussy. She's so fucking wet. I line my cock up and press inside.

With my cock buried inside her, she moans loudly.

"*Yes.* I need your cock so badly."

I give her slow, languid strokes. My hands caress her back, then play with her tits as I kiss the space between her shoulder blades.

Sophie arches her back, pressing her ass back into me. I know what she wants.

My hands move to grip her hips, my fingers digging into the flesh of her ass. I rock into her again, then draw my hand back and smack her ass. Sophie moans and I can feel her getting even wetter around my cock. It would normally spur me on, make me go wild. But when I look down at the pinkness of her ass cheek and think about our baby inside her, I struggle to continue.

Fuck. What is happening?

The passion and desire are still there.

I still want to tease her, whisper filth in her ear, and make her come so fucking hard, but I also feel the need to be gentle with her. To take care of her.

I deliver one more spanking before a breathy moan escapes from Sophie's lips and she pulses around my cock. Once her orgasm subsides, I lower her to her back.

"I want to see you."

Taking Sophie from behind is hot, but I've realized nothing compares to seeing the desire in her eyes, the way her lashes flutter and her lips part when she falls apart.

Lifting her left leg over my hip, I sink deep inside her again, then lift my head to look at her.

"This okay?" I ask, my tongue darting out to gently tease her nipple. I know how sensitive she is now.

She nods, pushing her fingers through my hair. My thrusts are careful and unhurried.

This is what *I* need.

Sophie's body tucked safely beneath mine while I fuck her slowly.

The thought sends me over the edge with Sophie tightening around me for a second time.

I spend an excessive amount of time kissing her, letting my fingers stroke over her skin. Finally, I make myself pull back to grab a washcloth from the bathroom to clean us up.

After I clean between her legs, Sophie sighs, a satisfied smile pulling at her lips as she snuggles into my side. I think she's about to fall asleep when her head pops up and she looks at me, her heart-shaped lips dipping at the corners. She looks a bit grumpy for a woman who just had two orgasms.

"You know you only spanked me twice. And it wasn't even that hard."

I know Sophie is sensitive to the fact that a lot of things are changing in her world. Her relationship with Griffin, her body, her career aspirations. The last thing I want to do is make her worry about what is happening between us. My feelings haven't changed, hell, I want her more than ever, but knowing our baby is growing inside her, I'm having a hard time being as rough with her as I was before.

"It's been harder for me to be rough with you, especially when I know you're not feeling well." I kiss her shoulder and trail my fingers down her spine.

She sighs. "I'm feeling good, a little tired, and if I don't eat every few hours, I might murder someone, but that was likely to happen even if I wasn't pregnant."

I chuckle, Sophie is not to be messed with when she's hungry.

My thumb plays with her bottom lip before I lean in and kiss her.

"I want to give you everything you need, but we'll need to talk to the doctor about what is safe."

"Okay." She rolls onto her side and nuzzles in next to me. "I'm starving."

"What sounds good?" I ask.

"Do you still have that truffle popcorn? Oh, and those deli pickle spears from Zucker's? And a black cherry Polar Seltzer?" Her eyes roll to the back of her head, and she moans. "That all sounds so good."

"You bet."

She moves to get off the bed.

"Don't get up, I'll get it."

"I have to get up for work anyway." She slides off the bed and reaches for the robe I got for her to keep here.

"What?" I ask her retreating back.

"My shift at The Penrose," Sophie calls from the hallway as she moves toward the kitchen.

I pull on my briefs and join her in the kitchen.

By the time I get there, she's already elbow deep in the bag of popcorn as she opens the refrigerator to grab out the pickles.

"I don't mean to sound patronizing, but now that you're pregnant, do you think you should be working a second job?"

Her brows lift. "It's even more reason to have a second job. Babies are expensive."

"Again, I don't want to come off the wrong way, but you know that as far as money goes, we're good, right?"

She pulls a jar of pickles from the refrigerator shelf. There are five more exactly like it behind that one. The entire sub-zero refrigerator looks like the neatly stacked shelves of the grocery store refrigerated section. The pantry is identical. I've had my housekeeper stock it full of Sophie's favorite foods, everything she's been craving.

"I get it. You're a billionaire, but I'm not. I need to be able to contribute."

"You are contributing." I point to her belly. "You're growing a whole person. That's a lot of work."

She's struggling with the pickle jar lid, so I take it and open it for her. She pulls one out and takes a bite, fixing me with a glare.

"Clearly, you have no problem with accepting help in certain situations." I indicate the open jar in her hands.

She thinks about this for a moment, then wrinkles her nose in defiance.

"We talked about this. One of my goals after graduating

college and moving here was to become more self-reliant. To not be leaning on Griffin like I have my whole life."

"I understand that you're trying to establish a new dynamic with your brother, but we're in a relationship and we're having a baby together. Taking care of you is my top priority now."

I wrap my arms around her back and pull her to me. That's when I hear it.

I wasn't sure if the sound was what I thought it was until Sophie jumps out of my arms, and I see the horrified look on her face. I can tell she's trying to not make it a big deal, but she's also embarrassed.

"Was that a—"

Sophie's eyes go wide. "Don't say it. Don't you even say it."

I press my lips together. *Do not laugh. Do not laugh.*

It's kind of funny, but Sophie looks like she's going to murder me. Leave no witnesses.

"Gas and indigestion at this stage of pregnancy is perfectly normal," I tell her. "There are a lot of changes going on in your body."

Sophie's eyes narrow at me, while she continues to chomp down on her pickle.

"I know! They're happening to me."

She's cute when she's pretending to be annoyed with me.

"You need to stop reading that book," she says.

"No chance. Besides, I need to be an informed partner."

She shakes her head and grabs another handful of popcorn before leaving the kitchen.

"So, we'll talk about this later?" I call after her.

"We will never talk about it."

"I didn't mean the—"

"Don't say it!"

While Sophie gets ready for her shift at The Penrose, all I can think about is how to show her what she means to me.

~

SOPHIE

After my shift at The Penrose, I'm exhausted. The tips I made tonight were good, but I'm realizing maybe Hunter is right. Working a second job on my feet, late at night is not what my body needs right now.

When I reach the bedroom, I find Hunter shirtless in bed, our *What to Expect When You're Expecting* book split open across his chest. The bedside lamp casts a shadow on his muscular frame. He must have fallen asleep reading.

He obviously did not take my request for him to stop reading that book to heart. I realize now that it was silly of me to say that. Of course, I want a partner that is invested in what I'm going through, but I was embarrassed about farting in front of him and didn't know what else to say. Hunter has seen and touched every inch of my body, but dealing with pregnancy hormones and the changes happening to my body makes me feel more vulnerable.

I quickly change and get ready for bed.

I do my best to quietly get under the covers, but Hunter wakes with my movement.

"Hey," he says, moving to place the book on the bedside table. He's groggy from sleep, but he reaches for me. "How was work?"

I think about telling him it was good, but I don't have the energy to fake it.

"Really hard. I was so tired and bloated all night."

"I'm sorry, baby." He rubs my back and it feels so nice, my muscles immediately relax. "Can I hold you?"

"Yes, please." I wiggle myself into the middle of the bed where Hunter wraps his arms around me. "But don't squeeze me too tight," I whisper on a yawn, referencing what happened earlier.

"Baby, if you need to pass gas, just let it go."

"And fart on your balls?" Desperately tired, I'm delirious now. My embarrassment from earlier gone with every other care in the world.

He chuckles softly against my neck.

"If it makes you feel better, then yeah."

"That's so sweet," I murmur, already half asleep. "Goodnight."

I'm on the edge of sleep, about to be pulled under when the muffled sound of Hunter's voice floats into my ear.

"Goodnight, Sophie. I love you."

Those last three words are so faint, I might have already been dreaming.

CHAPTER 36

Sophie

"Start of your last period?" Gianna, the ultrasound tech, asks.

"June 18th, I think."

She types it into the machine.

Beside me, Hunter squeezes my hand and gives me a supportive smile.

When we got here, I peed in a cup to confirm the pregnancy, then the nurse took my vitals and blood sample.

I have no idea when we got pregnant. We've always used condoms and I was on oral contraception. It's as much of a mystery as the *Up and Vanished* podcast I'm listening to.

Well, over the last few days, I haven't been able to listen to it. It's less intriguing, and more stressful now that another human being is growing inside me. I'm thinking that the pregnancy hormones are altering my brain chemistry, which makes sense because they're doing God knows what to the rest of my body.

While the ultrasound tech preps the machine, I study Hunter's profile.

I wonder what features our baby will have of his, of mine.

"Oh, are we going to be able to find out the sex today?" I ask.

She takes out the ultrasound wand and covers it with a giant condom.

"Not likely today. It depends on how far along you are, so we'll see."

"Is that going where I think it is?" Hunter asks wide-eyed.

"Yes, we'll be doing a vaginal ultrasound today. A little pressure," she says, inserting the wand in my vagina.

I should be watching the screen, but instead, I'm watching Hunter. The way his eyes stare intently on the screen, waiting for a glimpse at our baby while he's asking Gianna a million questions about the technology that makes the ultrasound possible.

I love him.

The thought materializes from a drawer in my brain labeled *overwhelming thoughts* where I've kept it neatly tucked away. It's there along with *I'm pregnant* and *I think my brother hates me now.*

My eyes start to water.

"Hey," Hunter meets my gaze. He lifts my hand to his lips, pressing a kiss there. "We got this."

This man is everything. And he's going to be the father of my child. My heart bursts with happiness at the thought. It's also filled with amazement and anxiety.

How is it possible that I found this big of a love right out of the gate? It's like hitting the bullseye on the first try, with your eyes closed, using your non-dominant hand after spinning in a circle ten times.

It feels special.

Gianna shifts the angle of the wand, drawing my attention to the display on the monitor. For a moment, the screen looks like black and white static. I have no idea what I'm looking at right now.

"Oh, that's interesting." She's the professional, but I'd argue when a phallic-like wand is in someone's vagina, the words 'that's interesting' shouldn't be used.

She moves the wand again. My bladder feels like it's going to burst with her poking around in there. I should have peed before. Why did they tell me not to pee before?

"What's interesting?" Hunter asks, giving me a reassuring wink.

"Just a second. Okay, there. I've got a good photo of them. Let me show you." She rotates the screen around toward us.

"Them?" I question, but then I realize she must be using they/them pronouns since we don't know the sex of the baby yet.

"Yes, them." She points. "Baby A is here. And let me just get a better angle," she moves the wand again. "There's Baby B."

"Baby B?" Hunter and I say in unison.

"Congratulations! You're having twins."

"I'm sorry, I must have misheard you. Did you say—"

"Twins?" Hunter fills in.

"Two babies." Gianna smiles, then looks at the chart. My chart. I have one of those now. "Twins."

"Please stop saying that word." That's all I can say. The idea that there could be two babies never occurred to me.

"Okay, let me get some measurements. That's going to pinpoint their gestational age and your guess date."

"Guess date?" I ask.

"We like to use the term guess date instead of due date. We don't want anyone to feel like they are 'due' at a certain time. It's an estimate after all."

Gianna uses her computer to measure the babies.

Babies. *Twins*. Holy shit.

"With multiples, these factors can vary, but with the information you've given me and the current measurements, it appears you conceived between June fifth and June ninth."

Hunter and I look at each other. It wasn't in Vegas. It was after. Probably the first time we slept together here.

"But I had my period in June," I argue.

"It likely wasn't a period. The spotting you experienced could have been from implantation. The embryos attaching to the uterine wall."

I think back to my nausea. That wasn't pregnancy. It was a stomach bug. My eyes widen. Oh, shit. I wasn't pregnant then, but when I was throwing up, it must have messed with my birth control. And when Hunter and I started having sex, my birth control wasn't effective.

And now there are two human beings growing inside my body. Not one, *two*. I can't wrap my head around it.

"Let's see." She moves the wand again and I think I might have peed a little. "I'm now looking for the placenta. It will help me determine if your babies are identical or fraternal."

Super-sleuth Gianna over here just keeps bringing the facts.

"Ah, there. Your zygotes appear to be sharing a placenta. You're most likely having identical twins, but we can confirm that with genetic testing."

My mouth opens, but nothing comes out.

"That's surprising," Hunter squeezes my hand. "And exciting."

"Let's listen to their heartbeats." She hits another button on the machine and the room fills with a whooshing sound. "It's difficult to distinguish two heartbeats at this stage as they're often beating at the same pace."

"That's their hearts beating? It's so fast," Hunter comments while I'm spiraling.

"That's typical. Perfectly normal."

"Wow." That's all I can say.

"I'm going to print you some pictures." She taps on the keyboard and the machine makes a sound as it prints out the black and white photos of our babies. She extends the photos to me, but ultimately decides I'm worthless in this moment, and moves to give them to Hunter instead. "I'll also send you some literature on what to expect when carrying multiples.

The doctor can go over that with you. And you can always call with any questions."

She pulls the wand out of my vagina and tosses the large condom type thing into the wastebasket.

She finishes cleaning up the space, then stands, handing me a wad of tissues to clean myself up.

"I'll give you two a moment, then I'll have you check out at reception to schedule your next appointment."

"Thank you," Hunter says.

When she's gone, we stare at each other for a moment before Hunter speaks.

"Would you like to process this over ice cream?"

HUNTER

With the shock of finding out we're having twins still fresh, Sophie and I walked to the park to get ice cream. We're now standing in line at the ice cream cart on the corner of Sixty-Fifth and Central Park West.

I think about the fuzzy picture on my kitchen counter identifying not one, but two babies that are currently nestled inside the lining of Sophie's uterus. That's where babies grow. Until we were standing in the ultrasound room, I thought I was a smart man. I run a multibillion-dollar real estate development company, but it turns out, I know nothing.

This entire experience has been humbling.

"I was just coming to terms with the one baby. Now, there are two in there?" She points to her flat stomach as we move up in line. "Do you have some kind of magic sperm that creates multiple babies?"

I can't help but smile at her question. "I'm sure my sperm is special, but the information the tech gave me says that identical twins are completely random. The fertilized egg split, making two babies."

"How are we going to tell the babies apart? If they're identical, how will we know which is which?"

I give her a comforting smile and a quick kiss to her temple. "I think we'll get to know them and be able to tell."

I don't have any more answers than Sophie does right now, but I can tell she needs me to be certain, so I do my best to be that for her.

"Would you want boys or girls?"

I shrug. "I'd be happy with either. I just want them to be healthy."

"You're right. I just thought kids were so far in my future, I haven't given any of this much thought. And names? Now, we'll need *two*. And not just any two. They'll have to coordinate. Give off the same vibe. We can't have a Lark, and a Barbara. Or a Theo and a Sheldon."

"These are all important things to think about, and the good news is, we've got time."

When it's our turn, Sophie orders salted Oreo and I select coffee with praline crunch.

The man hands Sophie her waffle cone, then reaches for another to start scooping mine up.

"Wait, I only ordered one scoop," Sophie says, pointing at her cone.

He motions with the ice cream scooper. "That is one scoop."

"No, it's two," Sophie argues.

"I push a small scoop down into the cone," he says with his thick Jersey accent, demonstrating his technique while scooping up my ice cream, "then I put the big scoop on top."

Sophie's nostrils flare. "So, you agree, it's two."

He looks to me for help.

I shrug. "It's technically two scoops."

"It's a BOGO situation, but I just wanted the BO, not the GO."

His brows lift. "So, you're complaining about getting extra ice cream?"

"It's been a big day," I tell him.

Sophie, having given up on arguing with him, quietly licks her ice cream while I pay.

Then out of nowhere, she announces, "Oh, did I tell you? We missed our window for anal."

She looks up from her cone to find me and the ice cream man staring at her, then glances down the line at the small children waiting.

"Oops," she cringes. "Did I say that really loud?"

The ice cream vendor shakes his head and waves us on, and I toss a twenty in his tip cup for his patience.

I place my free hand on her lower back, guiding her away from the ice cream cart.

I can see the storm of emotion behind her eyes. It's clear there is so much going on in her brain. Even if it doesn't make sense to me, I want to be supportive.

"What are you saying? We missed our window for anal?"

"The pregnancy book I started reading. The one you picked up this weekend says anal is not recommended during pregnancy. It can cause hemorrhoids, but then it says I might get them anyways, so should we just say fuck it and do anal?"

I take her in. A red dress and sandals. Wavy blonde hair cascading over her shoulders, her green eyes wild with uncertainty. She looks beautiful. We're eating ice cream in Central Park and we just found out we're having twins and she's talking about anal.

This sexy, creative, and adorably quirky woman has my heart.

"What do you think?" she asks, giving her ice cream another lick.

"I love you."

Her eyes go wide. "What?"

She seems as surprised by my 'I love you' as I was by her bringing up anal.

"I love you, Sophie. I've loved you for a while now, but I haven't told you because I didn't want to freak you out."

"And now is the best time to tell me because I'm already freaking out?" she asks.

"Yeah. Maybe. I don't know, I just couldn't keep it in any longer."

"Did you say it the other night? When I was falling asleep?"

"Yeah," I nod, thinking of the other night when she was in my arms and the words slipped out. "I thought you were already asleep."

She's quiet a moment and I wonder if it's too much. If confessing my love while she's still taking in all the information from the doctor's appointment was a good idea. But seeing our babies on the screen, hearing their healthy heartbeats fill the exam room, and knowing I'm undoubtedly in love with her, I needed to say it.

I study her for a moment. She's still slowly licking her ice cream cone.

"I don't expect—" I start.

"I wasn't ready for you," she says, her gaze caught on something in the distance.

I'm about to ask her what she means, but she continues.

"I wanted to focus on my career and get my own apartment. To travel, and figure everything else in my life out first. Then, when the time was right, I'd start dating and eventually, fall in love."

"Your five-year plan."

She nods, her focus still over my shoulder, but I can't take my eyes off her.

"Now, I'll never have my own apartment. My career is in limbo," she shifts her gaze up to mine, "and the only thing

I'm certain about is *you*." A smile spreads across her face. "There was a moment in the exam room today, before we found out about the twins. I looked at you and how excited you were and I had this sense of calm. Seeing you in that moment, that's when I knew for certain that I loved you."

With a huge grin on my face, I pull her to me and press my lips to hers.

We get lost in a heated kiss until Sophie yelps because her ice cream has melted onto her hand. There's so much to discuss, so many things we'll need to figure out, but for the rest of the evening, we cuddle up on the couch and watch a movie, enjoying it just being the two of us.

CHAPTER 37

Sophie

It's been two weeks since the dinner party at Emma and Griffin's. Other than our brief encounter at the charity event, I haven't seen or heard from my brother until he texted me on Friday and asked if I could come by late Sunday morning.

After working a wedding yesterday until the early hours of this morning, I'm exhausted, but while I was at the wedding, I got another idea for my internship presentation. A way to incorporate what I've learned this summer with my passion for sustainable weddings. I'm excited to keep working on the project. And while there's still a looming question mark of what I'm going to do when the internship ends, I'm hoping that finalizing my project will give me some clarity.

I hesitate outside Emma and Griffin's apartment door. Technically, I still live here, but with the way we left things between us, it feels odd to just walk in. He's expecting me, so I give up the debate and use the code to unlock the door.

The second I enter the apartment, the smell of chocolate chip pancakes causes an overwhelming sense of nostalgia.

"Hey, it's me," I call as I shut the door and slip out of my sandals.

I find Griffin in the kitchen, a dish towel thrown over his shoulder as he holds a bowl of batter over a stove top skillet. Even though the luxury high-end appliance kitchen is different, the visual of Griffin meticulously making pancakes for us is the same.

For a moment, it feels like nothing has changed. But then I think about seeing him at the charity event and how he couldn't even look me in the eye. My stomach flips with the uncertainty of how this is going to go.

"Hey." He smooths out the batter with a spoon, then turns to look at me. "Are you hungry?"

I swallow back the emotion that is threatening to spill out of me and force a smile.

"For happy face pancakes? Always." I glance around the kitchen. "What can I do to help?"

"The bacon's already in the microwave. Would you cut up the strawberries?"

I pull out a cutting board and paring knife, then grab the basket of fresh strawberries from the refrigerator. Even with the unresolved tension between us, it still feels good to be here together preparing our traditional Sunday breakfast.

"Where's Emma?" I ask, slicing into a strawberry.

"She went to brunch with Chloe and Jess."

It's important that it's just the two of us, but right now, I could use Emma's ability to fill awkward silence. Because that's what it is as we both work quietly.

Finally, Griffin brings two plates over with a large pancake on each, I set the fruit on top, and he takes the bacon out of the microwave to place as the mouth. He uses the can of whipped cream to spray on the hair, then I follow him to the table that is already set with napkins and silverware.

I was hopeful about clearing the air, but the longer we don't talk, the more anxious I'm becoming.

I take a bite, but I can't even taste it, my stomach too tied in knots to register the sweet pancake.

Griffin chews a bite of pancake, then sets his fork down.

"This is the last time I'm going to make these pancakes for us."

At his words, my heart drops out of my chest. This is not at all what I expected when he invited me over.

"What? Why?" The alarm is evident in my voice. *What does this mean?*

"Soph, we started happy face pancake Sundays twelve years ago to create a tradition. It was a way for us to bond and find stability after Mom died. It signified the start of me being your official guardian and you the young girl that I needed to take care of.

"I'll admit to being overprotective when you were growing up, but it was because I couldn't stand the thought of anything happening to you. I still can't, but I'm not your guardian anymore." He smiles ruefully. "Change is hard. I struggled with committing to Emma because I was afraid how it would impact you, and when you told me you got the internship here, I was relieved because I didn't have to face that change. I was able to stay in the same place with you. Finding out about you and Hunter, that you're pregnant, was a huge wake-up call. I was never mad at you, never disappointed in *you*. I was frustrated with myself that I couldn't be what you needed in that moment, a supportive brother, even a friend, because I was too wrapped up in being your protector. I couldn't let go of the relationship dynamic we've had, because I thought if I did, I'd lose you. But it turns out that was happening anyway."

"You didn't lose me." I shake my head adamantly, my eyes wet with unshed tears. "I wanted so badly to have a fresh start with you here. I've felt like I was a burden that you graciously took on all those years and I wanted to prove that I could be self-sufficient. I wanted to take that weight off your shoulders."

It's Griffin's turn to shake his head. "The situation was

hard, but I never thought *you* were a burden." His jaw tightens, like he's fighting back emotion. "I hate that you'd ever think that."

"But you gave up so much for me. You could have had such a different life if you didn't have to take care of me."

"No. Don't even say that. Sophie, you are my family."

He pulls me out of my chair and into his arms, holding me while I sob.

"You made sacrifices, too. We both had to grow up fast and lean on each other. And if given the opportunity, I would have done it all the same. Look at my life now." His voice is calm and soothing. "I'm living in New York City with my beautiful wife and I have a job I'm excited about." He squeezes me tighter. "And I'm going to be an uncle."

His sweet words make me cry harder.

"How are you doing? Are you feeling okay with the pregnancy?"

I nod, taking the tissue he hands me to wipe at my eyes and nose. Why does every conversation I have lately end in a full emotional meltdown? Pregnancy hormones are a real bitch.

"I'm feeling good. I'm tired and emotional." I motion to the waterworks still streaming down my face. "Oh, and we're having twins."

Griffin blinks. "*Twins?*"

The shock on his face makes me laugh through my tears.

"I had the same reaction. And they're identical. You're going to be Uncle Griffin times two."

"Wow." He looks overwhelmed, but then wraps his arms around me again. "That's incredible. Congratulations, Soph."

"It's wild and scary and I've been really sad because we weren't talking."

"I'm sorry I wasn't there for you the last few weeks. I needed to sort out my own shit. Emma helped me find a therapist to talk to about everything. I've only met with him a couple times, but it's been life-changing."

"That's great."

"I'm feeling better now. This helps." I motion between us. "And Hunter has been so supportive. I don't know what I would have done if he wasn't all in. He's already in love with these babies."

"And what about you?" Griffin asks.

"In love with the babies?"

He nods. "It's a huge change from what you had planned."

"Yeah, it is." Suddenly nervous again, I ball the tissue up in my hand. "There's still a plan, it just looks different. It may seem like it's too soon, but I love Hunter. I can't imagine not being with him."

"Does he feel the same?" Griffin asks.

"Yes. He told me he loved me."

"He told me that day, out on the balcony when we were fighting." Griffin presses his lips together. "When I was fighting him."

"That he loved me?"

He nods. "I was surprised. Not because I didn't think he could fall for you, but because of his reputation. I wasn't sure if he was just giving me lip service and trying to dissuade my anger."

"Please don't be mad at Hunter. You two were friends and I feel like him being with me has ruined that."

"I'm not mad at either of you. I was hurt to find out you were seeing each other behind my back, but I don't want you to worry about me and Hunter. I'll talk to him."

I nod. Now I'm thinking about my relationship with Hunter. How my need for independence is clashing with Hunter's desire to take care of me and the babies.

"Hunter wants to take care of me."

"As he should." Griffin nods.

I sigh.

"I know that you were looking to become more self-sufficient, to do things on your own, but you're not on your own. You'll have two babies to take care of and you know the saying…it takes a village. We're all going to be there for you and Hunter."

"I know this probably isn't what you want to hear, but I'm going to start my own business based off my blog. It'll be a slow start, especially once the babies are here, but it's what I'm passionate about and I think the flexibility that it'll give me is going to be huge as a new mom."

"Why wouldn't I want to hear that?" he asks with confusion.

"It never seemed like you were supportive of my blog being a career option before."

"It was never my intention to make you feel that way. I think that's great, Soph. I want you to be happy, and if that's the right path for you, then I think you should pursue it. I'm sorry if I made you feel like it wasn't the right thing to do."

I nod. "So, no more happy face pancakes?"

Griffin shakes his head, a small smile pulling at his lips. "I thought we'd start a new tradition. Sunday dinners together with our family and friends. A way to catch up with each other as our lives get busier."

The thought of getting everyone together, Griffin, Emma, me, and Hunter, maybe even Hannah and James, and Barrett and Chloe, it's the perfect kind of tradition. A gathering of the family that Griffin and I have found here.

"And happy face pancakes aren't going anywhere." He nods at my stomach. "They'll continue on with the next generation."

Now I'm imagining making happy face pancakes for the twins. Two toddlers with hands smooshed into the whipped cream and making a complete mess. It's exciting to imagine, but also nerve-racking.

From my evolving relationship with Hunter, to my changing career path, to now being pregnant with twins, I'm starting to realize that my plans completely derailing isn't as terrifying as I thought it would be.

CHAPTER 38

Sophie

I glance at Hunter's text again, then up at the building address in front of me. It's a luxury apartment building a few blocks from Hunter's current building and only a block from Central Park. Hunter asked me to meet him here on my lunch break. It's a little past twelve-thirty. I look around, but there's no sign of Hunter.

"Ms. Hart?" An older man in a suit approaches me.

"Yes?"

"I'm Kirk Landow, Mr. Cartwright is running a few minutes late and wanted me to escort you up to the property."

"The property?" I ask.

He motions in the front door where a doorman is already holding it open for us. "The building was built in 1910, but as you can see from the updated lobby, it has been refurbished and now boasts luxury amenities. It's a prime location being only two blocks from Central Park, the B subway line, and of course, only a mile to designer shopping at Columbus Circle."

I follow Kirk through the lobby and into the elevator where his history of the building and updated amenities spiel continues.

"This penthouse is 3,700 square feet and features park and city views."

I make my way over to the window to take in the views he's mentioning.

"Holy shit, that's breathtaking." Then, my eyes widen at the words falling from my mouth. "Sorry."

"No, Ms. Hart," he chuckles, "I think you described the view perfectly."

I'm so enthralled with the space I don't even register the front door opening and footsteps moving toward us.

"Sorry I'm late."

I turn to find Hunter there. His hair is mussed, likely from his hands. He's wearing a blue suit that matches his eyes, and a navy-blue tie. My stomach cartwheels at the sight of him. *Easy, girl.* While I'm quelling my excitement to see him, Hunter walks right over to me and pulls me into his arms. His kiss lingers on my lips. I can tell he wants more. That he'd greet me differently if Kirk wasn't here.

"It's good to see you." His hands find my hips.

"You, too."

"I was just about to show Ms. Hart the chef's kitchen."

"What do you think?" Hunter asks.

I look around. "It's amazing." My eyes return to Hunter. "I'm just not sure what we're doing here."

Hunter turns toward Kirk.

"Kirk, would you give us a moment?" he asks.

"Certainly. I'll step outside."

When Kirk is gone, Hunter pulls away and walks toward the floor-to-ceiling windows in the living area.

"Would you be comfortable living here?" He motions to our surroundings.

We haven't talked about me moving in again since he first asked me when he found out I was pregnant. He hasn't asked, and although my thoughts on the idea have changed, I haven't brought it up.

He must read the hesitation on my face, because he quickly fills in.

"The apartment isn't for us."

"Oh, it's not?" I ask, my brow furrowing in confusion.

"No," his eyes find mine. "It's for you."

"Me? What do you mean?"

He crosses back over to where I'm standing.

"You wanted the experience of living alone. Having your own place." He places his hand on my belly. "It won't be for long, but I want you to have that."

If he wasn't holding me in place, I'd fall backwards.

I look around in disbelief. "Hunter, you can't buy me a condo."

His smile tells me everything I need to know. He already did.

"Hunter, that's not—"

"Necessary? Prudent? What, Sophie?"

"Yes! All those things." I pull away and walk toward the window. More than finding out I'm pregnant, the hardest thing to manage has been the idea that I won't be able to stand on my own two feet. My goal to be more independent, not be a burden or someone else's responsibility like I was for Griffin growing up has now transferred to Hunter. I don't want to be that to him.

I recall my conversation with Griffin. I need to find balance. Because no matter what plans I had, the moment I found out I was pregnant, that I was going to be a mom, everything changed.

"I get wanting to be independent, to do things for yourself and not be indebted to anyone, but then there's being downright stubborn."

I whip around. "I'm being stubborn? What about you?"

"Wanting to take care of you is not unreasonable."

"And wanting to take care of myself is?" I snap back with

the frustration, that niggling feeling that I'm a burden to the people around me worming its way back in.

My emotions are a hurricane about to make landfall. Another woman would swoon at her baby daddy—ugh, I hate that phrase—buying her a luxury condo on Central Park West. But I'm still coming to terms with the guilt that Griffin did so much for me growing up and this feels like a setback. Hunter knows this.

"I thought this could be a compromise. The condo would be all yours, the title in your name. There's also an account set up for HOA expenses and utilities. Everything is in your name."

I swallow thickly because no matter how sweet the gesture is, I still can't help but feel frustrated by it.

"You didn't want anything from me. That was the original appeal of you and our arrangement. Just orgasms and fun times wrapped up in a neat bow. Now, I want to give you the world and you're not even asking for the bare minimum, afraid to be a burden to anyone."

He pushes a hand through his hair.

"You're going to be the mother of our children, but you're also Sophie, the woman I fell in love with."

He walks toward me. His steps are confident and measured, meanwhile, my heart is fighting to escape my chest. Stopping in front of me, one hand finds my jaw, the other grips my hip, pulling me to him. He tilts my head up until our gazes lock. My heart swells at the emotion I see behind those pools of blue. He already told me he loved me at the park last week, the day we found out we're having twins, and he's said it every day since, but I'll never get tired of hearing those words from his lips.

"I love you, Sophie. I want a life with you. I want you in every way, and I know it will take time to figure everything out. I see that you're overwhelmed, and I want to be the one to take that burden from you.

"I want to spoil you. I want to buy you things and take you places. Travel the world, then curl up in sweatpants with you on the couch. I want everything with you, Sophie, and I thought giving you a space that you can call your own, even for a little while, would make you happy. Yes, this is new, but also it feels like you've always been mine," his thumb ghosts over my lower lip, "and we're adding babies to the mix before we've had much time together, but I want it all with you. It's going to be hard and messy and we're going to be tired and irritated with each other sometimes, I'm sure. But there's no one I'd rather be all those things with than you."

My mouth hangs open, my brain starting to spin again, overwhelmed by this man in front of me and his thoughtful gesture. That's what it is. His way of showing me how he feels and wanting to take care of me. Like Griffin and I agreed to work on our relationship, finding a new dynamic, I need to apply that to me and Hunter. Find a balance between my need for independence and his desire to take care of me.

I look around the condo. It's beautiful, but I don't have to see the rest of it to know that it's not where I want to be.

"I love you, too." I reach up to cup his face. "And I want everything with you."

Hunter's mouth curves into a smile before it drops to mine. He pulls back and my fingers glide down the placket of his shirt.

"I can't accept the condo, Hunter."

A faint groan escapes from the depth of his chest but he continues to hold me close.

"I know I've been challenging lately. My emotions are all over the place, and you probably don't want to put up with me, but if the offer still stands to move into your place, I want to do that."

With my announcement, a huge smile transforms Hunter's face. "Are you kidding? Of course, it does. I want you there all the time."

"Good, because there's no getting rid of me now."

Hunter lifts me into his arms, kissing me passionately. Minutes pass until we're finally willing to separate. I look around the condo, then back to Hunter, giving him a sheepish grin.

"So, what's the return policy on this thing?"

CHAPTER 39

Sophie

The intern office is in party mode. While nerves were high this morning, with each person that has come back with their presentation complete, the excitement and office volume has increased. The office is decorated stylishly and there's a sheet cake with buttercream frosting that I've had my eye on since I saw it delivered, but I'm waiting until after my presentation to celebrate. Once it's over, I'll drown myself in sugar.

I can't believe the summer is over and I'm out of my first trimester. I'll be thirteen weeks next week. After this presentation, Hunter and I are driving to Lake George for the long weekend. We're meeting his parents and Hannah and James there. I'm so excited.

The time is flying by, but the last month has been exhilarating. I moved in with Hunter and I'm slowly setting up a home office in one of the extra bedrooms. We decided which bedroom would be for the twins and I've started a Pinterest board for nursery décor ideas.

Last month, the feature in *Brides* hit shelves. It was surreal, but I've still got the entire stack of issues Hunter and Emma collectively gave me to prove it happened. Since the article came out, my blog has received an insane amount of traffic and requests for advertisers. I'm making some good money with it now. And I was invited to attend a speaker panel at the Blushing Bride convention in Las Vegas next year. It'll be a challenging time because the twins will be only a month old, but Hunter said we could make it work if I wanted to do it.

One of the best parts of the *Brides* feature was the issue party that the editors hosted for all the bloggers and influencers. It was great to meet and network with so many others in the same space. I've also started reaching out to vendors in the industry that offer products and services that align with my sustainable wedding business.

All of that has helped shape my final presentation that I'll be giving this morning.

All the interns were randomly assigned a slot and I'm going last. The anticipation is killing me. I want to rip it off like a band-aid, but instead, I'm sitting here overthinking everything.

June walks through the door and my stomach flutters with nerves. Maxwell gathers his laptop and heads for the door. I'm after him.

"How'd it go?" I ask June as she approaches our desk.

"I don't want to be overconfident, but I think I nailed it." She beams, her dark hair swishing over her shoulders as she bounces happily.

I smile. "I'm positive that you did."

"How are you feeling about your presentation?" she asks.

"Like I was just informed I'm driving a car with no brakes."

Her brows lift. "Pretty optimistic, then?"

We both laugh, because if I don't laugh right now, I'll either vomit or cry, maybe both.

Our desk is packed up, all our personal belongings already taken home so that there's nothing to lug around when we go out for a celebration later. Job offers won't go out until next week, so everyone will be able to enjoy the last day together with no hard feelings.

I go through my notes again, clicking through the slides to make sure everything looks perfect. Even if I'm not angling for a permanent position here, I want to do my absolute best. I want Marion to see me as a resource, a businesswoman that she may want to work with someday.

Movement at the door catches my eye. Maxwell is back. He makes eye contact with me and my stomach twists tighter.

It's my turn.

I grab my laptop from the desk and make my way toward the conference room where Marion and the assistant event planners are gathered.

I plug my laptop into the connection to the video screen behind me and open my slideshow.

Marion nods in my direction. "Ms. Hart, when you're ready."

"My presentation shows how aspects of each of the weddings I assisted with this summer could have been made more sustainable by opting for lower waste products and environmentally-friendly practices."

The room is too quiet and my hand shakes with nerves as I click through the slides.

I go through my presentation, then launch into my business, Sustainable Wedding Chic.

I'm about to wrap it up when Marion interrupts me. "Ms. Hart, is this your internship presentation or a business proposal?" Her lips are pinched, her face discerning.

But then I look over at Johnathan and he gives me a reassuring wink and it calms my nerves.

"Both," I say as confidently as possible. "You see, I came to New York City, enraptured by the thought of planning luxury weddings alongside some of the best planners in the business under the elite company of Marion Adler Events, but what it reaffirmed is that not only do I want to help couples plan one of the most memorable days of their lives, but I want to do it sustainably. I'm looking to bring awareness of options to those looking to plan a more eco-conscious event and offer guidance to those who may not even know what is possible. There will be couples who want to make their entire wedding zero waste, and there will be those who might opt to focus on a few aspects of their wedding. Like print wedding invitations on seed paper or using recycled décor. And I want to be the person that can help them make those choices."

"Like a consultant?" Johnathan prompts.

"Yes." I smile, having his support is the best feeling.

"Interesting," Marion says with a nod. "Thank you for your presentation."

I unplug my laptop and leave. On the other side of the conference room door, I let out a sigh of relief.

At my desk, I find a text that Hunter sent before my presentation.

Hunter: *Thinking of you. I love you.*

I'm about to text back when June sets a plate with a heaping piece of cake on it at my desk.

"I checked and we can't actually inject the cake into your veins, so you'll have to eat it like everyone else," she says.

Along with Johnathan, she's been so supportive about my new business endeavor and my pregnancy.

"Thank you." I fork a bite and let the frosting melt on my tongue.

"So, how'd it go?" she asks.

"It wasn't a presentation to land a job, but it was what I wanted it to be."

She smiles. "I'm glad you went with your gut."

"Me, too."

That afternoon, I leave Marion Adler Events for the last time. My time here was nothing like I expected, but everything I needed.

CHAPTER 40

Hunter

"I can't decide on the napkins. White would look pretty with my centerpiece, but the dark blue is also nice. It contrasts with the blush and rose-colored flowers."

"They both look great." I wrap my arms around Sophie's waist from behind and place my hands on her growing belly. She's sixteen weeks now and has the most adorable bump that I can't help but constantly touch.

She sighs, leaning into me. "That's not helpful."

"It's a nacho bar with queso and salsa, so let's go with the blue."

Suddenly she stiffens, and gasps. "The queso!"

I follow her into the kitchen, but we don't find burnt queso, we find Emma there stirring it while Griffin pulls out a bowl for the chips. My dad's whipping up a batch of guacamole while my mom is perfecting a non-alcoholic margarita recipe.

She hands a glass to Sophie. "I added more lime. Let me know what you think."

Sophie takes a sip and nods. "Delicious."

Since Sophie has settled into my place—*our place*—we decided to have our friends and family over for dinner to announce the sex of our babies. She's been craving Mexican food lately, so a nacho bar made sense.

Sunday dinner is a new tradition that Griffin and Sophie decided to start when they patched things up after our dating and pregnancy news came out a few months ago.

"Remember, I'm the one in charge here today."

Her lips relax, and a smile pulls at the corners. "Okay, that's kind of a turn-on."

I smile and gently pat her ass. Everything turns her on right now.

"Save it for later, baby," I press a kiss to her lips.

My parents—okay, mostly my mom because she's crazy about babies—were over the moon when Sophie and I told them we were expecting. My mom cried and then promptly took up knitting so she could make baby blankets for the twins. It's something she says she wished she had done for me and Hannah. Her text updates on the progress of said blankets are downright comical.

Hannah and James were happy for us, too. Though Hannah had a moment of panic when she wondered if Sophie was due around the time of her wedding. She'd want us to be there of course. Luckily, Sophie's guess date is months in advance of Hannah's wedding. That's hard to believe. That the babies will be here before Hannah and James get married.

After we eat, Sophie and I go into the kitchen to get the cookies we had made at the local bakery where I get my cookie decorating kits. We gave the owner, Marjorie, an envelope with the babies' sexes in it and asked her to make some sprinkle-filled cookies to help us make our announcement.

"Are you nervous?" I ask Sophie.

"A little. Up to this point, it's been fun to daydream about either scenario. Now, we'll know for sure."

"We don't have to know. We could just toss these cookies out and be surprised."

"First, that's a terrible waste of cookies. Second, I said I was nervous, not terrified. We're going to find out."

"That's my girl." I press a kiss to her cheek.

With our family and a few of our close friends gathered, we each break into a cookie to find pink sprinkles.

"We're having girls!" Sophie exclaims, leaping into my arms so that the sprinkles go flying everywhere. I think she was secretly hoping for girls, but she didn't want to voice it.

"Congratulations, man." Griffin pulls me in for a hug. "Baby girls. That's going to be a heck of a ride."

My parents hug me and Sophie, teary-eyed and overjoyed. Hannah, Emma, and Chloe are already shopping online for clothes, while James and Barrett salute me with a shot of whiskey.

"Can you believe it?" Sophie asks, when we have a quiet moment together.

"At this point, nothing is shocking anymore."

She laughs, her green eyes sparkling as she wraps her arms around my neck.

"I'm so happy."

"Me, too, baby." I place my hand on her growing bump.

"You're going to be the best dad," she says. "So loving and thoughtful, and protective but not overbearing."

It suddenly hits me that there will be two little girls running around that will have some resemblance to Sophie.

Fuck. I'm screwed.

"When you say not overbearing, you mean that I'll approve of them dating when they're eighteen?"

"Hunter," she lifts her brows, "they're not even born yet, you can't set a dating age mandate."

"Right, but I think it would be good to have a plan. Start discussing possible curfew times. Tour the all-girl schools. I'm sure there are wait lists for the best ones."

She shakes her head at my declarations. "I think we'll figure it out along the way."

"Good plan." I pull her close. "I love you."

"I love you, too."

Epilogue

THREE MONTHS LATER

SOPHIE

"You in this swimsuit is very distracting." Hunter leans over me, placing a kiss against my cleavage, his hands gently squeezing my hips.

"You should probably get rid of it then, huh?" I say.

With a smirk, he pulls at the tie behind my neck and the material falls away from my breasts. Another pull and the knot behind my back is undone.

We'd been on the beach outside our private villa on the South Shore of Maui when a simple sunscreen application had turned heated. That's been the theme of the babymoon that Hunter had surprised me with right after Christmas. Eat. Beach. Sex. Repeat.

After discarding my bikini top, he kneels before me. He sweetly kisses my bump before lifting the weight of my breasts in his capable hands.

I arch my back. "That feels so good." Not only the way he's teasing my nipples with his thumbs, but simply taking the weight of my heavy breasts from my body feels amazing.

"Lie back." He guides me to the head of the bed, settling me onto the array of fluffy white pillows there while snaking my bikini bottoms down my legs as I go. His erection is clearly visible in his navy-blue swim trunks.

Hunter takes his time, kissing me everywhere. His large hands stroking me and massaging my achy muscles. By the time he discards his trunks, I'm so relaxed. It's funny that sex used to be rough and urgent, but now it feels like a massage with a happy ending. I'm sure times of urgency will return after the twins are born, but this is where we are right now.

His fingers trace over the tan lines on my back as he settles in behind me. One arm moves under my head, cradling me, while his other hand splays out over my belly.

While I like being on top during sex, sometimes when I'm feeling like I want to be taken care of, this is my favorite position. Hunter behind me, his fingers teasing between my legs until I cry out. Then, he rocks into me from behind, filling me completely.

My hand reaches up behind me to push into his hair. Whispered words between us, soft and sweet.

Yes, Hunter. Right there.

Sophie, you feel incredible.

I love you.

My orgasm hits, and the familiar sensation of my belly tightening with each pulse makes it even more intense.

Hunter cleans us up, then offers me the light cotton robe I love to lounge in. We cuddle up in bed, staying there until the sun drops low in the sky and my bladder starts screaming at me.

Then, we shower and get ready for dinner.

We walk to one of the restaurants at the resort where we're staying.

I wait while Hunter checks us in for our reservation.

"They're running behind. Should we take a walk on the beach?"

I glance at my watch. If I would have known dinner was going to be delayed, I'd have eaten that granola bar Hunter set out on the table for me. That's one thing I've discovered being pregnant, low blood sugar is no joke.

"How long did they say? Shouldn't we be here in case they call our name?"

He nods toward the beach, taking my hand. "Five minutes."

"Okay."

While the days are sunny and warm, the evening breeze is cool, so I've opted for a light sweater over my long dress.

"I'm happy you've been able to take some time away from working. I know you're anxious to get as much done as you can before the girls arrive."

He's right. Since I started my own business a few months ago, I've been working diligently on the few accounts I've decided to take on before the twins are here.

While I'm getting most of my business through my blog and social media following, Marion has also hired me as a consultant to offer my services to her clients. It's the best of both worlds, and I'm loving the projects I'm working on.

I'm also trying to be mindful of how much I can take on right now. I'm seven months pregnant, and while I'm feeling pretty good at this point, I know most of the projects started now will need to be finalized after the girls arrive. No amount of preparedness is going to ready me for life once the twins are here. I'm aware of that and am now seeing a therapist who is helping me to work through past family trauma and this transitional time in my life.

"You were right. It has been challenging, but it's also been the most fun."

When we come to the spot where the path ends and we have to take our shoes off to walk on the sand, Hunter kneels down to help me remove my sandals, then takes my hand again.

"And I'm impressed by you not taking a single work call."

"You know what I realized?"

"What?"

"That I was largely focused on work because I didn't want to make time for anything else. Anyone else. Now, it feels easy to prioritize you because I want to."

He kisses the back of my hand and I swoon.

"Are you excited for the baby shower next week?" he asks.

"Yes, and it's technically babies shower. I can't wait to see what they've come up with." June helped Emma and Hannah plan it. And of course, Johnathan wanted input as well.

June did get offered a permanent position at Marion Adler Events and has been loving her new job. Her boyfriend, Allen, ended up moving to the city to be with her there. We still see each other often when I stop by to meet with Marion or Johnathan or one of the other wedding planning associates.

"I'm sure it will be perfect."

I hit a patch of uneven sand and wobble sideways, but Hunter steadies me.

"How did you run on this?" I ask. "I can barely walk."

This morning Hunter ran four miles down the beach before I even got out of bed.

"It doesn't help that your center of gravity is off. You'll be back to it before you know it."

"I hope so."

Hunter squeezes my hand and I smile over at him. He's wearing a white button-down with the sleeves rolled up and dark blue pants. His skin is tan from the sun and his jaw unshaven in a five o'clock shadow that I've been really into lately.

"Are you excited for the groundbreaking ceremony next week?" I ask.

"Yeah," he nods, "it's been a long time coming. I'm happy that the project has finally made it to this point."

"Well, I'm excited to go. You've been so supportive of my new business; I can't wait to be there for one of your big moments. Do you get to dig with a shovel and everything or is the ground too hard for that?"

"Um," he says distractedly, "we should be able to shovel some dirt."

"Do you think we should head back?" I ask. "I'm sure it's been five minutes. I'm also getting hungry and you know that when I'm hungry I've got twenty minutes max before things start going downhill."

"We don't have a reservation at the restaurant."

"What?" I ask, panic starting to set in. "Hunter, I need to eat. Very soon."

"Don't worry, baby. We're going to eat. There's a nice beach dinner set up for us."

He motions down the beach to the glow of tiki torches where a table is set up on the quiet beach.

"Oh, thank goodness." I'm so relieved, I could cry.

"But first…" he takes my sandals from my hand and sets them down on the sand. Then, he drops to one knee.

"Sophie, you have brought so much love and joy to my life."

His throat works hard to swallow, and I can see the emotion in his eyes as my own start to water.

"I couldn't even imagine this," he reaches forward to palm my bump, "until I imagined it all with you. I can't wait to be a parent with you. To grow and laugh with you as we inevitably make mistakes. But there's another role I want…to be your husband. The man by your side every step of the way through life's ups and downs." He pulls out a small velvet box and opens it to reveal a diamond ring. "Sophie Renee Hart, will you marry me?"

I'm already nodding before I can get the words out.

"Yes," I finally say, wiping at the tears streaming down my

face while Hunter places the stunning diamond ring on my finger.

He stands to pull me into his arms, as best as he can with my bump in the way.

"I love you so much." He kisses me.

"I love you, Hunter."

He's right. Neither of us could have imagined what our secret relationship would turn into. It was perfectly unplanned.

Epilogue Part 2

SIX MONTHS LATER

HUNTER

When Sophie bends down, the back of her robe lifts to reveal her luscious ass.

I look up to find her eyes meeting my hungry gaze, but she shakes her head and laughs. "Don't even think about it. We're running late."

"But now that's all I can think about."

My mind returns to this morning when my face was buried between Sophie's thighs.

I set Finley down on her belly on the playmat next to her sister, Poppy, who is already enjoying tummy time. I didn't know that was a thing.

Parenting is filled with surprises.

Like their arrival at three o'clock on a Tuesday afternoon three weeks early. That was normal for multiples we were told.

From the moment they arrived, healthy and happy, we've been obsessed with them.

Finley Kate and Poppy Renee are two dark-haired beauties with green eyes like their mom, so it would be impossible not to be.

Would I have liked to have had more time as just the two of us? Sure, but I wouldn't trade our life together for the world. It's messy now. Early mornings that don't involve sex before we head out for our run, but instead, diaper changes and feedings before we load the girls into the jogging stroller and head out for the park.

Sophie working in her office for few hours in the evenings while I put the girls down.

We're figuring it all out as we go along.

Sophie rushes past me, her silk robe fluttering around her hips. I catch her elbow. Turning her to face me, I edge her back against the wall. My hand finds the back of her neck, my thumb tilting her jaw up until our eyes meet. I'm desperate to finish our interrupted quickie this morning, but more than that I want to hold her in my arms.

"I love you," I tell her, pressing a kiss to her jaw.

"I love you, too." Her hands move up my chest and over my shoulders until they connect behind my neck. "Hannah is not going to be pleased if I don't get to her room for hair and makeup by ten."

Today is Hannah and James's wedding. It's wild to think that a year ago the planning meeting I attended with Hannah, with Johnathan and Sophie, is what started all of this. That a year later, I'd be engaged to the love of my life and have two precious baby girls.

When Sophie left Marion Adler Events, Hannah and James continued their planning with Johnathan, and Hannah asked Sophie to be one of her bridesmaids. I'm a groomsman, so our nanny will be in tow to help with the girls while we're on wedding party duty.

I smile wickedly. "Two five-month-old babies are the perfect excuse to be late."

I crave Sophie's body even more after her pregnancy.

Seeing her as a mom, a successful businesswoman, and all the things she does for our family has only increased my desire for her.

Having the twins hasn't been all rainbows and unicorns, but I will say that we don't know any different. If the next one is a single baby, we'll think it's a piece of cake. I can't wait to have more babies with her.

"You've got that look again," she says.

"What look?" I ask.

She shakes her head. "I'm good with two." Her lips quirk. "For now."

She's got an IUD in now, and we've talked about timing and how important the next few years are for getting her business established. I have no doubt that Sophie will succeed, but I know it will take time.

"I know, but I think we should practice. A lot."

"Tonight. Besides, I need to shower. I smell like baby vomit."

"You think some baby puke is going to deter me?"

I run my nose along the column of Sophie's neck, finding that sensitive spot where her ear and jaw connect. I breathe her in. She smells like sunshine and *mine* and okay, there might be a faint hint of baby puke.

"My mom and dad said they'd take the girls tonight so we can stay later at the reception."

"That's so nice of them." She smiles, then suddenly, her eyes light up. "Or we could come back here early, have uninterrupted sex and get eight hours of sleep."

"I like where your head is at." I steal another kiss before I let her pull away.

"Hey," she says, still holding my hand. "Have I told you you're an amazing dad and partner and my best friend and lover all rolled into one?"

"I think you've mentioned it before, but I'd love to hear it again."

Sophie opens her mouth, but a cry from Finley interrupts the moment.

"I got her. You go shower."

Later, at Hannah and James's wedding reception, the uncoupled guests are participating in some game where they find their numbered match to share a dance, while I've got my arms wrapped securely around Sophie's waist as we sway to the music.

"Can you believe we're going to do all of this in a few months?" she asks, looking up at me.

"I can't wait." I kiss her lips.

"For the planning to be over?" she laughs.

"No, for you to be my wife."

She reaches up and presses her lips to mine again. "I love you."

"I love you, too."

Now that the ceremony, dinner, and speeches are over, I can relax. The girls are already back at my parents' hotel room with our nanny. They'll relieve her after the reception.

Sophie lifts her head from my chest.

"Who is that guy dancing with Colette?" she asks.

I scan the dance floor, looking for them.

"That's Rhys."

Sophie's brows shoot up. "The infamous Rhys? From summers at Lake George?"

"Yeah." I nod, watching the childhood friends across the dance floor. "He's back in the city now. My parents encouraged Hannah to invite him."

"They look good together," she says.

"Rhys and Colette *together*? That would be like oil and water mixing. They're complete opposites."

"In what way?" she asks.

I shrug. "Every way that counts. She's sweet and focused on her dance career and he's…what was it that Hannah called him? A fuckboy?"

Sophie laughs. "And you're one to talk?" Her lips quirk as she teases me.

I pretend to be offended. "What are you trying to say, Mrs. Cartwright?" I let one of my hands slip lower to cup her ass.

"We never saw this going anywhere. Never thought we'd have a happily ever after." Her fingers tease through the hair at the back of my neck. "And I'm not Mrs. Cartwright…yet."

I growl against the shell of her ear. "Doesn't matter, you're still mine."

I kiss her then because she's right, this happy ending was accidentally ours, but I have every intention of making it last forever.

THE END

Acknowledgments

This is the first book I've written where I didn't get 50,000 words in and scrap the entire thing to start over. I don't know what it means. Maybe I'm figuring out my writing process… no guarantees, but I'll take it as a win.

Thank you to my husband, Eric, my rock and my most enthusiastic cheerleader, and my three kids, for supporting me in my passion for writing. I couldn't do this without your love and support. Thank you for understanding when I've set unrealistic deadlines and need to work through the weekend. I'm going to try not to do that next time around…we'll see how it goes.

To my family, Mom, Dad, and Jenny, John, Adam and Debbie, Jill and Paul: Thank you for your continued love and support. It means the world to me! To Linda who is no longer with us, but who I know would be cheering me on and buying all the books.

Thank you to my friends who have supported me on this journey; asking how writing is going, buying my books and spreading the word. Thank you for your friendship and love: Amanda, Courtney, Erica, Hadley, Kate, and Sam.

Thank you to my outstanding beta reading team: Allie @allie_rambles, Anna P, Ashley O'Dell, Isabella, Jordan, Laura, Molly, and Shea. I'm always grateful for your candid feedback and encouraging comments. My books wouldn't be what they are without you.

Thank you to my copy editor, Chelly Peeler, and my proofreader, Isabella Bauer…maybe someday I'll figure out how commas, hyphens, and dialogue tags work. Ha!

Thank you to the team at Literally Yours PR, I am literally so grateful for everything you do!

Thank You

Dear Reader,

Thank you for taking the time to ready my book. There are so many books to choose from, so thank you for spending your precious time reading mine. If you have a minute, please consider leaving a review for Accidentally Ours. Reviews help indie authors so much!

XO, Erin

About the Author

Erin Hawkins is a spicy romcom author who lives in Colorado with her husband and three young children. She enjoys reading, working out, spending time in the mountains, reality TV and brunch that lasts all day.

Printed in Great Britain
by Amazon